unwanted

kristina ohlsson

Translated by Sarah Death

**SIMON &
SCHUSTER**

London · New York · Sydney · Toronto · New Delhi

A CBS COMPANY

First published in Sweden by Piratförlaget under the title *Askungar*, 2009
First published in Great Britain by Simon & Schuster UK Ltd, 2011
A CBS Company

This paperback edition first published, 2012

Paperback ISBN 978-1-84983-130-7
Ebook ISBN 978-1-84737-960-3

Printed and bound in Great Britain by CPI Group (UK) Ltd,
Croydon, CR0 4YY

For Thelma

PART I

Signs of Deception

MONDAY

Whenever he let his mind wander, for some reason he always came back to the case notes. It usually happened at night.

He lay motionless on his bed and looked up at a fly on the ceiling. He had never found darkness and rest easy to cope with. It was as though his defences were stripped away the moment the sun disappeared and fatigue and darkness crept up to enfold him. He hated feeling defenceless. A large part of his life had revolved around being on his guard, being prepared. Despite years of training, he found it incredibly hard to be prepared when he was resting. To be ready, he had to be awake. And he was used to not giving way to the fatigue that lingered in his body when he denied it sleep.

It was a long time since he had been woken at night by his own tears. It was a long time since the memories had hurt him and made him weak. In that respect, he had come a long way in his attempt to find peace.

And yet.

If he shut his eyes really tight, and if it was totally quiet all round him, he could see her in front of him. Her bulky form loomed out of the dark shadows and came lumbering towards him. Slowly, slowly, the way she always moved.

The memory of her scent still made him feel sick. Musty,

sweet and powdery. Impossible to breathe in. Like the smell of the books in her library. And he could hear her voice:

'*You stubborn wretch,*' she hissed. '*You worthless freak.*'

And then she would grab him and grip him hard.

Her words were always followed by the pain and the punishment. By the fire. The memory of the fire was still there on parts of his body. He liked running his finger over the scars, knowing that he had survived.

When he was really small, he had assumed he was punished because he always did everything wrong. So, following his child's logic, he tried to do everything right. Desperately, tenaciously. And still it all turned out wrong.

When he was older he understood better. There was simply nothing that was right. It wasn't just his actions that were wrong and needed to be punished; it was his whole essence and existence. He was being punished for existing. If he had not existed, She would never have died.

'*You should never have existed!*' she howled into his face. '*You're evil, evil, evil!*'

The crying that followed, after the fire, had to be in silence. Silent, always silent, so she wouldn't hear. Because if she did, she would come back. Every time.

He remembered how her accusations had caused him intense anxiety for a long time. How could he ever come to terms with what she said he was guilty of? How could he ever pay for what he had done, or compensate for his sin?

The case notes.

He went to the hospital where She had been a patient and read Her notes. Primarily to get some concept of the full extent of his crime. He was of age by then. Of age, but eternally in debt as a result of his evil deeds. What he found in the notes, however, turned him quite unexpectedly from a debtor into a free man. With this liberation came strength and recovery. He found a new life, and new and important questions to answer. The question was no longer how he could compensate someone else. The question then was how *he* was to be compensated.

Lying there in the dark, he smiled faintly and cast a glance at the new doll he had chosen. He thought – he could never be sure – but he *thought* this one would last longer than the others. She didn't need to deal with her past, as he himself had done. All she needed was a firm hand, *his* firm hand.

And plenty of love. His own special, guiding love.

He caressed her back gently. By mistake, or perhaps because he genuinely could not see the injuries he had inflicted on her, his hand passed right over one of the freshest bruises. It adorned one of her shoulder blades like a small dark pool. She awoke with a start and turned towards him. Her eyes shone with fear; she never knew what awaited her when darkness fell.

'It's time, Doll. We can begin.'

Her delicate face broke into a pretty, drowsy smile.

'We'll begin tomorrow,' he whispered.

Then he rolled onto his back again and fixed his gaze on the fly once more. Wide awake and ready to begin. There could be no rest.

TUESDAY

It was in the middle of that summer of endless rain that the first child went missing. It all started on a Tuesday; an odd sort of a day that could have passed by like any other, but ended up being a day that profoundly changed the lives of a number of people. Henry Lindgren was one of them.

It was the third Tuesday in July, and Henry was doing an extra shift on the X2000 express train from Gothenburg to Stockholm. Henry had worked as a conductor for Swedish National Railways for more years than he cared to remember, and he couldn't really imagine what would become of him on the day they forced him to retire. What would he do with all his free time, all alone?

Perhaps it was Henry Lindgren's eye for detail that meant he could later recall so well the young woman who was to lose her child on that journey. The young woman with light auburn hair, in a green linen blouse and open-toed sandals that revealed toenails painted blue. If Henry and his wife had had a daughter, she would presumably have looked just like that, because his wife had been the reddest of redheads.

The auburn-haired woman's little girl, however, was not in the least like her mother, Henry noted, as he clipped their tickets just after they pulled out of the station in Gothenburg. The girl's hair was a dark, chestnut brown and fell in such soft waves that it looked almost unreal. It landed lightly on her shoulders and then somehow came forward to frame her little face. Her skin was darker than her mother's, but her eyes were big and blue. There were tiny little clusters of freckles on the bridge of her nose, making her face look less doll-like. Henry smiled at her as he went past. She smiled back shyly. Henry thought the girl looked tired. She turned her head away and looked out of the window. Her head was resting against the back of the seat.

'Lilian, take your shoes off if you're going to put your feet up on the seat,' Henry heard the woman say to the child just as he turned to clip the next passenger's ticket.

When he turned back towards them, the child had kicked off her mauve sandals and tucked her feet up under her. The sandals were still there on the floor after she disappeared.

It was rather a rowdy journey from Gothenburg to Stockholm. Many of the passengers had travelled down to Sweden's second city to see a world-class star in concert at the Ullevi Stadium. They were now returning on the morning train on which Henry was conductor.

First, Henry had problems in coach five where two young men had vomited on their seats. They were hung over from the previous night's partying at Ullevi, and Henry had to dash off for cleaning fluid and a damp cloth. At about the same time, two younger girls got into a fight in coach three. A blonde girl accused a brunette of trying to steal her boyfriend. Henry tried to mediate, but to no avail, and the train did not really settle down until they were past Skövde. Then all the troublemakers finally dozed off, and Henry had a cup of coffee with Nellie, who worked in the buffet car. On his way back, Henry noticed that the auburn-haired woman and her daughter Lilian were asleep, too.

From then on it was a fairly uneventful journey until they were nearing Stockholm. It was the deputy conductor Arvid Melin who made the announcement just before they got to Flemingsberg, twenty kilometres or so short of the capital. The driver had been notified of a signalling problem on the final stretch to Stockholm Central, and there would therefore be a delay of five or possibly ten minutes to their journey.

While they were waiting at Flemingsberg, Henry noticed the auburn-haired woman quickly get off the train, alone. He watched her surreptitiously from the window of the tiny compartment in coach six that was reserved for the train crew. He saw her take a few determined steps across the platform, over to the other side where it was less crowded. She took something out of her handbag; could it be a mobile phone? He assumed the child must still be asleep in her seat. She certainly had been a little while ago, as the train thundered through Katrineholm. Henry sighed at himself. What on earth was he thinking of, spying on attractive women?

Henry looked away and started on the crossword in his magazine. He was to wonder time and again what would have happened if he had kept his eye on the woman on the platform. It made no difference how many people tried to persuade him that he couldn't possibly have known, that he mustn't reproach himself. Henry was, and forever would be, convinced that his eagerness to solve a crossword had destroyed a young mother's life. There was absolutely nothing he could do to turn back the clock.

Henry was still busy with his crossword when he heard

Arvid's voice on the public-address system. All passengers
were to return to their seats. The train was now ready to
continue on its way to Stockholm.

Afterwards, nobody could recall seeing a young woman
running after the train. But she must have done so, because it
was only a few minutes later that Henry took an urgent call
in the staff compartment. A young woman who had been
sitting in seat six, coach two with her daughter had been left
behind on the platform in Flemingsberg when the train set off
again, and was now in a taxi on her way to central Stockholm.
Her little daughter was therefore alone on the train.

'Bugger it,' said Henry as he hung up.

Why could he never delegate a single duty without something
going wrong? Why could he never have a moment's peace?

They never even discussed stopping the train at an interme-
diate station, since it was so close to its final destination. Henry
made his way briskly to coach two, and realized it must have
been the red-haired woman he'd been watching on the platform who had missed the train, since he recognized her
daughter, now sitting alone. He reported back to the commu-
nication centre on his mobile phone that the girl was still asleep,
and that there was surely no need to upset her with the news of
her mother's absence before they got to Stockholm. There was
general agreement, and Henry promised to look after the girl
personally when the train pulled in. *Personally*. A word that
would ring in Henry's head for a long time.

Just as the train went through Söder station on the south-
ern outskirts, the girls in coach three started scuffling and
screaming again. The sound of breaking glass reached
Henry's ears as a door slid open for a passenger to move

between coaches two and three, and he had to leave the sleeping child. He made an urgent and agitated call to Arvid on the two-way radio.

'Arvid, come straight to coach three!' he barked.

Not a sound from his colleague.

The train had come to a halt with its characteristic hiss, like the heavy, wheezing breath of an old person, before Henry managed to separate the two girls.

'Whore!' shrieked the blonde one.

'Slut!' retorted her friend.

'What a terrible way to behave,' said an elderly lady who had just got up to retrieve her case from the rack above.

Henry edged swiftly past people who had started queuing in the aisle to get off the train and called over his shoulder:

'Just make sure you leave the train right away, you two!'

As he spoke, he was already on his way to coach two. He just hoped the child hadn't woken up. But he had never been far away, after all.

Henry forged his way onward, knocking into several people as he covered the short distance back, and afterwards he swore he'd been away no more than three minutes.

But the number of minutes, however small, changed nothing.

When he got back to coach two, the sleeping child had gone. Her mauve sandals were still there on the floor. And the train was disgorging onto the platform all those people who had travelled under Henry Lindgren's protection from Gothenburg to Stockholm.

Alex Recht had been a policeman for more than a quarter of a century. He therefore felt he could claim to have wide experience of police work, to have built up over the years a significant level of professional competence, and to have developed a finely tuned sense of intuition. He possessed, he was often told, a good gut instinct.

Few things were more important to a policeman than gut instinct. It was the hallmark of a skilled police officer, the ultimate way of identifying who was made of the right stuff and who wasn't. Gut instinct was never a substitute for facts, but it could complement them. When all the facts were on the table, all the pieces of the puzzle identified, the trick was to understand what you were looking at and assemble the fragments of knowledge you had in front of you into a whole.

'Many are called, but few are chosen,' Alex's father had said in the speech he had made to his son when he got his first police appointment.

Alex's father had in actual fact been hoping his son would go into the church, like all the other firstborn sons in the family before him. He found it very hard to resign himself to the fact that his son had chosen the police in preference.

'Being a police officer involves a sort of calling, too,' Alex said in an attempt to mollify him.

His father thought about that for a few months, and then

let it be known that he intended to accept and respect his son's choice of profession. Perhaps the matter was also simplified somewhat by the fact that Alex's brother later decided to enter the priesthood. At any rate, Alex was eternally grateful to his brother.

Alex liked working with people who, just like him, felt a particular sense of vocation in the job. He liked working with people who shared his intuition and a well-developed feeling for what was fact and what was nonsense.

Maybe, he thought to himself as he sat at the wheel on the way to Stockholm Central, maybe that was why he couldn't really warm to his new colleague, Fredrika Bergman. She seemed to consider herself neither called to her job, nor particularly good at it. But then he didn't really expect her police career to last very long.

Alex glanced surreptitiously at the figure in the passenger seat beside him. She was sitting up incredibly straight. He had initially wondered if she had a military background. He had even hoped that might be the case. But however often he went through her CV, he couldn't find a single line to hint that she had spent so much as an hour in the armed forces. Alex had sighed. Then she must be a gymnast, that was all it could be, because no ordinary woman who had done nothing more exciting than go to university would ever be that bloody straight-backed.

Alex cleared his throat quietly and wondered if he ought to say anything about the case before they got there. After all, Fredrika had never had to deal with this sort of business before. Their eyes met briefly and then Alex turned his gaze back to the road.

'Lot of traffic today,' he muttered.

As if there were days when inner city Stockholm was empty of cars.

In his many years in the police, Alex had dealt with a fair number of missing children. His work on these cases had gradually convinced him of the truth of the saying: 'Children don't vanish, people lose them.' In almost every case, *almost* every case, behind every lost child there was a lost parent. Some lax individual who in Alex's view should never have had children in the first place. It needn't necessarily be someone with a harmful lifestyle or alcohol problems. It could just as well be someone who worked far too much, who was out with friends far too often and far too late, or someone who simply didn't pay enough attention to their child. If children took up the space in adults' lives that they should, they went missing far less often. At least that was what Alex had concluded.

The clouds hung thick and dark in the sky and a faint rumble presaged thunder as they got out of the car. The air was incredibly heavy and humid. It was the sort of day when you longed for rain and thunder to make the air more breathable. A flash of lightning etched itself dully on the clouds somewhere over the Old Town. There was another storm approaching.

Alex and Fredrika hurried in through the main entrance to Stockholm Central. Alex took a call from the mobile of the third member of the investigating team, Peder Rydh, to say he was on his way. Alex was relieved. It wouldn't have felt right starting an investigation like this with no one but a piece of office furniture like Fredrika.

It was after half past three by the time they got to platform seventeen where the train had pulled in to become the subject of a standard crime scene investigation. Swedish National Railways had been informed that no precise time could be given for the train to be put back in service, which in due course led to the late running of several trains that day. There were only a few people on the platform not in police uniform. Alex guessed that the red-haired woman looking exhausted but composed, sitting on a large, blue plastic box marked 'Sand' was the missing child's mother. Alex sensed intuitively that the woman was not one of those parents who lose their children. He swallowed hastily. If the child hadn't been lost, it had been abducted. If it had been abducted, that complicated matters significantly.

Alex told himself to take it easy. He still knew too little about the case not to keep an open mind.

A young, uniformed officer came along the platform to Alex and Fredrika. His handshake was firm but a little damp, his look somewhat glazed and unfocused. He introduced himself simply as Jens. Alex guessed that he was a recent graduate of the police training college and that this was his first case. Lack of practical experience was frightening when new police officers took up their first posts. You could see them radiating confusion and sometimes pure panic in their first six months. Alex wondered if the young man whose hand he was shaking couldn't be said to be bordering on panic. He was probably wondering in turn what on earth Alex was doing there. DCIs rarely, if ever, turned up to conduct interviews themselves. Or at any rate, not at this early stage in a case.

Alex was about to explain his presence when Jens started to speak, in rapid bursts.

'The alarm wasn't raised until thirty minutes after the train

got in,' he reported in a shrill voice. 'And by then, nearly all
the passengers had left the platform. Well, except for these.'

He gave a sweeping wave, indicating of a clump of people
standing a little way beyond the woman Alex had identified as the
child's mother. Alex glanced at his watch. It was twenty to four.
The child would soon have been missing for an hour and a half.

'There's been a complete search of the train. She isn't
anywhere. The child, I mean, a six-year-old girl. She isn't
anywhere. And nobody seems to have seen her, either. At
least nobody we've spoken to. And all their luggage is still
there. The girl didn't take anything with her. Not even her
shoes. They were still on the floor under her seat.'

The first raindrops hit the roof above them. The thunder
was rumbling somewhere closer now. Alex didn't think he'd
ever known a worse summer.

'Is that the girl's mother sitting over there?' asked Fredrika
with a discreet nod towards the red-haired woman.

'Yes, that's right,' said the young policeman. 'Her name's
Sara Sebastiansson. She says she's not going home until we
find the girl.'

Alex sighed to himself. Of course the red-haired woman
was the child's mother. He didn't need to ask such things, he
knew them anyway, he *sensed* them. Fredrika was entirely
lacking in that sort of intuition. She asked about everything
and she questioned even more. Alex felt his irritation level
rising. Detecting simply didn't work that way. He only hoped
she would soon realize how wrong she was for the profession
she had decided was suitable for her.

'Why did it take thirty minutes for the police to be alerted?'
Fredrika continued her interrogation.

Alex immediately pricked up his ears. Fredrika had finally asked a relevant question.

Jens braced himself. Up to that point, he had had answers to all the questions the senior police officers had asked him since they arrived.

'Well, it's a bit of an odd story,' Jens began, and Alex could see he was trying not to stare at Fredrika. 'The train was held at Flemingsberg for longer than usual, and the mother got off to make a phone call. She left her little girl on the train because she was asleep.'

Alex nodded thoughtfully. *Children don't vanish, people lose them.* Perhaps he had misjudged Sara the redhead.

'So anyway, a girl came up to her, to Sara that is, on the platform and asked her to help with a dog that was sick. And then she missed the train. She rang the train people right away – a member of staff at Flemingsberg helped her – to tell them that her child was on the train and that she was going to take a taxi straight to Stockholm Central.'

Alex frowned as he listened.

'The child had gone by the time the train stopped at Stockholm, and the conductor and some of the other crew searched for her. People were flooding off the train, you see, and hardly any of the passengers bothered to help. A Securitas guard who normally hangs round outside Burger King downstairs gave them a hand with the search. Then the mother, I mean Sara over there, got here in the taxi and was told her daughter was missing. They went on searching; they thought the girl must have woken up and, like, been one of the first off the train. But they couldn't find her anywhere. So then they rang the police. But we haven't found her either.'

'Have they put out a call over the public-address system in the station?' asked Fredrika. 'I mean in case she managed to get off the platform and onto the concourse?'

Jens nodded meekly and then shook his head. Yes, an announcement had been made. More police and volunteers were currently searching the whole station. Local radio would be issuing an appeal to road users in the city centre to keep an eye out for the girl. The taxi firms would be contacted. If the girl had walked off on her own, she couldn't have got far.

But she had not been spotted yet.

Fredrika nodded slowly. Alex looked at the mother sitting on the big blue box. She looked like death. Shattered.

'Put out the announcement in other languages, not just Swedish,' said Fredrika.

Her male colleagues looked at her with raised eyebrows.

'There are a lot of people hanging about here who don't have Swedish as their mother tongue, but who might have seen something. Make the announcement in English, too. German and French, if they can. Maybe Arabic, as well.'

Alex nodded approvingly and sent Jens a look that told him to do as Fredrika suggested. Jens hurried off, probably quailing at the prospect of somehow getting hold of an Arabic speaker. Cascades of rain were coming down on the people gathered on the platform, and the rumbling had turned into mighty claps of thunder. It was a wretched day in a wretched summer.

Peder Rydh came dashing along the platform just as Jens was leaving it. Peder stared at Fredrika's beige, double-breasted jacket. Had the woman no concept at all of the way you broadcast that you were part of the police when you weren't in uniform? Peder himself nodded graciously to the colleagues he passed on his way and waved his identity badge about a bit so they would realize he was one of them. He found it hard to resist the urge to thump a few of the younger talents on the back. He had loved his years in the patrol car, of course, but he was very happy indeed to have landed a job on the plain-clothes side.

Alex gave Peder a nod as they caught sight of each other, and his look expressed something close to gratitude for his colleague's presence.

'I was on my way from a meeting on the edge of town when I got the message that the child was missing, so I thought I'd pick up Fredrika on the way and come straight here,' Alex explained briefly to Peder. 'I'm not really planning to stick around, just wanted to get out for a bit of fresh air,' he went on, and gave his colleague a knowing look.

'You mean you wanted to get your feet on the ground as a change from being chained to your desk?' grinned Peder, and received a weary nod in reply.

In spite of the significant age gap between them, the two

men were entirely in agreement on that point. You were never so far up the hierarchy that you didn't need to see the real shit. And you were never as far from reality as when you were behind your desk.

Both men assumed, however, that Fredrika did not share this view, and therefore said nothing more about it.

'Okay,' said Alex instead. 'Here's what we'll do. Fredrika can take the initial interview with the child's mother and you, Peder, can talk to the train crew and also find out if any of the other passengers who are still here can give you any information. We should really play it by the book and interview in pairs, but I can't see there's time to organize that just now.'

Fredrika was very happy with this division of duties, but thought she could detect some dissatisfaction in Peder's face. Dissatisfaction that she, not he, would get to tackle the mother of the missing child. Alex must have seen it too, as he added:

'The only reason Fredrika's dealing with the mother is that she's a woman. It tends to make things a bit easier.'

Peder instantly looked a little more cheerful.

'Okay, see you back at the station later,' said Alex gruffly. 'I'm off back there now.'

Fredrika sighed. *'The only reason Fredrika's dealing with . . .'* It was always the same. Every decision to entrust her with a task had to be defended. She was a foreign body in a foreign universe. Her whole presence was questionable and demanded constant explanation. Fredrika felt so indignant that she forgot to reflect on the fact that Alex had not only entrusted her with interviewing the mother, but he'd also let her do it alone. She was virtually counting the days until her time in Alex Recht's investigation team was over. She was planning to finish her probationary period and then leave. There were other agencies where her qualifications were more desirable, albeit less urgently needed.

I shall look over my shoulder one last time and then never look back again, thought Fredrika, seeing in her mind's eye the day she would stride out of the police building, or HQ, as her colleagues generally called it, on Kungsholmen. Then Fredrika turned her attention to a more imminent task. To the missing child.

She introduced herself politely to Sara Sebastiansson and was surprised at the strength of the woman's handshake. It belied the anxiety and exhaustion in her face. Fredrika also noted that Sara kept pulling down the sleeves of her top. It looked like a sort of tic or habit, something she did all the time. It was almost as if she was trying to hide her forearms.

Maybe an attempt to conceal injuries she got when she was defending herself, thought Fredrika. If Sara had a husband who hit her, that was information to be brought to the team's attention as soon as possible.

But there were other questions to be asked first.

'We can go inside if you like,' Fredrika said to Sara. 'We needn't stand out here in the rain.'

'I'm all right here,' said Sara in a voice not far from tears.

Fredrika pondered this for a moment and then said:

'If you feel you have to be here for your daughter, you have my absolute assurance that she'd be noticed by everybody else here.'

What's more, Fredrika felt like adding, it's not particularly likely that your daughter will turn up right here and now, but she left the thought unsaid.

'Lilian,' said Sara.

'Sorry?'

'My daughter's called Lilian. And I don't want to leave this spot.'

She underlined what she was saying by shaking her head. 'No thank you, no coffee.'

Fredrika knew herself that she found it hard to be personal when she was on duty. She often failed dismally. In that respect, she was a classic desk type. She liked reading, writing and analysing. All forms of interrogation and conversation felt so alien, so hard to deal with. She would sometimes watch with pure fascination as Alex reached out a hand and laid it on someone's shoulder as he was talking to them. Fredrika would never do that, and what was more, she didn't want to be patted herself either, be it on the arm or on the shoulder. She felt physically unwell whenever any male colleague at work tried to 'lighten the mood' by slapping her on the back too hard or prodding her in the middle. She didn't like that sort of physical contact at all. And most people realized. But not all. Fredrika gave a slight shiver just as Sara's voice interrupted her very private musings.

'Why didn't she take her shoes?'

'Sorry?'

'Lilian's sandals were still there on the floor by her seat. She must have been in a terrible state about something, otherwise she'd never have gone off in her bare feet. And never without saying something to somebody, asking for help.'

'Not even if she woke up and found she was all alone? Maybe she panicked and dashed off the train?'

Sara shook her head.

'Lilian's not like that. That's not how we brought her up. We taught her to act and think in a practical way. She would have asked someone sitting nearby. The lady across the aisle from us, for example, we'd chatted to her a bit on the way.'

Fredrika saw her chance to divert the conversation onto another subject.

'You say "we"?'

'Yes?'

'You say that's not how "we" brought her up. Are you referring to yourself and your husband?'

Sara fixed her gaze on a spot above Fredrika's shoulder.

'Lilian's father and I have separated, but yes, it's my ex-husband I brought up Lilian with.'

'Have you got joint custody?' asked Fredrika.

'The separation's so new for us all,' Sara said slowly. 'We haven't really got into a routine. Lilian sometimes stays with him at weekends, but mostly she lives with me. We'll have to see how it goes, later.'

Sara took a deep breath, and as she breathed out, her lower lip was trembling. Her ashen skin stood out against her red hair. Her long arms were crossed tightly on her chest. Fredrika looked at Sara's painted toenails. Blue. How unusual.

'Did you argue about who Lilian was going to live with?' Fredrika probed cautiously.

Sara gave a start.

'You think Gabriel's taken her?' she said, looking Fredrika straight in the eye.

Fredrika assumed Gabriel must be the ex-husband.

'We don't think anything,' she said quickly. 'I just have to investigate all possible scenarios for . . . I just have to try to understand what might have happened to her. To Lilian.'

Sara's shoulders slumped a little. She bit her lower lip and stared hard at the ground.

'Gabriel and I . . . have had . . . still have . . . our differences. Not so long ago we had a row about Lilian. But he's never harmed her. Never ever.'

Again Fredrika saw Sara pulling at the sleeves of her top. Her rapid assessment was that Sara would not tell her then and there whether she had been abused by her ex-husband or not. She would have to check for officially lodged complaints when she got back to HQ. And they would certainly have to speak to the ex-husband, at any event.

'Could you tell me more precisely what happened on the platform at Flemingsberg?' Fredrika asked, hoping she was now steering the conversation in a direction Sara would feel more comfortable with.

Sara nodded several times but said nothing. Fredrika hoped she wasn't going to start crying, because tears were something she found very hard to deal with. Not privately, but professionally.

'I got off the train to make a call,' Sara began hesitantly. 'I rang a friend.'

Fredrika distracted by the rain, checked herself. *A friend?*

'And why didn't you ring from your seat?'

'I didn't want to wake Lilian,' came Sara's quick response.

A little too quick. What was more, she had told the policeman she spoke to earlier that she got off the train because she was in the so-called quiet coach.

'She was so tired,' whispered Sara. 'We go to Gothenburg

to visit my parents. I think she was getting a cold, she never sleeps for the whole journey usually.'

'Ah, I see,' said Fredrika, and paused for a minute before going on. 'So it wasn't that you didn't want Lilian to hear the conversation?'

Sara admitted it almost immediately.

'No, I didn't want Lilian to hear the conversation,' she said quietly. 'My friend and I have . . . only just met. And it would be a bad idea to let her find out about him at this stage.'

Because then she'd tell her dad, who was presumably still beating up her mum even though they'd separated, thought Fredrika to herself.

'We only talked for a couple of minutes. Less than that, I think. I said we were almost there, and he could come round to my place later this evening, once Lilian was in bed.'

'All right, and what happened next?'

Sara pulled her shoulders back and sighed heavily. The body language told Fredrika they were about to talk about something she found really painful to remember.

'It made no sense at all, none of it,' Sara said dully. 'It was completely absurd.'

She shook her head wearily.

'A woman came up to me. Or a girl, you might say. Quite tall, thin, looked a bit the worse for wear. Waving her arms and shouting something about her dog being sick. I suppose she came up to me because I was standing separately from the other people on the platform. She said she'd been coming down the escalator with the dog when it suddenly collapsed and started having a fit.'

'A fit? The dog?'

'Yes, that was what she said. The dog was lying there having a fit and she needed help to get it back up the escalator again. I've had dogs all my life, until a few years ago. And I could honestly see what a state the girl was in. So I helped her.'

Sara fell silent and Fredrika considered what she'd said, rubbing her hands together.

'Didn't you think about the risk of missing the train?'

For the first time in their conversation, Sara's tone was sharp and her eyes blazed.

'When I got off, I asked the conductor how long the train would be stopping there. He said at least ten minutes. At least.'

Sara held up her hands and spread her long, narrow fingers wide. Ten fingers, ten minutes. Her hands were shaking slightly. Her lower lip was quivering again.

'Ten minutes,' she whispered. 'That was why I helped the girl shove the dog up the escalator. I thought – I *knew* – I had time.'

Fredrika tired to breathe calmly.

'Did you see the train leave?'

'We'd just got to the top of the escalator with the dog,' said Sara, her voice unsteady. 'We'd just got the dog back up when I turned round and saw the train starting to pull out.'

Her breathing was laboured and her eyes were on Fredrika.

'I couldn't believe my fucking eyes,' she said, and a single tear ran down her cheek. 'It was like being in a horror film. I ran down the escalator, ran like mad after the train. But it didn't stop. It didn't stop!'

Although Fredrika had no children of her own, Sara's words aroused a genuine feeling of anguish in her.

She felt something akin to stomach ache.

'One of the staff at Flemingsberg station helped me get in touch with the train. And then I took a taxi to Stockholm Central.'

'What was the girl with the dog doing while this was happening?'

Sara wiped the corner of her eye.

'It was a bit odd. She just sort of made off, all of a sudden. She bundled the dog up onto some kind of parcel trolley that had been left there at the top of the escalator, and went out through the station entrance. I didn't see her after that.'

Sara and Fredrika stood for a while saying nothing, each absorbed in their own thoughts. It was Sara's voice that broke the silence.

'And you know what, I wasn't really too worried once I'd got through to the train. It felt pretty irrational to get worked up about a little thing like Lilian being by herself for that last little bit of the journey from Flemingsberg to Stockholm.'

Sara moistened her lips, and then cried openly for the first time.

'I even sat back in the taxi. Closed my eyes and relaxed. I *relaxed* while some bloody sick bastard took my little girl.'

Fredrika realized this was a pain she had no chance of alleviating. With great reluctance she did what she would never normally do: she reached out a hand and stroked Sara's arm.

Then she realized it had stopped raining. Lilian had been missing for another hour.

It was trickier than Jelena had expected to get out of Flemingsberg by bus.

'You mustn't take the commuter train, you mustn't take a taxi, you mustn't drive,' the Man had told her that very morning, as they went over every detail of the plan for the hundredth time. 'You're to go by bus. Bus to Skärholmen, then take the underground home. Understand?'

Jelena had nodded and nodded.

Yes, she understood. And she would do her very, very best.

Jelena felt at least ten anxious butterflies fluttering in her stomach. She hoped desperately that it had all worked. It simply had to work. The Man would be furious if he hadn't managed to get the kid off the train.

She peered at her watch. It had taken more than an hour. The bus had been late, and then she'd had a wait for a tube train. She would soon be home and then she would know. She wiped her sweaty palms on her jeans. She could never be really sure whether she was doing things right or wrong. Not until later, when the Man either praised her or told her off. Just recently she'd done almost everything right. It had even gone okay when she practised driving, and when she had to practise talking properly.

'People have to be able to understand what you're saying,' the Man would tell her. 'You don't speak clearly. And you've got to stop your face twitching like that. It scares people.'

Jelena had had a real struggle, but in the end the Man had given her his seal of approval. All she had now was a slight twitch at the corner of one eye, and really only when she was nervous or unsure. When she was calm, it didn't twitch at all.

'Good girl,' the Man said then, and patted her on the cheek.

Jelena felt all warm inside. She hoped for more praise when she got home.

The train got to her stop at last. It was all she could do not to rush out of the carriage and run all the way home. She must walk calmly and unobtrusively, so nobody would notice her. Jelena kept her eyes on the ground, and fiddled with a bit of her hair.

The rain was beating on the road when she came up out of the underground, impairing her vision. It didn't matter – she saw him anyway. For a brief second, their eyes met. She thought he looked as if he was smiling.

A highly sceptical Peder Rydh observed Fredrika's pathetic attempt to offer comfort. She was patting Sara Sebastiansson with the same reluctance as you would pat a dog you found utterly revolting, but had to pat because it belonged to a good friend. People like her had no business in the police force, where everything depended on how you handled people. Different sorts of people. *All* sorts. Peder gave an irritated sigh. It really had been a very bad idea to recruit civilians into the police.

'The force needs an injection of top skills,' was the explanation from certain individuals high up in the organization.

Fredrika had mentioned on several occasions what subject she had read at university, but to be honest, Peder couldn't have cared less. She used too many words, with too many letters. She complicated things. She thought too much and felt too little. She simply wasn't made of the right stuff for police work.

Peder could only admire the police union's persistent opposition to the position and status that civilians had been given in the force. Without any relevant work experience whatsoever. Without the unique set of skills that can only be gained by learning police work from the bottom up. By spending at least a few years in the patrol car. Manhandling drunks. Talking to men who hit their wives.

Giving pissed teenagers a lift home and facing their parents. Breaking into flats where lonely souls have died and just lain there, rotting.

Peder shook his head. He had more pressing things to think about than incompetent colleagues. He thought over the information he had garnered from talking to the train crew so far. Henry Lindgren, the conductor, talked too much, but he had a good eye for detail and there was certainly nothing wrong with his memory. The train left Gothenburg at 10.50. It reached Stockholm eight minutes after the time it was due, at 14.07.

'I wasn't the one in charge of the delay in Flemingsberg,' Henry pointed out. 'That was Arvid. And Nellie.'

He looked sadly at the train, still standing at the platform. All the doors were open, gaping like great dark holes along the side of the train. More than anything else on earth, Henry wished that the little girl would suddenly come stumbling out of one of those holes. That she had somehow lost her way on the train, gone back to sleep, and then woken up. But with all the certainty that only grown-up human beings can muster, Henry knew it wasn't going to happen. The only people getting on and off the train were policemen and technicians. The whole platform had been cordoned off, and a fingertip search of the damp surface for traces of the missing child was in progress. Henry felt a lump in his throat that proved impossible to swallow.

Peder went on with the interview.

'You say you were keeping an eye on the child; then what happened?'

Peder could see Henry literally shrink, as if he was ageing

as he stood there on the platform, faced with explaining what had made him leave the girl.

'It was hard, trying to be in lots of places at the same time,' he said dejectedly. 'Like I told you, there'd been trouble in several of the coaches, and I had to leave the girl and get to coach three, smartish. But I called Arvid on the two-way radio. I called him really loud, and I tried several times, but he never replied. I don't think he can have heard. I didn't seem to be getting through at all.'

Peder decided not to make any comment on Arvid's behaviour.

'So you left the child, and didn't ask any of the passengers to keep an eye on her?' he asked instead.

Henry threw out his arms in dramatic appeal.

'I was only in the next carriage!' he cried. 'And I thought, yes I thought, I'll be straight back. Which I was.'

His voice almost gave way.

'I left the girl for less than three minutes, I was back the minute the train stopped and people started getting off. But she'd already gone. And nobody could remember seeing her get up and go.'

Henry's voice was choked as he went on:

'How's that possible? How can nobody have seen a thing?'

Peder knew all too well how. Get ten people to witness the same crime and they will come up with ten different versions of what happened, the order it happened in, and what the perpetrators were wearing.

What *was* strange, on the other hand, was the way Arvid Melin had acted. First he let the train leave Flemingsberg without Sara Sebastiansson, and then he failed to answer Henry's call.

Peder quickly sought out Arvid, who was sitting by himself on one of the seats on the platform. He seemed very twitchy. As Peder approached, he raised his eyes and said:

'Can we go soon? I've got to be somewhere.'

Peder sat down beside Arvid deliberately slowly, fixed him with a look and replied:

'A child's gone missing. What have you got to do that's more important than helping to find her?'

After that, Arvid uttered hardly a word that was not a direct answer to a direct question.

'What did you say to passengers who asked you how long the train would be stationary at Flemingsberg?' Peder asked sternly, finding he was addressing Arvid like some kind of schoolboy.

'Don't remember exactly,' answered Arvid evasively.

Peder noted that Arvid, who must have been nearing thirty, responded in the way he expected his own kids would answer questions when they reached their teens.

'Where are you going?' 'Out!' 'When will you be home?' 'Later!'

'Do you remember a conversation with Sara Sebastiansson?' Peder enquired.

Arvid shook his head.

'No, not really,' he said.

Peder was just wondering whether he could give Arvid a good shake, when he went on:

'There were lots of people asking the same thing, see. I think I remember her, the girl's mother, being one of them. People have to take a bit of responsibility for themselves,' he said in a choked voice, and only then did Peder realize how shaken he really was. 'It's not a bloody promise that the train's going to be stopped for ten minutes, just because we say so. All the passengers, *all* of them, want to get there as fast as possible. There's *never* any problem about setting off earlier than we first said. Why did she leave the platform? If she'd been standing there, she'd have heard me make the announcement on the train.'

Arvid kicked an empty cola bottle that was lying at his feet. It bounced angrily against the train and went spinning across the platform.

Peder suspected both Arvid Melin and Henry Lindgren would be having some disturbed nights for a good time to come if the girl failed to turn up.

'You didn't see Sara Sebastiansson being left behind?' Peder asked gently.

'No, definitely not,' said Arvid emphatically. 'I mean, I looked along the platform, the way we usually do. It was empty, so we left. And then Henry says he called me on the two-way radio, but I didn't hear . . . because I'd forgotten to switch it on.'

Peder looked up at the dark grey sky and shut his notebook.

He would just have a brief talk to the rest of the train crew and the others on the platform. If Fredrika had finished getting the mother's statement, perhaps she would help him.

Peder saw Fredrika and Sara Sebastiansson out of the corner of his eye, exchanging a few words and then going their separate ways. Sara looked the picture of dejection. Peder swallowed. An image of his own family rose to the surface of his consciousness. What would he do if anyone tried to harm either of his children?

His grip on his notebook tightened. He would have to get a move on. There were more people to talk to and Alex did not like to be kept waiting.

They drove back to the HQ in Peder's car. As the car swished along the rain-soaked tarmac, Fredrika and Peder were both lost in their own thoughts. They parked in the basement garage and took the lift in silence up to the floor where the team had its offices. Close to the county police and National Crime Squad's base, close to the Stockholm Police Department. Nobody was ever willing to say it out loud, but Alex Recht's investigative team most definitely served two masters. Well three, really. A special resources group, comprising a small number of hand-picked people of different background and experience, who on paper were part of the Stockholm police, but who in practice worked very closely with, and could be called upon by, both the national and county departments. It was a political solution to something that shouldn't have been a problem.

Fredrika sank down wearily in the office chair behind her desk. Was there any better place for thinking and acting than behind her desk? She realized she had been naive to think that her specialized skills would be welcomed and made full use of within the police organization. She could not for the life of her understand police officers' deep-rooted, all-embracing contempt for advanced, academic qualifications. Or was it really contempt? Did they in actual fact feel threatened? Fredrika couldn't quite put her finger on it. She only knew that her current work situation was not tenable in the long term.

Her route to Alex Recht's team had taken her via an investigative role at the Crime Prevention Council, and then a couple of years with social services, where she had been an expert adviser. She had applied to the police force to broaden her practical experience. And she would not be staying on. But she was relaxed about her current situation. She had an extensive network of contacts that could gain her entry to plenty of other organizations. She just needed to hold her nerve, and some new opportunity would eventually turn up.

Fredrika was very conscious of the way she was perceived by her colleagues in the force. Difficult and reserved. As someone with no sense of humour or normal emotional life.

That's not true, thought Fredrika. I'm not cold, I'm just so damn confused about where I'm going at the moment.

Her friends would describe her as both warm and sympathetic. And extremely loyal. But that was in her *private* life. And now here she was in a workplace where she was expected to be private even on duty. It was completely unthinkable as far as Fredrika was concerned.

It wasn't that she felt nothing at all for the people she encountered in the course of her job. It was just that she chose to feel a little less.

'My job's not pastoral care,' she had said to a friend who had asked why she was so unwilling to get emotionally involved in her work. 'It's detecting crimes. It's not about who I am – it's about what I *do*. I do the detecting; someone else has got to do the comforting.'

Otherwise you'd drown, thought Fredrika. If I were to offer comfort to every victim I met, there'd be nothing left of me.

Fredrika could not remember ever having expressed a desire for a police job in her life. When she was little, her dreams had always been of working with music, as a violinist. She had music in her blood. She nurtured the dreams in her heart. Many children grow out of their earliest dreams about what they want to be when they grow up. But Fredrika never did; instead, her dreams developed and grew more concrete. She and her mother went on visits to various music schools and discussed which would suit her best. By the time she started at secondary school, she had already composed music of her own.

Just after she was fifteen, everything changed. For ever, as it turned out. Her right arm was badly injured in a car crash on the way home from a skiing trip, and after a year of physiotherapy it was obvious that the arm could not cope with the demands of playing the violin for hours every day.

Well-meaning teachers said she had been lucky. Theoretically and rationally, Fredrika understood what they meant. She had been to the mountains with a friend and her family. The accident left her friend's mother paralysed from the waist down. The son of the family was killed. The newspapers called their accident the 'Filipstad tragedy'.

But for Fredrika herself, the accident would never be called anything but The Accident, and in her mind she thought of The Accident as the most concrete of dividing lines in her life. She had been one person before The Accident, and became a different person after it. There was a very clear Before and After. She did not want to acknowledge that she had had any kind of

Luck. But even now, almost twenty years later, she still wondered if she would ever accept the life that came After.

'There's so much else you can do with your life,' her grandmother said reasonably, on the rare occasions when Fredrika voiced the dreadful sense of despair she felt at being robbed of the future opportunities she had dreamt of. 'You could work in a bank, for example, seeing as you're so good at maths.'

Fredrika's parents, on the other hand, said nothing. Her mother was a concert pianist and music had a holy place in everyday family life. Fredrika had virtually grown up in the wings of a series of great stages on which her mother had played, either as a soloist or as part of a larger ensemble. Sometimes Fredrika had played in the ensembles. There were times when it had been quite magical.

So Fredrika's discussions with her mother had been more productive.

'What shall I do now?' nineteen-year-old Fredrika had whispered to her mother one evening just before she left school, when her tears would not stop.

'You'll find something else, Fredrika,' her mother had said, rubbing her back with a sympathetic hand. 'There's so much strength in you, so much willpower and such drive to achieve things. You'll find something else.'

And so she did.

History of art, history of music, history of ideas. The university had an unlimited range of courses on offer.

'Fredrika's going to be a history professor,' her father said proudly in those early years.

Her mother said nothing; it was her father who had always

boasted far and wide of the great success in life he envisaged for his daughter.

But Fredrika did not become a professor. She became a criminologist specializing in crimes against women and children. She never completed her doctorate, and after five years at university she felt she had had more than enough of theoretical study.

She could see in her mother's eyes that this was unexpected. It had been assumed that she would not want to leave the academic world. Her mother never expressed her disappointment openly, but she admitted she was surprised. Fredrika would dearly have liked to possess more of that quality herself: never to be disappointed, only surprised.

Consequently Fredrika knew a fair bit about pleasure and idleness, about passion and not knowing which way to go in life. As she printed out the accusation of abuse that Sara Sebastiansson had now formally lodged against her ex-husband, she wondered as she so often did why women stay with men who batter them. Was it love and passion? Fear of loneliness and exclusion? But Sara had not stayed. Not really. At least not judging by what Fredrika could deduce from the documents in front of her.

The first formal accusation had been lodged when her daughter was two years old. Sara, unlike many other women, claimed then that her husband had never hit her before. In cases where women themselves came forward to make complaints, there was usually a history. At the time of the first report, Sara had come to her local police station with extensive bruising on her right side and face. Her husband denied all the accusations and said he had an alibi for the evening when Sara claimed to have been attacked. Fredrika frowned. As far as she understood it, Sara never withdrew her accusation as so many women do. But nor did it lead to any kind of prosecution. The evidence did not hold, as three friends of her husband could attest that he had been playing poker until two o'clock on the night in question and had then spent the night at the home of one of them.

Two years then passed before Sara Sebastiansson lodged another complaint. She then claimed that he had not hit her on any occasion in between, but when Fredrika read about the extent of Sara's injuries and compared them with those she had had the first time, she felt pretty much convinced Sara was lying. She had also been raped. There were no marks at all to be seen on her face.

It seemed unlikely, in Fredrika's view, for the husband not to have touched his wife for two years, only for the violence then to escalate as it obviously had.

There was no prosecution that time either. Sara's husband could prove by means of original tickets and the word of two independent witnesses that he had been on business in Malmö at the time of the alleged assault. The crime could not be substantiated, and the investigation was halted.

Fredrika was concerned by what she read, to put it mildly. She could not get the pieces of the picture to fit together. Sara Sebastiansson hadn't given the impression of being a woman who would lie. Not about anything, in fact. She had not mentioned the assaults, though she must have realized that the police would find out about them sooner or later, but Fredrika was not inclined to see that as a lie. The injuries that had been documented were also true and genuine. So her ex-husband must be guilty, but however did he manage his alibis? He was clearly a successful businessman, and twelve years older than Sara. Did he buy his alibis? But that many?

Fredrika continued working her way through the papers. The couple had separated shortly after the second assault, and only a few weeks after that, Sara was back at the police station lodging another complaint. Her ex-husband would not leave her alone; he stalked her in his car; he waited for her outside her flat and her workplace. Her ex-husband made a counter-accusation that Sara sabotaged all his attempts to maintain proper contact with their daughter. A real classic. A few more months passed – more official complaints to the police of unlawful threat, molestation and trespass – but he never actually hit her. Or if he did, it was not reported.

The last report was dated 11 November 2005, when according to Swedish Telecom's records Sara's husband had rung her over a hundred times the same night. That was the only time any accusation made against him could be substantiated, and a banning order was issued to prevent him visiting Sara.

Fredrika pondered this. During Fredrika's interrogation, Sara had said that she and her ex-husband had recently separated, but the official reports told another story: she and her husband had not lived together since July 2005, when Sara had made the second report of assault to the police. What had happened between 11 November 2005 and today? Fredrika rapidly checked her information against the national police files and sighed when she discovered the answer. They had, of course, got back together again.

The timeline became all too clear. On 17 July 2005, two

weeks after the second report to the police, Sara and Gabriel Sebastiansson were at different addresses. They never filed for divorce, but they did separate. On 20 December 2005, just weeks after the banning order was issued, they were back at the same address. Then it all went quiet.

Fredrika wondered what their lives had been like since. She wondered how relations between them were now. And she understood all too well that Sara would not want it to come to her ex-husband's attention that she had moved on in her life and was in a new relationship.

Fredrika turned to a new page in her notebook. She would have to talk to Sara as soon as possible about the earlier, or continuing, abuse. She would definitely have to talk to Sara's ex-husband, who was currently unavailable. And she would also have to interview Sara's new 'friend', as she called him. Fredrika slammed her notebook shut and hurried out of her office. There was still time to get a cup of coffee before the team assembled to pool their information about the missing child, Lilian. Maybe she could also fit in a call to Gabriel Sebastiansson's mother before the meeting. She might know her son's whereabouts.

Alex Recht opened the meeting in the Den with his usual efficiency. Peder always felt a slight quickening of his pulse when they were gathered there on operational business. The Den, or the Lions' Den to give it its full name, was what they called the only meeting room they had. Peder liked the name. He took it for granted that it hadn't been Fredrika's suggestion. She was entirely lacking in that sort of imagination and finesse.

It was nearly six and Lilian Sebastiansson had been missing for more than four hours. In view of the fact that she had disappeared in the middle of Stockholm, and in view of her age, this had to be considered a long time. It was clearly beyond all reasonable doubt that she had not gone missing of her own free will. She was far too young to have made her way anywhere unaided, and she had no shoes on her feet.

'I need hardly remind you that we have a very grave situation here,' said Alex grimly, surveying his colleagues.

Nobody said a word, and Alex took a seat at the table.

Besides Alex, those in attendance were Fredrika, Peder, and the team's assistant Ellen Lind. Also present were some officers from the uniformed branch, there to report on the search of the area round the Central Station, and a few people from the technical division.

Alex started by asking what the search had revealed. The

answer was as short as it was depressing: it had revealed nothing at all. Hardly anyone had responded to the appeal over the public-address system on the concourse, and talking to the taxi firms had not produced any leads either.

The result of the technical check of the train coaches was almost as scanty. It had been hard to secure any fingerprints on site, nor had they found any traces indicating where the girl had got off the train. If it was assumed that she was carried and was possibly still asleep when she was taken, the task became even more difficult. No traces of blood had been found anywhere. All that they had found, and been able to secure, were some shoeprints on the floor, right by the girl's seat.

Alex pricked up his ears when he heard that the train crew said the floors were cleaned between trips, which meant the prints the technicians had found must relate to the journey in question. The prints were from a pair of Ecco shoes, size 46.

'All right,' Alex said briskly. 'We'll have to see if we get any pointers from the other passengers on the train.'

He cleared his throat.

'Has the news gone out to the media yet, by the way? I haven't seen or heard anything.'

The question was really directed at Ellen, who was the nearest thing the team had to a press officer. She answered:

'It was on the radio quite quickly, as we requested, and on the web, of course. And an announcement went out through the Central News Agency about an hour ago. We can expect the story to be in all the big national dailies tomorrow. The statement we issued to the media says specifically that we want to hear from all the passengers on that train from Gothenburg as soon as possible.'

Alex nodded, feeling fairly satisfied. He had no objections himself to turning to the media for help. But he was well aware that putting out the appeal could prove counterproductive. It was the end of July, the summer was raining away, millions of Swedes were off work for the holidays, and the newspaper editorial offices were presumably suffering from a total dearth of news. He scarcely dared think what the following day's headlines would be if the girl was not found in the course of the evening. And he scarcely dared contemplate how many members of the public would pick up the phone and ring in with a tip-off. Far too many people had a tendency to imagine that they were in possession of some vital piece of information the police couldn't live without.

'We'll hold back on the press conference for now,' he said meditatively. 'And we'll wait a bit before we issue a picture of the girl.' He went on, now addressing the whole investigation team: 'As we know, we're only talking about a very short space of time when there was no adult with her. According to the statements we've taken, she was left unsupervised for fewer than four minutes. The train had been at a standstill for scarcely a minute when the conductor got back to her seat, and by then she was gone.'

Alex turned to Peder.

'Peder, did you get anything concrete from your interviews? What sense did you get of the people you spoke to?'

Peder sighed and flicked through his notebook.

'I didn't talk to anyone who was directly under suspicion, so to speak,' he drawled. 'Nobody saw anything; nobody heard anything. The girl was gone, that's all. The only one who behaved a bit weirdly was the other conductor, Arvid Melin. He not only gave the all-clear for the train to leave Flemingsberg without Sara Sebastiansson, he also ignored his colleague's call for assistance. But to be honest . . . No, I can't for the life of me say I really think Arvid M. had anything to do with it. He seems totally useless at his job, and that no doubt made it easier for whoever took Lilian, but he wasn't actively involved in her disappearance. I really don't think so. And he hasn't got a criminal record.'

'Good,' said Alex.

Fredrika frowned.

'I'm not sure I think Arvid Melin stands out as the shady one in all this,' she said. 'Can we assume it was a coincidence that Sara missed the train in Flemingsberg? What have we got on the woman who delayed her there?'

Alex put his head on one side.

'What's your take on it?' he asked.

'It depends how we view the girl's disappearance. If we think it was planned, and depended on the girl being unsupervised in Stockholm so she'd be easier to snatch, we have to see the woman with the dog as a suspect, too,' Fredrika replied.

'True,' said Alex with some hesitation. 'But then how did the perpetrator know that the adult who was supposed to keep watch on Lilian would be prevented from doing so?'

'He didn't, of course,' said Fredrika. 'The perpetrator must naturally have realized that Sara Sebastiansson would leap into action when she missed the train, and contact the crew. But maybe it still seemed less of a problem to take her from someone who didn't know her than from her mother. Whoever took Lilian might have tried to do it even if Henry Lindgren had been there.'

'So you think the priority was to get Sara off the train, so what happened in Flemingsberg was no coincidence?' asked Alex.

'Exactly,' said Fredrika.

'Hmm,' said Alex.

'Er,' said Peder.

Alex gave Peder an encouraging nod.

'Well, I think it seems a bit far-fetched,' said Peder with a doubtful expression.

'What's the alternative?' asked Fredrika. 'It was all pure chance?'

'Opportunity makes a thief,' said Peder, like a patient teacher.

Fredrika could not believe what she was hearing, and was about to argue when Alex broke in.

'Let's finish the run-through of our findings first, then we can continue this discussion,' he suggested.

He nodded to Peder to go on.

Peder waited demonstratively for a few seconds for Fredrika to start protesting, but to his disappointment, she did not. Ellen's mobile stated to ring, however, so she left the room. Referring to his rather sloppy notes, Peder passed on to his colleagues what little other information they had. Nobody had seen what happened in Flemingsberg and nobody had seen Lilian leaving the train.

'The interviews didn't produce much,' said Peder, feeling suddenly sheepish.

Alex shook his head as if to say it didn't matter.

'At this juncture, it's impossible to say what's important and what's not,' he sighed. 'Fredrika, can you give us Sara's story and what you've got on her ex-husband, please?'

Fredrika liked giving lectures. She spoke clearly and concretely, and in all the other places she had worked, her presentations had been praised. But she suspected that in the police she was considered supercilious and far too formal.

Fredrika briefly gave her own impression of Sara and her account of the events in Flemingsberg. She also explained what the files had turned up, and put forward her theory that Sara's husband was still a big problem for her.

It was Alex who spoke next, of course.

'Have you talked to her ex-husband?' he asked.

'His name's Gabriel, and technically they're still married, so he's not really her "ex-husband" but her husband,' Fredrika began. 'And no, I haven't managed to get hold of him. He's got a small house tucked away in a nice part of Östermalm. I got through to his mother just before the start of the meeting, and she said her son was on a business trip. She thought he'd be in Uppsala all day. I tried ringing, but his phone's turned off. He had to be informed of what's happened to his daughter, anyway, so I left a voicemail message.'

'What's his current situation? Does he live alone?' asked Alex, jotting something down on his pad.

'I haven't had a chance to ask Sara or his mother yet. But I shall look into it, of course.'

Alex pondered in silence. A father who had in all probability abused his ex-wife on numerous occasions, and was perhaps still doing so, was a very interesting person in a missing child investigation. The single most interesting person, in fact. Decades of police work supported that fundamental assumption.

'What were the custody arrangements?' he asked Fredrika, leaning back in his chair with his hands behind his head.

'What Sara herself told me was that it hadn't been a matter of dispute between them, but on the phone just now, the husband's mother expressed concern that her son didn't get to see Lilian more often. I got the impression that she, the grandmother, was well informed about her son's daily life. She told me, for example, that the time he rang Sara a hundred times on one evening he was, as the grandmother put it, "beside himself with worry for the girl". She claimed Sara had taken Lilian off on a short trip without telling Gabriel.'

'So they *had* argued about the girl, in fact, at least earlier on,' Alex said slowly. 'Are there any grounds at all for suspecting that Sara Sebastiansson has been lying, and never was abused and harassed by her husband?'

Fredrika gave an emphatic shake of the head.

'No,' she said, with some force. 'I simply don't see how that could be possible. Not when the injuries are so well documented.'

'But isn't there something fishy about this whole set-up?' asked Peder, glancing at Alex, who nodded.

'Yes, there's something fishy all right. But I can't quite put my finger on it.'

He looked at Fredrika.

'Have you spoken to Sara Sebastiansson about the abuse aspect?'

'No, I didn't see the reports until I got back here. But I'm going to see her later this evening and I'll bring it up then.'

A rattling sound filled the silence when Fredrika stopped talking. The ancient air conditioning made a lot of noise considering how little cool air it generated.

'But even so,' Peder persisted, with another look of entreaty at Alex. 'The father's got to be our hottest lead, if he really is such a bastard as Sara claims, that is.'

Alex saw Fredrika's face harden at Peder's insinuation that Sara Sebastiansson might be lying to the police.

'Definitely,' he said. 'Regardless of what Sara herself may think, the father is a main lead in this investigation until we have reason to write him off as uninteresting.'

Fredrika felt relieved, and her shoulders relaxed a little. Alex had often thought how attractive she could be when she smiled and relaxed. Shame she didn't do it more often, that was all.

'Right,' said Alex. 'You said the girl's mother had a new man. Is he of any interest?'

'I haven't got a definite ID on him yet. He's called Anders Nyström, and Sara's known him for such a short time that all she could give me was his year of birth and where he lives. He isn't recorded as living at the address where Sara went to see him, and his mobile number only traces back to an unregistered pay-as-you-go account. He isn't answering his mobile and the voicemail isn't working.'

'What the hell is that girl doing hanging around with creeps like that? Guys who hit her and guys she hardly knows,' sighed Peder, slumping in his seat.

Fredrika fixed Peder with a stare but said nothing.

Alex indicated she should go on.

'When Sara rang him from the platform, they arranged for him to come round this evening, after Lilian was in bed, about nine-thirty. I've come up with three possible Anders Nyströms born the same year as Sara's friend, none of them with criminal records. When I see him at Sara's tonight, I shall be able to get more details.'

'You're seeing him tonight . . . ?' began Alex uncertainly.

He got no further before Fredrika raised a discreet hand from her place at the table.

Alex suppressed a sigh.

'Yes?' he said patiently.

'The woman with the dog,' replied Fredrika with equal patience.

'Yes?' Alex said again.

Fredrika took a deep breath.

'How does the woman with the dog fit into the scenario if we assume the father took the girl?'

Alex gave a rather tight-lipped smile.

'If Lilian's father took her, then can't the woman with the dog just be a coincidence?'

He gave Fredrika a searching look and said firmly:

'We haven't forgotten the woman in Flemingsberg, Fredrika. But for now we're prioritizing other information. With good reason.'

Alex surveyed the group again and cleared his throat.

'I'd like to come round to Sara's with you,' he said, nodding in Fredrika's direction.

Her eyebrows shot up. Peder reacted, too, straightening his back.

'It's not that I'm questioning your competence,' Alex said hurriedly, 'but wouldn't it be a good idea for you to share the responsibility for these interviews with someone else? Sara's new boyfriend could turn out to be a nasty piece of work and I'd feel happier if there were two of us.'

Peder beamed at Alex. Alex thought for a minute he was going to slap him on the back. This investigation would be hard going if the team couldn't work together.

From Fredrika there was not a word. Nor were any needed – her fixed expression betrayed what she was thinking very plainly.

Ellen interrupted proceedings with a loud knock at the door.

'Just wanted to say that the switchboard is getting calls from the public already,' was all she said.

'Great,' said Alex, 'that's great.'

Soon, if the child did not reappear, he would have to consider calling in assistance from the National Crime Squad to go through all the tip-offs. He brought the meeting to a close.

'In spite of the shocking nature of the event,' he said on his way out of the room, 'I have to say I've got quite a good feeling about this case. It's bound to be only a matter of time until the girl's found.'

Once the parcel was ready, the Man put it in an ordinary paper carrier bag and left Jelena alone in the flat.

'I'll be back later,' he said.

Jelena smiled to herself. She wandered restlessly between the kitchen and the living room. She avoided going anywhere near the bathroom.

The television was on. The news that a child had gone missing from a train was covered in a couple of quick sentences. Jelena found that rather annoying.

Just wait, she thought. You'll all soon realize this isn't just some ordinary little bit of news.

She ran her hands nervously through her hair. The man would not have liked her doing that; he would have taken it as a sign that she did not have complete trust in his ability to plan and carry through his project. But still. There was so much at stake, so much that had to go right.

Jelena went out into the kitchen and decided to make a sandwich. She was just opening the fridge door when she saw them on the floor, right under the table. The blood went coursing round her body and her pulse rate rose. Her heart was pounding so hard that she thought it would explode in her chest as she bent down to pick up the little pair of panties from the floor.

'No, no,' she whispered in panic. 'No, no, how could I have done this?'

Her brain was working as if it was on autopilot, doing what had to be done. She must get rid of the panties, at once. The Man's instructions had been entirely clear. All the clothes were to be in the parcel. *All* of them. Jelena felt so terrified she was on the verge of tears as she screwed the panties into a little ball and put them in an old plastic bag from a supermarket. *Just as long as he doesn't stop on the way and double check everything's in the parcel.* She moved at the speed of light as she left the flat and raced down to the rubbish storage room in the basement of the block of flats. The door resisted as usual and was heavy to open. Jelena lifted the lid of one of the rubbish containers and threw in the bag. Her heart felt like a bolting horse as she ran back up to her flat, taking two steps at a time.

The door of the flat slammed shut behind her with a bang, and she fumbled with the lock. She had to take several deep breaths to stop her palpitations turning into a full-scale panic attack. Then she tiptoed over to the bathroom and swallowed quite a few times before she opened the door. Her relief when she switched on the ceiling light was indescribable.

At least everything in the bathroom was as it should be. The girl was still lying naked in the bath where they had left her.

Peder Rydh flicked distractedly through his little notebook. He could scarcely read what he had written in it. He fanned himself with the book in the close heat of the office and let his thoughts roam free. Life could throw up the most unexpected and nasty surprises. Lilian Sebastiansson had experienced that today, first hand. But Peder took the same view as Alex, expecting the team to solve this particular case with relative ease.

The ringing of his mobile intruded into his thoughts. He smiled when he saw it was his brother calling. Jimmy rang him at least once a day.

'You listening?' the voice on the phone asked indignantly after a bit of introductory banter.

'I'm listening, I'm listening,' Peder put in hurriedly.

He could hear the silent laughter at the other end, almost like a child's stifled giggles.

'You're cheating, Pedda, you're cheating. You're not listening.'

Peder had to smile. No, he wasn't listening. Not properly, not the way he normally did when he was talking to his brother.

'You coming soon, Pedda?'

'I'm coming soon,' Peder promised. 'I'll see you at the weekend.'

'Is that long?'

'No, it's not long now. Only a few days.'

Then they rounded off the conversation the way they always did: with extravagant promises of kisses and hugs and eating posh cake with marzipan together when they saw each other. Jimmy sounded relatively happy. He would be seeing their parents tomorrow.

'It could just as easily have been you, Peder,' Peder's mum had told him, more times than he could remember.

When he was little, she used to cup his face in her warm hands as she said it.

'It could just as easily have been you. It could just as easily have been you who fell off the swing that day.'

Peder still had very sharp visual images in his head from the day his brother fell off the big swing their father had hung from one of the birch trees in the garden. He remembered the blood running over the stone Jimmy's head had landed on, the grass smelling so strong because it was freshly mown, Jimmy lying on the ground, looking as if he was asleep. And he remembered rushing over and trying to cradle his little head that was bleeding so badly.

'You mustn't die,' he had shouted, thinking of the rabbit they had buried so sadly, a month or so earlier. 'You mustn't die.'

His plea had been answered, in one sense, for Jimmy stayed with them. But he was never the same again, and although his body grew as fast as Peder's, he remained a child.

Peder leafed through his notebook again. No, you never knew what surprises life would deal you. Peder certainly thought he knew more about that than most people. Not only in view of what happened to his brother when he was growing up, but also as a result of bitter experience gained later in

life. Not to mention just recently. But he'd rather not think
about that.

He was roused from his reverie by the sound of Fredrika in
the corridor outside.

Alex had told Peder a few weeks earlier, in confidence of
course, that Fredrika lacked the tact and sensitivity you needed
for this profession. Peder couldn't have put it better himself. To
be frank, Fredrika was your classic anally retentive type. And
she didn't seem to have any kind of proper man to give her a
proper seeing to at regular intervals, but Peder decided not to
mention that to Alex. Alex was remarkably uninterested in
thoughts and comments of that kind; he never wanted to talk
about anything except work. Maybe eventually, when they'd
been working together for longer, they'd be able to go for a
beer together one evening? He felt a tickle of excitement in the
pit of his stomach. There were few police officers who could
even contemplate that – a beer with Alex Recht.

It really annoyed him that Fredrika couldn't see, and therefore didn't acknowledge, Alex's greatness in the policing
world. There she sat in her little jacket – she always wore a
jacket – with her dark hair plaited in an improbably long plait
that hung like a riding crop down her back, looking so bloody
sceptical it made him want to throw up. There was something
about the way she held herself, and that cocky laugh she
would sometimes let out, that he simply couldn't stand. No,
Fredrika wasn't a police officer; she was a so-called academic.
She thought too much and acted too little. That wasn't how
police officers operated.

Peder cursed the fact that he'd been passed over in favour
of Fredrika yet again and not been sent to talk to Sara

Sebastiansson. At the same time, he cursed the fact that he hadn't any extra spare time to give to the job, anyway. His private life was still using up too much of his energy for him to be able to function effectively.

Even so. Hadn't Alex sounded confident the case of the missing Lilian would soon be solved? Wasn't it very often the case that a man feeling wronged by his wife would use their child to punish her? So the Lilian case was not to be considered particularly major or important. Seen in that light, it was more understandable that Fredrika was going with Alex to interview Sara at home. It was actually a good thing that she and not Peder had been asked to go, because she was the one who needed to hone her skills, not him.

What Peder hardly dared admit, even to himself, was that for all the criticism he directed at her, he found Fredrika remarkably attractive. She had perfect skin and lovely, big blue eyes. Blue eyes when everything else about her was dark created an effect that was frankly dramatic. Her body looked as though it belonged to someone who had just turned twenty, though her bearing and the look in her eyes were those of a mature woman. She certainly had the breasts of an extremely mature woman. Peder occasionally caught himself thinking really filthy thoughts about Fredrika. He strongly suspected that university student unions and pubs were places that turned many young students into really good sexual partners. He suspected equally strongly that Fredrika was one of them. He avoided catching her eye when she automatically glanced into his room as she passed the door. He wondered what going to bed with her would be like. Probably not bad at all.

In a top-floor flat under the eaves in Östermalm, Fredrika Bergman was rounding off her intensive working day in the company of her lover. Fredrika and Spencer Lagergren had been seeing each other for a good number of years. In fact, Fredrika didn't like to remind herself quite how many years it was, but on the rare occasions she did let herself remember, she always went back to the first time they spent the night together. Fredrika had been twenty-one at the time, and Spencer forty-six.

There wasn't anything very complicated about their relationship. Over the course of the years, Fredrika had sometimes been single, sometimes involved in another relationship. At the times when she had someone else, she would refrain from seeing Spencer. A lot of men and women seem to be able to see two partners simultaneously. Fredrika couldn't.

Spencer could, however, and Fredrika was always very much aware of it. Spencer and his wife Eva had got married one sunny day almost thirty-five years before, and he would never leave her for anyone else. Or only for the occasional weekday evening. Fredrika found this an entirely satisfactory arrangement. Spencer was twenty-five years older than her. Common sense told her that such an equation would prove impossible. Cold mathematical calculations also told her that if she really were to give her life to Spencer, if she chose to live with him, it would not be all that many years before she was alone again.

So Fredrika contented herself with seeing Spencer on a sporadic basis and accepting her role as the second, not the first, woman in his life. By extension of the same principle, she did not let it worry her either that their relationship never grew or developed. So Spencer Lagergren was just what she needed, on the whole. So she told herself.

'I can't get this cork out,' said Spencer, frowning as he struggled with the bottle of wine he had brought.

Fredrika ignored him. He would rather die than let her try to open it. Spencer was always in charge of the wine, Fredrika of the music. They both loved classical music. Spencer had once tried to persuade her to play him something on the violin she still kept. But she refused.

'I don't play any more,' came her firm, abrupt reply.

And no more was said on the subject.

'Perhaps soaking the neck of the bottle in hot water would ease it a bit,' Spencer muttered to himself.

His shadow played across the kitchen tiles as he moved to and fro with the bottle. It was a small kitchen; he was perpetually just a couple of steps away from treading on her toes. But she knew he never would. Spencer never trod on a woman's toes, except perhaps when he was expressing his not entirely modern views in feminist discussions. And even then, he did so in such a brilliant way that he almost always emerged from those discussions on the winning side. In Fredrika's eyes, and those of many other women, that made him an altogether very attractive man.

Fredrika noted he had finally won his fight with the wine bottle. Artur Rubinstein was playing Chopin in the background. Fredrika crept up behind Spencer and gently put her arms around him. She leant her head wearily on his back, her forehead resting against the body she knew best in the world apart from her own.

'Are you tired, or shattered?' Spencer asked quietly, pouring the wine.

Fredrika smiled.

She knew he was smiling, too.

'Shattered,' she whispered.

He turned in her embrace, and held out a glass of wine. She rested her forehead on his chest for a split second before she took the glass.

'Sorry I was so late today.'

Spencer raised his glass in a silent toast, and they enjoyed their first sip.

Fredrika had not been particularly keen on red wine before she met Spencer. Now she found it hard to forgo it for more than a few days at a time. The good professor had indisputably taught her some bad habits.

Spencer ran a gentle hand across her cheek.

'I was late last time, you know,' was all he said.

Fredrika gave a little smile.

'But it's eleven o'clock, Spencer. You certainly weren't that late, last time we met.'

For some reason – maybe because she felt guilty, maybe because she was tired – tears came to her eyes.

'Oh, don't get upset . . .' began Spencer, seeing the glint of moisture in her eyes.

'Sorry,' she mumbled, 'I don't know what's the matter with me. I . . .'

'You're tired,' said Spencer firmly. 'You're tired, and you hate your job with the police. And that, my friend, is a really bad combination.'

Fredrika drank more of her wine.

'I know,' she said in a low voice, 'I know.'

He put a steady arm around her waist.

'Stay at home tomorrow. We'll both stay here.'

Fredrika gave an imperceptible sigh.

'No chance,' she said. 'I'm working on a new case now. A little girl's gone missing. That's why I was so late: we were interviewing the child's mother and the mother's new boyfriend all evening. Such a horrible story you can hardly believe it's true.'

Spencer pulled her closer. She set down her glass and put both arms around him.

'I've missed you,' she whispered.

Saying anything like that was admittedly against the unspoken rules they agreed on, but Fredrika was too exhausted to worry about any agreement just then.

'I've missed you, too,' mumbled Spencer as he kissed the top of her head.

Fredrika stared into his eyes in astonishment.

'Now there's a coincidence, eh?' said Spencer with a crooked smile.

It was after one before Fredrika and Spencer finally decided to try to get some sleep. As usual, Spencer was able to put the decision into practice with little delay. Fredrika found it much harder.

The wide double bed stood along one wall of what was really

the only proper room in the flat. Apart from the bed, the flat was sparsely furnished with a couple of battered old English armchairs and a beautiful chess table. Over by the little kitchen there were also a small dining table and two chairs.

The flat had belonged to Spencer's father, and he had inherited it when his father died, nearly ten years ago now. Since then, Fredrika and her lover had never really met anywhere else. She had still never been to Spencer's main home, which felt logical. The only times they met somewhere other than the flat were when Fredrika occasionally discreetly accompanied Spencer to some conference abroad. She thought a number of his colleagues must know about their liaison, but quite honestly she couldn't have cared less. What was more, Spencer's status among his professorial colleagues was extraordinarily high, so he was never confronted with any direct questions.

Lying there in Spencer's arms, Fredrika curled up into a little ball. He was breathing deeply behind her and already fast asleep. She stroked a cautious finger over the hairs on his naked arm. She couldn't imagine a life without him. Such thoughts were indescribably dangerous, she knew that. Yet she could not banish them. And they always came when the night was at its darkest and she was feeling at her loneliest.

She shifted carefully until she was lying on her back.

The visit to Sara Sebastiansson's had been a strain in every way. Partly because of Sara Sebastiansson herself, of course. The woman was entirely unbalanced. But also because of Peder. He had been mightily pleased when Alex decided Fredrika should not go to see Sara Sebastiansson on her own. Fredrika had seen him straighten up, and his face had broken into a sneering grin.

'*It's not that I'm questioning your competence*,' Alex had said.

Fredrika knew all too well that that was exactly what he was doing. Expectations of her, a young woman with an academic background, were set extremely low. She was assumed to be barely capable of operating the photocopier. She could sense Alex's irritation whenever she dared put forward or develop a new hypothesis.

His attitude to the woman in Flemingsburg was a case in point.

Fredrika found it hard to exclude her from the investigation. It was frankly grotesque that Sara hadn't been asked for a description of the woman and that they hadn't done a photofit. On the way back to the office after they had seen Sara, Fredrika had tried to raise the question again, but a weary Alex had firmly interrupted her.

'It's obvious, completely bloody obvious, that the father of that child is as sick as they come,' he said agitatedly. 'There's nothing to point to there being any other lunatics in Sara's circle who would want to harm her child, or scare Sara by taking Lilian from her. And nobody's sent Sara a ransom note or anything like that.'

When Fredrika opened her mouth to point out that the perpetrator could be someone Sara was not actually in touch with at present, or did not realize she was in conflict with, Alex brought the discussion to a close with a:

'It would be to your advantage in this organization to respect the competence and experience we have here. I've been looking for missing children for decades, so believe me, I know what I'm doing.'

Things went very quiet in the car after that, and Fredrika saw no reason to continue the discussion.

She peered over at Spencer's peaceful face. Craggy features, grey, wavy hair. Good looking, you might even say handsome. Not cute, not ever. She had stopped asking herself how he could sleep so well, night after night, when he was being unfaithful. She assumed it was because he and his wife lived separate lives and had a mutual agreement about the extent of personal freedom they each had in the marriage. There had never been any children. Perhaps they had chosen not to have any. Fredrika wasn't sure about that.

Alex Recht really shouldn't have been particularly hard for Fredrika, of all people, to deal with. Not after almost fourteen years with a person whose views came from a time machine stuck somewhere in the mid-nineteenth century. Not after fourteen years with someone who still wouldn't let her open a bottle of wine. Fredrika smiled wistfully. Spencer still respected her infinitely more than Alex did.

'What is it he gives you that you feel you can't do without?' a succession of her friends had asked her over the years. 'Why do you carry on seeing him, when nothing can ever come of it?'

Her answer had varied over time. At the very beginning, it had been so incredibly exciting and passionate. Forbidden and invigorating for both of them. An adventure. But the relationship had deepened, within its given limitations. They had many interests and some values in common. Over time, closeness to Spencer developed into a sort of fixed point for her. As she commuted between various cities and countries while finishing her studies, Spencer had always been there to come back to. The same was true when she became entangled in a variety of love affairs, all relatively short-lived. Once disaster had struck and the house of cards had collapsed, he was always still there. Never without pride, but permanently bored with his marriage yet unable to leave his wife. Though Fredrika had been told the wife had flings of her own.

Fredrika's single status had been discussed in her own family on countless occasions over the years. She knew she had been a surprise to her parents in more than just her choice of profession. Neither of them had imagined she would still be single by her age. Her grandmother definitely hadn't.

'Oh, you'll find someone,' she used to say, patting Fredrika's arm.

It had been a while now since Fredrika's grandmother had done that. Fredrika had just celebrated her thirty-fourth birthday with some good friends out in the archipelago, and was still husbandless and childless. Grandma would probably have had a heart attack if she had known Fredrika shared a bed from time to time with the professor who had been her supervisor at university.

Her father delivered thinly veiled lectures on the virtue of 'settling for' some things in life and 'not being too greedy'. Only once Fredrika had grasped this would she, as her brother already did each Sunday, take her place at the parental dining table in the company of a family of her own. A year or two after Fredrika turned thirty and still seemed determinedly single (or 'alone', as her father put it), the Sunday dinners were putting such a strain on her mentally that she started to avoid them.

Lying in the dark beside a man she thought she loved in

spite of everything, Fredrika knew that the day she told him she was having a baby, Spencer would be on his way out of her life. Not because she was replaceable, but because there was no room for a child in their relationship.

Fredrika and Spencer hadn't talked about it for a long time, but after a long period of reflection, Fredrika was increasingly realizing that she might not find a man to start a family with, and that she might need to start thinking about the alternatives. It wasn't a decision she could postpone indefinitely; she had to decide. Either she did something about it, even though she was alone, or there might be no children at all. She found it unexpectedly painful trying to visualize a whole life without the experience of parenthood. To put it bluntly, it felt unfair and unnatural.

There were various alternatives to weigh up. The most unthinkable of them was to force Spencer into paternity: she could stop taking the pill without telling him. Less unthinkable was a trip to Copenhagen to buy a chance of motherhood at a fertility clinic. The option that seemed the most feasible was adopting a child.

'For fuck's sake just send in the forms,' Fredrika's friend Julia had said, a few months earlier. 'You can always back out, say you applied in too much of a hurry. You'll have oceans of time to think it over; it takes forever to be approved to adopt. I'd get in the queue straight away.'

At first she hadn't even seen it as a serious suggestion. What was more, it would amount to giving up somehow. The day she sent in her application to adopt would be the day she really gave up all hope of having a family of her own, with a partner. Had she reached that point?

The answer to that question came when Spencer didn't answer the phone, either his mobile or his job number. After several days of silence, she started ringing round hospitals. He was in the cardiac department of the University Hospital in Uppsala. He had suffered a major heart attack and been given a pacemaker. Fredrika cried for a week and then, with a new perspective on what is enduring in life, she sent in the application form.

Fredrika planted a light kiss on Spencer's forehead. He smiled in his sleep. She smiled back. She still hadn't told him about her plan to adopt a little girl from China. After all, her friend was right: she had oceans of time.

One last thought formed in her head before she succumbed to sleep. How much time did Lilian have? Did she have oceans of it, too, or were her days numbered?

WEDNESDAY

The woman on the TV screen was talking so fast that Nora almost missed the news report. It was early morning and her flat was shrouded in darkness. The only light came from the television, but since the blinds were down, Nora was almost certain its flickering gleam couldn't be seen by anyone looking in from the street.

For Nora, this was very important. She knew she was condemned to feel unsafe, but she also knew there were certain little things she could do to improve her odds. One of them was simply not to be seen. By requesting protected identity from the tax authorities, she became less visible; by never having the light on in the flat in the evening, she became even less visible. She had a minimal circle of friends. She only had sporadic contact with her grandmother, always ringing her from a phone box in the street, and always from some other town. Her job was useful in that respect; she had to travel a fair amount.

When she heard the news she was in the kitchen, making a sandwich, with the fridge door open. The light in the fridge was useful; it meant she didn't need to switch on any other lights to see what she was doing.

The woman's voice cut through the silence and reached Nora as she struggled with the cheese slice.

'A six-year-old girl went missing yesterday from a train travelling between Gothenburg and Stockholm,' the woman's voice intoned. 'The police are appealing for anyone who was on the train that left Gothenburg at 10.50 a.m. yesterday morning, or at Stockholm Central Station around . . .'

Nora dropped the cheese slice and ran to the television.

'Oh God,' whispered Nora, feeling her heart thud. 'He's started.'

She listened to the end of the news, then switched off the set and sank down on the settee. The words she had just heard sank slowly into her consciousness, one by one. Together they formed whole sentences creating violent echoes from a time she had tried so hard to put behind her.

'The train, Doll,' whispered the echo. 'You've no idea what people leave behind on the train. And you've no idea how unobservant all the rest are. The ones who don't leave things behind, but are just travelling. That's what people do on the train, Doll. They travel. And they don't see a thing.'

She sat there on the settee until her hunger reminded her of the sandwich she had made. Only then did she reach a decision about what to do. She switched the TV back on, and clicked to teletext. The police number for members of the public with any information was at the end of the item about the missing child. She keyed it into her mobile. She would ring later in the day. Not from her mobile, of course, but from a telephone box.

Nora pulled the blind aside and peeped cautiously out into the street. If only it would stop raining.

Alex Recht woke up just after six, almost an hour before the alarm clock was due to go off. Carefully, so as not to wake his wife Lena, he got out of bed and padded out of the room to make his first cup of coffee of the day.

The house was light on this bright morning, but the sun had already settled behind a clump of thick cloud. Alex suppressed a sigh as he measured the coffee into the filter of the machine. No, he honestly couldn't remember ever experiencing a worse summer. The rest of his holiday leave lay just a few weeks ahead. They would feel like totally wasted weeks if the weather didn't improve.

Mistrustful of the weather, he opened the back door to check whether it had started raining yet and made a brisk foray to retrieve the morning paper. He unfolded it even before he was back inside. A headline about the disappearance of Lilian Sebastiansson looked back at him from the front page of the national daily. 'Child of six missing since yesterday . . .' Excellent, even the big papers had been in time to run the story.

Alex took his cup of coffee and newspaper and crossed the little hall, painted a deep blue, to his study. It had been Lena's idea to paint the hall blue. Alex had been sceptical.

'Doesn't it make small spaces look even smaller if you paint them a dark colour?' he said doubtfully.

'Maybe,' said Lena. 'But more to the point, it makes them look nice!'

That, Alex realized, was an argument he had little hope of countering, so he allowed himself to be persuaded more or less without a fight. It fell to his son to do the painting job, and it certainly did look lovely. And cramped. But they didn't talk about that.

Alex sat down in the enormous desk chair that was more like a small armchair on wheels. He had inherited it from his grandfather and would never part with it. Alex gave the arm of the chair a contented pat. Not only was it handsome, it was also comfortable. Alex and the chair would soon be celebrating their thirtieth anniversary. Thirty years! That was a terribly long time to sit in one chair. Actually, thought Alex, it was a terribly long time in every way. Longer than he had been married to Lena, in fact.

Leaning back in the chair, Alex closed his eyes.

He didn't feel properly rested. He had not slept well last night. For the first time in several years, he had had nightmares. However much he would have liked to blame it on the weather, he knew the bad dreams had their origins elsewhere.

Alex was more than vaguely aware that in the course of his years with the police, he had come to be viewed as something of a legend. On the whole, he thought it was a reputation he deserved. The number of investigations and cases that had crossed his desk was too great for him to count, and he had solved most of them sooner or later. Never alone, but he had generally taken the lead. Just as he was doing this time. But now he was becoming aware of the passage of the years. They were talking about bringing the pension age for police officers down to sixty-one. Alex initially thought it sounded a lousy idea, but now he felt differently. It did no good for an authority like the police to be weighed down by a lot of tired and ageing officers. It was important to bring new blood into the organization.

In his years in the police force, Alex had encountered more desperate individuals than he could remember. Sara Sebastiansson was the latest of them. But she hadn't let any real despair show yet. She was keeping herself together in a quite remarkable way, thought Alex. He had no doubt that inside she was being torn apart by her anxiety and her desperate longing to see the child, but she was forcing herself not to show it. It was as if she thought that if she exposed for a single second – *a single second* – the horror she was going through, then the world would split apart beneath her feet and her daughter would be lost for ever. As Alex understood it, she hadn't even rung her parents yet.

'I'll do it tomorrow, if Lilian's not back by then,' she had said.

Now it was tomorrow, and as far as Alex knew, Lilian was still missing. He looked at his mobile phone. No missed calls, no missed news.

There were a few other basics to bear in mind where missing children were concerned. Almost all such children, the vast majority, were found. Sooner or later. And 'later' was seldom more than a day or so. That had been the case, for example, for the little boy out on the coast last year, when Alex was called in precisely because he had handled a number of missing child cases in the course of his career. The boy, perhaps five years old, had slipped away from his family's summer place at Ekerö when his parents were having an argument, and then simply run or walked so far from the house that he couldn't find his way back again.

They found him asleep under a spruce some ten kilometres from home, further away than expected, beyond the radius of the initial search. He was reunited with his parents early the next morning, and the last thing Alex heard as he left the place was the parents bickering loudly and bitterly about whose fault it was the boy had gone off.

Then, of course, there were cases Alex found it harder to reconcile himself to. Cases in which the child had been subjected to such abominations when it was snatched that it was basically a completely different child by the time it was restored to its parents. There was one particular little girl who always came back into Alex's mind when another child went missing. The girl had been gone for several days before she was found in a ditch by a motorist. She was unconscious for more than a week after she was admitted to hospital, and could never give any proper account of what had happened to her. Nor was there any need. The injuries to her body bore witness to the kind of scum that must have taken her, and though doctors, psychologists and well-meaning parents did everything in their power to heal her wounds, there were psychological scars that no medical treatment or words on this earth could remove.

The girl remained dysfunctional and disturbed as she grew up, not interacting with those around her at home or at school. She became more and more of a loner. She didn't finish secondary school. Still not of age, she ran away from home and turned to prostitution. Her parents brought her home time after time but she always made off again. And before she was twenty, she died of a heroin overdose. Alex could remember crying in his office when the news reached him.

Alex had felt an overwhelming urge to go and see Sara Sebastiansson for himself the previous evening, and that was why he had accompanied Fredrika Bergman to Sara's flat. He was afraid Fredrika took it as a sign that he questioned her competence in that area of work. Which he did, to some extent, but that wasn't why he had wanted to go with her. No, he had just wanted to get a better feel for the case. And he certainly had.

First Fredrika and Alex talked to Sara on her own for a while, and then her new friend Anders Nyström turned up. The checks on his personal data had not yielded anything, but Fredrika had nonetheless interviewed him briefly in Sara's kitchen, while Alex continued his conversation with Sara in the living room.

The information that emerged troubled him.

Sara had no enemies. At least none she was aware of.

On the other hand, she didn't seem to have many friends, either.

She told him that her ex-husband used to abuse her, but that it was no longer a problem, and she didn't believe for a moment that he had taken their daughter. That was why she had chosen not to mention the earlier abuse to Fredrika when they first spoke. She didn't want the police investigation getting unnecessarily sidetracked, as she put it.

Alex didn't believe a word of it. For one thing, he had explained in as lecturing a tone as he could without sounding downright arrogant, it was not Sara's role to evaluate the various avenues of investigation, if indeed there were more than one. And for another, Alex did not believe Sara's ex-husband was now leaving her in peace. It took him a while to talk her round, but eventually she showed him her forearms, which she had clearly been trying to hide inside her sleeves. Just as Fredrika had suspected, the arms showed clear signs of physical violence. A large and evidently very painful patch stood out sharply on her left arm. The skin was orangey-red and Alex could see signs of blisters that were now starting to heal. A burn, without a doubt.

'He burnt me with the iron, just before we separated,' Sara said in a flat voice, with an empty gaze that was trying to fix on a point somewhere behind Alex.

Alex took her arm gently in his hand and said quietly but emphatically:

'You'll have to report this, Sara.'

At that, she slowly turned her head and looked him straight in the eye.

'He wasn't here then.'

'What?'

'Haven't you read the police reports? He's never here when it happens. There's always someone who can confirm he was somewhere else.'

Again her eyes went to that point behind Alex.

It disturbed Alex to see the extent of Sara Sebastiansson's injuries. To his great annoyance and dismay, her ex-husband had not been in touch at all that evening. Alex sent a radio car to his address for the second time that day, but the officers reported back that the house was still in darkness and no one had answered the door. Fredrika then said she would contact

Gabriel Sebastiansson's mother again the following day, and ring the place where he worked. *Somebody* must know where he was.

Sitting there in his grandfather's office chair, Alex could feel the anger rising inside him. There were certain fundamental rules that he had grown up with and learnt to respect in his almost fifty-five years in this world. You did not hit women. You did not hit children. You did not lie. And you took care of the elderly.

Alex shuddered as he remembered the burn.

What made you do something like that to the person closest to you?

Alex found it hard to stomach the political mood that was now sweeping the country, talking of 'men's violence against women'. It would be unthinkable to make sweeping generalizations like that in other areas. To take just one example, a colleague had said at a police conference that 'the immigrant tendency not to obey laws or regulations is costing society untold sums of money'. That statement almost cost the colleague his job. If he went round saying things like that, it was argued, the public would think all immigrants chose to live outside society's rules, and that was definitely not the case.

No, thought Alex, it was definitely not the case. Any more than saying that all men hit all women. *Some* men hit women. A huge number of others did not. Unless that was the accepted starting point, the problem would never be properly addressed.

There had been no need for the team to meet again the previous evening. Alex had updated Peder once he and Fredrika left Sara Sebastiansson's flat. Alex was neither stupid nor gullible. Peder had an almost childlike urge to show how clever he was, and Alex was a little concerned that this might have a negative impact on his judgment in stressful situations. But at the same time he didn't want to inhibit Peder, who showed exemplary enthusiasm for his job and had so much energy.

It would have been nice if Fredrika could display a little more of that, he thought drily.

He glanced at the clock. Nearly seven. Time to get dressed and head into town. He was so lucky to live on an island like Resarö, so close to the city, yet just far enough away. He would never exchange this house for any other. It was a real find, as his darling Lena had said when they bought it a few years before. Alex got up from his desk chair and took the blue corridor back to the kitchen. By the time he stepped into the shower a short while later, the first rain shower of the morning was already drumming on the window.

The train service between Gothenburg to Stockholm is more or less hourly. Sara Sebastiansson's parents took the earliest train they could, leaving Gothenburg at six in the morning. This was not their first emergency trip from coast to coast, but it was definitely the gravest of its kind. On several previous occasions they had had to drop everything at home and at work to look after Lilian while Sara tried to recover from the damage done to her body as quickly as she could. They had systematically refused to have anything more to do with their son-in-law after the first attack. They had tried every way they could to persuade Sara to be strong and keep away from him. They had implored her to move back to the west coast. But she had always refused. She was not going to let Gabriel destroy any more aspects of her life, she told them. She had been away from Gothenburg for fifteen years, and would never move back. Never. Her life was in Stockholm now.

'But Sara, love,' her mother said, 'he could kill you. Think of Lilian, Sara. What will happen to Lilian if you're dead?'

But Sara hardened herself against her mother's tears, and carried on saying no.

Had she done the right thing?

Sitting at her kitchen table the morning after Lilian disappeared, she asked herself if she had made a mistake of incalculable proportions. She wondered if Gabriel really had taken Lilian. God knows the man had done monstrously evil things. Never directly aimed at Lilian, but affecting her indirectly all the same, since she had more than once been woken from her innocent sleep by her mother Sara's screams from an adjacent room. Once, Lilian had crept out of bed and tearfully found her way to where the sound was coming from.

Sara could still see the scene in her mind's eye. She was lying on the floor, prevented from getting up by the intense pain in her side where Gabriel had kicked her. Gabriel, seething with rage, bending over her. And in the midst of it all, Lilian's little voice.

'Mummy. Daddy.'

As if in a trance, Gabriel turned round.

'Oh,' he whispered, 'is Daddy's little darling awake?'

He took a couple of swift strides across the kitchen, lifted up the child and carried her out of the room.

'Mummy just fell over and landed all wrong, darling,' Sara heard him say. 'We'll leave her to have a little rest, and then she'll be as good as new. Do you want me to read you a story?'

Sara had done a university foundation course in psychology, and she knew that many men who beat their wives showed great remorse afterwards. Gabriel never did. He never said sorry; he never gave any hint of thinking what had happened was abnormal or wrong. He just looked at her injuries and bruises with such casual contempt that she wished she could fall dead on the spot.

She knew she was too exhausted to go on much longer. That night, the first night without Lilian, had been so relentlessly long.

'Try to get some rest,' Alex Recht had advised her. 'I know

it sounds impossible, but it really is the best thing you can do for Lilian, so you can be strong. Because when she comes back, she needs a rested mum to look after her. Okay?'

Sara had tried to hang on to that thought. She had tried to sleep, tried to prepare herself for her daughter's return. She clung on to Alex's last words: 'Because when she comes back . . .' Not *if* she comes back, but *when* she comes back.

As she lay there in bed, Sara realized almost at once that it had been a big mistake to send Anders away so soon. It had felt like a kind of betrayal of Lilian to have him around, as if his presence somehow worsened the odds of getting her daughter back. At two in the morning, she rang her parents. Her father went totally quiet, she heard him breathing into the phone.

Finally she heard his husky voice: 'We've always known we'd lose one of you,' he said. 'It could never end well with that evil man in your lives.'

Hearing those words, Sara dropped the phone and slumped to the floor. She clawed at the parquet floor of the kitchen as her tears flowed.

'Lilian,' she cried, 'Lilian.'

Somewhere in the background, from the telephone lying where it had fallen, she heard her father's desperate voice.

'We'll come right away, Sara. Mum and I will come right away.'

Sara cradled her cup of coffee. She liked the fact that it got light early in the mornings, despite the bad weather. She had slept for less than an hour in total. She tried to convince herself that this didn't make her a bad mother. A mother who didn't care at all must be worse than one who cared too much.

Sara was taken aback by her own thoughts. Was there really a limit to how upset you were allowed to be if your child vanished? She hoped not. She prayed not.

The shrill tone of the doorbell cut through the silence. Sara had just switched off the radio. She had heard the news of her daughter's disappearance on both television and radio. At first the girl newsreader's voice felt like a big, warm blanket. Somebody out there cared. Somebody out there wanted to help look for her child. But by the end of the third or fourth news bulletin, the warm blanket felt more like a noose, throttling her, an ever-present reminder of Lilian's absence, of which Sara was already all too painfully aware.

The doorbell rang again.

Sara considered. A quick look at the clock showed it was almost half past eight. She had been in touch with the duty officer at the police station an hour previously, and he had updated her. Still no news.

Sara peered cautiously through the peephole in the front door, hoping it would be Fredrika Bergman or Alex Recht. It was neither. No, there was some kind of postman standing there. And he had a parcel.

Sara opened the door, surprised.

'Sara Sebastiansson?' asked the man with the parcel.

She nodded. The thought occurred to her as she did so that she must look quite a sight, drained and exhausted as she was.

'I've got a parcel for you,' said the man, holding it out. 'It was to go directly to you, not to one of our collection points. Can you take delivery?'

'Yes,' said Sara warily, taking the package. 'Thank you.'

'Thank *you*!' said the man, smiling. 'Have a nice day!'

Sara made no reply to this, but shut the door and locked it. She gave the parcel a gentle shake. It weighed scarcely anything, and made no sound when she shook it. She looked for the address of the sender, there was none. It was a box about the size and shape for a DVD player or something like that. She turned it round, turned it over. Hesitant at first, then more deliberate.

'Contact the police immediately if anything unusual happens, anything you weren't expecting,' Alex Recht had urged her the night before. 'You've got to report it, Sara, whatever it is. Odd phone calls, odd rings at the door. Even though we're inclined not to think so, it could be that Lilian's been kidnapped, and in that case the perpetrator may try to contact you.'

Standing there with the package in her arms, Sara wondered if this should be considered an abnormal event. Her parents would be arriving any minute; should she wait for them to get there?

Perhaps it was lack of sleep, or the driving forces of desperation and curiosity, that made Sara Sebastiansson decide on the spur of the moment to open the parcel straight away. She laid it gently on the kitchen table and put her mobile phone beside it. She would open the parcel and then ring Alex Recht or Fredrika Bergman. If there was any reason to. It could just be something she'd ordered and forgotten about.

Sara peeled off the tape sealing the lid of the box. Her long fingers grasped both sides of the lid and lifted them up. A bed of polystyrene foam granules confronted her. Sara frowned. What was this?

She pushed the granules carefully aside. At first she could

not make out what it was she had been sent. Her eyes sought some kind of context they could comprehend. Hair. A mass of medium-length, wavy hair, chestnut brown. Dumbstruck, Sara touched the hair, revealing what lay beneath it. Then Sara instantly knew whose hair she was holding in her hands, and let out a loud, animal howl. She went on screaming until her parents arrived some minutes later and rang for the police and a doctor. Then the screams, which were starting to make her hoarse, turned into sobs of bewilderment and bottomless despair. The dam she had so skilfully built up to hold back her rising sense of panic had burst. *What had she done to deserve this? What in heaven's name had she done?*

Sara Sebastiansson's parents' call came through to the police just after 9 a.m. Alex was immediately informed and drove crazily fast to Sara's flat, taking Fredrika Bergman with him. To her unfeigned amazement, Fredrika noted as they left that Peder looked very unhappy about Fredrika being asked to answer the emergency call and not him.

Once the cardboard box with its nauseating contents had been sent off by special courier to the National Forensic Science Laboratory, SKL, in Linköping, Alex and Fredrika returned to HQ. Both occupants of the car derived a certain comfort from the silence that settled over them as they began the short return journey from Södermalm to the police building in Kungsholmsgatan. They swept up onto Västerbron and looked out from the bridge over a Stockholm wreathed in almost autumnal darkness. The next front of heavy clouds that had rolled in over the capital overnight were vividly reflected in the water spreading out beneath them. Fredrika reflected on the fact that they coloured the water grey, making the view a good deal less attractive than usual.

Alex cleared his throat.

'Sorry?' said Fredrika.

Alex looked at her and shook his head.

'I didn't say anything,' he said quietly.

He was reluctant to admit it, but Alex was shocked by what

he had just seen. The package turned the case from what initially seemed a routine investigation involving two adults going through a painful divorce in which their child had inevitably become a pawn, into a case with a much less predictable outcome. The experience had been made no less upsetting by Sara Sebastiansson's panic, which filled the whole flat and was made all the more tangible by her mother's tearful entreaties to her daughter to calm down. Alex could see at once that Sara Sebastiansson had gone beyond the point where a human being can simply 'calm down'. He decided the most efficient course of action was to wait for the doctor and then, when Sara had been given a sedative, to investigate the box and its contents himself.

It was clear from Sara's reaction to the parcel that the hair must be Lilian's. Tests would establish the fact for certain. Underneath the mass of hair were the clothes Lilian had been wearing when she disappeared. A green, knee-length skirt and a little white T-shirt with a green and pink print on the front. There were two little hairbands, too. Her panties were missing, for some reason.

Seeing the clothes made Alex's stomach lurch. Someone must have taken them off her. Of all the sick people in the world, he found none more repugnant than those who violated children.

There were no bloodstains or anything like that on the clothes. At least none that were visible, but SKL would establish that, of course, as well as checking for traces of other bodily fluids.

Alex thought he understood the message a package like that was intended to convey all too well. Somebody wanted to frighten Sara in a big way. Sara's hysterical reaction showed how very successful the sender had been. Later on, Sara would have to be asked about both the package and the person who delivered it, but any sort of conversation or interrogation was out of the question in her present state.

Soon, thought Alex. Soon.

He gripped the steering wheel hard, very hard.

'Did you get anything useful out of the call to where the ex-husband works?' he asked Fredrika.

Fredrika gave a start.

'Yes and no.'

She sat up straighter in her seat. She'd rung Gabriel Sebastiansson's employer earlier that morning.

'According to his boss, Gabriel Sebastiansson's on holiday at the moment, but he couldn't say where he is. He's been off since Monday.'

Alex gave a whistle.

'Interesting,' he said. 'Particularly as he clearly hasn't told his ex-wife about it, even though they have a child together. And didn't he tell his old mum he was on a business trip?'

'Yes, he did,' she said. 'Or at least, that's what she told me he said. But to be honest, I didn't have a very good feeling about her.'

Alex frowned.

'How do you mean?'

'I mean that just because she says he said he was on a business trip, it doesn't necessarily mean it's true. Her sense of loyalty to her son is so fierce, I presume she wouldn't have any objection to lying for his sake.'

Alex thought this over. They were almost back at HQ.

Fredrika wondered why it was that she was always the passenger rather than the driver when she went anywhere by car with her male colleagues. Presumably this fact, too, could be explained by her never having been to police training college, never having done her stint in a patrol car, so she must clearly be an incompetent driver.

'Go round to her place,' Alex said roughly, completely forgetting to applaud the moment of Fredrika's first ever admission that she was acting on an instinct. 'Go round and see the ex-husband's mother. We'll just have a quick meeting first.'

'I will,' said Fredrika.

They turned into the garage entrance and carried on down the tunnel to the parking area.

'Are we still sure it was the father took the girl?' Fredrika asked quietly, afraid of reigniting Alex's anger by questioning his working hypothesis. 'Would a father scalp his own daughter and send the hair to her mother?'

The question prompted Alex to think of the burn from the iron on Sara's arm.

'Normal fathers wouldn't,' he said. 'But Gabriel Sebastiansson is not a normal father.'

Peder Rydh was frustrated. The emergency call from Sara Sebastiansson's had taken the whole group totally by surprise, and then – just as the situation was at its most acute – Fredrika was asked to go along, rather than Peder. He had to carry on following up tip-off after tip-off. He felt he was worth better than being stuck on something so apparently unimportant, compared to a trip to interview Sara again.

Admittedly he was getting a lot of valuable help from Mats

Dahman, the data analyst from the National Crime Squad; Alex had asked if he could call him in to help with the investigation as soon as Sara's parents rang. Mats had a handy programme for sorting the information that had come in. You could easily identify who had reported things that happened too early, for example. All those who claimed to have seen Lilian Sebastiansson at Stockholm Central Station at quarter to two, for example, could be weeded out automatically, because Lilian hadn't disappeared by then. But the later ones were trickier. One woman who had been on the same train as Sara and Lilian said she had noticed a short man carrying a sleeping child when they got out onto the platform. But if the perpetrator took size 46 shoes, he was hardly likely to be particularly short. He was presumably quite tall, in fact. Assuming the shoeprints had anything at all to do with Lilian's disappearance.

Peder leant back in his desk chair and gave a dejected sigh. It hadn't been particularly great last night, either. He hadn't got home until ten, despite having made up his mind to get back earlier, and he'd found Ylva sitting at the kitchen table over a cup of tea. She'd been at home all day, but she was still feeling tired. For some reason, Peder found that infuriating, and had to make a real effort not to say anything critical or unkind. He made himself repeat the same old mantra that had been going round and round inside his head for the last ten or eleven months:

She's tired; she's not well. She can't help it. And if we take it slowly, one step at a time, she might improve. Things can only get better.

Until about a year before, Peder had been one of those

people who really enjoy their lives to the full. He considered it almost a duty for anyone lucky enough to have a healthy body and a decent situation in life. He enjoyed going to work every day. He enjoyed life in general, and a career that was finally taking off, and he enjoyed his Ylva and the thought of the family they were about to become. In short, he was a secure, straightforward, positive and harmonious person. Happy and outgoing. That was how he saw himself, anyway.

But things changed when Ylva gave birth to the twins, their first children. Life as Peder knew it evaporated, never to return. The boys were immediately put in a special care incubator, and Ylva disappeared into a vast darkness called 'post-natal depression'. In place of the life he had before, Peder got a different one: full of dissatisfaction and regret, of prescription drugs and long-term sick leave, and constant phone calls asking his mother to look after the children again. What was more, he had to cope with the misery of an everyday life with a total lack of sex. Peder felt instinctively that this was a life he had neither asked for nor deserved.

'Ylva is so depressed that she doesn't feel she wants any kind of physical relationship with you,' the elderly, not to say ancient, doctor had explained to Peder. 'You'll have to be patient.'

And Peder really had been patient. He tried to think of Ylva as incurably ill, almost the way he thought of Jimmy, with no prospect of getting better. Peder – and his mother, he mustn't forget – took over all the day-to-day running of things at home. Ylva slept her way through September, October and November. She cried all through December, except for Christmas itself, when she pulled herself together for a day for the family's sake. In January she was a little better, but Peder still had to be patient. In mid-February she had another setback and was down all month. In March things improved a bit again. But by then it was already more or less too late.

In March, the Södermalm police, where Peder was working at the time, held its big spring party, and Peder spent half the evening having sex with his colleague Pia Nordh. A delicious relief. Horribly sinful. Totally unforgivable. And yet – in Peder's world – entirely understandable.

Afterwards he felt the deepest and most awful remorse he had ever known. But then, as Ylva gradually got better and better, and the days longer and longer, Peder started to forgive himself. He had a right to a bit of physical pleasure now and then, after the hell he'd been through. He had the solidarity and support of some of his colleagues, who knew his secret. It was only natural for him to fancy screwing someone else. Not all that often, but occasionally. He felt sorry for himself, thought he deserved a better fate. Bloody hell, he wasn't even thirty-five. So he got together with Pia every so often. The damage was already done, after all.

He stopped like a shot when she asked him if he was think- ing of leaving Ylva, though. Was she crazy? Leave Ylva for some colleague dying for a fuck? Pia obviously had no idea about what was important in life, thought Peder, and dumped her by text message.

Soon after that, he got a new job, moving on from the uniformed branch to become a DI – sooner in his career than most people. He was allocated to the investigation team of the almost legendary Alex Recht, and threw himself whole- heartedly into the new job. At home, to Peder's genuine delight, Ylva started talking about the future, and how it would be in the autumn, when Peder was to take a spell of paternity leave, and then the boys would start at nursery; and they all went to Majorca for the last week in May. Peder and Ylva made love for the first time in over ten months, and after that some things seemed to start going back to more like what Peder thought of as normal.

'Don't be in too much of a hurry to get everything back to how it was,' his mother warned him. 'Ylva's still sensitive.'

Peder actually felt like saying that Ylva was still bordering on the unrecognizable, but the week away had given him new hope. Ylva was gradually showing more sides of herself that he could recognize. It really would be risking everything to tell her about the affair with Pia Nordh, he told himself. And anyway, he had so deserved a bit of fun just then.

Now it was the end of July. Two months since Majorca. He still had Pia's number if he felt miserable again. He hoped he wouldn't need to use it, but you never knew.

There were times when he simply could not accept his situation, times when it was all too much. The evening he screwed Pia Nordh had been one of those. Last night had been another one.

'Have you been working all this time?' Ylva asked.

Peder tensed. What the hell was this? An accusation?

'Yes, there's a kid gone missing.'

'I saw,' said Ylva, looking up from her teacup. 'I didn't know you were on that case.'

Peder took a beer from the fridge and a glass from one of the cupboards.

'She didn't go missing until this afternoon, before that there *was* no case. And now I'm telling you that I'm working on it.'

The cold beer chilled his hand as he filled the glass.

'You could have rung,' Ylva said.

Peder lost his temper.

'But I did,' he sputtered, and gulped down some of his beer.

'Yes, but not until six,' Ylva said wearily. 'And you said you'd be late, but you'd be back by eight. And now it's ten. Don't you realize how worried I've been?'

'I didn't know you cared where I was,' Peder said curtly, and regretted it the same instant.

Sometimes, when he was tired, stupid things like that just slipped out. He met Ylva's eyes over his beer glass, saw the tears come to her eyes. She got up and went out of the kitchen.

'For fuck's sake, Ylva, I'm sorry,' he called after her, keeping his voice down.

Keeping his voice down so as not to wake the children, sorry to try to get her back in a good mood. There was always somebody else whose needs he was supposed to prioritize over his own.

Peder felt anxiety and his guilty conscience clawing at him as he sat there at his desk. He simply didn't understand how it could all have turned out so wrong when he got home. He'd rung, hadn't he? The only reason he hadn't rung again was that he hadn't wanted to wake the children. Or he tried to convince himself that was the main reason, at least.

It had been a wretched night. The boys woke up and wouldn't settle again, and it ended up with the two of them lying in between their parents in the double bed. Peder had fallen asleep with his arm round one of his sons. The little boy slept less fitfully that way.

Driving home from work the evening before, Peder had

hoped that Ylva would still be awake and might feel like sex. How naïve of him, looking back. She'd only felt like sex once since they got back from Majorca. And he could hardly bring it up with his best mates when they were in the sauna after training on Thursdays.

It was bloody humiliating, thought Peder. Not being able to make love to your own wife.

And nobody humiliated Peder, that was for sure.

There had been so much life in Ylva when they met six years before. He could never for a moment have imagined then that he might cheat on her one day. But was it really cheating on someone when that person scarcely wanted sex all year? A year was an enormously long time, to Peder's way of seeing things.

Ylva, Ylva, where the hell have you gone?

Pia Nordh's number was burning a hole in his mobile.

If he just gave her a call and made himself sound really, really charming, and sort of hinted it was all his fault for handling it so badly when they broke up, she'd be sure to want to see him again. Peder straightened his back as he sat there. This enforced abstinence was affecting his judgment badly, he told himself. Affecting his judgment and making him frustrated. He'd do his job much better if he could just have a little distraction.

Peder's fumbling fingers located his mobile. It took her a few rings to answer.

'Hello.'

Husky voice, warm memories. *Crazy* memories. Peder cut off the call. He swallowed hard and ran his hands through his hair. He'd got to pull himself together. This wasn't the time to lose his grip on real life again. It just wasn't. He decided to ring Jimmy instead and see how he was doing.

Then Ellen, their assistant, stuck her head round the door.

'Alex rang and said he wanted you to make sure the media get a photo of the girl to spread around. They didn't get one yesterday.'

Peder braced himself.

'Fine, no problem.'

Alex Recht felt under pressure as he assembled his team again on his return from Sara Sebastiansson's. A pair of size 46 shoeprints belonging to an unidentified individual had been found just where Sara and Lilian were sitting on the train. Apart from that, there was no technical evidence to help the team in its work. Alex hoped the box that had gone off to SKL would give them some more leads.

But the parcel delivered to Sara was extremely alarming. The act was so calculated that it felt like the work of a not entirely healthy mind. What was brewing here, exactly?

'Fredrika, try to get Gabriel Sebastiansson's mother to tell you everything – and I mean *everything* – she knows,' he said sharply.

Fredrika gave a brief nod and jotted a few words in the notebook she always carried with her. It wouldn't surprise Alex if she turned up with a dictaphone one of these days.

'The parcel puts a different complexion on things,' he said. 'Now we know for sure that Lilian's disappearance was no coincidence, and that she didn't just wander off. Someone who knew who she was – someone who clearly wants to hurt her mother – is deliberately keeping her hidden. As things stand . . .'

Alex cleared his throat and went on.

'We haven't been able to interview Sara yet, but when I spoke to her yesterday there was no indication she might have any enemies apart from her ex. Until we get any information to take us in other directions, any tip-offs that come in, for example, we'll work on the hypothesis that Gabriel Sebastiansson's got the girl.'

Alex fixed Fredrika with a look, and she said nothing.

'Any questions?'

No one said anything, but Peder squirmed in his seat.

'How are you getting on with what's come in from the public?' Alex asked. 'Anything we can use?'

Peder shook his head.

'No,' he said hesitantly, with a sideways glance at the analyst from the National Crime Squad, who had been asked to join them for the meeting. 'No, we've nothing concrete to tell you. A few tip-offs have come in, but things won't really start happening until her photo's on TV and in the papers.'

Alex nodded.

'But they've had the photo?'

'Yes, of course,' Peder said quickly.

'Good,' muttered Alex. 'Good. Somebody out there must have seen something. It's just absurd that nobody on the train registered seeing Lilian leave it.'

He took a breath and then added:

'And naturally we'll keep quiet about the parcel sent to Sara. God knows what the headlines would look like if it got out that the kidnapper scalped the girl.'

Everyone was quiet for a moment. The air conditioning coughed and hissed.

'Okay,' said Alex in conclusion. 'We'll have another meeting this afternoon, when Fredrika's back from seeing Gabriel's mother. I've decided to send her on her own; I reckon we'll get more out of the lady in question if she doesn't have to entertain a whole delegation. Peder will carry on following up what comes in, and we'll hope to hear back from SKL about the parcel soon. Peder can also contact the courier company that brought it round. I've asked Sara's parents to draw up a list of people Sara knows, people we can interview and ask about Gabriel's whereabouts. It's going to be another busy day.'

With that, the meeting was over and the team dispersed. Only Ellen remained at the table for a few minutes, making notes.

It was only when Fredrika Bergman was actually sitting in the car with a road atlas open that it registered: Gabriel Sebastiansson's mother – Lilian's grandmother – lived in Djursholm. Big, expensive houses, huge gardens, and endless bisous on the cheek. Fredrika reflected for a moment that Sara Sebastiansson seemed to come from a very different background to her husband.

In her mind, Fredrika went over the day so far. She was feeling a lack of structure and direction in her work. It had not escaped her that Alex was *very* skilled and competent at what he did. She also readily conceded that he had a vast range and depth of experience that she lacked. But she felt contempt, to put it bluntly, for his inability to incorporate new suggestions into their work. Particularly in the current situation. Loose threads remained loose, and Fredrika could not see that any concrete measures were being taken either to discard them or to follow them up. They *were assuming* – perhaps entirely wrongly – that the girl was being kept hidden by her own father and therefore was not in any immediate danger. Now they knew for sure that Lilian had not disappeared by chance. So how could Alex decree that what had happened in Flemingsberg was still of no interest?

And how the hell could he let a National Crime Squad

analyst attend their meeting without introducing him properly? In conversations with Fredrika and Peder, Alex had only referred to him as 'the analyst'. Such an oversight that it almost made Fredrika blush. When she got the chance, she would take matters into her own hands and at least introduce herself.

Fredrika was unwilling to admit it, but as a woman she was treated differently by the boss she and Peder shared. Particularly as a *childless* woman, she felt, she was treated differently. Not to mention the sense of exclusion she faced because of her academic background. That was one thing she had in common with the National Crime Squad analyst, at least.

Fredrika considered making a quick phone call to Spencer before she got out of the car. But she decided against it. Spencer had hinted that they might be able to see each other again at the weekend. Best to leave him to get on with his work in peace, so he would have time to see her.

'But you only ever see each other on his terms,' Fredrika's friend Julia had objected, a few times. 'When have you ever been able to ring and suggest getting together on the spur of the moment, like he does?'

Fredrika found questions and observations like that quite upsetting. The terms on which they met were given: Spencer was married, and she wasn't. Either she accepted it, and the consequences – such as Spencer always being less accessible to her than she could be to him – or she didn't. And if she didn't, she might as well look for a different lover and friend. The same was true for Spencer. If he had not accepted that Fredrika occasionally had relationships with other men, and then came back to him, they would have split up long ago.

He doesn't give me everything, Fredrika would say, but since I don't happen to have anyone else at the moment, he gives me enough.

Perhaps the relationship was unconventional, but it was genuine and it was practical. And it neither demeaned nor ridiculed either of them. A mutual exchange, in which neither appeared a clear loser. Fredrika chose not to examine too closely whether either of them emerged a clear winner. As long as her heart carried on signalling desire, she surrendered herself to it.

An elderly woman, presumably Gabriel's mother, was already standing on the front steps as she braked and pulled up at the edge of the gravel forecourt. The woman gestured to Fredrika to wind down the window.

'Please park your car over there,' she said, her long, slim finger graciously indicating a space beside two cars Fredrika assumed to belong to the house.

Fredrika parked and climbed out onto the gravel. She breathed in the damp air and felt her clothes sticking to her body. As she walked over to Teodora Sebastiansson, she looked around her. The garden was larger than others she had passed on the way there, almost like a park, secluded and at the end of the road. The lawn was strangely green, and reminded her of the grass on a golf course. A wall ran round the entire garden. The gate through which Fredrika had driven was the only opening to be seen. She had a sense of being both unwelcome and shut in. Large trees of some species she didn't recognize were growing all around and immediately behind the house. But for some reason, Fredrika could not imagine children ever having played in them. On the lawn over near the wall was a little collection of magnificent fruit trees, and further back, beyond where Fredrika had parked the car, was a greenhouse of abnormally large proportions.

'We are pretty much self-sufficient in vegetables here in the summer,' the woman said, answering the question that Fredrika assumed to be reflected in her face as she caught sight of the glasshouse.

'My husband's father took a great interest in horticulture,' the woman added as Fredrika approached.

There was something in her voice that caught Fredrika's attention. It had a faint echo to it, with a sort of rasp to some of the consonants. The echo was hard to explain, coming from such a small person.

Fredrika held out her hand as she got to the steps and introduced herself.

'Fredrika Bergman, police investigator.'

The woman took Fredrika's hand and squeezed it unexpectedly hard, just as Sara had done at Stockholm Central the day before.

'Teodora Sebastiansson,' said the woman with a very slight smile.

It struck Fredrika that the smile made her thin face look older.

'It's very kind of you to let me come round,' she said.

Teodora nodded with the same gracious attitude she had displayed when pointing out the parking place. The smile vanished and her face smoothed out.

Fredrika noted they were about the same height, but that

was where the similarity ended. Teodora's grey and presumably quite long hair was pulled back from her face into a severe knot, high at the back of her neck. Her eyes were as icily blue as those Fredrika had seen in her son's passport photo when she retrieved it from the passport authority records.

Her body language was perfectly controlled. And her hands rested one on top of the other on her stomach, just where her blouse met her grey skirt. The cream blouse was enlivened only by the brooch fastened under her pointed little chin. Her ears were adorned with simple pearl earrings.

'Naturally I am deeply worried about my little granddaughter,' said Teodora, but her voice was so impersonal that Fredrika could not believe she really meant it. 'I shall do everything in my power to help the police.'

She extended one hand in a simple gesture of invitation. Fredrika took three quick steps into the large hall and heard Teodora close the door firmly behind them.

For a brief moment there was silence, while their eyes grew used to the dim lighting in the windowless hall. That moment also felt like stepping straight into a museum of the end of the last century. A tourist from outside Europe would probably be willing to pay a small fortune to stay in the Sebastiansson family mansion. The feeling of being in another age was if anything intensified as Fredrika was shown into what must be the family drawing room. Every detail in the choice of wallpaper, mouldings, stucco ceiling, furniture, every painting and chandelier, had been hand-picked with exquisite precision to give the sense of a home where time stood still.

Fredrika was amazed, and could not remember having seen anything like it before. There had been nothing to rival the sight in front of her even in the homes of her grandparents' most bourgeois acquaintances.

Teodora Sebastiansson was standing right beside Fredrika, observing the impression her home interiors were making with thinly veiled delight.

'My father left a huge collection of porcelain, including the china dolls up there on the top shelf,' she rasped, when she saw Fredrika staring wide-eyed at the tall, glass-fronted case that seemed to have pride of place right next to the gorgeous black grand piano.

Fredrika's thoughts strayed immediately to her mother. She knew that if she shut her eyes, she would instantly be transported back to the time before The Accident and see herself sitting at the piano with her mother.

'Can you hear the melody, Fredrika? Can you hear the games it plays before it settles in our ears?'

Teodora followed Fredrika's gaze and ran her fingers over the instrument.

I'm already losing it with this lady, thought Fredrika. I've got to take back the initiative; I wouldn't have been here at all if I hadn't invited myself round.

'Do you live in this big house all by yourself?' she asked.

Teodora allowed herself a brittle laugh.

'Yes, so there is going to be no question of an old people's home where I am concerned.'

Fredrika gave a fleeting smile, and cleared her throat.

'Well, I've come to see you because we've been trying to speak to your son, but we haven't been able to get hold of him.'

Teodora listened and did not stir. Then all at once, she turned to look at Fredrika and said:

'Would you like a cup of coffee?'
Fredrika had lost control of the conversation again.

Peder Rydh was trying to do at least ten things at once, with
the inevitable result that he perceived his work situation
appeared as to be even more chaotic than it really was. An
address stamped on the box delivered to Sara Sebastiansson
had identified the courier company that brought it. Full of
hope, he had rushed round to the company's unobtrusive
office on Kungsholmen. There was a good chance somebody
there had accepted the parcel and would be able to give a
description of whoever brought it in.

His hopes were dashed pretty soon.

The parcel had been left anonymously at the office the
previous evening after closing time. The staff had found it in
the morning, in the parcel deposit box that was open round
the clock. The system was that the sender of the parcel would
stick an envelope to the item, containing the recipient
address, requested delivery time and payment in cash.
Unfortunately the CCTV camera trained on the box had
been out of order for a long time so there was no picture of
the person who had left the parcel. The envelope with the
money and address details had been seized, of course, and
sent straight off to SKL by express courier, but Peder didn't
really expect them to find any trace of the kidnapper on
either the money or the envelope.

He swore to himself and went back to HQ to pick up Alex
so they could head off to interview Sara Sebastiansson again.

Then out of the blue, he had a phone call from Ylva. Her
voice was strained and she wanted to talk about what had

happened the previous evening. Peder said he would have to ring her back later; he was busy at the moment. Her call was an irritant and stressed him out. They were so indescribably remote from each other at the moment. They seemed to be living in separate worlds even when they were together. Sometimes it felt as though the boys were the only things they had in common.

Sara was sleeping and could not be woken when they visited her. The doctor who had been summoned that morning had given her a very effective sedative. Peder looked at her lying there on one side in her bed. A pale face framed in a tangle of red hair. A summery, freckled arm sticking out from under the cover. Another arm with a big burn that was just starting to heal. A blue bruise on her calf. Evil was fond of bright colours, Peder thought wearily.

Alex was in the kitchen, talking quietly to Sara's parents, who were keen to tell him about all their son-in-law's acts of cruelty to date. They had written down the names of people the police might be interested in talking to. It was a short list. Sara was very isolated, thanks to that dreadful husband of hers.

'She was never able to hang on to her friends,' said Sara's mother. 'Scarcely a single one.'

They warned Alex and Peder to be wary of Sara's mother-in-law. They had admittedly only met her once, at the wedding. But she had made a lasting impression on them.

'She'd go through fire and water for her son,' sighed Sara's father. 'She's not quite right in the head, that woman.'

Peder took the list of names and telephone numbers provided by Sara's parents with some help from her mobile phone. With Alex at the steering wheel on the way back to Kungsholmen, Peder started ringing round. The reaction at the other end was always the same. Oh no, not again. Was it so bad this time that the police had been called in? What had that madman taken it into his head to do now? No, nobody had heard from him or had any idea where he could be.

'But try talking to his mother,' said one man Peder spoke to, once a good friend of Sara and Gabriel.

Peder put his mobile away in his jacket pocket and spared Fredrika a fleeting thought.

'To be quite honest, I imagined my son would meet a different sort of girl,' said Teodora Sebastiansson, breaking the silence that had descended after Fredrika Bergman accepted the offer of a cup of coffee.

Fredrika raised an interested eyebrow over the cup she had brought to her lips.

Teodora fixed her gaze on something behind Fredrika. For a second, Fredrika felt tempted to turn round, but she took another sip of coffee instead. It was too strong, but was served in beautiful little cups that her grandmother would have sold her own grandchildren to drink out of.

'You see,' Teodora said rather hesitantly, 'I had certain expectations of Gabriel. Really just the sort all parents have of their children, but he showed us quite early in life that he wanted to go his own way. I suppose that was why he chose Sara specifically.'

She took a discreet sip of her coffee and put the cup back down on the table in front of her. Fredrika asked guardedly:

'Have you any idea how their relationship actually worked, Sara and Gabriel's?'

She realized her mistake a split-second later. Teodora sat back even more stiffly in her chair.

'If you are asking whether I, as Lilian's grandmother, have been informed of all the hateful lies my daughter-in-law has been spreading about my son, the answer is yes. I believe I told you that when we spoke on the telephone.'

The message was not difficult to interpret – either Fredrika backed off, or the interview would be brought to an immediate end.

'I realize this may be a sensitive issue,' said Fredrika hoarsely, 'but we are actually in the middle of a very serious investigation here, and . . .'

Teodora interrupted by leaning across the table that separated them and fixing her with eyes of steel.

'My grandchild – not yours, *mine* – one of the most precious things I have, is missing. Do you think,' she hissed, 'do you think you need to spend a single second telling me how serious the situation is?'

Fredrika took a deep breath and refused to drop her eyes, though she could feel herself shaking.

'Nobody doubts how anxious you are,' she said with a composure that surprised her. 'But it would be a very good idea for you to answer our questions, so we felt you really were trying to cooperate with us.'

Then she explained about the parcel that had been delivered to Sara that morning. Once she had finished, the room remained in eerie silence, and for the first time since her arrival, Fredrika saw she had managed to say something that Teodora took to heart.

'We're not saying,' Fredrika went on, stressing the word 'not', 'that your son is mixed up with this in any way. But we must – I repeat *must* – get hold of him. We can't and won't ignore the information about him that has come to our attention. About his and Sara's marriage. And there's no way we can cross him off our list of key people until we've spoken to him.'

There was no list of key people, but all in all, Fredrika felt pretty satisfied with her exposition. If she had not had Teodora's full attention before, she certainly had it now.

'If you do know where he is, this would be a really useful time to tell us,' Fredrika said, quietly but forcefully.

Teodora slowly shook her head.

'No,' she said at last, so quietly that Fredrika hardly heard the word, 'I don't know where he is. All I know is that he was going to be away on business yesterday. That's what he said when I spoke to him on the telephone on Monday. We talked about him and little Lilian coming to dinner here, once Sara was back from the latest of all those trips she drags the poor child along on.'

Fredrika observed her.

'I see,' she said, and then leant across the table herself. 'The only problem is,' she said, with a slight smile, 'that according to Gabriel's boss, he's been on leave since Monday.'

She felt her heart beat extra fast as she saw the colour drain from Teodora's face.

'So naturally we're wondering why he lied to his own mother about that,' she went on mildly.

She sat back again.

'Unless there's anything else you want to tell me?'

Teodora said nothing for a long while. Then she declared:

'Gabriel never lies. I refuse to call what he told me a lie, before he has himself admitted that it really was one.'

She pursed her lips and her colour slowly returned. She looked Fredrika in the eye.

'Are you conducting the same thorough investigation of Lilian's mother?' she said, her eyes narrowing.

'In a case like this, we investigate everyone in the child's immediate vicinity,' Fredrika replied tersely.

Teodora clasped her hands on the table in front of her and smiled a wry, superior smile.

'My dear girl,' she said sternly, 'it really would be most unfortunate if you didn't take a closer look at Sara.'

Fredrika sat up straighter.

'As I say, we're looking at everyone who . . .'

Teodora held up a hand to interrupt her.

'Believe me,' she said, 'you and your colleagues would gain a lot of time by focusing more on all those people Sara allows to come and go as they like in that flat.'

When Fredrika made no reply, she went on.

'You may not be aware of the fact, but in my opinion, my Gabriel has been more than patient in his relationship with Sara.'

She clicked her tongue in a way Fredrika knew she could never imitate, however much she might want to.

'He was put through total humiliation,' she said, and Fredrika was taken aback to see the old lady's eyes glinting with tears.

Teodora looked out of the window at the dark sky and dabbed the corners of her eyes. When she looked back at Fredrika, her face was white with rage:

'And then she told all those atrocious lies. As if Gabriel hadn't suffered enough, she then had to go and try to destroy his life by accusing him of being a wife-beater.'

She gave a sudden, shrill laugh that made Fredrika jump.

'If that isn't evil, you tell me what is.'

Dumbfounded, Fredrika could only watch the older woman's little theatrical performance, or whatever you could call it.

'Perhaps you didn't know that Sara had well-documented physical injuries each time she reported your son for assault?'

Teodora stopped her before she launched into her next point.

'Of course I knew,' she said, glaring at Fredrika as if to say the question was both unnecessary and lacking in judgment. 'Some of her other male friends must have lost patience with her, of course.'

Then Teodora reached across the table and took the cup of coffee Fredrika had scarcely more than tasted.

'I have rather a lot to do, as I'm sure you understand,' she said apologetically. 'So if you have no more questions . . . ?'

Fredrika swiftly took one of her cards from her inside pocket and put it on the table.

'Feel free to contact me any time you like,' she said firmly.

Teodora nodded and said nothing, but they both knew she would never ring.

When they were back in the gloomy hall, Fredrika asked:

'Does Gabriel still keep any of his things here?'

Teodora again pursed her lips.

'Naturally. This is his home, after all. He has his own room upstairs.'

And before Fredrika had time to respond, she went on:

'Unless you have a search warrant, I shall have to ask you to leave my house at once.'

Fredrika hastily thanked her and left. It was not until she was standing on the steps and Teodora was shutting the door behind her that she realized what she had forgotten to ask:

'By the way, what size shoes does your son take?'

Ellen Lind had a secret. She had just fallen in love. This made her feel terribly guilty, for some reason. Somewhere out there, she thought, looking out of the window, a child was being held captive by some deranged person, and down in Söder the child's mother was going through all the torments of hell. Ellen had children of her own. Her daughter was nearly fourteen and her son twelve. She had been on her own with them for quite a few years now, and had no words to describe what they meant to her. Sometimes at work she felt herself going all warm inside at the very thought of them. They had a good life, a full life, and occasionally – but only occasionally – the children's father put in a brief appearance. Ellen was waiting patiently for the children to get older and understand how badly their father had behaved all those years. At their age, there was no room for anything but pleasure when their dad got in touch. They never asked about him, and when he did turn up, Ellen noted they had stopped asking him where he'd been, and why he hadn't rung for weeks or months.

Ellen had found out from mutual acquaintances that he had a new girlfriend again, and that she had very quickly got pregnant, which Ellen did not find very amusing. In fact the thought of it made her gnash her teeth. Why have more children, when he didn't even look after the ones he'd already got?

But more than anything, Ellen thought about her new love. Rather unexpectedly, it was her interest in stocks and shares that had brought them together. She hadn't yet come across any colleagues who shared her enthusiasm, but outside work she had several friends who were eager to give her tips and advice. It was all just a big gamble for Ellen. She never invested large sums, and she was careful never to risk her profits. This last spring had enriched her life, and the children's, more than she had ever dared wish. A successful and in fact rather bold venture had paid so well that Ellen and the kids had been able to go on a package holiday abroad for a couple of weeks earlier that summer. They went to Alanya in Turkey, staying in a five-star hotel. All inclusive, of course. Masses of food and drink. Excursions and the beach or the pool in the daytime. Entertainment in the evenings. Ellen had realized how desperate she'd been for a break like that. She and the children, just as it always had been.

Ellen was no flirt. She was actually rather shy, and not used to being paid compliments. It wasn't that she was ugly or anything, absolutely not, but she did tend to create a rather 'ordinary' impression. Neither too much colour, nor too little. Not a fabulous wardrobe, but not a dull one, either. It was easy to make her laugh, and she had a pretty smile. Her eyes were narrow and her hair was straight. Her bust was maybe a little tired after feeding two babies, but the way Ellen dressed hid it well.

Then one evening in the hotel bar in Alanya he was suddenly standing there, asking if he could get her a drink.

Ellen loved to recall that moment and blushed every time. He was so good looking and his eyes had a lovely glitter to them. The top few buttons of his shirt were undone and Ellen could see dark hair. And he was tall and tanned. All in all, he was incredibly attractive.

Ellen wasn't a pushover by any means, but this man had really turned her on. He flattered and flirted, but never too much. Not so much that she had to take it seriously. They had such a lot to talk about. Ellen accepted several glasses of wine, and the time simply flew by. Just after midnight she said she had to go; the children – who had been keeping themselves amused – wanted to go back to the room, and Ellen didn't really want to let them go on their own.

'Will I see you tomorrow?' the man asked.

Ellen nodded eagerly – *so eagerly* – and smiled. She did very much want to see him again, and was pleased that the interest was mutual.

Perhaps she had had her doubts when it was time to come home at the end of the holiday. They'd tried to meet for a while every day, always when the children were busy elsewhere. They hadn't been to bed together, but he had kissed her on two different occasions. In the end it was Ellen who brought it up on their last evening.

'Shall we see each other in Stockholm when we get back?'

A slightly evasive look came into his eyes, trying to avoid looking at her.

Damn, was Ellen's immediate thought.

Then he drew himself up straight.

'I have to work long hours,' he said gently. 'Very long hours,' he clarified. 'I'd like to see you again, but I really can't promise anything.'

Ellen had assured him she didn't need any promises at all.

She just wanted to know there was some chance of them seeing each other again. Yes, there was, he assured her in his turn, clearly relieved she wasn't demanding any guarantees. But he didn't actually live in Stockholm, though his job brought him there fairly often. He would ring her next time he was passing through the city.

A week went by, and the rainy summer became a fact. And on one of all those rainy days he rang, and since then, Ellen hadn't been able to stop smiling. How totally ridiculous, but what a glorious relief. The only fly in the ointment was the fact that they really did only meet as rarely as he had hinted they might, and then there was the almost complete lack of interest he showed in her children. But of course she understood that, too. Making him part of the children's lives straight away would mean making the relationship too serious too fast. That was why, Ellen told herself, it was more rational to see him in his hotel room, the way he always suggested. They would go out for a meal at some expensive restaurant, and then go back to his room. Once they had spent that first night together, Ellen was sure. There was no way she would give this up without a fight. He was simply too good to be true.

Ellen looked at the calendar she had on her desk. She had counted the weeks since they got back from Turkey. Five weeks had passed. In those five weeks, she and her new love had seen each other four times. Bearing in mind that he didn't live in town, Ellen thought that felt like a very solid start, a verdict confirmed by the friend who looked after the children for her when she went on her dates.

'I'm so happy for you,' she whooped.

Ellen fervently hoped her friend's enthusiasm wouldn't wear off, because it looked as though she was going to need a baby-sitter again soon. She had just reached for her mobile to call her lover, when her desk phone rang. It was the central command unit, asking her to take a call from someone with something to report about the missing girl, Lilian. Ellen accepted the call at once, and heard a reedy female voice at the other end.

'It's about that child that went missing,' she said.

Ellen took it slowly.

'Yes?' she said.

'I think . . .' the woman went quiet. 'I think I might know who did it.'

More silence.

'I think it might be a man I met,' she said in a low voice.

Ellen frowned.

'What makes you think that?' she asked gently.

Ellen could hear the other woman breathing, not being sure whether to go on or not.

'He was just horrible. Just . . . out of his mind.'

Another pause.

'He was always talking about it, about doing it.'

'Sorry,' said Ellen. 'You've lost me there. What was it he talked about doing?'

'Putting everything right,' the woman whispered. 'He talked about putting everything right.'

The woman sounded as though she was starting to cry.

'What did he want to put right?'

'He said there were women who'd done things that meant they didn't deserve their children,' the woman said in a brittle voice. 'That was what he wanted to put right.'

'He was going to take their children from them?'

'I never understood what he said, I never wanted to listen,' said the woman, and now Ellen was sure she was crying. 'And he hit me so hard, so hard. Shouted at me: I'd got to stop having nightmares, I'd got to fight against it. And I'd got to help put everything right.'

'Sorry, but I don't think I understand all this,' Ellen said tentatively. 'The nightmares and all that.'

'He said,' the woman sobbed, 'that I'd got to stop dreaming, stop remembering what had happened before. He said that if I couldn't do it, that showed I was weak. He said I'd got to be strong, to join the fight.'

The woman was silent for a moment, and then she said:

'He called me his doll. He'd never be able to do it on his own; he must have another doll now.'

Ellen was so nonplussed that she really did not know what to say next. She decided to try to steer the conversation back to the bit about children.

'Have you got children of your own,' she asked the woman.

The woman gave a weary laugh.

'No, I haven't got any,' she said. 'And he hadn't, either.'

'Was that why he wanted to take another person's child?'

'No, no, no,' the woman protested. 'He wasn't just going to take it; he didn't want it for himself. The important thing was for the women to get their punishment, to have their children taken away from them.'

'But why?' Ellen asked in desperation.

The woman said nothing.

'Hello?' said Ellen.

'I can't talk any more now, I've already said too much,' the woman whimpered.

'Tell me your name,' pleaded Ellen. 'You've nothing to be afraid of. We can help you.'

Ellen admittedly doubted the confused woman's story had any relevance for the case, but she was quite convinced the woman needed help.

'I can't tell you my name,' the woman whispered. 'I can't. And don't you go saying you can help me, because you lot have never been able to. But the women weren't to be allowed to keep their children, because they didn't deserve to.'

Why not, Ellen wondered. Out loud she said:

'Where did you meet him? Tell me his name.'

'I can't tell you any more now, I just can't.'

Ellen thought the woman was going to hang up, and tried to keep her on the line by asking:

'But why did you ring if you don't want to tell us who he is?'

The question made the other woman hesitate.

'I don't know what his name is. And the women didn't deserve their children, because if you don't like all children, you shouldn't be allowed to have any at all.'

Then she ended the call, and Ellen sat there with the receiver in her hand, bewildered. She was sure she hadn't found out anything of particular value. She hadn't got a name, and the woman hadn't explained why the man she knew had taken that particular child. Ellen shook her head, replaced the telephone receiver and wrote a short memo of the incoming call, which she put with all the rest. She made a mental note not to forget to mention it to the others in the team.

They were all waiting for Fredrika in the Den when she got back to HQ from Teodora Sebastiansson's. It was several hours after lunchtime, and in a desperate attempt to boost her blood sugar level a little, Fredrika gulped down a chocolate wafer she found in the bottom of her handbag.

Alex Recht was standing by himself in one corner of the room. His expression was tense. He was deeply concerned. The case of Lilian Sebastiansson's disappearance was developing in a direction he could never have predicted. Initial tests had confirmed the hair and clothes were Lilian's. They had nothing else to go on at all. There wasn't a single fingerprint on the box, inside or out. There were no traces of blood or anything like that. And the call on that goddamned courier company had yielded no information either.

When Fredrika turned up, Peder slipped in through the door behind her. Alex opened their third meeting in the Den in a very short space of time.

He called on Fredrika to report back on her meeting with Lilian's grandmother. Alex had had misgivings from the very start about letting Fredrika conduct such vital questioning without the assistance of a more experienced colleague, but as Fredrika's story emerged, Alex – and even Peder – realized they could scarcely have sent anyone other than Fredrika to interview such an eccentric old lady.

'What was the overriding impression you brought away with you?' Alex asked.

Fredrika put her head on one side.

'I'm really not sure about her,' she had to admit in the end. 'I get the feeling she's lying, but I don't know how much or what about. I don't know if she believes herself that her son would never have hit Sara, and I don't know if she's lying because she knows something or because she's simply protecting her son, regardless of what he may have done.'

Alex nodded thoughtfully.

'Have we got enough on him to issue an arrest warrant? Arrest him in his absence?'

'No, I'm afraid not,' was Fredrika's forceful response. 'The only thing we could use would be the earlier wife-battering.'

Alex was opening his mouth to say something, when Fredrika added:

'And we know he takes a size 45 shoe and has a mother who's pretty bloody disturbed.'

Alex was so surprised to hear Fredrika Bergman swear that he completely forgot what he was about to say.

'Size 45 shoe,' he eventually echoed.

'Yes,' confirmed Fredrika. 'According to his mother he does. So it's not entirely unthinkable that he might own a pair in size 46, as well.'

'Well done, Fredrika, well done!' said Alex, elated.

Fredrika's face flushed blood red at the unexpected praise, and Peder looked as though he might like to kill himself. Or possibly Fredrika.

'Well maybe we should go after him on a charge of assault

and battery?' he suggested in an attempt to grab a bit of attention at the table.

He ignored the fact that Fredrika had said the same thing a few seconds before.

'Definitely,' said Alex, nodding in agreement. 'We're not crossing him off the list until we find him. Issue an arrest warrant, for the assaults on his wife.'

Peder gave a slight nod.

Fredrika stared at him with an empty expression.

Ellen broke in.

'There was a woman who rang a little while ago,' she began hesitantly.

Alex absent-mindedly scratched a mosquito bite. Those blessed mosquitoes; surely they got earlier every year?

'Yes?'

'Well,' sighed Ellen, 'I don't really know what to say. She wouldn't identify herself and what she told me was, er . . . a right old jumble, to put it mildly. But basically it came down to her thinking she knew the man who's taken Lilian.'

Everyone round the table turned their eyes to Ellen, who gave a deprecating wave of her arm.

'I mean, she sounded confused. And scared. But it wasn't at all clear what of. She said she thought it was a man she'd once been in a relationship with, and he had hit her.'

'Which we know Gabriel Sebastiansson did, hit the woman he's got now,' Alex put in.

Ellen carried on shaking her head.

'It was something else,' she said, trying to get her thoughts in order. 'She said she had nightmares that made him cross, and . . .'

'What?' interrupted Peder.

'Yes, it was something like that she said. About her having nightmares and the guy getting angry. He was waging some campaign he wanted her to get involved in.'

'What kind of campaign?' asked Fredrika.

'I couldn't make it out,' sighed Ellen. 'The whole thing was a jumble, like I said. Something about some women not deserving their children. Something about her being his doll, him using dolls somehow. But it was all pretty unintelligible.'

'And she didn't give his name? The man who hit her?' said Alex slowly.

'No,' said Ellen. 'And like I said, she wouldn't tell me her name, either.'

'But you got the technical department to trace the call?' asked Alex.

Ellen hesitated.

'Er, no, I didn't,' she admitted. 'It felt so weird, not serious. And you always get a few loonies ringing at times like this. But I can ring the technical unit as soon as the meeting's over,' she added.

'Good,' said Alex. 'My guess is that your assessment of it is about right, but it does no harm to check who the caller was.'

He was about to go on when Fredrika signalled that she, too, had something to say.

'Unless the woman wasn't confused at all, just scared,' she said.

Alex frowned.

'If the woman's been a victim of abuse, she might have turned to the police on other occasions, and felt she got no support. In that case, she's pretty traumatized by her whole relationship with the police service, and she's probably also still afraid of her ex. And in that case . . .'

'Wait a bloody minute!' Peder interrupted in frustration. 'What do you mean, "traumatized by her relationship with the police"? It's not the police force's fault that nearly every bit of skirt who rings in and reports her guy takes him back time after time after time . . .'

Fredrika wearily held up her hand.

'Peder, that's not what I'm saying,' she said calmly. 'And I don't think we need a debate on police tactics for preventing assaults on women right now. But if, and I mean *if*, she has been abused and felt she didn't get any protection from the police, she's probably very scared indeed. And that means it would be stupid to dismiss the call as confused.'

'But if we think the whole thing through,' interrupted Alex, 'isn't it a bit odd that she's rung as soon as this?'

Nobody said anything.

'What I mean is, how much do the media know as yet? The fact that a child has gone missing. That's all. We haven't told them about the parcel with the hair and there isn't really anything to point to the girl having suffered anything worse than all the other kids reported missing in the course of a year.'

Each individual group member digested what Alex had said.

'I still tend to think she doesn't really know what she's talking about,' he concluded. 'But of course we ought to follow up the call. We can't exclude the possibility that it was Gabriel Sebastiansson she had a relationship with.'

'But there must have been something in the story that she

recognized from what her ex had told her,' persisted Fredrika. 'You're quite right, Alex, when you say how little information we've released. It must be some tiny detail that caught her attention and rang a bell for her, and distinguished this story from all the other stories about missing children. And we can't take it for granted that it actually is Gabriel Sebastiansson popping up here again . . .'

Alex had had enough, and quite forgot that he had been full of praise for Fredrika just a moment before.

'Right, let's get on with the meeting,' he said brusquely. 'There are always a variety of leads in an investigation, Fredrika, but for now we only have the one, and it looks very plausible, to say the least.'

Alex turned to the National Crime Squad analyst, whose name he couldn't for the life of him recall.

'Have any other witnesses been in touch? Any train passengers?'

The analyst was quick to nod. Oh yes, lots of people – lots and lots – had got in touch. Almost all the passengers from carriage number 2 where Sara and Lilian had been sitting. None of them could remember hearing or seeing anything. All of them could definitely remember seeing the child asleep, but nobody remembered anyone coming to fetch her.

'The first time I talked to Sara, she said she and her daughter had chatted a bit with a woman sitting on the other side of the aisle. Has she rung in?' Fredrika wanted to know.

The analyst took a sheaf of paper out of a plastic folder.

'If the lady was sitting straight across the aisle,' he said, extracting a sheet of paper, 'that would mean she was in seat number 14. Nobody's been in touch from seats 13 or 14.'

'Let's hope they soon will be,' muttered Alex, rubbing his chin.

His eyes were drawn to the window. Somewhere out there was Lilian Sebastiansson. Most likely in the company of her sadistic father, who was prepared to stoop to anything to terrify his ex-wife. He fervently hoped they would find the girl soon.

Then Ellen's mobile rang and she slipped out of the room to answer it.

'Peder,' Alex said decisively, 'I want you to deal with the warrant for Gabriel Sebastiansson's arrest. I also want you and Fredrika to get a second interview with as many of his and Sara's family and friends as you can. Try to find out where on earth he might be.'

Or, thought Fredrika to herself, we might even find out something that gives us some new leads.

She chose not to say anything out loud.

Alex was about to round off the meeting when Ellen popped her head round the door:

'Our prayers have been answered,' she said. 'The lady sitting just across from Sara and Lilian on the train has just rung in.'

At last, thought Alex. At last things are starting to move.

Peder Rydh took Ingrid Strand's statement in one of the interview rooms on the same floor as the reception desk. The day had started so chaotically he could hardly get his thoughts in order. He was glad he had a colleague sitting in on the interview with the new witness. Otherwise there was an undeniable risk that Peder might miss some of the information she had to offer. Ingrid Strand might be sitting on the last crucial lead for solving the case, and he needed to be on the ball.

Peder was pleased to be the one taking the lead in the interview with the potential key witness. There had been a few shaky moments back there when he thought this witness was going to be given to Fredrika as well, but Alex had come to his senses, thank goodness, and entrusted the task to Peder.

Ingrid Strand was looking straight at him. So was his colleague Jonas. Peder stared back at them both.

He cleared his throat.

'Sorry, where were we?' he said, and looked up.

'I don't think we were anywhere,' said the elderly lady sitting opposite him.

Peder smiled his lopsided smile, the one that generally made even the toughest old ladies melt. Ingrid Strand thawed a fraction.

'I'm sorry,' he said. 'We've had an incredibly stressful day.'

Ingrid Strand nodded and smiled to show she accepted his apology. They could continue the conversation.

He took a furtive, appraising glance at Ingrid Strand. She looked nice. Like a safe, well-adjusted granny. Almost reminded him of his own mother. He immediately felt the pressure in his chest. He still hadn't rung Ylva back. That permanently nagging, guilty conscience.

'So you were sitting beside Sara and Lilian Sebastiansson on the train, across the aisle?' he asked, because he had to start somewhere.

Ingrid nodded obligingly and sat up straighter.

'Yes,' she replied, 'and I would very much like to explain why I haven't been in touch sooner.'

Peder leant forward attentively.

'We'd be very interested to know where you've been,' he smiled.

Ingrid smiled back, but then the smile faded.

'The thing is,' she said quietly, lowering her eyes. 'I've been with my mother; she's very poorly. Well she's quite old now, of course, no spring chicken. But she was taken ill without any warning, a few days ago, and that was why I had to come to Stockholm.'

Peder had worked out from her dialect that she couldn't be from Stockholm.

'We've lived in Gothenburg for nearly forty years, my husband and I, but my parents stayed here. Dad died last year and now Mum's time seems to have come. My brother is with her at the moment. He says he'll ring if there's any change.'

Peder slowly nodded.

'We're terribly grateful to you for making the time to come in,' he said patiently.

Jonas nodded in agreement and jotted something on his pad.

'Oh, of course I wanted to come, once I heard what had happened. Yesterday, you see, I was with my mother virtually the whole time. I was scarcely out of her room, and I slept in the chair beside the bed. We thought it might all happen more quickly, you know, it felt that way. But then my brother came, as I said, and I went to sit in the room for the relatives, and the television was on. And then . . . well, then I heard the girl had gone missing and realized I ought to get in touch straight away. I was sitting right by her and her mother. I rang as soon as I could.'

A slight shiver ran through Ingrid's body before she went on.

'Maybe I should have realized something was wrong,' she sighed. 'I mean, I was talking to the little girl and her charming mother on the journey, after all. The girl fell asleep quite quickly, but I talked to her mother for longer. And I was certainly aware of her not coming back to her seat after we left Flemingsberg. But the conductor, the older one, came and stood with the child. I didn't want to interfere; I thought he seemed so solid and "on top of things" as they say these days. And like I told you – I had other things on my mind.'

To make things easier for Ingrid Strand, Peder gave a nod of recognition.

'Of course that's how it is sometimes,' he said gently. 'Of course we all have other things on our mind.'

When Ingrid met his gaze, there were tears in her eyes.

'It never occurred to me that she could come to any harm,' she whispered. 'The train stopped in Stockholm in the normal way, and we all got up to collect our things and get off. And the conductor, he never came back. I wondered if I ought to do something, but for some reason I felt they must have made arrangements for the little girl.'

Ingrid sighed and a tear rolled down her cheek.

'I was just leaving the carriage when I saw she'd woken up. She looked round, still a bit dozy. She sat up in her seat and looked all round. And then he just came out of nowhere. All of a sudden I couldn't see the girl any more, just his back view.'

Peder stared at her.

'A man came up to her?' said Jonas, who hadn't spoken until now.

Ingrid Strand nodded and wiped her eyes.

'Yes, he did. And he seemed so sure of what he was doing that I thought ... I just assumed everything was all right. Because when I got out onto the platform, I saw her again.'

Peder sat motionless. His mouth felt dry.

'The man was holding her in his arms,' whispered Ingrid. 'I saw them just outside the other door of the carriage, just as I got out myself. He was holding the girl, and she looked all relaxed. I thought that was good; it must be someone she knew who'd come to pick her up.'

Ingrid blinked a few times.

'I only saw him from behind. He was tall. Tall and dark. Short hair, and he had a green shirt on, like the one my son-in-law wears when we're at the cottage. And he was rubbing her back, like a parent would. I saw his hand; he had a big gold ring, a signet ring.'

Peder noted it all down. Was the man tall enough for them to assume he might take size 46 shoes?

'I saw him whisper something in her ear,' Ingrid Strand

went on, her voice less shaky now, ' I saw him talking to her. And she was listening, even though she was hanging there so floppily in his arms.'

It all went quiet, totally quiet. Peder took slow breaths, in and out. Jonas shifted a little, and looked at him. If Ingrid had anything else to tell them, it would be best for neither of them to speak.

Her shoulders slumped and her face had a dejected look.

'I really didn't think there was anything wrong when I saw them,' she said under her breath, and more tears came into her eyes. 'It was so obvious the girl knew him. I thought he must be her father, in fact.'

Pia Nordh was waiting in Peder's office when he got back. Peder stopped in the doorway and just stared at her. She had a faint smile on her lips, and Peder could feel his stomach somersault as she moved her head and her pale blonde hair crept towards her heart-shaped face.

'Hi,' she said.

'Hi,' answered Peder, coming into the room.

He looked around him in confusion. *Shit.*

'I saw I had a missed call from you,' said Pia, and smiled. 'I must have picked up just as you ended the call.'

Yes, that was the plan.

Peder was too disconcerted to do anything; he just stood in the middle of the floor facing Pia. *Hell, what now?*

'But maybe you're busy right now?' Pia ventured softly.

Way too softly.

Peder shook his head fiercely. He took several quick steps past Pia and sat down at a safe distance behind his desk.

He straightened his back. He cleared his throat. *Control, Peder, control.*

'Yes, actually,' he said in a rather too authoritative tone. 'I'm working on an important case at the moment. Haven't really got time to ... you know, chat. No time for a coffee break just now, if I can put it that way.'

Peder knew he was laying it on thick. In the police, there was always an excuse for a coffee. Saying you had no time for a coffee break was tantamount to signalling you were faced with a very serious situation. Like the king getting shot, or Parliament being blown up by terrorists. But crimes like that would be dealt with by the security services, of course.

The security services. Just imagine getting a job there. Every policeman's wet dream.

They were interrupted when Ellen Lind rushed in, looking for Peder.

'Are you nearly ready? Alex wants the feedback from the interview as soon as possible,' she said, sounding stressed.

Ellen threw a surprised glance at the enchanting Pia, whom she had never seen before, but then looked back at Peder.

'I'll be right there,' he said quickly.

Ellen went out, leaving the door open.

'Maybe we could have a beer, after work?' asked Pia with a smile.

Peder grinned back. *Forget her, forget her, forget her.*

'I'll ring you later,' he said.

Peder looked at Pia one more time and left the room, relieved to avoid further confrontation with the very individual who personified his transgression, but painfully aware of the desire that seeing her aroused in him. *Forget her, forget her, forget her.*

Fate had been kind to Ellen Lind when she was born. Not only had she always been in the best of health, but she also had a number of talents to draw on. One of these was being able to spot when there was a spark between two people. That was how she had discovered her mother had met someone new, so she had not been surprised by her parents' divorce when it eventually happened. That was also, unfortunately, how she realized her husband was being unfaithful, which was how she had ended up on her own. And it was thanks to this gift, too, though she only had a millisecond to deploy it, that she knew the beautiful woman in Peder's office was more than just a colleague.

The discovery that Peder was cheating on his wife did not really come as a surprise to Ellen, but it made her absolutely livid. The papers that needed sorting on her desk got the rough treatment. Ellen knew Peder's wife had spent the last year with the misery of protracted post-natal depression that wasn't responding to treatment.

Ellen was all too well acquainted with that aspect of the male world not to realize what had happened. Peder had felt sorry for himself and treated himself to a fling. Ellen simply couldn't understand how that sort of man could live with himself. She couldn't understand, either, why anybody would want to be with a man on such contemptible terms.

On the other hand, Ellen's own situation in the love stakes was hardly ideal. Her man friend had just rung back and said something had come up at work that he couldn't get out of. Ellen had found it hard to hide her disappointment. It was as if he didn't understand that it wasn't always easy to juggle a love affair with being a single parent in sole charge of two children.

Talking to him on the phone this time, she had detected an entirely new note. His voice implied she was nagging and childish for voicing her displeasure. Suddenly he had completely changed his tune and more or less given her a telling off. Subtle, but still unmistakable.

'We've got to be reasonable in what we expect of each other,' he said. 'It worries me that you're so set in your ways, so inflexible, Ellen.'

Her first reaction was one of amazement. Then she considered hanging up. In the end she decided to ignore his killjoy comment entirely, and ended the call with a 'Let's speak later in the week.'

Why did it have to be so hard – *so hard* – to find a man to have a normal, functioning relationship with?

Alone on the road, under cover of the rain and the unusually dark sky, Jelena drove north in the car she and the Man had purchased for just that purpose. Jelena was so excited she could hardly sit still. Finally it was happening. After all the planning, all the waiting, it was about to happen at last. A smile played on her small, delicate face; a persistent bubble of happiness kept demanding her attention and begging to take over her body. But the Man's instructions had been extremely clear, as always.

'We won't count our chickens before they're hatched, Doll,' he had whispered, cupping her face in his strong hands. 'No celebrations – nothing – until it's all gone without a hitch. Remember that, Doll. Don't let anything go wrong. Not when we're so nearly there.'

She had looked him straight in the eyes and promised and sworn on all that was holy never ever to let him down.

'Do you love me?' he asked her.

'Yes,' she whispered, urgently, longingly. 'I love you so awfully much!'

His grip on her face tightened.

'I asked whether you loved me, Doll. That's a question best answered with just one word. Never use more words than you need. It could land us in a proper mess.'

She tried to nod between his rough hands, eager to please him.

'I know,' she answered, 'I know. But since it's only us here . . . I so much wanted to tell you how *much* I love you, not just that I do.'

He gripped her even harder; it hurt now. Slowly, he raised her up to his chest, up to his face. She had to stand on tiptoe or she'd be dangling in mid-air.

'It's nice that you want to say it, Doll,' he whispered. 'But you know we've talked about this before. The important thing isn't what you say, it's what you *do*. If I don't know how much you love me, if you have to tell me, then our love's worth nothing. Am I right?'

Jelena tried to nod, but it was impossible with him holding her head in such a tight grip. Tears came into her eyes, and she hoped desperately they wouldn't overflow. Then the evening would be ruined. And it would mean pain for her. A lot of pain.

'Do you understand what I'm saying?'

His grip relaxed very slightly, so she could nod.

'Say it,' he demanded, his voice its normal volume.

'I understand,' Jelena said swiftly. 'I understand.'

To her horror, his grip tightened again.

'That's good, Doll,' he said, lowering his voice again. 'Because if you don't understand, if I can't rely on you, then I've no use for you. You understand that, as well?'

Jelena understood. She understood very well indeed.

'So we'll say no more about it,' he said calmly, releasing her face enough for the soles of her feet to touch the ground again.

Her breathing eased. The muscles in her neck were taut.

'And you're my doll, aren't you?' he whispered, leaning forward to kiss her.

'Yes,' she whispered, deeply relieved that he had forgiven her for her mistake.

'That's nice, Doll,' he said. 'Very nice.'

And he had propelled her gently but firmly towards the bedroom.

Jelena hugged the steering wheel hard as she remembered their union in bed, both of them filled with a great and overwhelming joy that they had taken the first steps. The man was right, of course. She mustn't feel pleased yet, risk not concentrating properly. But when they had finished . . . Jelena felt a shiver of anticipation. It would be fantastic. It just had to be.

The car purred obligingly along the road. Even though Jelena hadn't even passed her test. She met hardly any other cars. She looked neither ahead nor behind. She felt very sure of the role she had to play now. When it came down to it, this stage was childishly simple. She just had to do exactly what they had arranged. Or the Man had arranged. Since he knew best, Jelena left all the planning to him.

She knew for sure that it would be the end of her if she messed up. She swallowed and concentrated on driving.

Dump the Foetus, she thought. Nothing else matters for now. Just got to wait for the right moment.

Fredrika Bergman ended her working day by making a list. She was exhausted. She'd had no idea the day might develop along the lines it had when she elected to drink too much wine and get too little sleep the night before.

Fredrika glanced at the clock. It was seven thirty. She hadn't had lunch until four. She would soon be hungry again.

Her mobile telephone buzzed. One new message. Fredrika was very surprised to see it was from Spencer. He hardly ever texted her.

'Hello again and thanks so much for the wonderful time last night. Hope to see you at the weekend too. S.'

Fredrika felt warm inside. There was somebody for everybody. And she had Spencer Lagergren. Sometimes, anyway.

Then the thoughts she had been having the previous night resurfaced. What was the relationship with Spencer really costing her? One of her girlfriends once pointed out that Spencer made her feel comfortable, which meant she never met anyone she could start a serious relationship with. Fredrika protested and said that wasn't the case at all. Spencer was a comfort blanket she could reach for whenever the longing to be close to someone got the better of her. If she didn't have him, she wouldn't have been *less* lonely; she'd have been *desperately* lonely.

Fredrika went back to her list, well aware that the thoughts would be back all too soon.

Why was there no other witness to corroborate Ingrid Strand's version of events? Why hadn't anybody else seen the girl being carried around on the platform by a tall man?

Alex's explanation was that it was quite simply the sort of everyday sight that people don't react to and therefore don't remember. A father carrying his child, who would see that as noteworthy?

Fredrika could buy that argument to some extent. She could also appreciate that Ingrid Strand remembered it because she had had some contact with the child in question on the train journey. But still. Fredrika had discreetly made enquiries of Mats, the analyst who Alex seemed uninterested in introducing to the rest of the team. Had there really been no calls to corroborate that version of events?

Mats, who was dealing with the information from the public one bit at a time, entering it into a database, pursed his lips and shook his head as he searched through the tip-offs. No, no one else had rung in with information to support Ingrid Strand's story.

Fredrika did not doubt that Ingrid Strand had really seen what she had told the police she saw. She simply wondered where Lilian and her father – if it was him Ingrid had seen – had gone once they left the platform. Why hadn't anyone else seen them after that?

They had questioned taxi firms and people who ran shops inside Stockholm Central Station, but not the slightest lead had been forthcoming. Nobody could remember encountering a tall man carrying a child who looked like Lilian. That didn't mean they hadn't seen them, of course, but no one remembered anything of the kind. And that troubled Fredrika, because there had been huge numbers of people with every opportunity of seeing them.

Alex didn't sound particularly concerned about their inability to pin down how Lilian had left the station.

'Give people a bit of time,' he said. 'Sooner or later somebody's going to remember something.'

Give people a bit of time.

Fredrika gave an involuntary shiver. How much time had they got, in actual fact?

Everything depended on who had taken the girl and why? Fredrika realized with a sinking feeling that she was the only one in the team who had still not discounted it being anyone other than Gabriel Sebastiansson.

The examining magistrate had largely gone along with Alex and Peder and thought it most likely to be Lilian's father who had taken her off the train. Admittedly, Ingrid Strand hadn't seen the man's face, but the information she had been able to give them pointed in that direction. But of course it was no crime to collect your daughter from a train. There was no order banning Gabriel Sebastiansson from contact with his daughter, even though it would naturally be desirable for him to keep her mother informed of where he was taking her. The fact that her hair had been shaved off, on the other hand, could readily be categorized as assault, the examining magistrate argued. But since there was no evidence to link her father to the parcel of clothes and hair, they could not exclude the possibility that something else entirely had happened to the girl, even though the magistrate said several times that this was highly unlikely.

After half an hour's deliberation, the magistrate reached her conclusion: the child had been abducted; her mother had not been informed; the child had suffered maltreatment and the parcel sent to the mother could be construed as a threat. That was sufficient for classifying the crime as a potential abduction, with Gabriel Sebastiansson as the prime suspect. A warrant could therefore be issued for his arrest, and Alex would issue a national alert.

Alex and Peder looked hugely relieved as they left the examining magistrate's office. Fredrika walked two steps behind them, frowning.

She peered at the list of Sara Sebastiansson's circle of acquaintances and family, people she would try to see the next day. Predictably enough, Peder was delighted to find her so willing to hand over the task of continuing to investigate Gabriel's contacts. He looked quite triumphant, as if he had just won the lottery.

But Fredrika preferred to maintain her sceptical stance.

She no longer doubted that the perpetrator was someone with whom Sara had some kind of relationship, wittingly or unwittingly. But she was not convinced that that person had to be Gabriel. She thought about the woman Ellen had spoken to that afternoon. The woman who had lived with a man who hit her, and who now believed him to be the man who had taken Lilian. There was a microscopic chance that the man she was talking about actually was Gabriel Sebastiansson, but even there, Fredrika was keeping an open mind. No one else had reported Gabriel to the police, and surely they would have done if he were the man the anonymous woman was talking about? That was if they worked on the hypothesis that the woman's call constituted an actual report of being assaulted by the man. Alex and Peder had impatiently dismissed her attempt to try to unravel the information in the woman's call, asking her to focus on 'real, concrete scenarios' rather than the invented variety.

Fredrika gave a grim laugh. Invented scenarios. Where did they get these expressions from?

Thanks to the analyst Mats, she had at least been able to find out what happened when they tried to trace the call. The woman had rung from a telephone box in central Jönköping. The lead stopped there. In Jönköping. Fredrika ran a quick check to see if Gabriel Sebastiansson had any contacts there, but drew a complete blank.

Fredrika, for her part, was sure the incoming call had nothing at all to do with Gabriel. The question was whether it was worthy of attention, even so. Ellen was right, of course: whenever the police appealed to the public for help, there always were a number of very odd people who rang in.

Fredrika frowned. Maybe Alex was right when he said she hadn't got the right feel for the job. On the other hand. Fredrika took a deep breath. On the other hand. If you took notice of what Alex and Peder classed as the nub of police work, then the work Fredrika was doing now could be classed as the very sharpest end of that work.

Because when it came down to it, in the case of the woman with the dog on the platform in Flemingsberg, and in the case of the woman who rang in with the tip-off, Fredrika had absolutely nothing to go on but her gut instinct. That was something those boys ought to approve of.

Gut instinct. The very phrase made her feel queasy.

She put one hand cautiously on her stomach while the other noted down yet one more thing that needed doing the next day. Pay a visit to Flemingsberg Station.

Her guts rumbled.

Dialogue, thought Fredrika. Right now, there was nobody apart from her own guts to have a dialogue with.

Peder Rydh felt relaxed as he left work later that evening. In fact, he felt great. For the simple reason that he was not intending to spoil his evening by going home to his sulky wife, but was heading out for a beer with some of his work-mates instead.

He felt curiously relieved. They had known all along that Gabriel Sebastiansson had taken the girl, of course, but now they knew it more definitely, they wouldn't have to grapple with the 'who' any more and could concentrate on the 'where'. *Where was the girl?*

Peder laughed out loud as he thought of Fredrika getting bogged down in every little tip-off and sidetrack that cropped up in the investigation. She was no bloodhound, that was certain. More a very tired little pug dog with short legs and a snub nose. Peder gave another laugh. A pug, that was her. And pugs shouldn't play with the big dogs like Peder and Alex.

Peder's legs found their own way to the bar. He was walking tall as he went in through the door. By chance, Pia Nordh was there. He noted that several of the lads recognized her and grinned at him. He grinned back. *No comments, guys.*

Peder was a man who liked relying on sheer chance. Chance had made him very happy on more than one occasion. Ylva had less faith in chance and liked to plan everything that possibly could be planned. Taking the day as it came was not something that appealed to her.

In fact, that was the spark in their relationship, the glow, Peder told himself. It was fun and a challenge to live with somebody who thought differently, followed a different pattern.

But there was a down side, too.

Chance lives a life of its own and isn't amenable to being structured out of existence. It was so ironic that chance was the very thing that had devastated their lives. Peder didn't like thinking along those lines, particularly when he was on the beer and a bit drunk, but that was precisely what had happened. Their lives were pretty much devastated, and sheer chance was to blame. Along with Ylva's inability to go with its flow.

When Ylva had the ultrasound scan, both she and Peder had been dumbstruck to discover they were expecting twins.

'But,' Ylva stuttered, 'there are no twins on either side of the family.'

The midwife had explained. Two-egg twins could be the result of genetic predisposition. Identical twins, on the other hand, from a single egg, are purely random.

Peder found the phrase energizing, a source of great strength. Random twins. But Ylva, he realized later, had started to fall apart from the very first moment she heard the words.

'But this wasn't what we planned at all,' she said repeatedly during her pregnancy. 'This wasn't how it was supposed to be.'

Peder remembered being surprised, since he had not in any way shared that clear image of 'how it was supposed to be'.

One of the other lads in the group interrupted his reverie by thumping him on the back.

'How're things going in the Recht team?' he asked, his eyes plainly signalling his envy.

Peder savoured the moment. To hell with all his gloomy thoughts; here was a source of energy to tap into.

'They're going bloody well,' he said with a genial smile. 'Alex is such a pro. He's got an incredible feel for the job.'

His colleague nodded attentively and Peder felt himself almost blushing. Who would have thought that after only a few years in the police department he'd be standing here referring to the great Alex Recht by his first name?

'Things have turned out bloody well for you, Peder,' said his colleague. 'Congratulations, you jammy bastard!'

Peder gave a self-deprecating wave of the hand and thanked him for the compliment.

'The next round's on me,' he said loudly, and instantly found yet more colleagues flocking round him.

He had to answer a steady stream of questions. The guys were all very interested in how things were done in Recht's team. Peder relished being the centre of attention and didn't bother to mention the elements of his new situation that for him felt distinctly negative. Like the fact they were often short of resources and had to borrow people right, left and centre. Like the fact that he had to work on his own to a far greater extent than ever before. And like the fact that Alex Recht didn't really live up to his amazing reputation in many ways.

After a while they switched to talking about the other members of the exclusive team. Almost immediately, the conversation turned to Fredrika Bergman.

'You know what,' said one of Peder's colleagues from the Södermalm police, 'we've got a so-called civilian appointment in our team, too. And I've never worked with a more useless individual. Goes on the whole time about databases and structures, draws diagrams and rules lines. All talk and no action, in fact.'

Peder eagerly swallowed a gulp of beer and nodded.

'Too fucking right!' he exclaimed. 'And, like, no feeling at all for which lines of enquiry are seriously worth following up. Trying to keep all the balls in the air at the same time, and impossible to work with as a result.'

Another mate from his time in Södermalm squinted hazily in Peder's direction, and gave him a crooked grin.

'But maybe she's a nice eyeful, that Fredrika?'

Peder grinned back.

'Well,' he said, 'I hate to say it, but . . . . yep, she's a very nice eyeful.'

Enthusiastic grins spread from face to face around the assembled party, and they ordered another round.

It was eleven before Peder was able to leave the bar with a modicum of discretion in the company of Pia Nordh. His head was spinning with alcohol and lack of sleep, but his gut instinct was telling him unmistakably that this was another of those rare occasions in a man's life when he has the right to go to bed with a woman other than his wife.

As Pia closed the door of her flat behind her a short while later, there wasn't a trace of bad conscience in his body. Just alcohol and desire. Overwhelming desire. He gave it a right royal welcome.

Teodora Sebastiansson was a relic of a bygone era, a fact she was very aware of, and it was a status she cherished. Sometimes she felt almost as though she had no place in the age in which she was now living.

Her own mother had never beaten about the bush when it came to telling Teodora what life was ultimately all about. You had to get an education, get married, and immortalize yourself. The last of these you achieved quite simply by reproducing. Education, husband and children: the holy trinity of womanhood. There was no room for a career within the strict boundaries of that trinity, and nor would you need one, since a husband was expected to support his wife. You only bothered with education as an aid to making conversation with cultivated people.

As she had told Fredrika Bergman, Teodora was of the firm opinion that her son could have made a far better match than Sara. Teodora had waited patiently in the wings, hoping her son would come to his senses and leave his wife while he still had the chance. To her aggravation, he never did, and it was Sara who bore Teodora her first grandchild.

Since Teodora had herself been brought up in one of life's harder schools, she had honestly seen nothing to object to in her son's desperate and justified efforts to bring his wife up to scratch. Despite what she had told Fredrika Bergman, she had considerable insight into her son's life with Sara and the turbulent aspect the relationship sometimes assumed. Teodora could not help regretting Sara's inability to please her husband. Sara had certainly – *certainly* – never tried to hide who she was. And Teodora accepted that her son had married Sara to a large extent as an embarrassingly delayed rebellion against his poor parents. Nonetheless, Teodora was in no doubt at all where her daughter-in-law's loyalties lay once things came to a head and she turned to the police for help. So the life of luxury Gabriel could offer didn't suit her after all!

It was stupid of Sara, very stupid, to think that a good mother like Teodora would let her husband and grandchild down, under any circumstances. She was thinking above all of Lilian, she told herself as she lifted the receiver and rang two of her husband's faithful old servants, who owed the Sebastiansson family large sums of money and considerable favours.

The simple part was saving Gabriel's skin by arranging the alibis he needed and deserved. The hard part was guiding and directing him in life from now on. After the second phase of trouble and the second report to the police, Teodora had had a serious talk to her son. She had no particular problem with his attempts to knock Sara into shape, but the police involvement had got to stop. It was awkward for the family, and clearing his name repeatedly could prove difficult in the long run. Particularly as his efforts to smarten Sara up left such visible marks, and particularly as she hadn't the sense to keep quiet about things one always sorted out within the family.

After the time Gabriel was legally banned from seeing his own wife, and therefore ended up ringing her a few times too many one evening, Teodora had finally had enough. He was either to see that he got Sara back, which from the outset she really did not favour, or he was to abandon his attempts to make her into a good person, and file for divorce. Divorce and sole custody.

Teodora didn't know exactly how her son had managed it, but suddenly he and Sara were living together again. It didn't last long. Sara carried on making trouble and soon it was time for another separation.

And now Sara had inconceivably pulled off the trick of depriving Teodora of her only grandchild. Her whole body was shaking. There was plainly no limit to the ways Sara imagined she could destroy the Sebastiansson family. Teodora, a mother herself, had seen how Sara treated her child, oh yes. No firm hand, and no particular maternal care, either. If the child was returned to her mother, Teodora was going to fight tooth and nail for her son to be allowed to bring the child up on his own. Sara would finally meet a foe impervious to police reports and threats. Sara would find out what happened when you lived your life in a way that was bound to destroy you, and tried to take your child with you to perdition.

In view of these feelings for her daughter-in-law and grand-child, she had had no difficulty at all in lying on her son's behalf, either the day before or during that day's interview with Fredrika Bergman. It was most regrettable, of course, that her son had not had time to inform her he was going on holiday, since that would have simplified the basis for further lies considerably.

She sighed.

'They'll be back, you know,' he said.

Teodora jumped at the sudden sound of his voice.

'Goodness, you gave me such a fright.'

Gabriel stepped over the threshold of his father's library, where Teodora had been sitting ever since Fredrika Bergman left the house. Teodora got to her feet and walked slowly towards him.

'I've got to know, Gabriel,' she said in a low, urgent tone. 'I've got to know for sure. Have you anything – *anything at all* – to do with Lilian's disappearance?'

Gabriel Sebastiansson gazed past his mother, out of the window.

'I think there's a thunderstorm brewing,' he said huskily.

There was a time, when Nora was much younger, when the darkness had been her enemy. Now she had grown up, she knew better. The darkness was her friend, and she welcomed it every evening and every night. The same went for the silence. She welcomed it, and she needed it.

Under the cover of darkness and silence, Nora quickly packed a suitcase of clothes. As usual in summer, the sky never turned completely black, but that deep, velvety blue was dark enough. The floor creaked under her bare feet as she moved about the room. The sound frightened her. The sound disturbed the silence, and the silence did not want to be disturbed. Not now. Not when she had to concentrate. Actually, it was quite simple packing this time. There was no need to take everything with her. She would only be gone a few weeks.

Nora's grandma had been glad to hear her voice when she rang.

'You want to come and stay for a bit, love?' she exclaimed when Nora revealed her plan to go and visit her grandmother in the country.

'If that's all right,' Nora said.

'You're always welcome here, dear. You know that, don't you?' her grandmother replied.

Safe Grandma. Wonderful Grandma. The one bright spot in a childhood that was otherwise painful to look back on.

'I'll ring again when I've booked the ticket and have a better idea what time I'll be arriving, Grandma,' Nora whispered into the telephone, and they hung up.

Nora tried to get her thoughts in order as she packed. She decided to travel in her red, high-heeled shoes. Shoes like the ones the Man had once said made her look cheap, but she loved wearing them now, and saw them as a badge of her independence. Perhaps it had been a mistake not to give her name to the police, but Nora really didn't want to let anyone crack open the shell inside which she had successfully built herself a safe existence.

Nora's case was packed and she felt ready to leave the flat.

She stood the suitcase on the floor and sat down on the edge of the bed. It was almost ten o'clock. She ought to ring Grandma to confirm when she'd be arriving, as promised.

Nora was just keying in the number when a sound from the hall caught her attention. Just a single sound, then it went quiet. Nora blinked. Then the sound came again, the sound of someone taking a step on the creaking floorboards.

Her mouth went dry with fear when he suddenly appeared in the doorway. Paralysed by the realization that it was all over now, she did not move from her seat on the bed. She had still not keyed in the whole number.

'Hello, Doll,' he whispered. 'You going somewhere?'

The telephone slipped automatically from Nora's hand and she shut her eyes in the hope that the evil would disappear. The last things she saw were the red shoes, still standing beside her suitcase.

THURSDAY

Dr Melker Holm had always enjoyed the night shift in Accident and Emergency. For one thing, he was the sort of man who liked things being on the go, when there was stuff happening, and for another, he found himself irresistibly attracted by the nocturnal calm that always followed the more turbulent hours.

Maybe when Melker went on duty that night, he already had a premonition that this shift would be different. The emergency ward was buzzing with a level of commotion and activity that could hardly be considered normal. A serious car accident involving several vehicles took a very long time to deal with, while in the waiting room, a group of patients with slightly less acute problems grew increasingly fed up with the long wait.

Melker heard Sister Anne's footsteps before he heard her voice. Sister Anne had uncommonly short legs, which meant she took unusually short, quick steps. Apart from that, Melker had not noticed a single defect in her overwhelming physical presence. Though he was never one to listen to or spread gossip, he had – most unintentionally – heard that Sister Anne had not been slow to see how she could capitalize on her beauty.

He could not have cared less about vulgar women prostituting themselves in their places of work. At the same time, Sister Anne, of all people, was someone in whom he felt a degree of trust. There was something fundamentally stable about her. She was reliable. And there were few personal qualities Melker valued more highly than reliability.

Sister Anne appeared in the doorway a few seconds after he first heard her.

'I think you ought to come, Doctor,' said Sister Anne, and Melker noted a tension in her features he had not seen before.

Asking no questions, he got up and went with her.

To his surprise, Sister Anne hurried right through the Emergency Department and out of the front entrance. Only then did Melker speak.

'Sorry, but what's going on?'

Sister Anne turned her head towards him and her steps faltered a little.

'A woman rang,' she said. 'She said she and her husband were on their way here by car. She said it was her first baby and she was afraid they wouldn't make it in time. Afraid the baby was going to be born on the way. She wanted us to go out ready to meet them.'

Sister Anne licked her lips and anxiously scanned the drive leading to the Emergency Department. She sensed Melker's quizzical look and turned back to him again.

'She said they were almost here, and I couldn't get hold of the obstetrician, so I thought . . .'

Melker interrupted her with a nod.

'That's all right. But they aren't here, are they? And anyway – why would they be coming to A&E? You should have sent them to Maternity.'

Sister Anne flushed.

'I'm sorry, I didn't mean to waste your time,' she said

quickly. 'It was just . . . Well, her voice. There was something about her voice that made me think it was much more urgent than it clearly is.'

Melker nodded again, graciously this time.

'I understand what you were thinking and I am at your disposal, absolutely. But if they ring again, do tell them to go to Maternity Reception, please.'

He turned on his heels and went back to his room. He happened to glance at his watch. It was just past midnight. A new day had begun.

It was just after one o'clock when Melker heard Sister Anne's footsteps in the corridor once more. He had time to register that it really sounded more as if she was running, and then she was at his door, rain-sodden and wild-eyed.

'You must bloody well come right now,' she said, and rapidly repeated herself: 'Bloody well come right now.'

Melker Holm was taken aback by the strong language, which was totally inappropriate in the working climate of the Emergency Department, and rushed after Sister Anne through the reception area and out into the car park.

'Carry on, to the parking area at the far end,' Sister Anne exhorted him.

At the end of the access road, just between the ordinary visitors' car park and the approach to A&E, in the middle of the pavement, lay a little girl. She did not have a thread of clothing on her body, and her empty, glassy eyes stared unseeing up into the night sky as it pelted her pale, naked body with rain.

'What on earth . . . ?' mumbled Melker, kneeling down

beside the girl and checking her pulse, though he could tell at a glance that she was dead.

Later, Melker was to envy Sister Anne her ready tears, mixing freely with the rain, for he was unable to shed any himself for several days.

'I popped out to check whether that couple were waiting out here in the car park, because they didn't ring again,' he heard Sister Anne say. 'Oh my God, she was just lying here. Just lying here.'

Against his better judgment, Melker Holm leant down and stroked the girl's cheek. His eye fell on her forehead, where someone had written a word, the letters blurred and sprawling. Someone had marked her body.

'We must ring the police right away so we can get the poor little thing into the warm,' he said.

Just as he was opening the front door to set off for work, Alex received the call from the police up in Umeå.

'DCI Hugo Paulsson here, from the Umeå Crime Squad,' bellowed a voice at the other end.

Alex stopped what he was doing.

Hugo Paulsson gave a sigh.

'I think we may have found your little girl, the one who went missing from the Central Station,' he said softly. 'Lilian Sebastiansson.'

Found? Alex would remember that moment later as one of the few in his career when time stood utterly still. He did not hear the rain beating on the window, did not see Lena who was watching him from just a few feet away, did not say anything in reply to what he had just heard. Time stopped, and the ground opened up beneath his feet.

How the hell could I mess up on this one?

When Hugo Paulsson found himself still getting no reply, he went on.

'She was found at the hospital here in Umeå, outside A&E, at one o'clock last night. It took a while to establish the likely identity, because we had another little girl up here who'd run away, you see, and we had to make sure it wasn't her first.'

'Lilian didn't run away,' Alex said automatically.

'No, of course not,' said Hugo Paulsson grimly. 'But anyway, now you know where she is. Or to be more accurate – where she probably is. Someone will have to identify her.'

Alex nodded gently to himself as he stood in his hall, waiting for time to start moving again.

'I'll get back to you as soon as I can on how we're going to proceed,' he said at last.

'Fine,' said Hugo Paulsson.

Then he added slowly:

'I don't know what it means, but the girl's clothes haven't been found. And her head's been shaved.'

Fredrika Bergman received the news that the case of the missing Lilian had become a murder investigation via her mobile phone. It was Alex who rang, and she could tell from his voice that he was in shock. She herself felt drained of all emotion. Alex asked her to go and see Teodora Sebastiansson again and then try to talk to as many people as possible on the list of names and contacts they had got from Sara's parents. They would have to try to work out why the child had turned up in Umeå, of all places.

Only once Fredrika had ended the call and looked out to see that summer had yet another day of rain ahead did she start to cry. She felt profoundly grateful that she was alone in her office, behind a closed door.

How on earth could the girl suddenly be dead?

Of all the questions raging in her head, one was more insistent than the rest.

What the hell am I doing here? she thought. *How did I end up working in a place like this on a job like this?*

Fredrika was on the point of ringing Alex back there and then and saying:

'You're right, Alex. I'm not cut out for this. I'm too weak, too emotional. I've never seen a dead person in my life and I hate stories with unhappy endings. And it doesn't get any unhappier than this one. I give up. I've no business being here.'

Fredrika ran her fingers gently over the scar on her right arm. Time had faded the operation scar to just a couple of white lines, but they were still fully visible to any eye. For Fredrika, they were a daily reminder not only of The Accident, but also of the life that never was. The life she never had.

Fredrika wiped the corner of her eye and blew her nose. If she carried on thinking like this in her present state, she definitely wouldn't be able to work properly. She was tired, worn out. It was only a few weeks until her holiday. She gave a stubborn shake of the head. Not now, she told herself, not now. Right now it would do the investigation more harm than good if she got up and left. But later, when the case was over . . .

Then I'll leave . . .

Fredrika blew her nose again. Crumpled the tissue into a ball in her hand. Threw it at the bin. Missed but left it lying on the floor.

Why was the picture refusing to come into focus?

Thoughts were flying through Fredrika's brain at lightning speed as she sat there at her desk, though it was not yet eight o'clock. She was the first to admit that she had not worked on many cases, but she did have a solid amount of analytical experience behind her. Considering the point they had now reached in the case of Lilian's disappearance, it ought not to be that hard for Fredrika to complete the jigsaw puzzle in front of her. But there was something missing. She could feel it in her whole body, but couldn't put it into words. Had they missed something? Was it something they should have seen or thought of earlier?

But then, Fredrika argued to herself, they still hadn't found a motive for the abduction itself. If it was Gabriel Sebastiansson who had taken Lilian, what was his motive? There was no tedious custody battle going on; there were no reports of his having previously harmed the girl.

Fredrika's encounter with Gabriel's mother had left her in no doubt that he really had physically assaulted Sara. There was something extremely unpleasant about the whole family. Fredrika went to the computer to put together a list of further questions for Mrs Sebastiansson. The mere recollection of that lady's bony finger pointing to where she was to park the car made her feel tense. No, there was definitely something sick about that family. The only question was: why had someone like Sara chosen to marry into it? After all, unlike her mother-in-law she seemed a straightforward, unpretentious, uncomplicated person. It was certainly going to be interesting to see what Gabriel was like, when the time came.

Then her mobile rang, forcing her to break off from the list she had barely started to compile. It was a man's voice on the line.

'Am I speaking to Fredrika Bergman?'

'Yes, you are. And who am I speaking to?' said Fredrika.

'I'm Martin Ek, from SatCom. We spoke briefly the other evening, when you rang to ask about Gabriel Sebastiansson,' the man replied.

SatCom, the company in which Gabriel had been working his way up over the past ten years, and was now one of the top executives.

Fredrika was immediately alert.

'Yes?' she said.

'Well,' Martin Ek began, sounding relieved that she remembered him. 'You asked me to ring if Gabriel got in touch, so I kept your card.'

'Ah, right,' said Fredrika with a little gasp. 'And he's been in touch now?'

Martin Ek initially said nothing. Fredrika sensed he was on the verge of hanging up.

'We haven't heard from him.'

Fredrika's shoulders slumped a fraction.

'But I think I may have found something you'd be interested in seeing,' he gabbled.

'Okay,' said Fredrika guardedly, pulling paper and pencil towards her. 'What have you found, exactly?'

Another pause.

'I'd really rather you came over and saw for yourself,' he said.

Fredrika hesitated. She had neither the time nor the inclination to go over there. And anyway, it was really Peder who ought to be dealing with this contact, since he was the one following up Gabriel Sebastiansson's circle of acquaintances.

'You won't even give me an idea of what this is about?' she asked. 'We've got a huge amount on at the moment.'

Martin Ek was breathing heavily at the other end of the line.

'It's something I found on his computer,' he said finally.

He took a few more deep breaths before he went on.

'Photos. Disgusting photos. I've never seen anything so bloody sick. I'd really, really appreciate it if you could come round. Straight away, if possible.'

Fredrika felt her throat constrict.

'I'll ask my colleague to get back to you right away. Okay?'

'Okay.'

Fredrika was about to ring off when Martin Ek added:

'But please come quickly.'

The desert.

Thirst.

Pain. A whole head full of pain.

Peder Rydh was hung over and barely awake when Alex rang to tell him that a little girl who in all probability was Lilian Sebastiansson had been found dead in Umeå. Alex also told him to get round to Sara's and make sure she, or one of Lilian's other close relations, caught the ten o'clock flight to Umeå. Alex would be on that plane himself, and would meet whoever was going at the airport. He also instructed Peder to pull out all the stops to work out how Umeå fitted into the picture.

Peder's first reaction was one of near panic.

How the hell could the child be dead?

She had been missing fewer than forty-eight hours, and since getting the information from the woman sitting beside Sara and Lilian on the train, they'd been looking for the girl's father, suspecting him of involvement in her disappearance. Had Gabriel Sebastiansson gone off his head? Had he murdered his own daughter and dumped her outside a *hospital*?

Then came his second reaction: *Where the fuck was he?*

Peder fought desperately against the hangover, which was completely paralysing his powers of thought. Several long seconds passed before it dawned on him that he had fallen asleep at Pia Nordh's. Heck, this was going to be tricky to explain to Ylva.

The phone had woken Pia, and she lay on her side, watching him. She was naked and her expression was quizzical. She realized from the short call that something very serious had happened.

'They've found her,' Peder said curtly, getting up from the bed far too fast.

The floor rocked beneath his feet, his head throbbed and his eyes ached. He sat down on the edge of the bed and rested his head in his hands. He'd got to think, pull himself together. He ran his fingers through his hair and reached for his mobile again. He had a missed call from Jimmy and eleven from Ylva, who had admittedly been told to expect him home late, but would hardly have expected him not to come home at all. When had he rung her, exactly? His memories of the previous evening were one big whirl, impossible to separate out. Had he rung at all, when it came to it? The shadow of a recollection flitted by. Peder, half undressed in Pia's bathroom. One hand on the washbasin for support, keeping himself upright, the other hand holding his mobile, sending a text.

'Don't wait up. Back later. Speak soon.'

Peder wanted to crawl out of his own skin. This wasn't good. Or rather . . . it didn't get any worse than this. If this wasn't rock bottom, then he didn't want to be part of it all any longer.

'I've got to go,' he said gruffly, and stood up again.

His legs carried him all the way from the bedroom, out into the hall, into the bathroom. How much had he drunk? How many beers had it added up to?

He was just getting out of the shower when he heard his mobile ring again. He raced out of the bathroom, almost skidding on the wet floor tiles. Pia met him in the hall, his mobile in her hand.

It was Fredrika.

'There was a call from the place where Gabriel Sebastiansson works,' she said tersely. 'They want one of us round there at once, to see something they found on Gabriel's computer. Some horrible photos.'

Peder retreated into the bathroom so as not to drip all over Pia's hall floor, but had to come back out again because there was no signal in there. He tried to towel himself one-handed with the towel while he was still on the phone.

'Right,' he began, 'Alex has asked me to make sure Sara Sebastiansson knows what's happened first. Then I can deal with the Gabriel thing.'

He could hear Fredrika was about to say something, so he went on quickly:

'What sort of photos, anyway? We can't just go checking people's computers without getting the examining magistrate to grant a search warrant.'

Fredrika informed Peder with her usual cheek – *always that cheek* – that she was quite well aware the police couldn't go snooping in people's computers whenever they felt like it, but that this could be viewed as a tip-off in a very important investigation, and there was no law forbidding the police from going to look at something somebody else had discovered and . . .

'Okay, okay,' Peder interrupted her wearily. 'Give me their number and I'll ring them now and arrange something.'

'Good,' said Fredrika, sounding a bit washed out herself.

'They didn't say anything about what was in these pictures?' Peder asked.

'No,' said Fredrika, 'they just said they were disgusting.'

'What are you going to do now, by the way?' Peder enquired curiously.

'Alex asked me to go and see Mrs Sebastiansson again,' Fredrika said. 'And there are a few other things I need to get done . . .'

'Wasn't I supposed to be handling the interviews with Gabriel's family and friends from now on?' Peder said irritably.

'Clearly not this one,' came Fredrika's crisp retort.

Peder ended the call with a scowl and went back into the bathroom.

Pia appeared at the doorway. She was still stark naked. Peder looked at her in the bathroom mirror. Was she really that attractive when it came to it? He thought her tits looked a bit on the droopy side. Or was his hangover clouding his judgment? Well it was all the same to him, he was on his way out of the flat anyway.

For some reason he felt reluctant to turn round and meet her eye.

'So where do we go from here?' said Pia, folding her arms.

'Have you got any Panadol?' asked Peder wearily, and started brushing his teeth. With Pia's toothbrush.

Without a word, Pia opened a bathroom cabinet and got a strip of tablets out of a box. Peder took the lot from her; he'd be needing the rest later in the day.

'You might at least say something.'

Peder hurled the toothbrush impatiently into the basin.

'Don't you understand how I'm feeling right now?' he thundered, afraid his head would explode the moment he raised his voice. 'The kid's been found dead, murdered! Don't you understand that I can't think about anything else at the moment?'

Pia stared at him.

'Just go, Peder,' she said.

She left the bathroom without waiting for a reply.

Peder sat down on the floor and took several deep breaths.

He had let his wife down.

He had let his employer down by being in such a state.

He had very likely let little Lilian down as well.

And now Pia Nordh wanted to make out he had let her down, too. What the hell did the woman want of him?

Peder straightened up. He'd got to focus. He'd got to get up and get out. How he would get to Sara Sebastiansson's flat would be a question for later. He most probably wouldn't be able to drive.

Peder got up from the floor, put on his clothes and shoes and hurriedly left Pia's flat.

A short while later he was standing on a pavement in the rain with wet hair, ringing for a taxi. He blinked a couple of times and peered up at the sky.

He stopped for a moment.

For the first time in ages, it looked as though the sun might manage to break through the cloud cover. Summer had arrived.

Jelena was on her way back to Stockholm. In a plane. She had ditched the car as planned. She had never flown before. She leant forward and looked out of the plane window in fascination. Incredible, she thought. *Bloody incredible.*

Anxiety came washing over her. The man hated it when she swore. He had punished her very severely for it at the beginning. Well, not punished, *reprimanded* was the word he generally used. And only for her own good.

Jelena smiled as she sat there. The man really was the best thing that had ever happened to her. She squeezed the armrest of her seat. The man was in actual fact the *only* good thing that had happened to her. He was so generous. And smart. Jelena loved seeing the man working and planning. He was so, so handsome when he was doing that. The fact that he had worked out how to hold up that stupid cow in Flemingsberg so she missed the train, for example, had impressed Jelena enormously.

And besides, thought Jelena, in Flemingsberg they had had several strokes of luck.

The man naturally wouldn't have agreed with her, but they really had been served Sara Sebastiansson on a plate when she decided to get off the train to make her call. The original plan had been for Jelena to attract Sara's attention by knocking on the window by her seat and trying to lure her out onto the platform by frantic gesticulations. And if that hadn't worked, they would have tried to snatch Lilian the day after instead, when her mother handed her over to her father. But they hadn't needed to do any of that, after all.

Jelena didn't really know why the man had chosen her. She had been so lucky. The man must have known there were loads of other young girls who'd give their right arm to be part of his battle. He must have had so many to choose from. He had actually said as much.

'I could have taken anybody, Doll,' he whispered every evening when they were going to sleep. 'I could have taken anybody, Doll, but I chose you. And if you disappoint me, I'll choose someone else.'

Jelena hardly had words for the terror she felt whenever he hinted that she was replaceable. Jelena had been replaceable for almost as long as she could remember. It was not at all nice remembering the years she had lived before she met the man, so she seldom did. It was only at night, in her dreams, that the memories would not leave her in peace. Then she remembered all the disgusting things, every detail. Sometimes the dreams refused to end, and then she would find she had woken herself by sitting up in bed and howling.

'I won't, I won't, I won't.'

The man never wanted to hear about her dreams. He would just pull her back down into bed and whisper to her:

'You're the one in charge of your sleep, Doll. You've got to understand that. If you don't, you'll carry on dreaming things you don't like. And if you do that, Doll, if you carry on dreaming things you don't like, and you don't try hard enough, then you're a weak person. And you know what I think about weak dolls, don't you?'

To start with, she had tried to object, tried to tell him she was doing her very best, but the dreams came anyway. To start with, she had cried.

Then he would lie down on top of her in the bed, so heavy she could hardly breathe.

'There is nothing, Doll – *nothing* – more worthless than tears. Try to understand that. Know that you *have* to understand it. I don't want to see anything like that again. Ever. Do you understand?'

Jelena nodded beneath him, felt him making himself even heavier.

'Answer so I can hear, Doll.'

'I understand,' she whispered hastily. 'I understand.'

'If you don't understand,' he went on, 'I'll be happy to reprimand you.'

His fingers twined their way into her hair, and she saw his other hand clench into a fist.

'Do you understand?'

'I understand,' she said, her eyes wide with fear.

'Maybe you'd understand better if I reprimanded you, like I had to do in the beginning?'

Jelena started to tremble involuntarily beneath him, and tossed her head from side to side on the pillow.

'No, no,' she whispered. 'Please, no.'

He lowered his raised fist and stroked her cheek.

'Now come on, Doll,' he said, his voice silky. 'We don't plead. Not you and me.'

She took slow breaths, still with the heavy weight of his body on top of hers. Waited for his next move.

'You don't need to be afraid of me, Doll,' he said. 'Not

ever. Everything I do, Doll, I do in your best interests. In *our* best interests. You know that. Don't you?'

She nodded between breathing in and breathing out.

'Yes, I know.'

'Good,' he said, and rolled off her. 'Because when our fight begins, when we start our campaign to rouse those damned sinners from their slumbers, there'll be no room for mistakes.'

lex Recht just found time to pop into HQ before he had to head for the airport. Fredrika was able to tell him that someone had rung from where Gabriel Sebastiansson worked, and then he spoke to Peder, who had just left Sara's flat. Peder confirmed that Sara would be going to Umeå, accompanied by her parents, to identify the dead girl. Alex reminded both Fredrika and Peder of the need to establish whether the Sebastiansson family had any links with Umeå.

Very soon Alex was in a taxi on his way out to Arlanda. He wasn't expecting to stay long up in Umeå, in fact he'd probably fly back later that day. Somewhat reluctantly, he had sent Peder with the duty clergyman to break the bad news to Sara. Peder could hardly be called ideal for the job, but sending Fredrika would have been even more unthinkable.

People whose own emotional lives were dysfunctional could scarcely be entrusted with a demanding task like breaking the news that someone had died.

Alex leant back on the headrest in the back seat of the taxi. Lilian's body had been found outside the A&E department in Umeå at about one o'clock the previous night. Alex understood that she had been found by a nurse and a duty doctor, and had been lying stretched out on her back on the footpath, naked and wet in the rain. Someone had written the word 'Unwanted' on her forehead.

The child was already dead when they found her. There had been no attempt at resuscitation. Cause of death had not yet been established, but an initial examination of her body indicated that she had been dead for about twenty-four hours when they found her. That in turn meant she had lived only a few hours after the time when she was abducted. A few hours. If they'd known that was the sort of margin they had to play with . . .

But that was the thing. They hadn't known. And they'd had no reason to expect it. Or had they?

Alex felt a large lump in his throat, and swallowed to try to banish it. His thoughts went to his own children. With quick, fumbling fingers he got out his mobile and rang the home number of Viktoria, his daughter. She answered at the fifth ring and Alex could tell from her voice that he had woken her.

'I'm so glad you answered,' he said, his voice almost cracking.

His daughter, used to her father occasionally trying to ring her at odd times, didn't say much, and rang off without really discovering why he had called. It didn't matter. Experience told her that she would eventually find out. Maybe not until the next time he rang, but then if not before.

Alex, happy and relieved, put the phone back in his inside pocket.

Some part of him had always hoped, as all parents do deep down, that one of his children would choose the same career as him. Or at least something similar. But neither of them had.

Viktoria had become a vet. For a long, long time, Alex had

clung to some sort of hope that her all-embracing interest in horses might make her join the mounted police, but as she took her final school exams and prepared to go to university, he had to admit it was very unlikely.

He couldn't really object. After all, he had chosen a career path quite different from the one expected of *him*. It was more a case of having nurtured some kind of hope that Viktoria, physically the very image of her mother, might turn out to be her father's daughter in spirit. But she didn't. Alex would swell with pride whenever he thought of her, though he was aware of letting it show far too infrequently. He could sometimes detect something anxious and quizzical in her steady gaze.

'Are you happy with me, Dad?' it whispered. 'Are you satisfied with the person you made me into?'

Alex felt another lump in his throat. He was so unutterably satisfied that the very word 'satisfied' seemed banal in a context such as that.

He reminded himself that he was satisfied with both his children, not only Viktoria but also her younger brother, Erik. His son, the eternal seeker. Alex knew it was rather harsh of him to classify his younger child as a seeker when he hadn't even reached twenty-five, but he honestly couldn't see Erik ever putting down roots. Not really. Not the way he lived.

For a brief period, when he had just left school, it looked as though Erik might find a niche in military life. Alex didn't really want a son in the armed forces, but if it proved a good opening for Erik, then he would have no objections. But Erik left the officer training course he had enrolled on, and said he wanted to become a pilot instead. And though nobody could quite work out how, the lad got into some kind of flying school down in Skåne. Then something else got in the way, and to his parents' unfeigned amazement, he left the training course and the country, and moved to Colombia to live with a woman he had met at evening classes in Spanish. The woman was ten years older than him and had just left her husband. Alex and Lena simply didn't know what to say, so they let their son go without much of an argument.

'He'll soon get tired of her, too,' said Lena, trying to console him a bit.

Alex merely shook his head in resignation.

News of his son's life on the other side of the globe filtered through in the form of emails and calls from the boy himself, but also via Viktoria. Sure enough, the relationship with the woman petered out, but they were not surprised when he soon found someone else and decided to stay on a bit longer. He had now been living there for two years, and Alex hadn't seen him in all that time.

We should go out there, Alex thought in the taxi. Show him we care. Then maybe he'll come back home. Then maybe we won't lose him.

He looked distractedly out of the taxi window. The sun was shining. Alex's mouth felt dry. This was a fine bloody day for summer to make its appearance.

A very bright Stockholm enfolded Peder Rydh as he stood there outside Sara Sebastiansson's block of flats. Peder felt absolutely terrible. His flesh was crawling. Sara's howls and cries were still echoing in his head. Poor beggar, he thought to himself. He couldn't, *wouldn't*, simply refused, to imagine anything like that happening to him. Peder's children would never go missing. Those children were *his* children and no one else's. He made a solemn vow to himself to keep watch over them better than he had until now.

The sound of the door opening behind him made him jump. Sara Sebastiansson's father stepped gingerly out onto the pavement and waited right by the wall. Peder could swear the man had aged in the fifteen minutes that had elapsed since Peder and the clergyman came to the flat. His grey hair looked lifeless and his eyes were so full of despair that Peder found it hard to meet his gaze. He felt even more ashamed of the fact that he was again forced to ring for a taxi, as he was still not in a fit state to drive.

'Tell me,' said the older man before he had a chance to be the one to break the silence, 'if there's any chance it might not be our little girl they've found.'

Peder swallowed and felt his stomach knot as he saw the other man was crying.

'We don't think so,' he said thickly. 'We've had pictures to help us and we're almost completely sure we've identified her. And then there's the fact that she didn't have any hair when she was found . . . I'm sorry, but we're pretty convinced.'

He took a deep breath.

'We won't take it as positive identification until you've had a chance to see her, of course, but as I say, we're not in any doubt.'

Sara's father nodded slowly. His tears fell like heavy drops of rain onto his dark jumper and the spots grew into little wet patches weighing down his already weary shoulders.

'We knew all along this would end badly, Mother and I,' he whispered, and Peder took a step towards him.

Took a step towards him and put his hands in his pockets. He realized what he had just done and took them out again.

'You see,' said the man, 'Sara's mother and I have only got Sara. And we knew, we knew *straight away* when Sara met that man that things would turn out badly.'

His voice quavered, and his look vanished far, far away beyond Peder.

'The first day she introduced him to us, I said to Mother that he was no good for our girl. But they were so in love. *She* was so in love. Even though he started mistreating her almost straight away. Not to mention his witch of a mother.'

Peder frowned, and put in:

'But from what we understood from the police reports, it was a few years before he started abusing her. Isn't that right, then?'

The older man shook his head.

'He didn't hit her, but there are other ways of hurting another person. He had other women, for example, all the time. Almost from the start. Disappeared off some evenings without saying where he was going, stayed away whole weekends. And she always took him back. Over and over again. And then they had Lilian. Then she was as good as stuck.'

The air suddenly seemed too heavy to breathe in, and the older man gave a sort of shudder. When he breathed out, his shoulders slumped and the tears ran more swiftly down his cheeks.

'When the little girl was born, we thought the game was up. All our friends congratulated us, but . . . It was the start of something new, after all, and yet . . . After that there was no way back, after that it was bound to end in disaster.'

'Do you think,' Peder began tentatively, 'do you think Gabriel Sebastiansson could have anything to do with what's happened to the little girl?'

The other man raised his head and looked Peder in the eye.

'That man is evil incarnate,' he said in a voice that was tired but firm. 'There are no limits to what he'd do to harm and wound Sara. No limits at all.'

He seemed to be about to fall forwards, so Peder rushed to catch him. But the man hung there in his arms, crying like a child.

Before too long, Peder was on his way out of the centre of town, heading for Gabriel Sebastiansson's workplace. He had to keep swallowing to keep back his own tears. Then it struck him that he still hadn't rung Ylva.

He clenched his mobile. Now he was in big trouble. But she'd just have to wait. He was already late for his appointment with Gabriel's colleague.

Martin Ek met him outside the front entrance of SatCom. Peder could see he was tense and nervous. Generally Peder was no great genius when it came to reading other people, but Martin Ek was plainly on edge. *Very much* on edge.

'Thanks for coming so quickly,' Martin Ek said, with a firm shake of the hand.

Peder noted that the palms of the other man's hands were sweating profusely, and saw him wipe them on his suit trousers. Charming.

Martin Ek said no more until they were in the lift on their

way up to the executive floor. Peder's intuition told him the lift was too small and they were standing too close together. He hoped he didn't smell of drink.

'I went into his office this morning,' said Ek, staring straight ahead of him. 'There was an important quarterly report I needed, and Gabriel didn't answer his mobile. I tried him over and over again. But he never replied.'

Peder recognized that Martin Ek was trying to justify going into his colleague's computer, which wasn't necessary at all.

'I understand,' he said reassuringly, stepping out of the cramped lift with relief as soon as the doors opened.

Martin relaxed a little and discreetly showed Peder through the open-plan office to his own room. Peder noted a number of raised eyebrows and wondered whether he ought to ask to be introduced to the rest of the staff. He decided it could wait.

Safely inside his room, Martin nodded obligingly towards the visitor's chair, and took a seat behind his desk. He clasped his hands on his blotter and cleared his throat.

Behind him, Peder could see a row of photos in colourful frames. The pictures radiated warmth and harmony. Peder saw that Martin had three children, all of them probably under ten, and a lovely wife. If the pictures were telling the truth, Martin had a good marriage and loved his wife enough to want to look at her every day. Peder felt himself shrivel as he sat there in the visitor's chair. He was a disgrace to the male sex. Alex had loads of family photos in the office too, didn't he?

'So I went to Gabriel's room to get the report,' Martin began again, forcing Peder to focus on what he was saying.

'We're authorized to do that,' he added, 'if there's no

alternative. And our boss, mine and Gabriel's, gave me the go ahead.'

Peder nodded again, somewhat more impatiently this time.

'I didn't find the report,' Martin went on. 'I looked in his filing cabinets; we've got special, secure cabinets where we keep sensitive material, and our receptionist has a master key to them all.'

Another pause for effect.

'When I couldn't find the report, it occurred to me that he must at least have a working copy in his computer that I could print out.'

Martin shifted the position of his desk chair a little, and suddenly his whole family was hidden from view, for which Peder was truly grateful.

'That was when I came across the photos,' he said, his voice lowered almost to a whisper. 'Do you want to see them now?'

Peder had had a few words with Alex on that subject. If the photos really were criminal in content, it would be extremely important for the computer to be handled correctly, so it did not appear that the police had illicitly come by the information about what Gabriel Sebastiansson stored on the hard disk of his computer at work. But if the information was presented by a third party who had gone into Gabriel's computer of his own volition, there was no reason why Peder could not take a passive look at them. Peder, however, felt instinctively that looking at the photos was one of the last things he wanted to do.

'You didn't want to say any more about the photos on the phone,' he said softly, 'but maybe you could just give me a rough idea of what's in them before we take a look?'

Martin Ek squirmed in his seat. His eyes went to a small photo on the desk in front of him, presumably showing his youngest child. He cleared his throat again, looking pale and rigid. His gaze was fixed as it met Peder's. Then he answered in just two words:

'Child pornography.'

Fredrika Bergman drove swiftly out of town and down to Flemingsberg. She wondered if what she was doing amounted to official misconduct. Alex had expressly asked her to concentrate on interviewing Sara's family and closest acquaintances. He had asked her to see Teodora Sebastiansson again as a matter of priority, and to work out how Umeå fitted into the picture. He had definitely *not* asked her to go out to Flemingsberg to check out a station nobody else in the team thought of any interest.

But here she was on her way there, all the same.

Fredrika parked outside the local public prosecution office, close to the station. She looked about her as she got out of the car. The brightly coloured apartment blocks, where she had occasionally gone to see friends in her student days, were outlined against the sky in the middle distance on the far side of the tracks. The hospital was just beyond them. Her stomach lurched as she saw the signs pointing the way to it and her thoughts turned automatically to Spencer.

I could have lost him, thought Fredrika. I could have been left all on my own.

The walk from the car to the station made Fredrika quite hot. She took off her jacket and rolled up the sleeves of her shirt. It was disconcerting to find herself thinking about Spencer so much nowadays. Shouldn't she be thinking instead about the adoption application she'd sent in a while ago? Dear Spencer seemed suddenly to be pursuing her, day and night. Fredrika felt a slight tremor in the ground beneath her. Was she just imagining things, or had her relationship with Spencer changed since the start of the summer? They met more often and it felt . . . different.

But it was hard to pin down exactly what was different.

I've coped with my relationship with Spencer for over ten years without starting to assume anything or make it something it's not, Fredrika thought. There's no reason to complicate matters now, either.

She went into the station and looked around. There was an escalator down to each platform. At the far end were the escalator and steps down to platform one, where the intercity trains heading north to Stockholm came in. Sara must have gone pelting down there when she missed the train, thought Fredrika.

She went over to the girl in the ticket window by the barriers down to the local commuter services on platforms two and three, and showed her ID. She introduced herself and briefly explained why she was there. The girl in the cramped space of the ticket booth instantly sat up straight. She realized from Fredrika's earnest look that it was important to answer the questions properly.

'Were you working last Tuesday?' Fredrika asked.

To her relief, the girl at the ticket window nodded. This wasn't going to take long.

'Do you remember seeing a woman with a sick dog any time that day?'

The girl frowned, but then nodded eagerly again.

'Yes,' she said. 'Yes, I do. You mean a tall, lanky girl? With a big Alsatian?'

Fredrika's heart skipped a beat as she remembered Sara's description of the woman who had held her up in Flemingsberg.

'Yes,' she said, trying hard not to sound too excited. 'That fits the description we've been given.'

The girl smiled.

'I definitely remember her,' she said, almost triumphantly, reminding Fredrika of the assistant police officer at Stockholm Central at the time Lilian was reported missing, and the way he had received her and Alex.

'I saw it later on the news, like, about that little girl going missing from the train,' said the girl at the ticket window. 'The girl with the dog was here at the same time as that train from Gothenburg came into the platform, and had to wait there for a while. I remember, because I was the one who helped the little girl's mum make the call to our control centre after she missed the train.'

Fredrika smiled. Excellent.

'Where was she travelling to?' she asked. 'If you can remember, that is.'

The girl looked confused.

'The one who lost her kid?'

'No,' said Fredrika patiently. 'The one with the dog.'

'I don't know. She just wanted to go down onto the platform to meet someone off the train. She asked me where the train from Gothenburg comes in.'

'Ah,' Fredrika said quickly, 'and what happened then?'

'Well, I could see there was something wrong with the dog,' the girl said. 'It could hardly stand; she was yanking it by its lead. Then sort of shoving it along in front of her. I saw them go down the escalator, and after that I heard her shouting. The girl with the dog, that is.'

She paused.

'And it was only a minute or two later she came up again with the redheaded woman, who was helping her. At first I thought they were together, but when the X2000 pulled out, the one with the red hair almost had hysterics, and rushed down onto the platform again. She was yelling, "Lilian", the whole time.'

Fredrika felt her throat constrict.

She cleared her throat.

'And what did the dog woman do after that?'

'She bundled the dog onto a mail trolley that was parked just over there,' said the girl at the ticket window, pointing out through the glass.

Fredrika looked, but saw no trolley.

'I've never seen one of those trolleys in here before, now I come to think of it,' said the girl, 'but I just assumed the postmen had left it behind, or something.'

Fredrika made a sharp intake of breath.

'Anyway, that was when I realized they didn't know each other, the dog girl and the other one,' the girl went on. 'And as far as I could see, the dog girl wasn't, like, with anyone else. I assumed that the person she'd come to meet hadn't shown up, and she thought she'd better get a move on because the dog wasn't well. Though in fact, it seemed poorly from the word go.'

Fredrika nodded slowly, but inside she felt a growing conviction that the woman with the dog had gone down onto the platform with the sole purpose of delaying Sara Sebastiansson, to make her miss the train.

'Do you think the girl with the dog has anything to do with the kid who went missing?' the girl in the ticket window asked curiously.

Fredrika forced herself to smile.

'I don't know,' she said swiftly. 'We're just trying to have a word with everyone who might have seen something. Would you be able to give a clear description of the woman with the dog if I sent someone over to do an identikit drawing?'

The girl sat up straight and looked earnest.

'Definitely,' she said.

Fredrika took her contact details, and also asked for the phone number of the Swedish Railways control centre. She thanked the girl for her time and said she would be back later on that day.

She was just on her way out when the girl shouted after her:

'Wait a minute!'

Fredrika turned round.

'What about the little girl? Have you found her?'

There are pictures that speak a thousand words. And there are pictures you just don't want to see, because you want nothing to do with the words associated with them. Those were the kind of pictures stored on Gabriel's office computer. To avoid the risk of sounding the alarm for nothing, Peder looked at one of them. He instantly regretted it, and would regret it for the rest of his life.

The pictures were hidden in a folder labelled 'Reports 2nd

Quarter Version III', the one that had caught Martin Ek's attention. Having failed to find the report he needed anywhere else, he had opened this folder full of loathsome material that no normal person would wish ever to see.

In a taxi on the way back to HQ, Peder rang his colleagues to have another arrest warrant issued for Gabriel Sebastiansson, on a charge of child pornography. Gabriel would soon be detained in his absence and a nationwide hunt for him would be in progress. Analysis of the pictures – *How would that happen? Who had the stomach to pore over vile stuff like that?* – would show whether Gabriel was guilty of the sexual exploitation of children, or had contented himself with watching others do so. Inside Peder there was also a growing sense of horror that they might find pictures of Lilian, but he hadn't yet dared to think the thought consciously.

He had had a word with Alex, who was just off the plane in Umeå, to inform him of developments.

'We still don't know where this takes us,' Alex said circumspectly. 'But something tells me we're getting a bit closer.'

'But this must bloody well mean we've got him?' said an agitated Peder.

'No mistakes now,' Alex warned him. 'Until we find Gabriel Sebastiansson, we've got to keep our minds open to possible alternatives. Fredrika will need to go through Sara's acquaintances with a fine-toothed comb and see if any alternative suspects present themselves. And you can do the same on Gabriel's side. Get all the skeletons out of his cupboard.'

'Aren't child porn and wife beating enough?' objected Peder doubtfully.

Alex paused to heighten the effect of what came next.

'When we find this man, Peder, there mustn't be any doubts. No doubts at all, okay?'

'Okay,' said Peder, and ended the call.

Then he rang Fredrika. He glanced out of the taxi window. The sun was still shining. Amazing.

Peder couldn't stop himself sounding elated when Fredrika answered.

'We've got him!' he said, pressing the mobile to his ear in his exhilaration.

'Who?' Fredrika asked vaguely.

Peder was astonished and irritated.

'We've got the father,' he said exaggeratedly clearly, but avoided saying Gabriel's name in the taxi.

'All right,' was all Fredrika said.

'Child porn charges,' Peder said in triumph, and saw the driver staring at him in the rearview mirror.

'What?' said Fredrika in surprise.

'You heard what I said,' said Peder, leaning back in satisfaction. 'But we can talk about it back at HQ. Where are you, by the way?'

Fredrika didn't respond straight away, and when she did, she said:

'There was just something I had to check, but I'll be back at work in fifteen minutes. I've got some news as well.'

'Can hardly be anything of the same calibre as mine,' sneered Peder.

'See you,' said Fredrika brusquely, and rang off.

Peder felt pleased with himself as he ended the call. This was police work at its best. The investigation team had done a great job, in actual fact. Okay, the girl had died. That undoubtedly had to be seen as a police failure. But still. Looking back, it seemed somehow inevitable, almost as if the job of the police had never been to save her. It had been to find the person who took her life. What Peder fixed on was that they seemed to have cleared up a macabre crime in no time at all. Soon, very soon, they would find Gabriel Sebastiansson. Peder would insist on being present at all the interrogations. Presumably Fredrika wouldn't be trying to compete for that particular task.

His phone rang again.

He wrenched it out of his pocket.

It was only when he saw who was calling that it all came back to him. He had completely forgotten to ring Ylva.

Alex Recht had only been to Umeå once before. In fact his sorties north of Stockholm had been embarrassingly few in number overall. He'd been to visit Lena's relations in Gällivare on one occasion and once – back in his youth – went to see a girlfriend up in Haparanda. And that was about it.

After he had spoken to Peder, his mood was considerably better than it had been on boarding the plane. The news that Gabriel Sebastiansson's colleagues had found pornographic images of children on his computer didn't really change things much, but confirmed what they already knew in several respects. There was too much pointing at Gabriel for it not to be him, when it came down to it. He still hadn't been in touch, he had abused his wife, and he had child porn on his computer.

For Alex, it was all fairly clear-cut.

He was perhaps slightly dubious about the motive. It bugged him that he still hadn't encountered Gabriel, hadn't got any sense of what he was like. Was he a madman who had gone off his head and calculatingly planned and carried out the murder of his own daughter? Or was it something else? Did he hate Sara so much that he had to punish her by murdering their child?

DCI Hugo Paulsson met him at the airport. The men shook hands gravely and then Hugo showed him to where the car was parked. Alex made a comment about the airport being bigger than he remembered it and Hugo mumbled something about memory not always being reliable 'as we get older'. They said no more until they were on their way into Umeå. Alex peered sideways at Hugo Paulsson. 'Older', he had called them. Alex didn't really think either of them could be classed as older. The two of them looked about the same age. His colleague's hair was possibly a shade greyer and a touch thinner, but generally they both seemed equally young and healthy.

'It's the children who keep us young, Alex,' Lena sometimes said.

He noted without comment that Hugo was not wearing a wedding ring. Maybe he had no children, either?

'Recht, is that a German name?' asked Hugo, making an attempt at small talk.

'Partly German,' said Alex. 'Jewish.'

'Jewish?' echoed his colleague, looking at him as if it was utterly remarkable to have a Jewish surname.

Alex gave a slight smile.

'Yes, but it's a long story. For various reasons, my grandfather on my father's side took his mother's surname when he was born, the Jewish Recht. But since his father wasn't Jewish, the family never observed any Jewish traditions. So my nearest Jewish relation is my grandfather.'

Alex could have sworn that Hugo looked relieved, but he made no further comment on the subject. Instead he said:

'The file's in the glove compartment. You're welcome to look, but be prepared for the pictures.'

Alex nodded and took out the file. He opened it carefully, almost reverently, and took out the little bundle of photographs. He nodded to himself again. It was definitely Lilian, no question.

He felt a pang. Sara Sebastiansson and her parents would be on the next plane – they had been held up in traffic on the way to Arlanda – and then the identity of the child would be formally established. Alex looked at the photos again, leafing through the heart-rending pile. In actual fact, the identification process would be unnecessary and cruel. There wasn't the least doubt that the child was Lilian.

Alex shifted his weight. The old Saab had nasty, hard seats that were giving him backache even on this short journey.

'I thought we ought to go straight to the hospital,' said Hugo Paulsson. 'We're seeing the pathologist, who can give us a preliminary report on the cause of death. Then I assume the forensics people in Stockholm will take over, once the girl's been identified?'

'Yes, I expect so,' said Alex. 'You said she'd been dead about twenty-four hours when she was found, didn't you?'

'Yes, that's right,' Hugo confirmed. 'And they found her around one in the morning.'

That meant Lilian had been alive for less than a day from the time of her disappearance from the train. And she had definitely been dead by the time her mother took delivery of the parcel of clothes and hair.

'Have you interviewed the people who found her?' Alex asked.

Hugo nodded. Yes, they'd asked both the doctor and the nurse about what had happened. They had both given very matter-of-fact accounts of the evening's events, and there was no reason to suspect them of being involved.

'Is there anything to indicate the girl could have been killed here in Umeå?' Alex asked delicately.

The question was important, because the answer would determine which police authority took formal responsibility for the investigation. It was the scene of the crime, not the scene of the discovery of the body, which decided it.

'Hard to say,' said Hugo. 'The girl had been lying there in the rain for a while – up to half an hour maybe – and we're afraid a good number of clues could have been simply washed away.'

Alex was opening his mouth to say something when Hugo went on:

'She had a funny smell, the girl, acetone or something like that. We think somebody tried to wash her, but was in too much of a hurry to finish the job. And her nails had been cut right down, as short as they could possibly be.'

Alex sighed heavily. For some reason, the details made him more convinced than ever that it was Gabriel Sebastiansson who had taken the girl. Somebody had tried to wash all the evidence off the child. Somebody had cut her nails so no evidence could be scraped from under them. The murderer was evidently a person of some intelligence.

But why ever had they dumped her outside the hospital in Umeå, of all places? That was clearly where Lilian's murderer had wanted her to be found. But why?

He's mocking us, Alex thought grimly. He's mocking us, and laying the girl at our feet. *Look*, he's saying, *look how close I can get. And you still can't see me.*

Hugo pointed out of the window.

'Here we are. This is the hospital.'

Fredrika Bergman rang Swedish Railways as soon as she had finished talking to Peder. She introduced herself as a police investigator and said she was ringing about the child who disappeared from the X2000 train from Gothenburg two days before. The man at the other end knew at once what she was referring to.

'I've just got one quick question,' she said.

'Yes?' said the man, and waited.

'I wonder what caused the delay. Why did the train have to be held in Flemingsberg?'

'Er, well,' the man said hesitantly, 'in the end the train was only delayed a couple of minutes . . .'

'I know that,' Fredrika interrupted him, 'and I'm not really interested in exactly how many minutes it was delayed. I just want to know what the problem was.'

'It was what we call a signalling problem,' the man replied.

'Right, and what caused that problem, as it were,' Fredrika asked.

The man at the other end sighed.

'It was probably some foolhardy youngsters playing on the track. A few kids die that way every year, you know. Usually it doesn't cause too much disruption, it's just like in Flemingsberg; it takes a few minutes and then it's all working again.'

Fredrika swallowed.

'So it was some kind of sabotage that delayed the train?'

'Yes,' said the man. 'Or it could have been some animal getting at the transmitter. But I don't think that's very likely in this case, because the problem was only just outside Flemingsberg station.'

Fredrika nodded to herself.

'Thanks, that's all for now,' she said, committing the man's name to memory. 'I expect I'll be back in touch soon with a few more questions or a formal request for a written statement.'

When she had rung off, she gripped the steering wheel hard.

She scarcely dared to think what the investigating team had lost by not following up such an obviously important line of enquiry.

It might simply mean, of course, that Gabriel Sebastiansson had been working with the woman in Flemingsberg. Fredrika swallowed. She didn't really think that, but that was how she would present it to the team. She'd never get the authorization to pursue it any further, otherwise.

Fredrika felt anything but elated. It was a wretched business from start to finish. Fredrika's vision clouded as she wondered whether Sara would be able to summon the strength to identify her dead child.

Some years before, Alex couldn't recall exactly how long ago, his mother-in-law had been admitted to hospital. The diagnosis, incurable cancer of the liver and pancreas, had plunged Lena into despair. How could her father carry on? How would it be for her and Alex's children growing up without their grandma?

Alex had not been too worried for the children's sake.

Naturally they would miss their grandma, but their sense of loss could hardly be compared with what his father-in-law would go through.

'We've got to be there for Dad now,' Lena said the evening they heard the bad news.

'Yes of course,' Alex replied.

'No, more than that,' Lena said. 'More than that, of course, Alex. These are the times people need all the support and love they can get.'

The memory of the time his mother-in-law lay ill ached in Alex as he sat there in Sonja Lundin's office at Umeå University Hospital. Hugo Paulsson sat beside him.

Sonja Lundin was the pathologist who had reached a preliminary verdict on the cause of Lilian's death.

'We weren't initially sure which forensic unit was going to take the body,' Sonja Lundin said with a frown. 'We don't know where the crime was committed, of course, here or in Stockholm.'

Alex stared at Sonja Lundin. She was very tall for a woman, and looked very much on the ball. Alex was drawn to people with that look. He had occasionally reflected that Fredrika Bergman had it, too. Shame she had such shortcomings in other departments.

'But we checked what happened in previous cases, and decided we had to do at least an initial examination here, so as not to hold up the police in their preliminary enquiry,' Sonja Lundin went on. 'So now it's done.'

She gave them a swift summary of what she had found.

'There's nothing to indicate the child was subjected to any violence or, from what I could see with the naked eye, any sexual assault,' she began, and Alex felt himself give a slight sigh of relief.

Sonja Lundin noticed, and held up a hand.

'I really do have to stress that sexual assault can't be ruled out until after a more thorough examination.'

Alex nodded. Naturally he knew that.

'At first I couldn't work out what had killed her,' said Sonja Lundin, frowning again, 'but because her head was shaved, I soon discovered it when I looked a bit closer.'

'Discovered what?' asked Hugo.

'A wound in the middle of the head. And a much smaller puncture at the back of the neck.'

Hugo and Alex both instantly raised their eyebrows.

'I can't say for certain without more comprehensive tests and examinations of course, but my preliminary conclusion is that someone tried to stab the girl in the head, and when that didn't work, injected poison into her neck instead, and that was what killed her.'

Hugo, looked at her, his brow furrowed:

'Is that a usual way of going about it?'

'Not that I'm aware,' said Sonja. 'And it's not clear why they would try to stab her skull first, anyway.'

'Can you say what poison was used?' asked Alex.

'No, we'll need to run tests before we can say,' she said, with a defensive gesture.

Hugo couldn't keep still.

'But,' he began, 'would she have been conscious when they stabbed her? I mean . . .'

Sonja smiled slightly. It was a warm smile.

'I know what you're wondering,' she said, 'but I'm afraid I

have no answer to that. The girl could have been given some kind of sedative first, but I'm afraid I can't confirm that either, at this point.'

There was silence. Hugo quietly cleared his throat and Alex caught himself fiddling with his wedding ring.

He cleared his throat, too, a bit more loudly than Hugo.

'And what's the procedure now?' he asked.

'Your colleague knows that better than I do,' said Sonja Lundin, nodding in Hugo's direction.

'We wait for the mother and grandparents to identify the child,' he said firmly. 'Unless we manage to link the case more closely to Umeå in the course of the day, the girl's body will be sent to the forensic unit down in Solna this evening, so the complete autopsy will be done there. When did you say the mother and her parents were due?'

Alex glanced at his watch.

'They should be landing in about an hour.'

Fredrika was very happy to find Peder far too absorbed in his own activities to ask where she had been and why she hadn't gone to see Gabriel's mother yet.

Peder was just preparing a draft application to the examining magistrate when Fredrika came into his office.

'We're going to get him detained in his absence,' said Peder, his eyes unnaturally wide open from the sudden boost to his adrenalin level.

Other than that, he looked pretty rough. What had he been up to since the evening before? He really did look quite wild.

Fredrika chose not to comment on Peder's appearance out loud.

'And we're going to get a search warrant from the magistrate,' he went on. 'So get yourself off to his old ma's. You said he had a room there, didn't you?'

Fredrika stopped short. Had she said that?

'Yes,' she said eventually, 'he has.'

'Right, then we need a warrant to let us search his house in Östermalm, his room at his mother's, and his office,' said Peder.

'What are we looking for, officially I mean?' said Fredrika.

'Officially we're looking for child porn, unofficially every fucking thing that can give us a clue where the guy's got to. I just spoke to Alex, and it sounds as if the kid had poison injected straight into her head. So sick it's beyond belief.'

Fredrika swallowed. Yet another grotesque detail that had no natural place in the way she viewed the world.

'We're getting extra backup,' Peder added. 'Two more investigators to help us interview all the friends and acquaintances.'

'Okay,' Fredrika said guardedly.

She considered asking who was standing in for Alex in his absence, but was reluctant to ask a question to which she didn't want to hear the answer. Finally she asked it anyway.

'Alex said *I* was,' Peder said, so triumphantly that Fredrika felt rather sick.

He'd been waiting for her to ask, just so he could answer. Typical of her to fall into the trap.

'But Alex will be back this evening,' Peder added, 'unless we come up with anything to link this mess to Umeå.'

Then he went on:

'I'll take one of the new pair with me out to Gabriel's company and introduce him there. Gabriel and some of his colleagues seem to have been big buddies, so he might just have confided in them. You can set the other one – it's a girl – to work on the people Sara knows.'

Fredrika was about to comment on this when he burst out:

'Heck, this is *big*! Three search warrants in one go, it's not every day you get to be in on setting up a big operation like that,' he said, so elated that Fredrika started wondering if he'd taken something to get so high.

'A child has died,' she said instead, her voice a monotone. 'Pardon me for not joining in with your transports of delight.'

And she walked out of Peder's room to find her new workmate.

Peder wondered initially whether he ought to go after Fredrika and give her a good dressing down. Who the hell was she to tell him he was out of order?

Then he stopped himself. Fredrika was right, at least about this being a murder enquiry. But she was the one not respecting the fact, not him. Well he wasn't going to sink to her level. And he certainly wasn't going to let her spoil his good mood. If he could survive his talk with Ylva, or strictly speaking *from* Ylva, then he wasn't going to let some stupid colleague get the better of him.

Peder shuddered at the memory of Ylva's call. She had been furious, to put it mildly, and it didn't help that none of his fellow officers who she had rung during the night had been able to tell her where he was. Ylva had considered reporting him missing. Peder was deeply grateful that she hadn't, but had fallen asleep on the sofa instead. He had promised they would talk properly when he got home, but also told her about the latest developments in the missing child case. He was likely to be late home tonight, as well.

He found it rather hard to admit it, but Ylva had been really shaken to hear that the girl had been murdered, and had immediately mellowed towards him. Suddenly she was a lot more understanding about his job. But unfortunately she still didn't sound as though she quite believed he'd been work-ing all night. He would have to learn to lie better, that was all there was to it. Or give up his sessions with Pia Nordh. He didn't honestly think he could manage either of those things, but there was never any harm in having ambitions.

Jimmy rang and wanted to talk. He was worried and anxious. He was going on a cookery course with the other people from his assisted living unit and wanted to know if Peder thought it would go all right.

'Of course it will!' said Peder in that extra positive tone he always used for talking to his brother. 'You can do anything, you know!'

'You sure?' asked Jimmy, still not entirely convinced.

'Sure,' echoed Peder.

Then the pictures came flooding into his mind again. From a time when everything had been different, when Jimmy had dared and Peder had been the scared one.

'I can swing as high as anything, Pedda! I can swing higher than anybody else!'

'Don't believe you, don't believe you!'

'Yes I can, Pedda, I can swing highest in the whole street!'

If Jimmy had been able to grow up undamaged, thought Peder, would he have turned out the stronger of the two of them? Or would he have got softer over time?

Peder turned his attention back to his job. He knew Jimmy was the only person in the whole world he had never let down in his adult life. On the other hand, there was no one else to whom he owed so much. And maybe no one else he loved so unreservedly.

He had almost all the basic data in place for the examining magistrate. A couple of little details, and then it would be ready. Once he had dropped off his new colleague at the SatCom place, he would follow Fredrika out to Sebastiansson's mother's house. It wasn't every day you got the chance to rummage about in a real-live rich man's mansion.

Thoughts were circulating more smoothly in Peder's head now a few hours had passed since his brutal awakening. He had drunk loads of fluid and taken more Panadol. He debated whether he should drive himself to the various search premises. Probably not. But then who would check on a policeman on his way to execute a search warrant? Who could be so unlucky? Not Peder Rydh, anyway. He was convinced of that.

Ellen Lind was very upset. She had always expected Lilian Sebastiansson to be returned to her mother in the long run, and now they knew she had been murdered, Ellen was badly shaken. She tried to ring her lover on his mobile, even though he had not been very nice the day before, but all she got was his voicemail.

'You're through to Carl. Please leave a message after the tone and I'll get back to you as soon as I can.'

Ellen sighed. Maybe they could see each other for a while later in the evening? There was little likelihood of getting hold of a babysitter at such short notice, but some day there would have to be an end to all this hassle. She needed him. And she wanted to feel she had a right to feel that way. She wanted to feel it was okay – sometimes – to need him. Was that too much to ask?

She left him a voicemail message and could not stop herself crying as she explained what had happened. That poor girl, just lying there outside the hospital. Naked, on her back, in the rain.

Ellen stared blankly at her computer screen. She hardly knew what she was supposed to be doing. She was speechless with admiration at the sight of Peder and Fredrika dashing up and down the corridor, always caught up in some new stage of the investigation.

Alex had left clear instructions for Ellen by telephone before he set off for Umeå: she was not to say a word about the developments in the Lilian case until the girl's mother had formally identified her. Under no circumstances was she to go into any detail. She was definitely not to say anything about the child being scalped, or about the child pornography found on the computer of the dead girl's father. Ellen had been following the online news outlets and had seen that the discovery of the child was the top story on every paper's website.

Mats, the National Crime Squad analyst, broke into Ellen's reverie with a knock at her door.

'Sorry to butt in,' he began politely.

Ellen smiled.

'No problem, I was just sitting . . . thinking.'

Mats gave a tight little smile.

'Peder said something about us having the go-ahead from the examining magistrate on intercepts for Gabriel. Do you know anything about that?'

When Ellen didn't reply at once, Mats clarified:

'Wiretapping and phone records.'

Ellen gave a curt little laugh.

'Thanks, I know what you mean.'

She went on:

'It always takes an hour or so before the listening gets underway; you can ask the technical department if you want the exact timings. And then Tele2 was going to send us the logs of calls from Gabriel's mobile for the past two years, but I don't know when we can expect those.'

'I got them an hour ago,' Mats interrupted her. 'I've checked the activity of his phone in the past few days. Since the child was taken he's only made three calls, longish ones: one to his mother, one to a lawyer and one international number I haven't been able to trace. All I can see is that the prefix is the one for Switzerland. And he's had a few incoming texts.'

Ellen stared at him in surprise.

'Switzerland?'

Mats nodded.

'Yes, but I don't know who to, as I said. And if his mother's still claiming not to have seen him in the past few days, she's lying. I've checked the mobile phone mast records. Gabriel Sebastiansson's phone has been active in the vicinity of his parents' home several times since Tuesday. Right up to six this morning, in fact.'

Ellen whistled.

'Things are really hotting up,' she said thoughtfully.

'They certainly are,' said Mats.

Fredrika drove far too fast to the Sebastiansson family home. This time she did not ring to announce in advance that she was coming. And when she arrived, she did not wait for Teodora Sebastiansson's finger to show her where to park. Instead she skidded to a halt right outside the house and was out of the car almost before it came to a complete stop. She took the steps up to the front door in three strides and rang twice on the doorbell. When she heard nothing, she rang again. A moment later, she heard someone fumbling with the lock inside and the door slid open.

Teodora was incensed to see Fredrika.

'And what in heaven's name is this supposed to mean?' the diminutive woman barked, with surprising force in her voice. 'Roaring onto our estate and almost knocking the door down like this!'

'Firstly, I don't know that your home can best be described as an "estate"; secondly, all I've done is ring urgently on your doorbell; and thirdly . . .'

Fredrika was taken aback by the power with which she was countering Teodora's attack, and paused to heighten the effect.

'And thirdly, I'm afraid to tell you I have some very bad news. Could you let me in, please?'

Teodora stared at Fredrika. Fredrika stared back. This time, too, the older woman had a large brooch pinned to her blouse, right under her chin. It almost looked as though the brooch was there to keep her head held high.

'Have you found her?' she asked quietly.

'I really would prefer us to go in,' Fredrika said more gently.

Teodora shook her head.

'No, I want to know now.'

She did not drop her eyes from Fredrika's face.

'Yes, we've found her,' Fredrika said, after a brief consideration of the possible implications of breaking such news to a woman of Teodora Sebastiansson's advanced age on her own doorstep.

Teodora stood stock still for a long time.

'Come in,' she said at length, standing aside to let Fredrika enter.

This time, Fredrika did not spare a glance for the decor as she walked the short distance from the front door to the drawing room.

Teodora sat down slowly on a chair by the table. To her relief, Fredrika was not offered anything to drink. As discreetly as possible, she slid into the chair on the other side of the table and rested her chin on her clasped hands.

'Where did you find her?'

'In Umeå,' said Fredrika.

Teodora gave a start.

'In Umeå?' she repeated with genuine surprise. 'What on . . . Are you sure it's her?'

'Yes,' said Fredrika, 'I'm afraid we are. Her mother and maternal grandparents are about to identify her formally, but yes, we're completely sure it's her. Have you any links with Umeå? Or do you know if Sara or your son have?'

Teodora put her hands slowly in her lap.

'As I believe I explained last time, I know very little about exactly how my daughter-in-law lives her life,' she said gruffly. 'But no, as far as I know, neither she nor my son have any particularly strong links with Umeå, and nor do I, for that matter. No links at all, in fact.'

'Have you got friends there?'

'My dear girl, I've never even been there,' said Teodora. 'Nor do I know anyone who has. In my family, that is. It's possible Gabriel's been up there for work, but I honestly don't know.'

Fredrika waited a few moments.

'Speaking of your son,' she said more resolutely, 'have you heard from him?'

Teodora stiffened.

'No,' she said. 'No, I have not.'

'Are you sure of that?' Fredrika asked.

'I'm quite sure,' said Teodora.

The two women looked each other straight in the eye, a trial of strength across the tea table.

'May I see his room?' asked Fredrika.

'My answer is the same as before,' Teodora snapped. 'You can't see a single square metre of this house unless you have a search warrant.'

'As it happens, I do,' said Fredrika, hearing at that very moment the sound of several vehicles crunching to a halt on the gravel drive outside.

Teodora's eyes widened, radiating genuine astonishment.

'It does your son's cause no good at all if you refuse to work with the police in the hunt for your granddaughter's murderer,' said Fredrika, getting to her feet.

'If you had any children of your own, you would know that

one never, ever lets them down,' Teodora said in a broken voice, leaning towards Fredrika. 'If Sara had understood that, Lilian would never have come to any harm. Where was she, *worthless individual that she was*, when Lilian vanished?'

She was caught in a trap, set by somebody who really meant her ill, Fredrika thought to herself.

She said nothing. It had only been for a second, but she had still seen it. Weariness in the older woman's eyes. And vulnerability.

This is causing her vastly more suffering than she is prepared for people to see, thought Fredrika.

Then she accompanied Teodora to the front door to let in the waiting police officers.

Peder Rydh stood in the middle of Teodora Sebastiansson's living room, and could not believe his eyes. The whole interior was like a museum, and made him feel thoroughly uncomfortable. Matters weren't improved by having that fragile-looking little old lady staring at him from the other end of the room. She hadn't batted an eyelid since she met him at the door and he told her why he and the others were there. She'd just gone over and planted herself in an armchair in one corner.

Peder did a quick circuit of the ground floor. Not a trace of Gabriel Sebastiansson. But Peder knew he had been there. Recently. He was aware of Gabriel's presence in a way he couldn't explain.

'When did you last see your son?' Peder asked again when he had completed his circuit and come back to the living room.

'Mrs Sebastiansson will not be answering any questions for the time being,' said a curt voice right behind him.

He turned.

A man Peder didn't know had suddenly appeared in the living room. He was broad-shouldered and extremely tall. His features were heavy and his complexion and hair were dark. Peder felt an immediate and involuntary respect for him.

The man held out his hand and introduced himself as the Sebastiansson family lawyer.

Peder took his hand and told him in brief why the police were searching the premises.

'Child pornography offences?' cried Teodora, swiftly on her feet. 'Are you entirely out of your mind?'

She tripped lightly across the room to the two men.

'I thought you were looking for Gabriel!'

'As I explained when we arrived, that's just what we *are* doing,' Peder said evenly. 'I can also tell you that there's a nationwide arrest warrant out for your son. By helping him, you risk committing a criminal act yourself, depending what crime he's eventually prosecuted for. Your lawyer will confirm that.'

But Teodora had a distant look in her eyes again, and did not seem to be listening to what he said. Peder suppressed a sigh and left the room.

He strode up the wide staircase to the first floor. Gabriel's room was just off the landing at the top.

'How's it going?' he called. 'Have you found anything?'

A small policewoman who was down on all fours, looking under the bed, scrambled to her feet.

'Nothing,' she said. 'But we're damn sure he was here. The bed was very untidily made; the sheets were all crumpled. I'm pretty sure he slept here last night.'

Peder gave a resolute nod.

'He must have a laptop,' he said.

'He's bound to,' agreed a colleague. 'But he's likely to have taken it with him, in that case, wherever he's gone.'

'You're right,' Peder said wearily. 'You haven't found any photos and so on about the place?'

'Not a trace,' said the policewoman.

'All right,' said Peder in conclusion, 'but we think we can say with some degree of certainty that he spent last night here?'

They all nodded in agreement.

'Good,' muttered Peder. 'I'll ring the other teams to check what they found at his office and his Östermalm place.'

His first call, however, was to HQ, where Ellen confirmed that Mats had been able to link Gabriel Sebastiansson to his parental home by means of mobile telephone mast connections. But no, she said, there hadn't been any calls of note from the public, even though the girl's picture was now in every newspaper and all over the media. Though yes, there was someone who'd seen little Lilian being carried off along the platform in Stockholm just after the train pulled in, so that version of events seemed to be confirmed. Other than that? No, nothing new.

Peder rang the team that was busy with Gabriel Sebastiansson's office. His computer had been taken away and its contents would be scrutinized as soon as they assembled a team of volunteers willing to deal with such distressing material. The computer's email correspondence would be looked at separately, and considerably more quickly. Gabriel's boss also confirmed that Gabriel had the use of a laptop belonging to his employer, but he had no idea where it was. As might have been expected, the team had found no trace of any child pornography in the office apart from what was on the computer.

Peder then tried to talk to the new investigator he had put onto interviewing Gabriel's colleagues, but he said he was busy interviewing and promised to ring back within the hour.

Peder did not know quite what to make of the information

generated by the search to that point. It was satisfying to have confirmation that Gabriel was deliberately avoiding the police. It was also good to have confirmation that his mother had lied to protect her son. It was very good that they now knew where he had been over the past few days.

And yet . . .

Why was he stupid enough to keep child pornography on his computer at work, when he had a laptop? Why had he hidden at his mother's, when he could reasonably expect that to be the first place the police would look? And if it was Gabriel Sebastiansson who murdered Lilian, had the murder taken place at his mother's house? Had the child's grandmother even been an accomplice?

Peder felt instinctively that she could not have been. But could Gabriel have had Lilian in the house without his mother knowing? If one supposed the child had been sedated, or something like that? Probably not.

Peder looked around him. Was this really the house where Lilian died? If that were the case, he wanted the examining magistrate's immediate permission to turn the entire place upside down to find the scene of the crime. Though Alex had told him in their most recent phone call that the hospital reported Lilian had died of some form of poison, injected into her skull. A murder like that wouldn't exactly leave many clues behind.

Then something struck Peder. Mats the analyst had said Gabriel's phone hadn't once gone north of Stockholm. But it had clearly gone south. If you assumed Gabriel had had his phone with him the whole time, how the heck could Lilian's body have been taken to Umeå?

Fatigue descended on Peder once again. His brain refused to cooperate and his headache came back with a vengeance.

Then he had a call from the colleagues searching Gabriel Sebastiansson's home in Östermalm. They had not found anything much except a large box of sex toys. It was debatable whether that could be considered abnormal. They had also seized a number of unlabelled DVDs. It was possible that they might yield something.

'Did you find any trace of the child in the flat?' Peder asked disconsolately.

'She's got her own room in the flat, of course,' came the answer, 'but no, we can't say we found anything to indicate she's been here over the past few days. In fact no one seems to have been here at all. No rubbish in the kitchen bin, and the fridge has been left empty. Either no one's been here for a while, or somebody came in and cleared out the fridge.'

Peder was inclined to think the latter. It would be interesting to know whether the flat's landline had been used in recent days. But then on the other hand, Gabriel Sebastiansson's boss said Gabriel had been at work as usual all the previous week, and he'd been at the office as late as last Saturday.

Then something had happened to make Gabriel go to ground, take some leave at short notice and lie to his mother about a business trip. Why had he been so heavy-handed about it, though? It was obvious his mother was incredibly loyal to him. Yet if there was one iota of decency in the woman, that loyalty could not extend to child pornography and child murder.

Peder went back to the others in Gabriel's bedroom and told them he was going to look in on the Östermalm flat. He left the house. Teodora Sebastiansson and her lawyer had locked themselves away in the living room, and Peder saw no need to inform them of his departure.

A strange and overwhelming sense of relief flooded over him as he came out onto the gravel drive where his car was parked. He stared for a few moments at the big, brick mansion. Then he stared at the plot of land it was built on, the size of a park. At this particular spot on earth, time had stood still for far too long.

Jelena nervously put the key in the front door. Her hand always shook a bit when she was excited or nervous. Just now she was both of those things. She had done it. She had done absolutely everything the Man had instructed her to do. She had driven the car up to Umeå, got rid of the Foetus in almost exactly the way and exactly the place he wanted, and then caught the plane back. No one had seen her, no one had suspected what she was doing. Jelena was sure she had never performed better in her whole life.

Silence received her as she shut the door behind her.

She fumbled as she took off her shoes and arranged them precisely beside each other, the way the Man always insisted their shoes should be lined up in the little hall.

'Hello,' she said tentatively, going further into the flat. 'Are you there?'

She took a few more steps. Wasn't it strangely quiet?

Something was wrong, so wrong.

He suddenly detached himself from the shadows. She sensed rather than saw the great fist coming towards her and hitting her right in the face.

No, no, no, she thought desperately as she flew backwards through the air and landed hard on her back, her head hitting the wall.

Pain and fear were throbbing in her body, which had learnt

that in situations like this, by far the safest thing was not to react at all. But the blow was so unexpected and so ominous that she almost wet herself in terror.

He came swiftly towards her and pulled her to her feet. There was blood running from one corner of her mouth and her head was spinning. Darts of pain were shooting through her back.

'You bloody whore, you complete bloody misfit,' he hissed through clenched teeth, and his eyes seethed with a fury she had never seen before.

'Oh no, no, please, somebody help me,' she mumbled to herself.

'She should have been lying in a foetal position,' he said, holding her face so close to his own that she could see every tiny detail of it. 'She should have been lying in a foetal position and quite apart from that – *quite apart from that!* – what the fucking hell was she doing on the pavement? How bloody hard can it be to understand?'

He yelled the last bit with such force that she was struck dumb.

'I . . . ,' she began, but the Man broke in.

'Shut up!' he yelled. 'Shut up!'

And when she made another attempt to explain, explain that there hadn't been time to arrange the Foetus *exactly* as they – *as he* – had planned, nor in *exactly* the right place, he yelled at her again to shut up, and silenced her with another punch in the face. Two punches. A knee in her stomach. A kick in her side once she was on the floor. Ribs cracked, making the same sound as when frosty branches snap in a forest in winter. Soon she could no longer hear his yelling or feel his blows. She was scarcely conscious as he tore off her clothes and dragged her into the bedroom. She began to whimper as she saw him get out the box of matches. He kept her quiet by stuffing a sock in her mouth, and then lit the first match.

'How do you want things, Doll?' he whispered, holding up the burning match in front of her wide, terrified eyes. 'Can I rely on you?'

She nodded desperately, trying to get the sock out of her mouth.

He grabbed her by the hair and leant forward. The match was burning.

'I'm not sure,' he said, bringing the match closer to the thin skin where her neck met her chest. 'I'm really not sure.'

Then he lowered the match and let the flickering flame lick at her skin.

Alex Recht and Hugo Paulsson met Sara Sebastiansson and her parents in a so-called family room an hour or so after they had identified Lilian. Warm colours on the walls. Soft armchairs and sofas. Indian wood tables. No paintings, drawings or photos on the walls. But there was a bowl of fruit.

Alex scrutinized Sara.

Unlike when she had been given the box with the hair, and later the preliminary news of the death, she now seemed more composed. With the emphasis on 'seemed'. Alex had met enough suffering, grieving people in his professional life to know that Sara had a very long road ahead of her before she got back to anything resembling a normal, everyday life. Bereavement had so many faces, so many phases. Somebody, Alex couldn't remember who, had said it was as hard to bear intense grief as it was to walk on thin ice. One moment it feels all right, the next it suddenly gives way and you are suddenly plunged into the darkest darkness of pain.

Just at the moment, Sara seemed to be standing on a very small, but solid piece of ice. Alex felt he was viewing her from a distance. She was not really present, but not really absent, either. Her eyes were still red and puffy from crying, and she had a paper tissue in her hand. From time to time, her hand went up and wiped her nose with the tissue. The rest of the time, it lay motionless in her lap.

Her parents sat quietly, their eyes bright with moisture.

It was Hugo who broke the silence. First with the offer of coffee. Then with the offer of tea. And then with a promise that the interview would not take long.

'We're wondering why Lilian ended up here in Umeå,' Alex began hesitantly. 'Has the family got any connections in the town, or the area?'

At first no one said anything. Then Sara herself replied.

'No, we've no connections here,' she said quietly. 'None at all. Nor has Gabriel.'

'And you've never been here before?' asked Alex, turning to look at Sara again.

She nodded. It was almost as if her head was not properly fixed to her neck, as it was wavering around in all directions.

'Yes, once. My best friend Maria and I were here, the summer after we finished school,' she whispered, and then cleared her throat. 'But that was – let me see – seventeen years ago. I went on a writing course at a centre a little way outside the town, and then I got a summer job there as an assistant to one of the teachers. But I wasn't here long, as I say, maybe three months in all.'

Alex regarded her thoughtfully. In spite of the fatigue and grief that seemed to envelop her whole face, he could see a very slight twitch in the corner of her eye as she spoke. There was something bothering her, something that had nothing to do with Lilian.

Her lower lip trembled a little and her chin was jutting out. Did she perhaps look a bit defiant, despite the tears welling in her eyes and threatening to overflow?

'Did you make any new friends up here? Maybe a boy or something?' Alex asked vaguely.

Sara shook her head.

'Nobody at all,' she said. 'I mean, I met some nice people on the course, and some of them lived here in Umeå, and we saw each other a bit after I started working at the centre. But you know how it is, you go back home, and then it all seems so far away. I lost touch with most of them.'

'And you didn't make any enemies here?' Alex asked kindly.

'No,' said Sara, and closed her eyes for a moment. 'No, not one.'

'And the friend you came with?'

'Maria? No, nor did she. Not as far as I can remember. We don't keep in touch these days.'

Alex leant back in his chair and indicated with a nod to Hugo that he was free to ask any questions he wanted. Alex and Hugo both felt a bit dubious about the link to the writing course, but to be on the safe side Hugo took down the names of all the other people on the course that Sara could remember. There was, after all, nothing else to go on as they tried to find out why the girl's body had turned up in Umeå.

For now, the team in Umeå was working on the basis that the girl had been killed in Stockholm and that Alex's team should therefore take the lead in the enquiry.

Hugo's group had, however, collated all the information about the discovery of Lilian's body. The telephone call that had initially lured Anne the nurse out into the car park had come from a mobile with an unregistered top-up account. The call had come from thirty kilometres south of Umeå. The phone had not been used since. No woman about to give birth had showed up at the hospital with her partner that night, so the investigating team assumed the call had only been made to get a member of staff out to the car park. Someone wanted the child to be found, without delay.

There was so much that baffled Alex about this case. And he felt very clearly that he wouldn't be able to focus his mind on it properly where he was. He needed to get back to Stockholm as soon as possible, so he could sit down in peace and think things through. He felt a disturbing sense of anxiety. The story just didn't fit together. It just didn't.

Sara Sebastiansson's husky voice broke into his thoughts.

'I never regretted having her,' she whispered.

'Pardon?' said Alex.

'It said "Unwanted" on her forehead. But it wasn't true. I never regretted having her. She was the best thing that ever happened to me.'

Fredrika spent the rest of the day trying to get through as many interviews as possible with Sara Sebastiansson's friends, acquaintances and colleagues, using the contact details supplied by Sara and her parents. The list had expanded as a result of the first ring round. She allocated some of the people on the list to the extra investigator.

It was an unambiguous picture of Sara that emerged. She was basically seen as a very warm and positive person, a *good* person. Almost everyone, even those not so close to her, thought her private situation had been very difficult for the past few years. Her husband was inconsiderate and inflexible, cold and controlling. Sometimes she was limping when she came to work, and sometimes she wore long-sleeved tops even in the middle of summer. They couldn't be sure, of

course . . . but . . . how many times could a person acciden-
tally trip and hurt herself?

None of the people Fredrika and her assistant spoke to recognized Teodora Sebastiansson's picture of Sara as an irresponsible
mother and unfaithful wife. But one of Sara's closest friends told
them Gabriel had been cheating on Sara with other women from
the very start. She was crying as she spoke, and said:

'You see, we all thought she'd get away from him, find the
strength to leave him. But then she got pregnant. And then we
knew, then we knew almost for sure that the game was up.
She would never be rid of him.'

'But she left him, didn't she?' asked Fredrika, frowning.
'They're getting divorced.'

Sara's friend cried even harder, and shook her head.

'None of us really believe that. People like him always come
back. Always.'

One thing Fredrika picked up on in the course of the interviews was that even the individuals Sara referred to as 'friends
from way back' turned out to be people she had got to know
in adult life. She had not retained a single friend from when
she was growing up in Gothenburg. To judge by the list, her
parents were the only contacts she had on the west coast.

'Sara once told me she had to break off with almost everybody once she met Gabriel,' her friend explained. 'The rest of
us got to know Sara and Gabriel as a couple, pre-packaged,
but I think Sara's friends from before could never accept that
she was with him.'

The information coming out of interview after interview
indicated that Sara did not have an enemy in the world, apart
from her husband.

Fredrika returned to HQ exhausted, clutching a hot dog in her hand. She fervently hoped Alex was back. And if he wasn't, Fredrika was going to take the opportunity to shut herself in her room and try to relax for a little while. She needed to put her feet up and listen to a piece of music her mother had recommended, which she had downloaded to her MP3 player.

'Something to meditate to,' her mother had said with a smile, knowing that Fredrika, like her, considered music as important an element of everyday life as food and sleep.

But it was Peder she ran into first.

'Ooh, hot dog!' he exclaimed.

'Mmmm,' answered Fredrika with her mouth full.

To her surprise, Peder followed her into her office and virtually collapsed into her visitor's chair. Clearly there would be neither rest nor music for her at the moment.

'How was your day?' he asked, sounding tired.

'Good and bad,' she said evasively.

She still hadn't told him that she had taken herself off to Flemingsberg, still less that she had then sent an identikit artist there to make a sketch of the woman with the dog who had held up Sara Sebastiansson and made her miss the train.

'Did the searches reveal anything?' she said instead.

Peder took his time to frame his thoughts and eventually said:

'They certainly did. And it all seems a damn sight murkier than we thought, to be honest.'

Fredrika sat down at her desk and studied Peder. He still looked the worse for wear. Her attitude to him had at times been one of casual contempt. He was childish, puppylike, and unhealthily fond of showing off. But this particular afternoon, when they were all feeling the effects of what had happened over the past few days, she could see him in a different light. There was a human being inside Peder, too. And that human being was not coping well.

She quickly ate up her hot dog.

Peder somewhat hesitantly laid a thin sheaf of papers on her desk.

'What's this?' Fredrika asked.

'Print-outs of emails from Gabriel Sebastiansson's work computer,' replied Peder.

Fredrika raised an eyebrow.

'I got them about an hour ago,' said Peder, 'just after I got back from interviewing Gabriel's uncle. Fat lot of bloody use that was.'

Fredrika gave a wry smile. She'd had a few interviews like that herself in the course of the day.

'What's in them?' she asked.

'Read them and see,' responded Peder, 'because I'm not sure I can believe they say what I think they're saying.'

'Okay,' said Fredrika, leafing through the sheets.

Peder just sat there. He wanted to watch as she read. Uneasy and eager at the same time.

She read the top sheet first.

'It's an exchange,' Peder explained. 'It starts some time in January.'

Fredrika nodded as she read.

The exchange was between Gabriel Sebastiansson and someone calling himself 'Daddy-Long-Legs', which Fredrika with her scanty knowledge of children's literature assumed to come from a harmless series of picture books she knew.

Gabriel and Daddy-Long-Legs were discussing various types of wine and planning dates for wine tastings. By the time she had read two pages, Fredrika could feel a wave of queasiness rising inside her.

Daddy-Long-Legs, 1 January, 09.32: The others in the circle don't want to taste wines of any vintage earlier than 1998. What's your view?

Gabriel Sebastiansson, 1 January, 11.17: I think 1998 grapes would be fine, but preferably a younger wine. I am sceptical about long storage.

Daddy-Long-Legs, 2 January, 06.25: Questions have also been asked about the countries of origin of the wines, and the grape varieties. Is this important to you?

Gabriel Sebastiansson, 2 January, 19.15: I naturally prefer blue grapes to red. I am less concerned about the regions from which the wines come. I might like to sample something a little more exotic than I did last time our eminent circle met. Perhaps from South America?

'Oh good God,' whispered Fredrika, her throat tightening.
'It isn't wine tasting they're talking about, is it?' said Peder dubiously.
Fredrika shook her head.
'No,' she said. 'No, I really don't think so.'
'Red grapes, could they be girls? And blue grapes boys . . . ?'
'I reckon so.'

Fredrika's stomach churned.

'My God,' she said under her breath, and put her hand over her mouth as she read on.

Daddy-Long-Legs, 5 January, 07.11: Esteemed Member! Our next wine tasting will take place next week! Our supplier will provide us with delicious wines to sample and enjoy through the evening and night. Payment in cash on the day. Further details of the venue will follow as previously arranged.

They could work out that Gabriel Sebastiansson had attended four 'wine tastings' in all, since the start of the year.

'How do they find out about the venue?' Fredrika asked.

'Don't know,' Peder said in a weary voice. 'But I rang a friend of mine in the National Crime Squad who deals with this kind of shit. He said they have all sorts of ways: could even be by text message from unregistered mobiles.'

'How absolutely horrible,' said Fredrika in agitation, and reluctantly went back to the print-outs.

'Read the last sheet,' Peder demanded a little impatiently.

Fredrika was more than happy to skip some of the text, and leafed to the end.

Daddy-Long-Legs, 5 July, 09.13: Esteemed Member! The high point of the summer is almost upon us! We have taken delivery of an unexpected consignment of wonderful wines made from numerous grape varieties and all from the incredible vintage of 2001! Come and enjoy them next week! Venue to be announced separately as usual, but you can mark Tuesday July 20th in your calendar as the red-letter day. You can assume our event will start at around 4 p.m. Please note that this event is not to be held in our own wonderful part of the country, and you should allow at least five hours for the drive. Let me know as soon as possible if you can attend!

Fredrika instantly raised her eyes and stared intently at Peder.

'But . . . the 20th of July was the day Lilian went missing,' she said with a deep frown.

Peder nodded without a word.

They held each other's gaze for a few moments more.

Then Fredrika flicked through the print-outs. There were no messages with dates any later than the email she had just read.

'According to Gabriel's employer, he was on leave on Monday to Wednesday this week,' she said reflectively. 'He left it very late to apply for the leave, said he needed some days off for private reasons.'

'And as far as we can tell from the movements of his mobile, he was somewhere near Kalmar just after 10 p.m. the day Lilian was taken. The phone hadn't been used since that morning, but late in the evening he turned it on again.'

'And who did he ring?'

'That was when he rang his mother,' said Peder.

Fredrika gave Peder a long look.

'Just say their little, what can I call it . . . "event" . . . was in Kalmar,' she began, and Peder nodded to show the same thought had occurred to him. 'That would more or less fit with the journey down taking five hours.'

'So he must have left town at about eleven to get there for four when it all kicked off,' Peder supplied.

'Exactly,' said Fredrika eagerly, putting the print-outs on the desk. 'Have we got anything to fix when the phone left Stockholm?'

'No, there's no registered activity after eight in the morning,' Peder said, thinking it over.

'Okay, doesn't matter,' said Fredrika. 'We know that at ten he was in Kalmar, ringing his mother, at any rate. We can assume that by then the whole thing was over and he was on his way home.'

She looked at Peder.

'In that case, he can't have taken Lilian from the train,' she said, summing up what they had just pieced together. 'Not unless he was in a car on his way to Kalmar at the same time.'

Peder squirmed.

'Or,' he said, 'it could have been that he decided to arrive at the "event" late and took Lilian with him.'

Fredrika shook her head.

'Well,' she said, 'it could have been. But wouldn't that make it a very muddled story? First he has to take Lilian and get her into the car. Then he drives down to Kalmar and . . . goes to some sort of sick club, or whatever you want to call it. Then he drives back home with Lilian, scalps her, sends the hair to her mum, murders her and gets someone to drive up and dump her at the entrance to Umeå Hospital? The records from Tele2 say the phone wasn't active north of Stockholm during the period in question, don't they?'

Peder drew himself up. Fredrika could see that the new information was stressing him out.

'Correct,' he acknowledged, 'and it certainly does sound a bit too much when you put it like that.'

He thought for a moment and then thumped his fist on Fredrika's desk.

'Fuck it,' he said, 'everything's happening too fast in this goddamned mess! How the heck did he manage it all? It just doesn't fit! Maybe he gave his phone to someone else?'

Fredrika put her head on one side and looked briefly into the distance over Peder's shoulder. She thought she could hear Alex out in the corridor.

'Or,' she said slowly, 'it could be that these two stories have nothing to do with each other.'

A lex Recht left Umeå just after four. Lilian Sebastiansson's body was to be flown air freight down to Stockholm later that evening.

'Let's hope you find that evil person before he murders any more children,' Hugo Paulsson said darkly as he took his leave of Alex.

'Murders more children?' repeated Alex.

'Yes, why should he stop now? If he sees that he can get away with it, I mean,' said his colleague.

That little conversation hardly did anything to dispel Alex's sense of disquiet.

He landed in Stockholm an hour or so later and went straight back to HQ.

Fredrika, Peder, Ellen, the National Crime Squad analyst and two people Alex had never seen before, but assumed to be the new backup staff, were waiting for him in the Den.

'Well, my friends,' began Alex as he sat down. 'Where shall we start?'

It was late. He wanted a short, efficient meeting. Then he wanted to go home and think the case through, undisturbed.

'What do we know? Let's start there.'

Most of the information that had come to light that day had already been shared among the team members by telephone. Alex had not, however, heard the latest details about

Gabriel Sebastiansson's email and telephone activities. He saw Peder and Fredrika exchange a few quick looks when he asked someone – anyone, as long as they were quick – to update him on that point. Then he would run through what little he had not already told them about what had happened in Umeå.

Peder gathered his thoughts for a moment and then told them. He handed out copies of the email correspondence between Gabriel and 'Daddy-Long-Legs' to all those present. Then, to Alex's genuine amazement, he showed them an over-head transparency showing two timelines.

Alex glanced at Fredrika.

This must have been her idea, he thought.

To judge by the look of satisfaction on her face, he had guessed correctly.

It wasn't a bad idea, just a bit different. Sometimes it was good to have something different, Alex admitted to himself.

'So,' said Peder, indicating the timelines. 'We, well, that is, Fredrika and I, have come up with two possible theories on the basis of what we now know.'

He ran rapidly through his own theory. Then he handed over to Fredrika, who spoke without leaving her seat.

'The alternative to the theory that Gabriel drove to Kalmar and back with Lilian, which is fully possible if a bit tight time-wise, is that we're dealing with two completely different stories here, two completely unconnected crimes.'

Alex frowned.

'All right, let me clarify,' Fredrika said quickly. 'We know Gabriel has abused Sara, we know he looks at child porn at work, and I think we can assume from this email traffic that he's an active paedophile. He's part of a paedophile network we know nothing about, and he's been meeting up with them regularly since the start of the year. Then an extra event is suddenly announced, in Kalmar. He applies for some leave straight away and – understandably enough – decides to lie about it to his mother and tell her he's going on a business trip on the days in question. He promises to be back in time for dinner with Lilian when Sara and Lilian get back to Stockholm from Gothenburg.'

Fredrika paused for a moment to assure herself everyone had followed so far. Nobody sitting at the table looked confused.

'So,' she said, aware of being so worked up that she was blushing. 'So, he drives to Kalmar some time on Tuesday morning. Just after two, Lilian goes missing. An hour or so later, people start ringing to ask him about it. His mobile is turned off. Gabriel happens to be unavailable just then, and stays unavailable until ten that evening, when he switches his phone back on.'

Fredrika paused for added effect.

'The man's just been committing the most disgusting crime our society can conceive of when his daughter goes missing and he's wanted by the police in connection with that. He probably knows we've already found the records of his reported abuse of his wife, and imagines we'll also have had contradictory statements from his mother and his company about where he is. It's late and he's hours from home. Maybe it's panic, pure and simple. He doesn't want to drive home and he doesn't want to talk to the police. He knows he didn't take Lilian, but he really doesn't want to say where he was when she disappeared.'

Fredrika took a deep breath before going on.

'But he's wedged himself into a really tight corner, because his old mum who usually conjures up alibis for him finds it tricky this time, because he lied about where he was going to be. Naturally it's still her he rings; there's nobody else who'll offer him such unconditional help. It's hard to say exactly what plan they cook up between them, and exactly how much he tells his mother, but presumably they decide to assume Lilian will soon be found and they'll lie low until then.'

'And when Lilian's safely back, the police won't be interested in where he's been?' Alex added.

'Just so,' said Fredrika, taking a drink of water after her long exposition.

The room fell silent.

Alex looked through the emails Peder had handed out, reading a passage here and there.

'Christ almighty,' he said, putting the papers aside.

He leant forward across the table.

'Has anyone come up with information of any kind to make Fredrika's version seem unfeasible?' he asked softly.

Nobody said anything.

'In that case,' Alex said slowly, 'I'm inclined to believe that our friend Gabriel, who we've been hunting so frantically, most probably *isn't* the one who took Lilian.'

He looked at Peder, who was now sitting beside Fredrika.

'I agree it's not impossible for Gabriel to take Lilian and pay his visit to Kalmar all on the same day, but as Fredrika pointed out: it would be a terrifically tight schedule.'

Alex shook his head.

'But in that case,' Peder said, 'what about Ingrid Strand's

evidence? The woman who was sitting by Sara and Lilian on the train. I mean, she saw Lilian being carried off . . .'

' . . . by someone who "must have been her daddy",' Alex supplied calmly. 'I know, it's all as clear as mud. Who else would Lilian let herself be taken by? Unless she was already drugged, but we'll have to wait for the tests before we can know that.'

Fredrika swallowed.

'Was she . . . ,' she started. 'Could the pathologists tell if she'd been assaulted in any way?'

Alex shook his head.

'They think probably not, but that's something else we'll get a formal report on tomorrow morning.'

Alex lapsed into silence. Regardless of whether Gabriel Sebastiansson could be linked to Lilian's disappearance, a whole bundle of information about a paedophile network had suddenly landed on his desk. Goodness knows it wasn't his problem; it would have to be handed over to the regional or even national crime squad.

'Does this mean we're right back to square one?' asked Peder doubtfully.

Alex smiled.

'No,' he said, pondering. 'It just means that the information we've got doesn't hang together quite the way we first thought. But as I said, I do think we can write off Gabriel as chief suspect, at least for the time being.'

Peder sighed and Alex held up a warning finger.

'But,' he added, 'that doesn't necessarily mean Gabriel didn't know whoever took his daughter. We can't rule that out, knowing the circles he moved in.'

Fredrika raised a tentative hand to request permission to speak.

Alex gave her a nod.

'But we do know,' Fredrika said softly, 'that the person who took Lilian directed his attentions to Sara and not – as far as we know – to Gabriel. The hair was sent to Sara's address, not his.'

'So you think the murderer has links to Sara rather than Gabriel?' interpreted Alex.

'Yes,' came Fredrika's straight answer.

'Have we got any other information to back that up?' Alex asked, surveying those assembled.

Fredrika asked to speak again.

'Yes, we have,' she said, and flushed. 'You see, I went on a little visit to Flemingsberg today.'

Alex and the others listened to Fredrika's brief account of what she had found out in Flemingsberg and from Swedish Railways. She concluded by assuring them she didn't think any of this was proof, but she still maintained that too many things had happened at the same time for it to be pure coincidence.

Alex absorbed this in silence. Then he furrowed his brow.

'I ought really to say you shouldn't be sending yourself off on little missions of your own when I specifically asked you to do other things, but I'll let that pass for now.'

Fredrika gave a sigh of relief.

'If we assume the information you gathered to be true in the sense that it indicates this was a minutely planned series of actions, directed at Sara, then we're dealing with a real sadist,' Alex said quietly. 'And a very intelligent and successful one, at that. There's just one thing I wonder: why haven't we found an explanation for this? Why isn't Sara aware of who she could have upset to that degree?'

'Maybe because she didn't notice,' Peder put in. 'If it was some real psycho who took Lilian, and it seems like it, the reason might well not seem logical to anyone except the perpetrator himself.'

'We'll have to sift through all the information again,' said Alex, with audible tension in his voice. 'We must have missed something. When will the identikit of the woman with the dog be ready?'

'It already is,' said Fredrika, 'but we just want the girl at the ticket window to see if it needs tweaking, and she's doing that tonight.'

'Right, let's move on,' said Alex, thanking Fredrika with a quick nod.

Fredrika tried to interrupt, but Alex stopped her.

'Can I just run through what I found out from Sara and her parents in Umeå?'

Fredrika nodded, as curious as everyone else.

Alex was aware he was disappointing them.

He repeated what had been said in his interview with Sara and her parents after the formal identification. He saw Fredrika giving him a penetrating look as he told them about Sara's time in Umeå after she left school.

When he had finished, Fredrika was the first to comment.

'I've been talking to quite a few of Sara's friends and colleagues today,' she said, 'and it's struck me that she basically has none of her old friends left.'

'Yes,' said Alex. 'I understand she broke off with them when she met her husband.'

'That's right,' said Fredrika eagerly, 'but it means that when we try to chart her social network, our timeline's starting quite late. That is, we're not taking account of anything that might have happened in Sara's life *before* she met Gabriel.'

'And you mean that might be it? That someone who might have been brooding and plotting vengeance for decades snatched Lilian?'

'I mean we can't rule it out,' clarified Fredrika. 'And I mean that if that *is* the case, we've no chance of unearthing it as things stand, because we're looking at completely the wrong timespan.'

Alex nodded thoughtfully.

'Right, my friends,' he said, 'let's rest our brains tonight. Everybody go home and do something they enjoy. And when we meet tomorrow, we'll start again in the sense that we'll go through our material again. All of it. Even calls from the public we discounted previously. Okay?'

Alex had surprised himself by using the word 'friends' twice in one meeting. The thought made him smile.

Ellen Lind was feeling a touch disappointed as she left work. She'd really been working hard since the girl went missing, and though she was only an assistant, the boss ought to remember to give her credit for her contribution, too. Alex wasn't always very good at that. Not to mention the way he treated the poor analyst. Did he even know that Mats's name was Mats?

All such thoughts evaporated when she got out her mobile and saw she had several missed calls from the man she loved. He had left her a short, concise voicemail message saying he would very much like to see her that evening at Hotel Anglais, where he was staying the night. He also apologized for the stupid way things had gone between them last time.

Ellen's heart missed a beat for sheer joy.

At the same time she felt a little stab of irritation. She didn't like these sudden temperature changes in the relationship.

For a price, Ellen's niece agreed to look after the children in the end. She was actually already round at Ellen's to lend a general hand, since Ellen had had to work late.

'Do they really need a babysitter?' asked the girl, who was nineteen and had just left school.

Ellen's thoughts went to Lilian Sebastiansson and she said a firm:

'Yes.'

Then she hurried home so she would at least have time to say goodnight to the kids and change.

Ellen's niece watched her as she dashed around in her underwear looking for something to wear.

'You look like a teenager who's just fallen in love,' she giggled.

Ellen smiled and blushed.

'Yes, I know it's a bit silly, but I feel so happy every time he says he can see me.'

The girl gave her a warm smile back.

'Wear the red top,' she said. 'Red really suits you.'

Before long, Ellen was in a taxi on her way to the hotel. She didn't realize how tired she was until she sank into the back seat of the taxi. It had been hard work and tough going these past few days. She hoped Carl wouldn't mind listening while she told him about all that dreadful stuff, because she really needed to get it out of her system.

Carl met her in the lobby. His face broke into a warm smile when he saw her.

'Just think, twice in one week,' Ellen murmured as they embraced.

'Some weeks are easier than others,' replied Carl, holding her tight.

He stroked her back, praised her choice of top and said she looked radiant, even though she felt shattered.

The hours until they fell asleep passed in a haze. They drank wine, had a bite to eat, and a long, earnest talk about all that had happened, and then made passionate love until they decided it was time for some sleep.

Ellen relaxed in his arms and was almost dropping off as she whispered:

'I'm so glad we met, Carl.'

She could feel his smile tickle the back of her neck.

'I think exactly the same,' he said.

Then his hand cupped her left breast, and he kissed her shoulder and said:

'You truly give me all I need.'

PART II

Signs of Anger

FRIDAY

It was dark in the flat when Jelena came to. She opened her eyes and found she was lying on her back. One eye didn't want to open at all. She just had time to wonder why that eye was so heavy before the wave of pain washed through her. Through her and crashing against her. Impossible to ward off, impossible to endure. It coursed through her body and made her shake. When she tried to turn in the bed, the sheet stuck to the skin of her back in the places where the blood had clotted and dried.

Jelena almost immediately abandoned her efforts not to cry. She knew the Man would not be at home. He never was after a Reprimand.

The tears could run freely down her cheeks.

If only he had let her speak, if only he had listened and not rushed straight at her.

Such fury.

Jelena had never seen anything like it.

How could he do this? she thought as she cried into the stained pillow.

That was a forbidden thought, really. She was not to question anything about the Man, those were their rules. If he reprimanded her, it was only for her own good. If she could not understand that, their relationship was doomed to be weakened and destroyed. How many times had he told her?

But still.

Jelena was a woman who had lost her faith in herself and those around her bit by bit. She was alone, and that was because she deserved to be. That was why she had become the person who felt grateful and cherished when someone like the Man wanted her.

But there was still a vestige of strength in her that the Man had not managed to wipe out. Nor had that been his intention: without strength, she could never become his ally in the war that lay ahead of them.

Lying naked on the bed, alone and abandoned with wounds all over her body, Jelena used that last drop of strength to dare to sample the salty taste of protest. When she was younger, in a time she and the Man had done everything to make her forget, her whole being had been one big protest. The Man took that out of her. The kind of protest she indulged in was to be condemned. He had told her that the very first time he picked her up in the car. But there were other kinds of protest. If she wanted to and dared to, he could help her move forward.

Jelena wanted nothing better.

But the road to perfection, which the Man claimed was imperative for the fight, was far longer and darker than Jelena had ever imagined. Long and painful. It nearly always hurt somewhere. It hurt most of all when he burned her. Though really that had only been a few times, and only right at the start of their relationship.

Now he had done it again.

Jelena was hot and feverish. Her chest hurt when she breathed and she had burns on more parts of her body than she dared to think of. The pain was driving her insane.

A desperate thought flashed through her mind.

I must get help, she thought. I must get help.

Summoning all her willpower she slipped off the edge of the bed and slowly began to crawl out of the room. Seeking help for her injuries was another infringement of the rules, but this time she was sure she would die if she didn't get medical help.

The Man always came home sooner or later and helped her. But this time Jelena did not have time to wait for him. Her strength was draining away too quickly.

Got to get to the front door.

Somewhere inside her, the panic was growing. What would this betrayal mean for the relationship between her and the Man? What would be left of it, in fact, after she had gone behind his back?

Of course the Man would never accept her showing enough independence to leave the flat in her present state. He would come after her, and he would kill her.

Time, thought Jelena, as she kneeled up, trembling, and gripped the handle of the front door. I've got to think.

She struggled to raise her other hand so she could reach the lock. Unlock the door and open it. She remembered nothing more.

The door swung open and cold marble met Jelena's face as she hit the floor.

Alex Recht began his working day by dispatching Fredrika to Uppsala to question Sara Sebastiansson's former friend Maria Blomgren, who had been with her on the writing course in Umeå.

Then he sat behind his desk with a cup of coffee in his hand. Quiet and alone.

Later on, Alex would wonder just when had this case turned into a wild animal that paralysed his whole team by stubbornly and persistently choosing its own path. The case seemed to be living a life of its own, with the sole purpose of confusing the team and leading it astray.

Don't you dare control me, came a whisper inside Alex. *Don't you dare tell me which way to go.*

Alex sat stiffly at his desk. Although the night had only allowed him a few hours' sleep, he felt full of energy. He also felt pure, livid anger. There was such insolence to the perpetrator's whole plan. The hair was couriered to the child's mother. The child was dumped in a car park outside a big hospital. Somebody even rang the hospital to make sure the child would be found. Without leaving a single trace behind them. Or at least nothing personal, like fingerprints.

'But nobody on the planet is invisible, and nobody is infallible, that's for sure,' Alex muttered doggedly to himself as he lifted the receiver and dialled the forensics unit in Solna.

The pathologist who took Alex's call sounded surprisingly young. In Alex's world, skilled doctors were usually over fifty, so he always felt slightly anxious when he had to work with someone younger than that.

Despite his prejudices, he found the pathologist to be a very competent person who expressed himself in terms that even an ordinary police officer could understand.

That was good enough for Alex.

The pathologist up in Umeå had been right in her preliminary assessment. Lilian had died of poisoning, an overdose of insulin. The insulin had been injected directly into the body, high at the back of her neck.

Alex reluctantly found his anger now mixed with surprise.

'I've never seen anything like it,' said the pathologist, sounding concerned. 'But it's an effective and – how shall I put it – clinical way of killing someone. And keeps the victim's suffering to a minimum.'

'Was she conscious when she was jabbed?'

'Hard to say,' the doctor said doubtfully. 'I found traces of morphine in her, so presumably someone had tried to keep her calm. But I can't swear she was unconscious when she was given the lethal injection.'

He went on:

'It's hard to say what the murderer hoped to gain by injecting the insulin straight into her skull, or the back of her neck. At that concentration it would have been lethal even if injected into an arm or leg.'

'Do you think he's a doctor? The murderer?' Alex asked quietly.

'Hardly,' said the pathologist tersely. 'I'd call the way the needle was used amateurish. And as I say: why did he initially try putting it straight in the girl's head? It almost seems like some kind of symbolic act.'

Alex wondered at what he had just heard. Symbolic? How?

The cause of death seemed as bizarre as the rest of the case.

Had she eaten anything after she was abducted?

The pathologist took a few moments to answer.

'No,' he said eventually. 'No, it doesn't look like it. Her stomach was entirely empty. But if she was kept drugged for a period, that's not so surprising.'

'Can you tell us anything about where the body's been?' Alex asked wearily.

'As they noted in Umeå, the body had been at least partly washed with alcohol. I looked for traces of the perpetrators under her nails, but I didn't find anything. In a few places I was able to secure the remnants of a particular kind of talc, which shows they wore rubber gloves, the sort they have in hospitals.'

'Can they be got hold of anywhere else?'

'We'll have to do some more tests before I'm completely sure, but they probably are hospital gloves. And they're not difficult to get hold of if you know somebody who works at a hospital, but you can't just buy them at the chemist's.'

Alex nodded thoughtfully to himself.

'But if the murderer had access to hypodermic needles and hospital alcohol and gloves . . .' he began.

'Then it's likely one of the people involved moves in health service circles,' the doctor finished for him.

Alex went quiet. What had the pathologist just said . . . ?

'You always talk about the murderer as if it was more than one person,' he said enquiringly.

'Yes,' said the pathologist.

'But what are you basing that on?' asked Alex.

'I do beg your pardon, I thought you'd been given that information when you were up in Umeå,' the pathologist apologized.

'What information?'

'The girl's body is completely undamaged apart from the lesion to the scalp. She hasn't been subjected to any kind of external bodily harm and nor has she been sexually abused.'

Alex sighed with relief.

'But,' the pathologist went on, 'there are distinct sets of bruises on her arms and legs. They were probably the result of a struggle as someone tried to hold her down. One of the pairs of hands that made them was very small, probably a woman's. Further up the arms there are also larger bruises, which appear to have been inflicted by much larger hands. Probably a man's.'

Alex felt his chest tighten.

'So there are two of them?' he said. 'A man and a woman?'

The pathologist's hesitation was audible.

'Could be, yes, but I can't be entirely sure, of course.'

He went on:

'But I can say that the bruising must have occurred several hours before the child died. Possibly when they were shaving her head.'

'The woman held her down while the man shaved her,' Alex said softly. 'And Lilian put up too much of a fight, so they changed places. The woman shaved and the man held her down.'

'It's possible,' said the pathologist again.

'It's possible,' said Alex under his breath.

By the time Fredrika Bergman got to Uppsala, the picture of the woman who had held up Sara Sebastiansson in Flemingsberg was already all over the media. Fredrika heard it on the radio as she pulled up outside Maria Blomgren's.

The police are now looking for a woman who is thought to have been . . .

Fredrika switched off the engine and got out of the car. The media were now following the Lilian case extremely closely. They didn't know all the repulsive details yet, but sooner or later they would get their hands on them. And then all hell would break loose, that was for sure.

It was warmer in Uppsala than in Stockholm. Fredrika remembered she'd always thought so when she was a student as well. It was always a bit hotter in Uppsala in summer, and a bit colder in winter.

As if you were travelling to an entirely different part of the world.

Meeting Maria Blomgren soon shook Fredrika out of her reverie. Maria Blomgren looked unmistakably as though she came from exactly the same part of the world as Fredrika herself.

We even look a bit like each other, thought Fredrika.

Dark hair, blue eyes. Maria was perhaps a little fuller in the cheeks, a bit taller and slightly darker-skinned. Her hips were broader and more rounded.

She must have had a baby, thought Fredrika automatically.

And Maria gave an even more earnest impression than Fredrika, if that was possible. She did not smile until she had seen Fredrika's ID. Then she smiled a thin little smile showing not even a glimpse of her teeth.

But there was not much reason to smile, when it came to it. Alex Recht had called Maria Blomgren in advance to explain what the visit was all about. Maria said she didn't think she had anything particular to tell them, but of course she would cooperate with the police.

They sat down at the kitchen table. Sand-coloured walls, white mosaic tiles, modern kitchen units. The table was elliptical in shape, and the chairs were hard and white. Apart from the walls, almost everything in the kitchen was white. The whole flat was pedantically tidy and looked clinically clean.

So different from Sara Sebastiansson's, thought Fredrika. It was quite hard to imagine the two women once having been best friends.

'You wanted to ask me about that summer in Umeå?' Maria said straight out.

Fredrika delved in her handbag for her notebook and pen. Maria was demonstrating unequivocally that, while not unwilling to talk to the police, she wanted it over and done with as soon as possible.

'Maybe you could start with how you and Sara became friends? How did you get to know each other?'

Fredrika detected distinct hesitation in Maria's face. Then scarcely perceptible irritation. Her eyes darkened.

'We were friends in upper secondary,' said Maria. 'My parents separated around then and I had to change schools.

Sara and I happened to be in the same German group; we were with the same German teacher for three years.'

Maria fiddled with the vase of beautiful flowers on the table in front of her. It struck Fredrika that she had not been offered so much as a glass of water.

'I don't really know what sort of things you want me to tell you,' Maria said slowly. 'Sara and I soon became close friends. Her parents were going through some sort of crisis just then, too, and arguing a lot. We understood each other, both being in the same boat. We were both typical model pupils, the kind who lend their pens to everybody and don't like the sort of classmates who disrupt lessons.'

When Maria raised her eyes, Fredrika saw moisture glinting in them.

She's grieving, thought Fredrika. That's why she's being so buttoned up. She's grieving for the relationship she and Sara once had.

'In the last year at secondary school, Sara changed,' Maria went on. 'She wanted to rebel. Started wearing make-up, drinking and messing around with boys.'

Maria shook her head.

'I think she got tired of it. That phase ended pretty quickly, round about the time her parents got back together again. I think they'd separated for a while, but I'm not sure. Anyway, on the whole things were fine again. And then we went on to college and made sure we were on the same course. We'd already decided what we wanted to be: interpreters at the UN.'

Maria laughed heartily at the thought, and Fredrika smiled.

'You were both good at languages?'

'Yes, oh yes, our German and English teachers couldn't praise us enough.'

Maria's look turned grave again.

'But then Sara had more trouble at home. Her parents changed church and Sara didn't get on with the new, stricter rules they suddenly expected her to follow.'

'Church?' Fredrika echoed in surprise.

Maria raised her eyebrows.

'Yes, church. Sara's parents were Pentecostalists, and there was nothing odd about that. But then a group of them broke away and started a Swedish branch of an American Free Church movement. They called themselves Christ's Children, or something like that.'

Fredrika listened with growing interest.

'And what was the conflict with her parents about?' she asked.

'Well it was so stupid, really,' Maria sighed. 'Her parents had always been quite liberal although they were such believers. They didn't mind us going out or anything like that. But in the few years they were part of that new group, they changed, got more radical. They were much more restrictive about clothes, music, parties and so on. And Sara couldn't cope with the change. She refused to take part in anything to do with the church, which her parents accepted even though the pastor tried to force them to be stricter in their parental role. But that wasn't enough for Sara; she wanted to push the boundaries even more.'

'With more booze and boys?'

'With more booze and boys, and sex,' sighed Maria. 'It wasn't too early for it, really, we must have been seventeen

when she got going, so to speak. But it was a bit worrying
that she seemed to be trying to go with boys just to annoy
her parents.'

Fredrika found herself crossing her legs under the table.
She hadn't been with a boy until she was well over eighteen.

'Anyway,' Maria went on, 'she met a really nice boy the
year after that. And I got together with the boy's best friend,
so we were like a little gang, always going round together.'

'How did Sara's parents take it? Her having a boyfriend, I
mean.'

'They didn't know at first, of course. And when they found
out . . . Well, I think they thought it was quite okay. Sara
calmed down a bit, and they genuinely had no idea about all
the boys she'd been with before that. If they had known, I
think it would have been a different story.'

'And what happened?' asked Fredrika, who was really
caught up in the story.

'Then time passed and spring came,' said Maria, who was
a good storyteller and knew when she had a good listener in
front of her. 'Sara suddenly felt a bit unsure about the relationship. They were spending more time apart, and our little
group wasn't together so often. Then I split up with the other
boy, and after that Sara didn't want to be with hers, either.'

Maria took a breath.

'He made a bit of a fuss at first, Sara's boyfriend. He didn't
want it to be over. Kept ringing her and wouldn't give up. But
he found a new girl not long after, and then he left Sara in
peace. It was only a few weeks before we finished college, and
Sara had already booked us on the writing course in Umeå.
There were so many things I was looking forward to.

College-leaving celebrations, the writing course, starting at university.'

Maria bit her lip.

'But there was something worrying Sara,' she said softly. 'At first I thought it must be because that boy wouldn't leave her alone, but then he backed off. And then I thought she must have fallen out with her parents again, but it wasn't that either. I could see there was something, though. And I was terribly hurt that she wouldn't confide in me.'

Fredrika made some notes on her pad.

'So you went off to Umeå?' she prompted quietly, realizing Maria had lapsed into total silence.

Maria gave a start.

'Yes, that's right,' she said. 'We went off to Umeå. Sara kept saying things would be better once she got away. And then she just came out with something on the way: said it was all arranged that she would be staying up there all summer, and we wouldn't be coming back together. I was really upset; it felt like an insult and a betrayal.'

'You didn't know she'd applied for a summer job up there?'

'No, I had no idea. Nor did her parents; she rang them a few weeks later to tell them. Made it sound as if it was an opportunity that had just come up, when it wasn't at all. Sara knew when she left that she'd be there all summer.'

'Did she explain at all?' Fredrika asked reflectively.

'No,' Maria said with a shake of the head. 'She just said it had been a difficult year and she needed to get away. Told me not to take it personally.'

Maria leant back in her seat and folded her arms on her chest. She looked steely.

'But I couldn't really get over it,' she said, sounding almost defiant. 'We did the course and then I went home by myself. We'd planned to share a flat or something in Uppsala when term started there, but over the summer I decided I'd rather be on my own, in student accommodation. Sara got in quite a state about it and thought I was letting her down, but she let me down first. And then . . .'

She lapsed into silence. A big red car went past in the road outside. Fredrika's eyes followed it while she waited for Maria to go on.

'And then everything was sort of fine again,' she said in a low voice. 'Not really, not like it had been before. We saw a lot of each other in Uppsala, and we shared the same interests and confided in each other to some extent, but . . . no, it was never like before.'

Fredrika felt a strange, gnawing feeling inside her. How many people had she grown apart from over the years? Did she grieve over it the way Maria seemed to regret the loss of Sara?

'Let's just go back to the time in Umeå,' Fredrika said briskly.

Maria blinked.

'How were things there? Did anything particular happen?'

'Things were . . . Well, fine, I think. We stayed at a course centre and got to know some people.'

'Anyone you're still in touch with?'

'No, no, no one at all. It felt like drawing a line under it all when I came home. The course was over and I was going to work for the rest of the summer. Work, and then move to Uppsala.'

'And Sara? Did she have anything to say for herself when she got back?'

Maria knitted her brow.

'No, scarcely a thing.'

'Was there anyone else she was as close to as she was to you?'

'No, I'm sure there wasn't. She had friends, of course, but no one that close. It felt to me as if there were lots of things she just wanted to put behind her when we moved to Uppsala. Before she met Gabriel, then she was pretty much on her own again, I suppose.'

Fredrika snapped this up at once.

'Were you seeing much of Sara when she met Gabriel?'

'Yes, we seemed to be starting to find each other again properly just about then. It was a few years since the Umeå thing, and we were soon going to be taking our exams and looking for jobs. We were on the brink of a new phase in our lives, a more adult one. But then Sara met Gabriel and everything changed again. He took over her life completely. At first I tried to stay in touch to . . .'

Maria stopped, and Fredrika was in no doubt this time. Maria was crying.

'To . . . what?' Fredrika asked quietly.

'To save her,' Maria sobbed. 'I could see how she was getting knocked about in that relationship. And then she got pregnant. After that we lost contact completely, and we haven't been in touch since. I couldn't bear seeing her with him. And to be honest, I couldn't stand seeing the way she just gave up and died when she was with him, and didn't lift a finger to break free.'

Fredrika instinctively disagreed with Maria about Sara Sebastiansson not lifting a finger to break free from Gabriel, but she kept it to herself. Instead she said:

'Well, she's definitely broken free now. In fact, she's desperately alone.'

Maria wiped away a tear from her cheek.

'How does she look?'

Fredrika, who was just packing away her things to get up and go, raised her head.

'Who?'

'Sara? I wonder how she looks today.'

Fredrika gave a slight smile.

'She's got striking red hair, long. Beautiful, you could say. And her toenails are painted blue.'

The tears rose in Maria's eyes again.

'Just like before,' she whispered. 'That's the way she's always looked.'

Peder Rydh was reflecting on life in general and his marriage to Ylva in particular. He scratched his forehead, as he always did when he was stressed and unsettled. He discreetly scratched his groin, too. He itched all over this morning.

An inveterate fidget, he dashed out into the corridor for his second coffee of the morning. Then he slunk back into his room again. To be on the safe side, he shut the door. He wanted a bit of peace.

Yesterday evening had been a nightmare.

'Go home and do something you enjoy,' Alex had said.

Enjoy wasn't really the way Peder would describe how he felt about last night. The boys had been asleep when he got home. It was several days since he had got home early enough to play with the boys and spend some time with them.

And then there was Ylva. They started by talking to each other as 'grown-up human beings', but after a few short exchanges, Ylva went completely crazy.

'Do you think I don't know what you're up to?' she shouted. 'Do you?'

How many times had he seen her cry this last year, for Pete's sake? How many?

Peder had only one weapon to defend himself with, and he almost died of shame recalling how he had used it.

'Don't you get how serious this case is?' he shouted back.

'Don't you get how bloody awful I feel with dead kids popping up all over Sweden when I'm a dad myself? Holy shit, is it that odd if I sleep over at work now and then? Eh?'

He won, of course. Ylva had no concrete proof of her suspicions, and she was so worn down by the past difficult year that she didn't really trust her own intuition any longer. It ended up with her sitting on the floor, crying and saying she was sorry. And Peder took her in his arms, stroked her hair and said he forgave her. Then he went in to the boys and sat silently in the dark between their beds. *Daddy's home now, guys.*

Peder's face went hot as he remembered it.

Arsehole.

He had been a complete arsehole.

The memory of it made him start to shake. *God al-migh-ty.*

I'm a bad person, he thought. And a bad dad. A useless dad. A disgusting man. A . . .

Ellen Lind broke into his thoughts with her insistent knocking on his door. He knew it was her although he couldn't see her. She had a special way of knocking.

She opened the door before he had a chance to call 'Come in'.

'Sorry to barge in,' she said, 'but a detective from Jönköping has just called, asking to speak to someone in Alex's team. Alex wants you to take it, because he's on the phone to someone in Umeå.'

Peder, confused, stared at Ellen.

'All right,' he said, and waited while she went back to transfer the call.

He heard a woman's voice at the other end. It sounded

pleasant, assured; Peder guessed he was speaking to a middle-aged woman.

She introduced herself as Anna Sandgren and said she was a DI with the crime squad in the Jönköping county force.

'Uhuh,' said Peder, mainly just to have something to say.

'Sorry, I didn't catch your name,' said Anna Sandgren.

Peder squirmed.

'I'm Peder Rydh,' he said. 'DI with the Stockholm police, and I'm one of Alex Recht's special investigation team.'

'Ah, right,' said Anna Sandgren, still with that slightly singing intonation she had. 'I'm ringing about a woman we found dead yesterday morning.'

Peder listened. That was the same morning Lilian was found.

'Her grandmother reported her missing. She said her granddaughter had rung on the Wednesday evening and said she was coming to stay. She apparently had protected identity status after some violence in an earlier relationship, and she also used to come and hide up at her old granny's when things got difficult.'

'Right,' said Peder guardedly, waiting for an explanation of how this could possibly have anything to do with him.

'But there was no word from her that evening as she'd promised,' Anna Sandgren went on, 'so the old lady rang the police and asked us to go round there to see if anything had happened to her. We sent a patrol car and everything seemed normal. But the grandmother insisted we ought to go into the flat. And when we did, we found her murdered in her bed. Strangled.'

Peder frowned. He still could not fathom why the call had been put through to him, of all people.

'We made a brief search of the flat and found her mobile. There weren't many numbers in it and it hadn't been used much. But one of the numbers she'd saved was yours.'

Anna Sandgren stopped.

'Ours?' gulped Peder, not really understanding what she meant.

'We checked all the numbers on her phone, and one of them was the number the Stockholm police issued to the media for anyone with information about that missing child who turned up in Umeå.'

Peder sat up straighter.

'As far as we can see, though the number's saved there, she didn't ever ring it from her mobile. But we thought you ought to know. Especially as we have so little to go on at our end.'

Peder swallowed. *Jönköping*. Had Jönköping come up in any context in the investigation?

'Do you know when she died?' he asked.

'Probably a couple of hours after she rang her grandmother and told them she was coming to stay,' Anna Sandgren replied. 'Forensics will be getting back to us with a more exact time, but preliminary observations indicate she died around ten on Wednesday evening. She'd bought her ticket online for the train up to Umeå where the grandmother lives, and was meant to . . .'

'Umeå?' Peder interrupted.

'Yes, Umeå. She was meant to be catching the train from Jönköping the morning we found her dead. Yesterday, that is.'

Peder's heart was beating faster.

'Does the grandmother know who he is? The man who abused her so she needed a protected identity?'

'It's a terribly complicated story,' sighed Anna Sandgren resignedly, 'but the short version is this: Nora, that's the victim's name, got together with a man when she was living in a small place not far from Umeå, six or seven years back. It wasn't what you'd call a healthy relationship. Nora wasn't very well herself at the time. She was off work with depression, seems to have had it very tough growing up in a series of foster homes. Both her parents are dead.'

Peder took a deep breath.

'You ought really to talk to Nora's grandmother face to face,' said Anna Sandgren. 'We've only spoken to her on the phone, and she was very shaken by the news of Nora's death. But she was able to tell me that she'd never met the man in question, and that Nora suddenly felt the need to get away from the Umeå area and just went. She was able to get protected identity without having to identify the man, because she had such well-documented injuries. I don't think the police made any particular efforts to find him. It would have been the same here, if we hadn't even had a name to go on.'

'And here,' Peder said without thinking.

'Well now you know what's happened, anyway,' said Anna Sandgren to wind up the call. 'We'll keep you informed on the progress of our investigation, of course, but as things stand we've no leads on the murderer at all.'

She gave a dry laugh.

'Well no, that was a slight exaggeration. We have got one, and that's a footprint we found in Nora's hall. A man's Ecco shoe, size 46.'

Fredrika Bergman got back to HQ about lunchtime. She was mystified to see Alex sitting alone at the table in the Den. His brow was knitted, and he was writing furiously on a sheet of paper in front of him.

He's woken up now, Fredrika thought to herself. He lost his bearings early on and wandered off in the wrong direction, but now he's back on track.

'Are we having a meeting?' she asked out loud.

Alex jumped.

'No, no,' he said. 'I'm just sitting thinking. How did it go in Uppsala?'

Fredrika reflected.

'Fine,' she said. 'Fine. But there's something weird about that writing course.'

'How do you mean, "weird"?'

'Something happened up there, or just beforehand, that made Sara decide to stay up there much longer than her friend.'

Alex stared ahead, pondering what she had said.

'I'd like to go up to Umeå,' said Fredrika, taking one step over the threshold.

'Umeå?' Alex repeated, surprised.

'Yes, and talk to whoever was running that course, ask them if they know what it was that had that effect on Sara.'

Before Alex could reply, Fredrika added:

'And I thought I'd have another word with Sara herself. If she's up to it, that is, and assuming she's back in Stockholm.'

'She's back,' said Alex. 'She and her parents got back this morning.'

'Did you know the parents are very religious?'

'No,' said Alex. 'No, I didn't. Could that be relevant here?'

'It could,' said Fredrika. 'It could.'

'I see,' said Alex. 'Well then, you'd better come in and tell me more about it.'

He ventured a smile as Fredrika came into the room. She sat down at the opposite side of the table.

'Where's Peder?' she asked.

'On his way to Umeå,' said Peder, right behind her.

He had come into the meeting room with a holdall slung over one shoulder.

Like a boy, thought Fredrika. Like a boy on his way to football practice.

She raised her eyebrows.

'What's happened?'

Peder surveyed the room irritably.

'Are we supposed to be having a meeting now?'

Alex gave a chuckle.

'No, not really. But since you're both here . . .'

Peder sank onto a chair. He had already told Alex everything, so he briefed Fredrika in a single sentence.

'They've found a murdered woman in Jönköping who had our public hotline number stored in her mobile, and her grandmother lives in Umeå.'

Fredrika gave a start.

'In Jönköping?'

'Yep. We've no idea of course why she had it in her phone, especially as she doesn't ever seem to have used it to make a call, but . . .'

'But she *did* make a call,' Fredrika broke in.

Alex and Peder stared at her.

'Don't you remember? Ellen told us about a woman who wanted to stay anonymous, who thought she knew the perpetrator and had once lived with him.'

Alex was suddenly tense.

'You're right,' he said quietly. 'You're right. But how do you link that to the woman in Jönköping?'

'The call was made from a public telephone in Jönköping,' said Fredrika. 'Mats, the analyst, checked it out.'

'How long have we known that?' asked Peder indignantly.

'We dismissed the call as unimportant,' Fredrika retorted, equally indignantly. 'And Jönköping wasn't in the picture at all at that point.'

Alex raised a hand to stop them.

'And it's all there in Mats's database, for anyone who asks,' Fredrika swiftly added.

Peder's face dropped.

'I didn't check this with him,' he admitted.

He glanced in Alex's direction.

Alex gave a couple of dry little coughs.

'Okay, okay,' he said. 'Let's assume it was the murdered woman who rang. Is there any written record of what she said?'

Fredrika gave an eager nod.

'Ellen made a note; I think that's in the database, too.'

Peder leapt to his feet.

'I'll go and talk to Mats,' he said, and was out of the room before either Alex or Fredrika had time to say anything.

Fredrika gave an almost imperceptible sigh.

'Wait a second,' called Alex, and Peder came back into the room.

'Fredrika apparently needs to go to Umeå as well. But I don't see any point in sending you both up there just now.'

Fredrika and Peder listened, both on tenterhooks.

'We've already had several calls about the woman with the dog in Flemingsberg,' said Alex. 'I've been with the analyst, er . . .'

'Mats,' supplied Fredrika.

'Yes, Mats, and we went through them all, and there are two that definitely need following up. One was from the proprietor of a car hire place. He thinks he hired out a car to a woman who looked a bit like the one in the picture. And then a woman rang and said she was the girl's foster mother some years ago. She gave us a provisional description to go on.'

Silence descended on the room. Fredrika and Peder glanced at each other.

'It might just be,' Alex said slowly, enunciating every syllable, 'that it would be more appropriate for Fredrika to go to Umeå to take care of a poor old grandmother and a writing teacher. And for you, Peder, to deal with the car hire man and the foster mother.'

Peder and Fredrika nodded to each other in agreement.

'Is there anything else I should know about the dead woman in Jönköping?' asked Fredrika.

Peder stuck a memo under her nose.

'Here's everything we've got,' he said curtly.

Fredrika began to read.

'A pair of Ecco shoes size 46,' she said softly.

'We mustn't get our hopes up,' said Alex, who had already seen the memo, 'but it's certainly a coincidence, isn't it?'

Fredrika read on, frowning.

'Good, that's decided then,' said Alex.

A sceptical Fredrika watched Alex and Peder as they hurried out of the room.

Chaos, she thought. These men live at the epicentre of chaos. I honestly don't think they'd be able to breathe anywhere else.

At that moment, Alex turned round.

'By the way,' he said very loudly.

Peder and Fredrika both listened. Ellen put her head out of her office.

'I contacted the National Crime Squad with what we got from Gabriel Sebastiansson's emails,' he said. 'Apparently "Daddy-Long-Legs" is well known in those circles. The Crime Squad is gearing up for a major move against him and his network and was very glad of our input. I was to pass on their thanks.'

Peder Rydh had had certain preconceptions about the police world when he applied for a place on the training scheme ten years before.

The first was that the police force was a place where stuff really happened. The second was that being a police officer was an important profession. And the third was that other people looked up to the police.

That third point had been a crucial one for Peder. Getting respect. Not that he wasn't used to people showing him respect. But this was a *different kind* of respect, one that went deeper.

And he certainly did find himself respected. The only slightly strange thing was that since he had left the uniformed branch and was in plain clothes, people perceived him as less of an authority figure and treated him accordingly.

The proprietor of the car hire firm who had rung in to say he recognized the picture of the girl at Flemingsberg station was a case in point. When Peder arrived the man regarded him very suspiciously until he showed his ID. He then lowered his guard a little but still wasn't entirely satisfied.

Peder glanced around him to get the measure of the place. It was a little office in the heart of Södermalm. The posters in the windows offered both car hire and driving lessons. Not a very usual combination. And there was nothing in the office to indicate that any kind of driver instruction was conducted on the premises.

The other man saw Peder surveying the scene.

'The driving school's downstairs,' he said peevishly. 'If it's them you're looking for.'

Peder smiled.

'I was just taking a little look round,' he said. 'Good place for a car hire firm, I should think.'

'How do you mean?'

What a bloody misery guts, thought Peder angrily, but kept his smile on and said, 'I just meant there can't be too much competition round here. Most of the car hire places are at the big petrol stations, aren't they, so they're a fair way out of the city centre?'

When the man did not respond, and went on looking annoyed, Peder decided not to waste any more energy trying to be pleasant.

'You rang and said you thought you'd seen this woman,' he said briskly, putting the drawing of the Flemingsberg woman on the counter separating him from the other man.

The man studied the picture.

'Yes, that looks like her, the one who was here.'

'When was she here?' Peder asked.

The car hire man frowned and opened a large desk diary he had in front of him.

'Is she the one who murdered the kid?' he asked insensitively. 'Is that why you're looking for her?'

'She's not under suspicion for anything,' Peder said rapidly. 'We just want to talk to her; she might have seen something of interest to us.'

The man nodded as he looked through the calendar.

'Here', he said, stabbing a fat finger onto the open page. 'That's when she was here.'

Peder leant forward. The man turned the calendar round. He had his finger on the left-hand page. June the seventh.

Peder's spirits fell.

'What makes you remember it was that day?' he said dubiously.

'Because it was the day I was having my goddamned wisdom tooth taken out,' said the car hirer, looking very pleased with himself as he drummed on a straggly doodle on the page. 'I was just going to close the shop and go to the hospital when she came in.'

He leant over the desk with a glitter in his eye that made Peder feel very uncomfortable.

'Petrified little beggar,' he said in a thick voice. 'Stood staring around her like a little animal caught in the car headlights. Those ones that never shift even though the danger's right on top of them. That's the way she looked.'

He gave a short, coarse laugh.

Peder ignored the other man's attitude, though he suspected some of what had just been said ought to be stored away in his mind for future reference.

'Which car did she hire, and how long for?' he asked.

The man seemed nonplussed.

'Eh?' he said, eyeing Peder in confusion. 'Whaddya mean, which car? She didn't want a car.'

'Didn't she?' said Peder, looking foolish. 'What did she want, then?'

'She wanted a driving licence. But that was before I'd

started that business, so I told her to come back at the beginning of July. But she never turned up again.'

Peder's brain was working overtime.

'She wanted a driving licence?' he echoed.

'Yep,' said the car hirer, slamming his desk diary shut.

'Did she give her name?' Peder asked, though he already
knew the answer.

'No, why should she? I couldn't put her down for lessons.
I hadn't got the paperwork sorted by then.'

Peder sighed.

'Do you remember anything else about her visit?'

'No, only what I've already told you,' said the car hirer,
massaging his beard with one hand and his belly with the other.
'She was scared shitless, and she looked washed out. Her hair
must've been dyed, it was so dark it didn't look natural. Almost
black. And someone had been knocking her about.'

Peder pricked up his ears.

'There were bruises on her face,' the man went on, indicating his left cheek. 'Not new ones, more the sort that've been
there a while, know what I mean? Looked quite nasty. Must've
been painful.'

Neither of them said anything. The door behind Peder
opened and a customer came in. The car hirer waved to the
man to wait.

'I'm just going,' said Peder. 'Anything else you can
remember?'

The car hirer gave his beard a vigorous scratch.

'No, only that she talked strangely.'

'Talked strangely?' repeated Peder.

'Mmmm. It was kind of disjointed. I s'pose it was because

she'd been beaten up. Women usually learn to hold their tongues then.'

Once Peder and Fredrika had left HQ, the same feeling descended on Alex that he used to get when his children still lived at home and had gone round to a friend's for the evening. It was so quiet and peaceful.

Peder and Fredrika were not the only ones who worked on the same corridor as Alex, far from it, but he still had a palpable sense of their absence, which he sometimes found a positive blessing.

His wife rang him on his mobile.

'So what about this holiday?' she asked. 'In view of this case you're working on, I mean. The travel agent rang about confirmation and payment.'

'We'll get our holiday, don't worry,' was all Alex said.

'Are you sure?'

'Do I generally lie about things like that?'

He smiled, and knew she was smiling back.

'Will you be late home this evening?'

'Probably.'

'We could have a barbecue,' Lena suggested.

'We could go to South America.'

Alex was surprised to hear himself utter the words. But he didn't take them back, just left them hanging there between them.

'What did you say?' asked Lena at length.

Alex felt his throat go dry.

'I said we should go and visit our son, who lives there, sometime. So he knows we still want to be part of his life.'

Alex's wife took a little while to respond.

'Yes, we certainly should,' she said softly. 'This autumn, perhaps?'

'This autumn, perhaps.'

Love for a child wasn't like anything else, thought Alex when they had rung off. Love for a child was so fundamental, so unnegotiable. Alex sometimes thought it was actually love for the children that had made it possible for him and Lena to be married for nearly thirty years. What else explained the way they'd come through every setback, every spell of dreary, day-to-day boredom?

Admittedly Alex was the boss, but he was aware of the gossip circulating in the corridor. He knew what they said about Peder, that he had a woman in the Södermalm force. Alex had never been unfaithful to his wife, but he could still visualize quite easily how a situation like that could arise.

If you were really, really down. If you were really, really weighed down with a huge burden of problems.

But not when you had young children at home, as Alex knew Peder did. And definitely not with a work colleague and so indiscreetly that other people noticed. That was low and irresponsible.

Alex felt a stab of irritation. Young people were so spoilt these days. He knew he sounded old-fashioned and even a bit reactionary, but he had some genuine objections to young people's way of viewing the world, and what they expected from it. Life was supposed to be one long walk in the park with no obstacles in your way. The world had turned into an enormous playground where anybody could play wherever they fancied. Could Alex have done what his son was doing?

Could he have moved to South America? No, he could not. And that was just as well, because if you had options like that open to you, how could your spirit ever settle? You would be bound to end up like Peder.

Alex was starting to feel guilty about sitting there, thinking. He had no business having opinions on how his colleague lived his life. But still. He was thinking of Peder's wife and children. Why wasn't Peder doing that?

His gloom was dispelled somewhat by a call from Peder. There was at least something driven in that voice, something to tell Alex that Peder liked what he did in his days at work. It was hard to see that as anything but positive.

But this time his young colleague sounded less than happy.

'The only new thing we've found out is that she tried to get a driving licence,' he said morosely. 'Even assuming it's her.'

Alex stopped Peder in his tracks.

'We also know she gets beaten up at regular intervals, which indicates pretty strongly that we've found the right girl. And the right man,' he said firmly, and went on rather more eagerly. 'Just think about it, Peder. The girl who was murdered in Jönköping had had protected identity since she broke up with a man who abused her. When she was on the phone to Ellen, she talked about some kind of campaign, about the man wanting to punish certain women. Just suppose that lunatic's found himself another girl as a partner and assistant. Another girl whose life has gone off the rails – way off – and who for some reason falls for this man. If, and I mean *if*, it's the man who took Lilian that murdered the girl in Jönköping, then we also know he must have had help to get Lilian – dead or alive – to Umeå, since he can hardly have been in two places at once. And that means it would have been very handy if his sidekick could pass her driving test in time.'

Peder was thinking and took a while to respond.

'Shall I go round to all the driving schools I can find in Söder and show them the picture, while I'm here? She might have tried another one when that car hire place couldn't do it.'

'Good idea, as long as we don't overlook the woman who thought she might have fostered the girl.'

'I'll get that sorted, too,' Peder said swiftly. 'Heard anything from Fredrika yet?'

'No,' sighed Alex. 'I think she's on her way to have an extra little chat to Sara. She was going to call before she went on to the airport.'

Alex was about to hang up when Peder said:

'There's one more thing.'

Alex waited.

'Why did he go to Jönköping and murder that girl just then? I mean, he must have had his hands full with Lilian. Why would he draw even more attention to himself?'

Alex nodded to himself.

'I've been thinking about that, too,' he said unsurely. 'There seems to be some plan behind it all. First he holds up the train and Sara in Flemingsberg; then he sends the box of hair and clothes. Maybe the Jönköping murder was part of the ritual, though we can't see it yet?'

'I thought the same,' said Peder, 'but it doesn't fit. It feels more like the Jönköping murder was an emergency measure. He didn't even wipe the floor. He's been so bloody careful everywhere else, and then suddenly he leaves evidence behind him.'

'Well he did that on the train, too,' Alex objected.

'Because he had no choice,' said Peder. 'He couldn't go cleaning the floor in there, and he could hardly get on the train barefoot or in his socks. That would really attract attention. And anyway, he probably felt relatively safe on the train, where there'd be lots of other footprints.'

'So you think he murdered the woman in Jönköping to shut her up?'

'Yes,' Peder replied after a brief pause. 'That seems the only plausible explanation.'

Alex pondered this.

'All right, but how did he know?'

'Know what?'

'How did he know she needed shutting up?'

'Yes, that's the thing,' Peder said uneasily. 'How the hell did he know she'd rung the police? Or can we assume he would have topped her anyway?'

Ellen Lind felt happy, elated even. She thought about the previous evening and night and felt all warm inside.

'Perhaps he loves me,' she murmured.

She was so glad she had been able to see him last night. He had been such a good listener, just when she needed to get all that wretched Lilian stuff off her chest. Even though he had no children of his own, he really seemed to understand how traumatic it was for everyone involved.

Then they had talked about new films they might go and see. Ellen felt a tingle of excitement. They had never been to the cinema together before. Their socializing had always been geographically confined to whatever hotel he happened to be staying at on the evening they met, and the pattern of their dates was always the same: they had a meal, they talked, they made love, they slept.

It would be good for us to do something new, thought Ellen with a roguish smile.

If she was able to get him to a film, then it ought not to be a problem to persuade him to meet her children, too. If he really did love her, he would understand that the kids were part of the package.

Ellen smiled as she took out her mobile. She had just sent a text and was waiting for him to answer. But she had no new messages.

When they parted that morning, Ellen had asked when she would next see him. He had hesitated for a few moments and then said:

'Soon, I hope. We'll have to see when I can make it.'

'When I can make it,' Ellen repeated silently to herself with a wry smile. Why was it always on his damn terms?

The sun had finally made Stockholm quiver a little in the heat, Fredrika Bergman noted, as she hastily parked outside her block of flats. She raced up the stairs, key at the ready, and was inside her flat in what felt like seconds. It would not take long to pack an overnight bag for her Umeå trip.

Her case was on the top shelf of the walk-in wardrobe. Fredrika caught a glimpse of the violin in its case, tucked in behind. She tried not to see it, not to remember. But the usual thing happened. The speed of her thoughts won out over the strength of her will not to remember. The words flew through her head as automatically and painfully as ever.

I could have been somebody else, I could have been somewhere else today.

Fredrika's mother had brought up the subject a while back.

'The doctors never said you couldn't play at all, Fredrika,' she said softly. 'They just said you couldn't play professionally.'

Fredrika shook her head obstinately, tears burning her eyes. If she couldn't play as much as she once had, then she didn't want to play at all.

The message light on the telephone was flashing when she went out into the kitchen. Surprised, she played the message.

'Hello. Karin Mellander here,' said a rather throaty, elderly-sounding female voice. 'I'm ringing from the adoption centre, about your application. I'd appreciate it if you could call me back, whenever it's convenient, on 08 . . .'

Fredrika stood dumbly as the woman recited a number. The figures flew across the room and into Fredrika's head, where they dissolved into thin air.

Shit, thought Fredrika. Shit, shit, shit.

Panic and stress had a way of making Fredrika very rational. This time was no exception.

She went swiftly back to the wardrobe and started packing. Knickers, bra, top. She hesitated over an extra pair of trousers; would she really be away more than one night? And couldn't she wear the same trousers two days running, if it came to it? Her brain was far too busy concentrating on other things to worry about such trivia. She threw in the trousers.

Fredrika tried to concentrate as she packed her sponge bag. For some reason, she couldn't get Spencer out of her mind.

I've got to tell him, she thought. I've really got to tell him.

Her case was ready and the door slammed shut behind her.

Air, she thought. I need some air.

Hot tarmac breathed warmth onto her legs as she stood outside on the pavement.

Shit, what was all this about? If the adoption was so badly thought through that she was reacting like this, maybe she should give up the whole idea.

Fredrika swallowed hard.

One look at the billboards of the kiosk in the next block brought her back to the here and now.

'Who murdered Lilian?' shrieked the billboards.

That's what I ought to focus on, Fredrika thought, gritting her teeth. I ought to focus on Sara Sebastiansson, who's just lost her child.

She wondered what was worse. To have a child, and then lose it. Or never to have a child at all.

For some reason, Fredrika had not been expecting Sara herself to open the door, and was surprised to find herself standing face to face with her. Fredrika had not seen Sara since Lilian's body had been found. She knew she ought to say something. She opened her mouth but then closed it again. She had no idea what she was expected to say.

I'm a monster, she thought. There's no bloody way I should be allowed to have children.

She took a breath. Again she tried to speak.

'I'm truly sorry.'

Sara gave a stiff nod.

Her red hair flamed around her head. She must be exhausted.

Fredrika took a few hesitant steps into the flat. The light hall began to look a little familiar, and the living room off to the left. That was where she had interviewed Sara's new boyfriend that first evening.

How long ago it felt.

Sara's parents filed in behind her. Like a fighting unit, ready to attack. Fredrika said hello and shook their hands. Yes, that's right, they had met before. When the box of hair . . . yes, then.

Hands pointed, indicating where Fredrika was to go. She was to sit in the living room. The settee felt hard. Sara sat in a big armchair, her mother perched on one of its armrests.

Her father took a seat on the settee, a little too close to Fredrika.

Fredrika would really have preferred not to have Sara's parents in attendance. It was wrong, and broke all the rules where the art of interrogation was concerned. She felt instinctively that there were things that could not be said in their presence. But both Sara and her parents were demonstrating very clearly that either Fredrika spoke to all of them together, or to no one.

A big, old grandfather clock dominated one corner of the room. Fredrika tried to recall whether she had noticed it there before. It was two o'clock.

I've been efficient, thought Fredrika. I've been to Uppsala and HQ and home to pack.

Sara's father cleared his throat to remind Fredrika she was not making very good use of her time.

Fredrika turned to a new page of her notebook.

'Well,' she began cautiously, 'I've got a few more questions about your time in Umeå.'

When Sara looked blank, she clarified:

'When you were on the writing course.'

Sara nodded slowly. She tugged at the sleeves of her top. She still did not want the bruises to be seen. For some reason, this brought a lump to Fredrika's throat. She swallowed several times and pretended to read through her notes.

'I interviewed Maria Blomgren this morning,' she said eventually, raising her eyes to look at Sara again.

Sara did not react in any way.

'She asked to be remembered to you.'

Sara went on staring at Fredrika.

Maybe she's on tranquillizers, thought Fredrika. She looks drugged up to the eyeballs.

'Sara and Maria haven't been in touch for years,' Sara's father said brusquely. 'We told your boss that, in Umeå.'

'I know,' said Fredrika quickly. 'But a few things came up in my chat with Maria that mean I need to ask a few more questions.'

She tried valiantly to catch Sara's dulled eye.

'You were going out with a boy just before you went up there,' she said.

Sara nodded.

'What happened when you broke up?'

Sara shifted in her seat.

'Nothing much happened,' she said slowly. 'Nothing at all, really. He sulked and made things awkward for a while, but he let me go once he realized we weren't compatible.'

'Was he ever back in touch later? After the summer maybe, or did he even turn up in Umeå?'

'No, never.'

Fredrika paused for thought.

'You stayed on in Umeå longer than Maria,' she began. 'Why was that?'

'I got a summer job there,' Sara said listlessly. 'It was too good an offer to refuse. But Maria was cross. And jealous.'

'Maria says you knew before you went to Umeå that you weren't coming home to Gothenburg when the course was over, and that you fixed up the summer job before you went.'

'Then she's lying.'

Sara's answer came so rapidly and vehemently that Fredrika almost lost her thread.

'She's lying?'

'Yes.'

'Why would she lie about something like that that happened so long ago?' Fredrika asked warily.

'Because she was jealous of me getting that chance when she didn't,' Sara said fiercely. 'She never got over it. She even used it as an excuse for backing out of our plan to share a flat in Uppsala.'

Sara seemed to shrink in the armchair.

'Or maybe she misunderstood the whole thing,' she said wearily.

'Maria told me she had a summer job waiting for her back home in Gothenburg,' said Fredrika. 'Hadn't you?'

Sara appeared not to understand.

'I mean, hadn't you got anything planned for the rest of the summer? The course in Umeå was only going to last a fortnight, after all.'

Sara's eyes had a shifty look.

'Once I got the chance to work there, I couldn't just throw it away,' she said quietly. 'That had to take priority.'

Sara's mother shifted uneasily on the arm of the chair.

'But it's just come back to me that I ran into Örjan who ran that guest house where you used to work in the summer holidays, and he said you'd turned down the job he offered you that year, because you were going to be out of town all summer.'

Sara's face darkened.

'I can't help what that old man went round saying,' she hissed.

'No, of course not,' Sara's father put in. 'And our

memories let us down at times like this. We all know that, don't we?'

He knows, thought Fredrika. He knows Sara's trying to hide something, but he doesn't know what it is. He knows it's something worth hiding, and that's why he's helping her out.

'All right,' said Fredrika, trying to find a more comfortable position on the settee. 'What happened when you got there, then? How come you were the one to be offered this job?'

'They needed an assistant for the writing tutor,' Sara said quietly. 'And my creative writing was so good, they thought, so they made me the offer.'

'Sara's always been good at writing,' her father added.

'I don't doubt that,' Fredrika said honestly. 'But I imagine it must have felt quite competitive in the writing group. We all know what it's like at that age . . .'

'No one else seemed put out,' Sara said, tugging at some strands of her hair. 'They said when we arrived that they were looking for an extra staff member for the rest of the summer, and that anyone interested could let them know.'

'And then they chose you?'

'And then they chose me.'

It went quiet. The hand of the grandfather clock took another peck forward. Outside, the sun went behind a cloud.

'She's lying,' Fredrika said indignantly into the phone when she rang Alex to report on her way out to the airport.

Alex listened to her story and then said:

'I'm not saying there's nothing there worth getting to the bottom of, Fredrika. But Sara's very sensitive at the moment, and her parents are watching over her like hawks. See what you get from the Umeå trip and then we'll decide how to take this forward.'

'I can't stop thinking about that boyfriend she had,' Fredrika went on. 'According to Maria Blomgren, he went a bit crazy when Sara chucked him.'

'He must have been more than a bit crazy if he was angry for fifteen years and then got even by killing Sara's little girl,' sighed Alex.

'I've got his ID,' said Fredrika. 'I rang and asked Ellen to run a records check, and he seems to have had a finger in various pies since he left school.'

'Like what?' Alex enquired dubiously.

'He was found guilty of beating up his ex's new boyfriend,' answered Fredrika. 'And receiving stolen goods. And car theft.'

'Certainly sounds like the criminal type, but not exactly capable of carrying out something as well planned as Lilian's abduction,' Alex objected.

'But still,' Fredrika persisted.

Alex sighed.

'Where does this crook live nowadays, then?'

'He seems to move about a lot, but at the moment he lives in Norrköping. He moved away from Gothenburg after he finished his military service.'

Alex sighed again.

'Jönköping, Norrköping, Umeå,' he said crossly. 'This investigation's getting totally farcical. It's far too spread out.'

'But at least it's moving!' Fredrika persevered.

'Okay,' said Alex. 'I'll see how Peder's fixed. He's on his way to Nyköping at the moment to interview the woman who claims the Flemingsberg woman was her foster child.'

'Nyköping!' exclaimed Fredrika. 'Well, that's on the way.'
Alex took a deep breath.

'You're right,' he said. 'I'll ring Peder straight away. Has
Ellen got the crook's details?'

'Yes,' Fredrika confirmed.

'Fine. Let me know when you've landed,' said Alex.

Then he just sat there with the receiver in his hand. For the
first time since Fredrika Bergman had joined his team, she
was displaying a bit of enthusiasm for her job. Until now
she'd just sat there looking self-conscious, full of objections.
Alex thought she even sounded as if she was enjoying what
she was doing.

It went against the grain to admit it, but the fact was,
Fredrika had been the first of them to see the lead that had got
the investigation to where it was now. Not that the others
couldn't have found it without her, but she had actually been
faster. She was quick to identify connections in the vast array
of information that Alex generally needed longer to digest.
On the other hand – if Gabriel Sebastiansson *had* been the
culprit, Fredrika would have been the last person in the group
to pick it up. And that was hardly encouraging.

Alex peered at a diagram he had made of what they knew,
and felt his spirits sink.

Regardless of how they had got to this point in their
enquiries:

What did they really know for certain?

Alex felt they could be virtually sure that there were two
perpetrators, not just one. The woman with the dog in
Flemingsberg, and the man with the Ecco shoes. He looked at
Ellen's note of the call from the woman in Jönköping. Nora.

If it was the same woman. Alex gave a sigh of frustration. What the hell, he'd work on the assumption that it was.

Ellen had written that the woman seemed confused. She was scared, and she rang in a hurry, Alex interpreted.

The woman had said she thought the perpetrator was someone with whom she had been in a relationship. Someone who often hit her. Alex's thoughts went automatically to what Peder had said after his visit to the car hire firm. The Flemingsberg woman had been knocked about, too. Ellen had also jotted down a few little quotes. The woman had said the man was waging some kind of battle and wanted the woman to be part of it. 'The women weren't to be allowed to keep their children, because they didn't deserve to.' Hmm. Alex read on. 'The women didn't deserve their children, because if you don't like all children, you shouldn't be allowed to have any at all.'

No beating about the bush there, Alex thought grimly.

He did not understand what he was reading. What did it mean: 'if you don't like all children'? It goes without saying that people don't like all children equally. And above all, that there are no children you like better than your own, Alex reasoned.

He read Ellen's note again. The women had to be punished, the women couldn't be allowed to keep . . . *The women*? His stomach knotted.

'You're wrong, Fredrika,' he mumbled to himself.

The man's fury was not directed only at Sara Sebastiansson. Not if what the woman in Jönköping said was true. The man's fury was directed at *a number of* women. Women who didn't like all children equally. And if the woman in Jönköping was telling the truth, the man had tried to put his plan into action earlier, but not carried it through.

What's this madness, thought Alex. And who are the other women?

It had taken Magdalena Gregersdotter several years to start feeling at home in Stockholm. So she and her husband had put off having a family until she felt a bit more settled in her new hometown.

'I don't want any children until I feel as if I've got a social network of my own to fall back on,' Magdalena said firmly.

Torbjörn, her husband, went along with it of course. For one thing, he always did, and for another, he knew better than to insist on starting a family when the prospective mother didn't feel ready for it.

But things did not really go the way they had planned. When they eventually did launch their baby project, it turned out they could not have any children. They tried on their own for a whole year – *oh how they hated that word 'tried'* – and then spent the following year having tests. Then another year of 'trying'. They endured eleven rounds of IVF treatment in all. Then Magdalena suffered an ectopic pregnancy.

'To hell with it,' she wept in her hospital bed. 'I can't take any more of this.'

Nor could Torbjörn, so they took some unpaid leave and went round the world for six months. Then they decided to adopt.

'But then it won't really be yours,' Torbjörn's mother said.

It was the only time in her life Magdalena considered hitting another person.

'Of course she'll be ours,' Magdalena hissed emphatically.

And of course, she was. Torbjörn and Magdalena travelled to Bolivia, returning one March day with Natalie, and not a single day had passed since without Magdalena waking with a smile on her lips. It sounded ridiculous when she said it out loud, but it was completely true, all the same. It was also true that she was now no longer dreading her imminent fortieth birthday, not even a bit.

'You're beautiful,' Torbjörn had whispered into her ear that morning.

'Of course I am. I'm young, you know,' she had responded.

Anyone with young children must be young, too, the way Magdalena saw it. And little Natalie still hadn't turned one, so by that token, Magdalena must be especially young.

In retrospect, she could not remember why she had suddenly felt the urge to look at Natalie. Though Natalie was growing fast, she still slept outside in her pram every day. First Magdalena would take her out for a walk in the pram to get her off to sleep, and then she would park it in the little patch of garden that went with the ground-floor flat. The garden was shielded from view by a tallish hedge that Torbjörn had fortified still further with a little fence.

So Magdalena felt comfortable leaving Natalie asleep in her pram. She always left the garden door open, and she always had a baby monitor in the pram. Through it, she could hear if even a tiny bird hopped near the pram, and the faintest sound that should not have been there. Maybe it was such a sound that suddenly alerted her attention and caused her to worry. Maybe it was such a sound that made her cover the distance between the kitchen and the garden so quickly.

She saw the pram through the glass door as she approached and slowed her steps.

A little gust of wind crept in at the open door and the long, linen curtains stirred. A flower petal dropped from a potted plant and floated gently to the floor. Later, it was these two details she would remember most vividly, and never forget.

Magdalena bent over the pram. It was empty. As if in a trance, she straightened up and ran her eyes along the hedge and beyond. There was nobody to be seen.

Where was Natalie?

Peder Rydh trekked round Söder from one driving school to the next. He found two other people who thought they could identify the woman in the picture, but nobody could say for sure. Peder, however, felt pretty confident they had all encountered the same woman, since their accounts were identical. For one thing, she had seemed nervous. For another, she had bruises on her face and arms. And for a third, she wanted to know the quickest possible way to get a driving licence. Both driving school proprietors had suggested an intensive course, but when she realized it was a residential course, several days in length and in another town, she had immediately lost interest. She couldn't get the time off work, she said. And left.

What the hell did she need a driving licence for? Peder thought, feeling frustrated. So she could take the body to Umeå while her sick boyfriend went off to Jönköping to snuff out an old flame?

He glanced at his watch as he got into the car to head for Nyköping for his appointment with the woman who thought she had fostered the Flemingsberg girl. He'd have to make sure he didn't run too late.

Ylva had said she was taking the twins to the swimming beach at Smedsudde on Kungsholmen. He had felt like saying he didn't think it was a very good idea. She always found it too much when she was on her own with the boys. She hadn't really thought through what taking them to the beach would involve. But on the other hand, Ylva could hardly be accused of being the irresponsible one in the family.

Peder hardly dared look at his mobile. If he saw he had a missed call from Ylva or Pia, he would drive off the road. He started wondering if he might be ill. Hadn't he read an interesting article about men with extra-strong sexual urges? It seemed unlikely that everybody felt as driven by them as he did. The only problem was, it hadn't been like that before the twins were born. What had gone and happened to his old life? And what sort of person had he turned into?

Ylva and Peder had tried for a baby for nearly a year before it finally 'worked'. They had been so happy. Terrified, but happy.

'Holy shit,' Peder said when Ylva did the pregnancy test. 'There's someone growing in here.'

Then he put a warm hand on her bare belly and tried imagining what life must be like in there. They had made love at every possible opportunity until the results of that bloody ultrasound scan. There certainly hadn't been anything wrong with Ylva's urges. She couldn't get enough of him. One time, she had even rung to summon him home in his lunch hour.

'Must be the hormones,' she giggled as they got dressed again afterwards.

The notion of Ylva calling him home over lunch for a good screw seemed so distant that a dry laugh burst out of him. It wasn't even about the sex, really. It was about closeness, and feeling needed. And being allowed to have needs yourself. The times she did ring him at work had to do with strange, other needs. Difficult needs that were impossible to meet if you had a job to hold down. Peder's needs had ceased to exist. One night he got home from work after he and some other officers found two pensioners who had been robbed and murdered. Shot in the face. He tried to sleep close to Ylva that night. She had wriggled and squirmed.

'Do you have to lie so close, Peder? I can't sleep with you breathing in my face.'

He retreated. So Ylva could sleep. Though he shut his eyes as tight as he could, sleep did not come to him. Either that night or the next.

Peder had cried so few times in his adult life that he thought he could remember them all. He cried when his grandfather died. He cried when the twins were born. And he cried two weeks after they found the pensioners who had been shot. Like a child he cried, in his mother's presence.

'It just goes on and on,' he whispered, referring to his problems with Ylva. 'It just goes on and on.'

'Things will change,' his mother replied. 'Things will change, Peder. Misery has its natural limits. There comes a point when you know for certain that things can't get worse, only better.'

This from a woman who had once believed she would bring up two healthy boys into adult manhood, and had then had to accept that one of them would never be anything other than an overgrown child.

Peder somehow felt he had now passed beyond that misery limit his mother had talked about. Above all by taking up with Pia again. Something was on its way towards ending. Peder's whole body could sense it. His marriage. It genuinely hadn't been his intention, and he certainly wasn't following any conviction that this was the way to extract himself from his hell. But there was a risk it would happen.

At least if he went on seeing Pia.

The road to Nyköping felt much shorter than he had expected. It didn't take long to get there at all. Had he already missed the turning off, in fact?

He had just found the right address and parked outside when his mobile rang. He answered as he climbed out of the car. It was still quite hot, though the sun had once again stubbornly taken cover behind heavy cloud. Peder surveyed the houses around him. Middle class. No brand new cars, but no dented old ones, either. No new bikes, but decent, used ones. Some clean, wholesome looking children were playing a little way along the road. The safety and security many a Swede hankered after.

Alex's voice put an end to his impromptu analysis of the neighbourhood.

'Are you there yet?' he asked.

'Yes,' said Peder. 'Just got out of the car. What's up?'

'Nothing. It was just . . . if you were still on the road. I had a thought. But we can take it later.'

Peder saw out of the corner of his eye that the door of the house he was heading for had opened.

'Sure it can keep?' he asked.

'Yes, I'm sure,' Alex replied. 'I'll carry on refining my little theory, and call you later. Though there was one other thing, too.'

Peder guffawed. 'A theory?' he said. 'You ought to be ringing Fredrika, not me.'

'I will, naturally. But as I said, there was another thing. Sara Sebastiansson's got an ex in Norrköping. A small-time crook she was with just before she went on that writing course in Umeå. Think you could have a quick word with him before you come back to Stockholm?'

'In Norrköping?' Peder said dubiously.

'Yes,' Alex said cautiously, 'it's on your way . . .'

'Okay,' Peder said. 'Okay. As long as you can fill me in on the background.'

Alex sounded relieved.

'I'll get Fredrika to give you a ring later,' he promised. 'Best of luck!'

'Thanks,' said Peder, and ended the call.

He smiled at the lady standing on the front steps of the house and went towards her.

Birgitta Franke served homemade cinnamon buns and coffee. Peder couldn't remember when he'd last been offered such delicious looking buns. He took two.

Birgitta Franke seemed a kindly but no-nonsense sort of woman. Her voice was gruff, but the expression in her eyes was warm. She had grey hair, but a fairly young-looking face. She was, in short, a woman who had learned from what life had thrown at her, Peder surmised.

Peder asked discreetly if he could check her ID card, and saw then that she had just passed her 55th birthday. He wished her a belated happy birthday and praised her baking again. She thanked him and smiled. Her smile made little wrinkles appear round her eyes. They suited her.

'You rang the police hotline about an identikit picture we'd issued,' he put in at last, to get away from the small talk about buns and kitchen furnishings.

'Yes,' said Birgitta. 'I did. And what I'd like to know first of all is why she's wanted.'

Peder drank some more of his coffee, looked at Birgitta's curtains and thought of his grandmother for the first time in years.

'She's not wanted as such, nor formally under suspicion. It's just that we'd like to have a talk to her, because we think she has information that has a crucial bearing on this case. I'm afraid I can't go into what sort of information it is.'

Birgitta nodded thoughtfully.

For some reason, Peder's mind went to Gabriel Sebastiansson's mother. That old hag had plenty to learn from Birgitta when it came to how to communicate with other people.

Birgitta leapt up from the kitchen table and went out into the hall. Peder heard her open a drawer. She came back carrying a large photograph album, which she put down in front of Peder, and then turned over a few pages.

'Here,' she said, indicating the photographs. 'This is where it starts.'

Peder stared at the pictures, which showed a younger version of Birgitta, a man of the same age who Peder could not identify, and a girl who with a little stretch of the imagination could be said to resemble the Flemingsberg woman. There was a boy in two of the shots, as well.

'Monika came to us when she was thirteen,' Birgitta began her story. 'It was rather different being a foster parent in those days. There weren't as many children in need of a new home as there are nowadays, and the general view was that a bit of love and tolerance could solve most problems.'

Birgitta gave a slight sigh and pulled her coffee cup towards her.

'But it wasn't like that with Monika,' she sighed. 'Monika was what my husband called damaged, not entirely normal. To look at these pictures, you might think she was almost like anyone else. A blonde girl with lovely eyes and delicate features. But inside, she didn't function. Wrongly programmed, you might say these days, if you worked with computers.'

'How do you mean?' asked Peder, leafing through the album.

More pictures of Monika and her foster parents. Monika was not smiling in a single one. But Birgitta was right. She had nice eyes and fine facial features.

'Her background was so dreadful that looking back, we hardly understood how we could have taken her on in the first place,' said Birgitta, resting her head in her hands. 'Though I can honestly say we weren't given the full picture until after disaster struck. And by then it was too late. More coffee?' she said.

Peder looked up from the album.

'Yes please,' he said automatically. 'Where's your husband, by the way?'

'He's at work,' answered Birgitta. 'But he'll be back in an hour or two if you'd like to stay and eat with us this evening.'

Peder had to smile.

'That's kind of you, but I'm afraid I won't have time.'

Birgitta smiled back.

'What a pity,' she said, 'because you seem such a nice lad.'

She reached for the coffee jug and poured some for them both.

'Where was I?' she said, and supplied the answer herself. 'Oh yes, the girl's background.'

She got up and went out to the hall again. She came back with a file.

'This is where my husband and I kept all the information we were given about our foster children,' she said proudly, putting the file in front of Peder. 'You see, we couldn't have any children ourselves, so we decided to foster instead.'

She had a rather satisfied expression as she flicked through the file for Peder.

'Here,' she said, 'this is what social services sent us before she came. The rest was classified, so I've no copies of that.'

Peder pushed the photograph album to one side and read the papers from the social service department.

13-year-old girl, Monika Sander, from a very unsettled background, requires immediate placement with a loving family within a stable, structured framework. The child's mother lost custody when Monika was three, and has had very limited contact with her since.

Monika was taken into care as a result of her mother's alcohol and drug addiction problems. The mother has had a succession of male sexual partners since the girl's birth, and is probably a prostitute. The father disappeared off the scene at a very early stage when he was killed in a car crash. The mother's problems began after the father's accident.

The girl was in her first foster home for three years. The foster parents then separated and the girl could not be kept on. She went through a succession of short-stay fostering arrangements until she was eight, and then lived in a children's home for a year. She was then placed in a foster home that was expected to offer her a long-term solution.

The girl's schooling has been disrupted from a very early stage by her difficult circumstances. There were suspicions that she had been abused, but investigations could not substantiate this. Monika has found it difficult to socialize with other children. From her third school year, she has been receiving individual remedial tuition, and has been placed in a special class with only six pupils. This has worked relatively well, though it is still not entirely satisfactory.

Peder read two more pages detailing how the girl's schooling had fallen by the wayside. By the time she came to live with the Frankes, she had already been arrested once, on suspicion of shoplifting and theft.

His thoughts flew at once to the woman in Jönköping. Hadn't she, too, grown up in a succession of foster homes?

'I see,' he said when he had finished reading. 'And you mean there was other information you and your husband should have been given, apart from all this?'

Birgitta nodded and took a few sips of coffee.

'We meant so well,' she said, looking Peder in the eye. 'We thought we could be the support the girl needed in life. And God knows we tried. But it was all futile.'

'Did you have other foster children here at the same time?' Peder asked, thinking of the boy in some of the photographs.

'No,' said Birgitta. 'If it's the young man in the photos

you're thinking of, that's my nephew. He was the same age as Monika, so we thought they might enjoy each other's company. And they were due to go to the same school.'

Birgitta gave a faint smile.

'It didn't work, of course. My nephew was very tidy and organized even at that age. He couldn't stand her, said she was nuts, disturbed.'

'Because she stole stuff?'

'Because she was frightened of odd things,' said Birgitta. 'She found any kind of social occasion difficult and made herself scarce. She could be angry and all over you one minute and collapse into a tearful little heap the next. She had violent nightmares about her past; she'd wake up in the middle of the night, yelling. Drenched with sweat. But she never told us what she'd been dreaming, we could only imagine.'

Peder felt weary. That was the obvious drawback to police work: you hardly ever got to talk to, or about, easy-going, unproblematic people.

'How long was she with you?' he asked.

'Two years,' Birgitta told him. 'Then we'd had enough. She gave up going to school almost entirely; she would disappear for long periods and then turn up and not tell us where she'd been. And then there were her various illegal activities: stealing, smoking hash.'

'Boyfriends?' Peder asked.

'I never met any, but of course she had boyfriends.'

Peder frowned.

'And what was it you wish they'd told you before you took her on?'

Birgitta crumpled.

'That she was originally adopted,' she said quietly.

'Sorry?'

'That the woman who was identified as her mother in the social services report you just read wasn't Monika's biological mother. Monika was adopted.'

'But how on earth could a woman like that get approval to adopt?' Peder asked in bewilderment.

'Because what the report says is true: the adoptive mother's problems only started when her husband died. Or quite possibly they started much earlier, but until then she was living a perfectly normal life with a home, a job, a car. Then things went rapidly downhill. The mother had apparently moved in some pretty socially unacceptable circles when she was younger, and she drifted back to them when she was left alone with the girl and lost her job.'

'Where did Monika come from originally?' asked Peder.

'Somewhere in the Baltic states,' replied Birgitta, and then shook her head. 'I don't quite remember which country, or the exact circumstances of the adoption.'

Peder's brain was working furiously to process all this new information.

'Who told you? That she was adopted?'

'One of the case workers,' Birgitta sighed. 'But I never saw it in black and white. The social service department really mismanaged the whole Monika case. They should have intervened much sooner in her life. You could say she was doubly let down: first by her biological mother and then by her adoptive one.'

Birgitta hesitated.

'And then maybe by another foster family, too,' she said, 'but that isn't clear.'

Peder read the social services report again. Then he flicked randomly through the album. The photographs showed the little family in various settings. At Christmas and Easter. On holidays and outings.

'We tried,' said Birgitta Franke, her voice faltering. 'We tried, but we just couldn't.'

'Do you know what happened to her afterwards?' asked Peder. 'After she left you?'

'She went into some kind of residential treatment centre for six months, but she must have run away, oh, ten times or more. Once she even came back here. Then they tried to place her with another family, but that didn't work out, either. And then all of a sudden she turned eighteen and wasn't a minor any longer, and since then I haven't heard a thing about her. Until I saw the picture in the paper, that is.'

Peder gently closed the album in front of him.

'But how did you recognize her?' he asked. 'I mean, I can see some similarities between the drawing and the girl in your photos, but . . .'

He shook his head.

'How do you know it's the same girl?'

Birgitta's eyes shone.

'The necklace,' she said with a smile. 'She's still wearing the necklace we gave her at her confirmation, just before she moved out.'

Peder grabbed up the identikit picture of the woman at the station. He had not registered the fact before, but sure enough she had a necklace on. It was a silver lion on a chunky silver chain.

Birgitta opened the album again, and flicked through to the middle.

'See?' she asked, pointing.

Peder did see. It was the same necklace. The necklace in conjunction with the photo was enough to convince him. It must be the same girl.

'She was obsessed with star signs,' Birgitta told him. 'That was why we gave it to her. At first she didn't want to get confirmed at all, but we tempted her with a course at a lovely centre out in the archipelago, and said we'd give her a nice present, too. We thought that kind of social group might be good for her. But she made trouble, of course. She stole things from the others, it emerged later.'

Birgitta began clearing the table.

'That was when we decided we'd had enough, really,' she said. 'If you steal when you're on a confirmation course, then there can't be much decency in you. But we let her keep the necklace, since she liked it so much.'

Peder started noting down Monika's details from the social services report. Monika Sander. Then he had a better idea.

'Could I take this with me and make a copy?' he asked, waving the document at Birgitta.

'Yes, of course,' she said. 'You can post it back to me. I like to keep tabs on which foster children I've had.'

Peder nodded.

He took the papers and got up slowly from the table.

'And if anything else occurs to you, do give me a ring,' he said in a friendly tone, putting his card on the table.

'I promise I will,' said Birgitta.

She added, 'I must say, we never thought she would turn up in such ghastly circumstances.'

Peder stopped.

'However could she have got drawn into such a web of horrible events?'

'That's what we're wondering,' said Peder. 'That's just what we're wondering.'

Fredrika Bergman reached Umeå late in the afternoon. By the time the plane landed, her whole body was aching with fatigue. She turned on her mobile to find she had two new messages. It would be too late now, unfortunately, to interview Nora's grandmother and Sara's course tutor before the next day. She looked at her watch: it was almost half past five. Her flight had been delayed. She shrugged. There wasn't really any rush. As long as she got the interviews done tomorrow, everything would be fine.

Fredrika had not had a chance to ring Peder with the background story on Sara's ex as she had promised. She hoped he had somehow managed to get the information he needed before the interview.

Though she was tired, Fredrika felt strangely buoyed up. The investigation had finally broadened out, and in some peculiar way, she felt it was now on the right track. She wondered briefly where their first main suspect Gabriel could now be. It seemed likely his mother would have helped him leave the country. Fredrika gave a shiver at the thought of Teodora Sebastiansson's house. There was something creepy about the whole property.

The evening sun was caressing the tarmac as Fredrika left the terminal building. While she waited for Alex to answer his phone, she allowed herself to stand with her eyes closed, basking a little in the sunshine. A warm breeze stirred the air.

Spring weather, thought Fredrika. This isn't summer weather, there's spring in the air.

Neither Alex nor Peder were answering their phones, so Fredrika resolutely picked up her case and walked towards the nearest taxi. She had booked a room in the plush old Town Hotel. Maybe she could treat herself to a glass of wine on the verandah while she drew up the outline of the next morning's work. Maybe while she was there she could have a proper think about the phone message from the adoption centre, too?

Fredrika almost panicked when the message came into her mind. Was she going to be called on to a decision at last? Was it time to start planning for life as a single mother? She suddenly found herself sobbing.

She tried to take a few deep breaths. She did not know why the call had upset her so much. There was no reason to be reacting like this. It was ludicrous for everything to come to a head this very minute, at a kerbside outside the terminal building at Umeå Airport. She looked about her in confusion. Had she ever been here before? She didn't think so. She could not recall it if she had.

Fredrika's phone rang as she got to the taxi. She and the driver slung her bags into the boot and she climbed into the back seat to take the call.

'Another child's been taken, a baby girl,' Alex said, the strain audible in his voice.

Fredrika's whole attention was suddenly focused. There wasn't enough air in the back seat of the taxi. She pressed the button and the glass slid down.

The driver protested from in front.

'You can't just open the window like that!' he barked. 'What about my air conditioning?'

Fredrika hushed him with an urgent gesture.

'How do we know it's got anything to do with our case?' she asked Alex.

'About an hour after the baby went missing, the police found a parcel on the edge of the flowerbed near the front door of the block, and it had the baby's clothes and nappy in it. And he'd chopped off a tiny tuft of hair that her mother had put a hairslide in.'

Fredrika did not know what to say.

'What in God's name . . . ,' she began, and was taken aback by the force of her own language. 'What do we do now?'

'We work round the clock until we find whoever did this,' Alex answered. 'Peder should be in Norrköping to talk to Sara Sebastionsson's ex just about now, and then he's coming straight back to Stockholm. I'm on my way to the car to go and see the missing baby's mother.'

Fredrika swallowed hard, several times.

'Check if she's got any links with Umeå,' she said in a weak voice.

'I most certainly will,' said Alex.

Fredrika could tell from the sounds at the other end that Alex had reached his car.

'It all seems to be happening faster this time, if it's the same man,' she said slowly.

She heard Alex pause.

'What do you mean?' he asked.

'Sara didn't receive her parcel of hair until the day after her daughter went missing. But you're telling me these clothes and hair were delivered to the parents almost as soon as the baby had gone.'

Alex said nothing for a moment.

'Shit, you're right,' he whispered.

Fredrika shut her eyes, the phone clamped to her ear. Why was the perpetrator suddenly in such a hurry? And why take another child so soon after the first? And . . . if the clothes and hair had already been given back to the parents, did that mean the baby was already dead?

What's driving him, Fredrika thought to herself. What on earth is driving him?

Peder Rydh was heading back to Stockholm at the speed of light. Alex had rung with news of the second child's disappearance just as he got to Norrköping. They agreed that the interview with Sara Sebastiansson's ex-boyfriend should still go ahead. There was a microscopic chance, in spite of everything, that he was behind Lilian's abduction, and had now taken another child to make it look as though Lilian had fallen victim to a serial killer rather than her mother's former boyfriend.

But the instant Peder saw Sara's ex, his hopes were dashed. In short, there wasn't a cat in hell's chance that the man Peder had before him in Norrköping could have kidnapped, scalped and murdered a little child. He had a few offences to his name, to be sure, and he admitted he had felt bitter about Sara for a surprisingly long time after they broke up, but it was a huge step from there to the murder of Sara's child fifteen years later.

Peder gave a weary sigh. This was another day that hadn't

turned out the way he'd envisaged. But he was very glad indeed that it was Fredrika and not him who had been sent to Umeå. For one thing he felt too shattered for the journey, and for another it was good to have Fredrika out of the way now things were hotting up with another missing child.

Peder was not at all happy about the way the case was developing. It seemed to be moving beyond the stretch of his imagination. As long as they were working on the hypothesis that it was Lilian's own father who had first taken and then murdered her, Peder had known what he was doing. The guilty party in cases like this was nearly always someone close to the victim. Nearly always. This was an indisputable fact that should inform every normal policeman's thinking. There had been no other circumstances to take into consideration. There were no other children missing; there was no one else Sara was in conflict with.

Fredrika had been more flexible in her thinking virtually from the word go. She had identified Sara, rather than Gabriel, as the parent who must be linked to the murderer, and had tried to get them to consider alternatives to Gabriel as Lilian's kidnapper. The fact that nobody had listened to her had unfortunately cost the investigation valuable time. Peder knew this to be the case, but he also knew he would never admit it out loud. Least of all to Fredrika.

But Peder was still doubtful whether they had ever had any reasonable chance of saving Lilian from her death. He didn't think so. Even Sara Sebastiansson had not thought there could be anyone in the world who hated her so much that they would murder her daughter to punish her. So how could the detectives possibly understand the course of events?

And now another child was missing. Peder felt his guts churn. A baby. What normal person could possibly bring himself to hurt a baby? Naturally there was a simple answer to Peder's question: anyone who you could imagine killing a baby or a child was not normal.

It distressed Peder to have to think it, but it did not seem likely that the investigation team would be able to find or save this child, either.

Peder slammed his fist down on the steering wheel.

What the hell was he thinking? It went without saying that they would do their utmost to find the child. But he felt instantly deflated again. Unfortunately it also went painfully without saying that if the murderer intended to kill child number two within fewer than twenty-four hours, too, then the team was not going to find it in time.

We'll find it when he wants us to, Peder thought dejectedly. We'll find it where he puts it, when he wants to show it to us.

The police could be heroes, but they could also be helpless. Peder wondered what he'd actually achieved that day. He thought he had the identity of the woman who had helped the man with the Ecco shoes. But what did that connect her to, in fact? She had behaved oddly with a dog at Flemingsberg station. Maybe to delay Sara Sebastiansson. She had tried to get a driving licence. Maybe to drive Lilian's body to Umeå. There were too many maybes for comfort.

Peder swallowed. If she was who they thought she was, and had played the role in all this that they suspected she had, then it was absolutely vital to the investigation to find her and talk to her.

Alex had decided straight away to release Monika Sander's

name and picture to the press and issue an appeal for her to get in touch. Or anybody who knew who she was. And *where* she was. They would also ask Sara if she recognized the name or picture; there was always a chance that she might be able to confirm it was the same woman. They would ask the parents of the missing baby, too.

But both Alex and Peder were convinced that Monika Sander could hardly have been behind the baby's disappearance. If the picture her foster mother had painted of her was not misleading, the plan was too precise and sophisticated for Monika to have conceived it and made everything happen at the right time. Yet she was still clearly a key figure in the story.

Peder shook his head. There was something he should have thought of, something he ought to be remembering.

The dryness in his throat persisted. He was thirsty but there was no time to stop to buy something to drink. Priority number one had to be to get back to Stockholm and get underway with the new investigation, to see if they could link it into the existing one.

There must be a connection. It couldn't be a coincidence that the baby's clothes and hair had been put in a box and left in the garden, or wherever it was. The details of Lilian's abduction were still not known to the press; the team had not released them.

Peder had only one thought in his head as he neared Stockholm and saw the silhouette of the Globe Arena away to the east. If only they could find Monika Sander. And quickly.

The nurses in Ward Four of the Karolinska University Hospital in Solna, just outside Stockholm, had been instructed to be very gentle with the patient lying alone in Room Three. The young woman patient had been brought to A&E by ambulance during the night. Her neighbour had been woken by strange noises in the stairwell and had looked through the spyhole in his front door to see if it was burglars making the most of everyone being away for the summer. What he actually saw was the girl in the next-door flat lying on the landing floor, badly beaten up, with her feet still inside the flat and her body resting on the hard, marble floor.

He immediately rang for an ambulance and then sat on the landing to keep watch over the little slip of a girl, who was barely conscious as the ambulance crew lifted her onto the stretcher and carried her down the stairs.

The neighbour was asked what the girl was called.

'Jelena, or something like that,' he told them. 'But the place isn't hers. The actual owner hasn't lived here for several years. The girl's just the latest of all his sub-lets. There's a man who stays here sometimes as well, but I don't know his name.'

There was no name on the door of the flat. The injured woman mumbled something scarcely coherent when a paramedic gave her a gentle slap on the cheek and asked her what her name was. A nurse who had come with them thought she could make out a name. It sounded as if she was saying Helena.

Then the battered woman slipped into unconsciousness.

When she was seen on arrival at A&E, her injuries were assessed as extremely serious. Examination revealed her to have four broken ribs, contusions to her cheekbones, a dislocated jaw and several broken fingers. She had bruising to her entire body, and when an X-ray of her skull showed that her brain was swollen as a result of all the blows to her head, she was put in intensive care.

The hospital staff were taken aback by the sheer number of bruises, cuts and broken bones the patient had. What shocked them most of all were her burns. There were more than twenty, inflicted with what they assumed to be lighted matches. The thought of how painful the burns must be made the nurses' flesh creep as they took it in turns to keep watch at the bedside.

At about ten o'clock the woman, admitted under the name 'Helena', began to come round, but she was still groggy from all the morphine they had given her for pain relief. The intensive care consultant determined that she was now well enough to be moved to a general ward, and her bed was wheeled up to Ward Four.

She was initially in the care of nursing assistant Moa Nilsson. It wasn't that there was a lot to do, but Moa found it quite traumatic watching over the slim figure, her face a patchwork of bruises. It was impossible to say what she normally looked like. They hadn't found an ID card. But Moa thought she had some idea how the girl had lived, anyway. Her nails were bitten right down and she had small, amateurish tattoos on her arms. Her hair was red, but anyone could see it was dyed. Moa hazarded a guess that it had only just been done, too. The sad, dry hair spread across the pillow around the woman's head. Her hair was so red that it looked as if her head was resting in a pool of blood.

Moa's nursing colleagues kept popping along to see how things were going, but the situation was still unchanged by the time the dinner trolley clattered past the door. Then the patient slowly opened the one eye that was not swollen shut.

Moa put aside her magazine.

'Helena, you're in Karolinska University Hospital,' she said gently, and sat down on the edge of the bed.

The girl said nothing. She seemed very, very frightened.

Moa cautiously stroked her arm.

The girl murmured something.

Moa bent closer, frowning.

'Help me,' the girl said faintly. 'Help me.'

SATURDAY

Spencer Lagergren had many good points, but one thing Fredrika Bergman had always missed in their relationship was any element of spontaneity and surprise. To some extent, of course, this was because Spencer was married; scope for spontaneity was rather restricted. But she attributed the absence of surprises more to Spencer's rather limited imagination in that area. Spencer could only surprise you with the help and guidance of fate.

But every rule has its exception.

Fredrika gave a little smile as she hurriedly tried to put her dark hair up. She had visualized herself spending the evening in Umeå alone with a glass of wine and her notebook. And that was indeed how the evening had started. But as she sat in the verandah of the Town Hotel drinking her over-priced wine, she suddenly heard a voice behind her.

'Excuse me, is this seat free?'

Fredrika was so amazed to hear Spencer's voice that her jaw literally dropped, and the sip of red wine she had just taken dribbled down her chin.

Spencer looked dismayed.

'Are you all right?' he said in some agitation, grabbing a serviette from the table and wiping her face.

Fredrika, struggling with her hair, blushed and laughed at the recollection.

Spencer's bold move had impressed her. They had a very clear agreement, and it said in principle that their relationship did not bind either side to any particular obligations, or promises to support each other. In that respect, Spencer's role in her life was unambiguous. Yet he had still come. Probably not just for her sake, but also for his own.

'You have to seize chances when they come your way,' Spencer said as they raised their glasses to each other, not long after his unexpected arrival. 'It's not every day one gets the opportunity to go to Umeå and live in style at its top hotel.'

Fredrika, completely knocked sideways, tried to thank him and explain to him simultaneously. It was wonderful to see him again so soon, but did he realize she had to work the next day and then fly back home? Yes, he did. But he had found himself missing her too much. And on the phone she had sounded really down, really frayed.

Fredrika thought that Eva, Spencer's wife, must know about his relationship with her. That would explain how he could so easily get away from home one night a week. And Eva had had affairs of her own over the years.

Spencer had once brought up the subject of why he didn't intend to get divorced. There were various sensitive relationships on the fringes of his marriage – the one between him and his father-in-law, for example – that made a divorce unthinkable. And the fact was, Spencer added, that in some strange way he and his wife felt quite strong ties binding them together, in spite of everything. Ties that could be stretched even more than they had been, but still they would never break entirely.

And that wasn't really a problem, thought Fredrika, because she wasn't sure she would appreciate sharing her day-to-day life with Spencer full time.

They had a quiet but memorable evening. Wine on the verandah, then a meal at a nearby restaurant where a young pianist crowned the warm evening with live music. At one point, when Fredrika – light-headed from the wine and the temporary peace of mind – was sitting staring at the pianist a little too intently, Spencer reached out across the table and gently stroked the scar on her arm. Wondering. Fredrika carried on observing the man at the piano and avoided Spencer's gaze. But she did not pull away.

A serious expression came into Fredrika's face as she slipped her hairbrush into her handbag and pulled her jacket straight. The only source of anxiety triggered by Spencer's visit was the fact that she still hadn't brought herself to tell him about the call from the adoption centre.

I've got to tell him, she thought. Regardless of the state of our relationship, I've got to tell him. And soon.

It was nine o'clock before Fredrika left the hotel and set off to the home of the tutor from the writing course Sara Sebastiansson had attended all those years ago. Parting from Spencer was quite a complicated ritual. They never knew for certain when they would next see each other, but that didn't matter; the main thing was that they knew they *wanted* to. They would just have to see when it turned out to be.

Fredrika had a quick word with Alex on the phone before she got out of the car to ring at the tutor's front door. The media were going mad, he said, a fact that had not escaped Fredrika when she caught sight of all the newspaper headlines that morning. No dead baby had been found, for which everyone involved was truly grateful, even though they knew they probably had very little time.

'Report back as soon as you get anything,' Alex said at the end of the call. 'We followed up a few leads last night, but to be honest . . .'

Fredrika could visualize him shaking his head.

'To be quite honest we've drawn a blank on all fronts,' he sighed.

Fredrika left the car and walked swiftly to the front door of the little house. It reminded her of the witch's house in Hansel and Gretel. Pretty, with sweet little decorative details that looked almost painted on. It seemed a quiet, rather elegant neighbourhood. No children or young people. The words 'retirement homes' flew through Fredrika's mind before the door opened, and she found herself eye to eye with a man with thick, ginger hair.

Fredrika blinked in surprise.

'Magnus Söder?'

'That's me,' replied the man, holding out his hand.

Fredrika was relieved to find she recognized the voice from their earlier phone calls, and took his hand. She gave a tight little smile and looked into his hard eyes. Was there something faintly aggressive about him?

Magnus Söder, recently retired, with coffee stains on his hand-knitted waistcoat, was so far removed from anything Fredrika had imagined he would be that she almost blushed. For some strange reason, she had expected him to be younger, darker and more attractive. And not as tall. It always made Fredrika nervous when she felt small in the company of someone she did not know.

Magnus went ahead, right through the house and out to the back, where he had a lovely terrace. He did not offer her anything to eat or drink, but simply sat down opposite her and looked straight at her.

'As I said on the phone, I don't remember much of those years,' he said curtly.

And before Fredrika could comment, he added:

'I'm a recovered alcoholic, and the time you're asking about was a bad patch for me.'

Fredrika gave a slow nod.

'As I tried to explain,' she said, 'my questions aren't particularly detailed.'

Magnus put up his hands as if acknowledging defeat.

'I found some paperwork from that summer,' he sighed. 'I've always been terrible at throwing out old papers.'

He put a green file on the table between the two of them. The sound of the file banging down on the tabletop made her jump.

'Who is it you want to know about?' Magnus said gruffly.

'Someone called Sara Lagerås,' replied Fredrika quickly, congratulating herself on remembering Sara's maiden name.

Magnus stared at a document in the file.

'Yep,' he said at length.

Fredrika's brows knitted.

'Yep,' he said again. 'I've got her here. She was from Gothenburg, wasn't she?'

'That's right,' said Fredrika.

'And now she's lost her kid? The one that was on the news?'

'Yes.'

Magnus uttered an indeterminate sound.

'I've just got a few questions,' said Fredrika, adjusting her blouse as she sensed Magnus's eyes on her cleavage.

Magnus gave a slight smile and raised his eyes. He said nothing.

'Can you see from your paperwork whether Sara stayed on as an employee of the centre when the writing course was over?'

Magnus leafed through the file.

'Yes. We asked her to stay on for the rest of the summer. We always asked someone to do that; the other tutor and I – he lives in Sydney now, by the way – needed some help with the admin and so on.'

'How did you decide who got to stay?' Fredrika asked.

'It was either decided in advance, or by us once we could see if any of the students were particularly gifted. I mean, they all wanted to stay on; I suppose it was seen as some kind of feather in their cap.'

'And how did you come to pick Sara Lagerås?'

Magnus consulted his file again.

'She wrote to us beforehand,' he said. 'I've got the letter here. Says she wants to work in Umeå for the summer, and she sent in some stuff she'd written, for us to see. She seemed capable, so we gave her a chance.'

'May I see the letter?'

Magnus passed her the file.

There was nothing interesting in the letter from Sara. It

was just a straightforward application for a summer job at the centre.

'She didn't mention any other reasons she might have had for wanting to stay?' asked Fredrika.

'None that I can recall,' sighed Magnus.

Seeing Fredrika's expression, he went on:

'The thing is, though I do honestly remember this girl, she was only one of the many summer-job students we've had here. She lived at the centre and used to hang out with some of the students from previous courses. I can't remember even talking to her all that often. We definitely didn't discuss anything personal. We talked work and creative writing.'

Magnus reached for the file, and Fredrika passed it back automatically. She sat in silence as he leafed through it again.

He suddenly straightened up.

'Oh, yes,' he said under his breath.

He looked at Fredrika.

'There was one thing a bit out of the ordinary: a fuss about a particular date.'

Fredrika pulled an enquiring face.

'The girl, Sara, suddenly told us she absolutely had to have a particular day off, and it happened to be the day we'd planned a seminar that we really needed her to help with. But she wouldn't budge; claimed she'd given us plenty of notice. My memory was pretty poor even then, so even if she had told us well in advance, I didn't remember. I was bloody cross with her, but it didn't seem to make any difference.'

Magnus peered at the contents of the file again.

'The twenty-ninth of July, it was.'

Fredrika made a careful note.

'And what was the upshot?' she asked.

'She took the day off, of course. She evidently couldn't reschedule this activity of hers. But it was a bit odd, we all thought so. And the seminar was totally chaotic without her there to help.'

Magnus shook his head.

'You never asked her where she was that day?' queried Fredrika.

'No, she just said she really had to see someone,' Magnus said. 'Someone who was only in town that one day. I don't think she said anything about it to anyone else, either. She was a bit standoffish. I remember I made some note about her being rather antisocial. Her thoughts were always somewhere else.'

Fredrika gave a slow nod.

'Anything else you can remember?'

Magnus gave a short laugh.

'I remember I ran into her later on that day, in the evening. She was so white in the face it wasn't true. Really put the wind up me. But she said she'd be fine if she could go and rest. I assumed it was something to do with whoever she'd been to see, and things not going the way she'd hoped.'

He shrugged.

'She wasn't a minor, I couldn't damn well force her to go to the police or a doctor.'

Fredrika gave a rather stiff smile.

'No, you're right,' she said.

Then she put her card on top of Magnus's green file.

'In case you remember anything else,' she said, and got to her feet.

'Or feel like a bit of company,' said Magnus with a wink.

Fredrika managed another stiff smile.

'I'll find my own way out,' she said.

A lex Recht felt miserable. Miserable, and infuriated. In the course of his long police career he had made mistakes, of course he had. No one was perfect. But this. This whole child abduction thing. Sitting there in his office, Alex felt like punching somebody – anybody. He had completely disregarded the possibility of more children being snatched. They all had. Even after the investigation had ruled out Gabriel Sebastiansson as its prime suspect, he had been quite sure that all the events revolved round Sara's life. Not for one second, until it was too late, had he considered that they might be dealing with evil personified. And by then it was too late – again.

Alex's chest hurt as he breathed out. His anger was aching somewhere deep down in his throat.

He fiddled with the desk diary in front of him. It was Saturday, and five days since Lilian had been reported missing from an X2000 train from Gothenburg. *Five days*. That was hardly any time at all. That was what had thrown the police investigation, more than anything else: the speed at which the case had developed. Just as they felt they were in control of the situation, the case was already heading in a different direction entirely. Alex turned over the expression 'one step behind' in his mind. He and the team were not one step behind – they were miles behind.

Alex listened to the sounds from the corridor outside. Generally there was hardly anyone there at weekends, but now everything was bustling. The analyst from the National Crime Squad was working himself to death with all the tip-offs coming in on the police hotline. Alex vaguely wondered if there was any point in feeding them all into a database. It hadn't done them any good at all so far. Admittedly that was to some extent because of the way his team of investigators chose to work. Peder, for example, had not talked to the analyst when the call came through about the woman's death in Jönköping. If he had, they would have made the link to their own case more quickly. But Fredrika had supplied the necessary information soon enough. That confirmed what Alex had maintained ever since computers started taking over more and more of the paperwork – they had a limited range of applications, because there was always somebody who kept the facts in their own little head. If a team was welded closely enough together, information flowed as it should, even without the help of computers.

Alex heaved a sigh and looked out into the blue sky, flecked with cloud.

Maybe he was getting old and grumpy. Maybe the spark was going out of him. Or still worse – maybe he was turning into the sort of reactionary DI no newly qualified police officer wanted to work with. How long could you carry on being known as a legend if you didn't deliver the goods? How long could you live on your reputation?

He shuffled the papers on his desk. Fredrika had just rung from Umeå to confirm that Sara Sebastiansson had been lying about when she first knew she would be staying at the course centre after her friend left. Alex frowned. It was depressing that Sara was lying about her Umeå links. He felt the anger flare in him. He would go out to his car and go round to Sara's himself. He didn't give a damn that she was suffering the deep hurt of bereavement. She was obstructing the work of the police, and that could never be permitted. No matter how distressed a person felt.

Then Alex retreated into his room again. Sara hadn't really lied about her links to Umeå, she'd lied about one particular *detail*. A detail she had thought she could conceal from the police, but which the police, by contrast, believed to be an important piece in the jigsaw. The team had been working on the assumption that something happened in Umeå which decided the future course of Sara's life, but that must be at least partly wrong. Something must have happened *before* Sara went on the course that summer, something Sara had tried to remedy by staying away longer.

And now she was being punished for it by someone murdering her child. Possibly the person she had claimed she had to see that day.

Alex rooted through his papers to find the horrible pictures of the dead Lilian. Why had someone marked her with the word 'Unwanted'? Why had someone decided she was a child no one wanted? And why had she been found outside A&E? Was the location important? Could she just as well have been dumped somewhere else in Umeå? Or in any old town?

Alex fidgeted uneasily. The obvious question was whether the next body would also turn up outside Umeå hospital.

Alex tried valiantly not to think about the missing baby. He hoped Fredrika's interview with the Jönköping woman's grandmother would produce something. And he hoped they would soon find the mysterious Monika Sander. Without her, everything for the moment looked pretty hopeless, he was afraid to say.

He got to his feet with fresh resolve. A cup of coffee was what he needed. And he must shake off all this anxiety. If he was already speculating about where the next dead child would be found, then he had lost the battle.

Peder Rydh had slept incomprehensibly well the previous night. He and Ylva hadn't had much to say to each other when he got home just after ten. The boys were asleep, of course. He stood at the end of one of their beds, watching the sleeping child. Blue monkey pyjamas, thumb in mouth. A slight twitch in his face; was he dreaming? Peder gave a wan smile and ran a gentle hand across the boy's forehead.

Ylva asked questions about the second missing child, and he gave minimal answers. Then he had a glass of wine, watched TV for a while, and went to bed. Just as he put out the light, he heard Ylva's voice in the darkness.

'We've got to have a proper talk one day, Peder.'

At first he said nothing.

'We can't go on like this,' she continued. 'We've got to talk about how we feel.'

And then for the first time he told it like it was:

'I can't take any more. I just can't.'

And he added:

'I don't want this to be my life. No way.'

He was turned towards her in the bed as he said it, and despite the darkness he saw her face fall and heard the change in her breathing. She was waiting for him to go on, but he had nothing more to say. Then he fell asleep, strangely relieved but not a little concerned by the fact that he felt nothing. No regret, no panic. Just relief.

In the car on the way to work, he tried to think clearly about the abducted children case.

Initially his thoughts were distracted by remembering that he hadn't rung Jimmy to say he wouldn't be able to come and see him as planned. They would have to have their posh cake with marzipan another day, because Peder was busy. How much Jimmy understood of what Peder told him was always hard to gauge. His brother seldom got the subtler points in conversations, and Jimmy related to time in an entirely different way to other people.

There was something nagging at the back of Peder's mind, something he'd overlooked. Some simple but crucial detail that had vanished out of his head. The newspapers had dutifully printed Monika Sander's name and picture and said she was wanted by the police. The identikit drawing was published again, along with a passport photo taken some 10 years before. Alex and Peder had asked themselves whether it was a good idea to publish the old photo they had got from Monika's foster mother. It bore little resemblance to her current appearance and there was a strong risk that all sorts of people from her past would dash to the phone to report things from a time that had no bearing on the life she was living now. They were also aware of the need to share every last scrap of information they had. The investigation could not afford any more gaps in its knowledge. Monika Sander had to be dragged into the open – at any price.

Peder had spoken to Alex that morning. Nobody had rung in with any sensible information to date. Peder felt a sudden weariness and dejection. How far did they really think they were going to get with an ancient photo, a useless identikit drawing and a name that Monika Sander might not even use any longer?

Then it suddenly came back to Peder what he had overlooked when they released the information about Monika. He parked outside HQ and rushed up to the department.

Alex had just come back to his room with a cup of coffee when Peder came hurtling through the door.

Alex hardly got his 'Good morning' out before Peder started.

'We've got to issue a double name,' he gabbled.

'What are you talking about?' asked a bewildered Alex.

'Monika Sander,' Peder blurted. 'We've got to ring the tax people and find out what her name was when she first came to Sweden. She was adopted, wasn't she? She might have found out the name she was born with and be using it as an alias or something.'

'Well we've already gone public with the name Monika Sander, but . . .'

'Yes?'

'I was just going to say that it's a very good idea, Peder,' Alex said evenly. 'Get Ellen on the case; she can ring the tax office.'

Peder dashed out of the room and sprinted off in the direction of Ellen's room.

Alex gave a wry smile. It was amazing to see a human being with that much energy.

In another part of Stockholm, two people with considerably less energy than Peder Rydh were also busy. Ingeborg and Johannes Myrberg were down on their hands and knees at either end of their large garden, weeding conscientiously between the shrubs and flowering plants. The rain had kept them from any sort of work in the garden until now, but at least summer seemed to have arrived. Admittedly there were a few clouds loitering around the sun, but as long as it was still shining and shedding its warmth, Ingeborg and Johannes Myrberg were more than happy.

Ingeborg took a quick glance at her watch. It was almost eleven. They had been out there for nearly two hours. Without a break. She shaded her eyes with her hand and looked across to her husband. Johannes had had a few prostate problems in recent years and was usually hurrying off to the toilet all the time. But not this morning. No, this morning they had both worked on undisturbed.

Ingeborg's face broke into a smile as she watched her husband weeding round the rhubarb. They still took a child-like delight in their domain. In their heart of hearts, they had never really believed the house would be theirs. So many properties had passed them by. Either they were too expensive, or they turned out to have mould in the basement or damp patches on the ceilings.

Ingeborg surveyed the big, white house. It was attractive and a good size. There were enough rooms to accommodate all the children and grandchildren when they came to visit, but was still compact enough to retain its charm and the sense of really being someone's home. *Their* home.

'Johannes!' Ingeborg called into the quietness of the garden.

Johannes almost overbalanced at the sound of Ingeborg's shout, and she laughed.

'I was just going to say: I'm going in for a minute to get a drink. Would you like one, too?'

Johannes gave that slightly lopsided smile, so familiar to her throughout their married life. For thirty-five years, to be exact.

'A glass of the strawberry cordial would be nice.'

Ingeborg got slowly to her feet, her knees protesting slightly. When she was young, she had never considered that her body would feel weaker and frailer one day.

'What a summer we've had,' she said under her breath as she stepped into the house from the terrace.

Then she froze. Afterwards she couldn't really explain why she had stopped just there, just then. Or how she had sensed without going any further that something was wrong.

She walked slowly through the guest room that gave onto the terrace, and out into the corridor between the four bedrooms. She looked left, where the bedrooms were, but nothing was moving. She looked right, towards the main hall, the kitchen and the living room. She could see nothing strange or out of the ordinary there, either. Yet she still knew that someone had been there, that her home had been violated.

She shook her head. What a ridiculous thought; was she getting paranoid in her old age?

She regained control of her thoughts and her home by striding off to the kitchen and making two big glasses of cordial for herself and her husband.

She was just on her way out with the little tray when she decided it would be as well to pop to the toilet while she was in. She just couldn't fathom how Johannes had managed to go for so long without a pee.

The bathroom was at the far end of the house, beyond the bedrooms. Afterwards, she couldn't really remember how she got there. She only remembered putting the tray down and being aware that she needed to go to the loo. Whether she remembered it or not, she must have gone from the kitchen to the hall, and along the corridor to the bathroom. Put her hand on the handle, pressed it down, opened the door, turned the light on.

She saw the baby straight away. It was lying naked on the bathroom mat, curled up in a foetal position.

For a few seconds, Ingeborg did not really understand what she was seeing. She had to step forward and bend down. Automatically her hand went out to touch the baby. It was only when her fingers made contact with the hard, cold body that she started to scream.

Fredrika Bergman got the call about the discovery of the dead baby at the elderly couple's house just as she was being served tea by Margareta Andersson, grandmother of Nora who had been found murdered in Jönköping. Fredrika had to excuse herself and go out onto the balcony.

'On a bathroom mat?' she repeated.

'Yes,' said Alex grimly, 'in a house in Bromma. With the same word on her forehead, I'm heading there now. Peder's on his way to see some psychologist.'

Fredrika frowned.

'All this must have really got to him, then?'

Alex gave a chuckle of surprise.

'No, no,' he said. 'It's for the case. He decided we could do with the help of one of those profilers, and it would be good if he could get us one.'

Alex was expressing himself so badly and casually that Fredrika thought he must have been drinking. 'One of those profilers' and 'some psychologist'. They didn't grow on trees.

'He read about him in the paper,' Alex explained. 'That's what gave him the idea.'

'Read about who?' Fredrika asked, at a loss.

'An American profiler who works for the FBI is over here lecturing to some behavioural science scientists at the university,' Alex said, more controlled now. 'Peder was going to try to arrange a meeting with him through some friend of his who's on the course.'

'Okay,' Fredrika said slowly.

'Is everything all right your end?' Alex asked.

'Yes, fine. I'll get back to Stockholm as soon as I've finished here.'

She was silent for a moment.

'But why ever should the baby turn up in Bromma?' she went on.

'You mean he's breaking the pattern?'

'I don't know about any pattern,' mumbled Fredrika. 'Maybe we've just been imagining there was a clear link to Umeå.'

'No, I don't think so,' said Alex. 'But I do think we need to find a better common denominator.'

'A common denominator of a bathroom in Bromma and a town in Norrland,' Fredrika sighed.

'Yes, that's our second challenge,' Alex said firmly. 'To try to understand the connection between the bathroom in Bromma and the A&E department at Umeå hospital. Assuming the geography has any relevance at all, that is.'

If the situation hadn't been so grave, Fredrika would have allowed herself to laugh.

'Are you there?' Alex asked, when she said nothing.

'Sorry, I was just thinking. What's our first challenge?' Fredrika responded. 'You said the connections were the second one.'

'Finding Monika Sander,' said Alex. 'I don't think we're going to understand a bloody thing about this whole mess until we talk to her.'

Fredrika couldn't help smiling, but immediately felt guilty. She felt awful, smiling when a baby had just been found dead.

'Okay,' she said soberly. 'We'll just have to do our best.'

'You bet your life we will,' Alex said with a sigh.

Fredrika put her mobile away and returned to the flat. She apologized to her hostess.

'I'm sorry. I had to take that call.'

Margareta nodded to show she accepted the apology.

'Have you found the baby now, as well?' she asked, to Fredrika's astonishment.

'Yes,' she said hesitantly, after a pause. 'Yes, we have. But it isn't official yet, so I'd really appreciate it if . . .'

Margareta gave a dismissive wave of the hand.

'Of course I won't say anything,' she said. 'And I don't talk to anybody anyway, except Tintin.'

'Tintin?' Fredrika echoed.

'My cat,' grinned Margareta, and indicated a seat for Fredrika at the table laid with teacups and a plate of sliced bun loaf.

Fredrika liked Margareta's voice. It was deep and throaty, dark yet still feminine. Margareta herself was as broad-shouldered as a wrestler. She was not fat or heavy looking, but simply stable in the purest sense of the word. Safe was another word that came spontaneously into Fredrika's mind.

She automatically ran over all the information she had had from the Jönköping police about Nora, the murdered woman. Spent her childhood in various foster homes; mental problems; recurring periods of sick leave. In a relationship with the man suspected of having murdered her, Lilian Sebastiansson and now the baby. Moved from Umeå to Jönköping. Held down a job, looked after a home, but had no family and few acquaintances.

Fredrika decided to start from the beginning.

'How did Nora come to be in a foster home?'

Nora's grandmother grew very still. So still that Fredrika thought she could hear Tintin purring as he lay there in his basket.

'Do you know what, I wondered that, too,' she said slowly.

Then she took a deep breath and laid her wrinkled old hands in her lap. She plucked at the hem of her frock. The fabric was red and brown. To Fredrika's mind, it was definitely a winter frock.

'You always try not to have too many expectations of your children. Well my husband and I did, at least. And when he died, I carried on the same way. But . . . But you do have certain basic expectations, you can't help it. Of course you want your children to grow up and be able to look after themselves. But Nora's mother never really did, I'm afraid. And we didn't have any more children.'

Margareta tailed off, and Fredrika did not realize until she raised her head from her notebook that the other woman was crying.

'We can take a break if you like,' she said uncertainly.

Margareta gave a weary shake of the head.

'It's just that it hurts so much to think I've got neither of the girls left now,' she sobbed. 'I felt so wretched when Nora's mother died. But I knew what sort of life she'd lived, how *hard* it had been for her. There was really only one way it could end. But then I could console myself that at least I had Nora left. And now she's gone, too.'

Tintin came out of his basket and approached the table. Fredrika quickly pulled her legs aside. She had never liked cats.

'Things went wrong for Nora's mother early on in her life,' Margareta told her. 'Very early on. When she was still in secondary school, just after her dad died. She got into bad company and brought home one boyfriend after another. I was beside myself when she decided to leave school as soon as she could and go out to work instead. She got a job in a sweet factory; it closed down years ago. But she didn't stick to the rules, and she got the sack. I think that was when she turned to prostitution and the more dangerous drugs.'

In Fredrika's family there was a very conservative saying that went: 'In every woman of every age there lives a Mother.' She wondered if she herself was harbouring one. And she wondered what she would have said in that position, if her daughter had dropped out of school, started work in a factory and gone on the game.

'Who was Nora's father?' Fredrika asked cautiously.

Margareta gave a bitter laugh and wiped away her tears.

'You tell me,' she said. 'It could have been literally anybody. Nora's mother didn't register a father's name when Nora was born. I was with her for the birth. It was several days before she would even hold little Nora.'

The sun vanished briefly behind a cloud and it went darker inside the flat. Fredrika felt cold, sitting there.

'Nora was as unwanted as a child could possibly be,' Margareta whispered. 'Her mother hated her even when she was still in her stomach; she hoped for a long time she might have a miscarriage. But she didn't. Nora was born whether she liked it or not.'

Fredrika felt the floor lurch beneath her.

'Unwanted,' she repeated softly.

She immediately saw the pictures of Lilian Sebastiansson's body in front of her eyes. Somebody had written 'Unwanted' on her forehead. 'Unwanted.'

Fredrika swallowed.

'Did she know about this when she was growing up, about being unwanted I mean?' Fredrika asked, trying not to sound too eager.

'Yes, of course she did,' sighed Margareta. 'Nora lived with me for most of the time until she was two, since her mother didn't want her, but then social services found out about it and they said it would be better for Nora to be in a foster home, "A real family," as they put it.'

Margareta gripped the edge of the table hard.

'The girl would have been much better off with me,' she said in a shrill voice. 'It would have been much better for her to live with me than to keep being moved from family to family. She could always come and visit me, but what good did that do? There was no chance of making something decent of her with so many other people allowed to mess her up.'

'Did you both live here in Umeå while all this was going on?' asked Fredrika.

'Yes, the whole time. It's hard to believe one person can have lived at so many addresses in the same town as Nora, but that's what she did. The only thing that cheered me up a bit was that she stuck with school right until the end of upper secondary. She chose an odd course, social this and social that, but at least school gave her a bit of structure.'

'Did she get a job when she left?'

'I wouldn't say that,' sighed Margareta. 'Just like her mother: she started going off the rails, too much booze, too many parties, too many men. She could never hang on to her job. She always looked haggard and drawn. And then she met that man.'

Fredrika held her breath.

'I remember, because it was the same year my brother got married for the third time. That was seven years ago.'

Tintin the cat took an agile leap from the floor to Margareta's lap. She put her tired hands on his back and started stroking his fur.

'At first I thought she'd found something decent for herself,' Margareta recalled. 'He got her to stop drinking, stop taking drugs. At first I thought it was wonderful, a sort of Cinderella story. The girl in the gutter got her prince and was saved from her horrible life. But then . . . everything changed. And I was terrified, to put it bluntly.'

Fredrika frowned.

'I never met him,' Margareta suddenly asserted. 'I might just as well tell you that straight away, so you don't go expecting me to whip out a pile of photos for you or anything.'

'But what you can tell me is important, all the same,' Fredrika said quickly, but with a growing sense of disappointment.

Part of her had hoped she might be coming away from Margareta's with at least a description of the suspected murderer.

Margareta looked quite pleased with herself. Fredrika could see she liked being the centre of attention.

'She met the man in early spring. I'm not sure how they first met, but I think he saved her from some awkward situation in the street one time.'

'Was Nora a prostitute, too?'

'No, no,' Margareta said indignantly, 'but you can still find yourself with that sort of people, can't you?'

Fredrika was not so sure about that, but she said nothing. She wished Margareta would get a move on with her story. Her wish was instantly granted.

'She told me about him right away. Said he was a psychologist, very clever and good-looking. Then she told me he was always saying she was "chosen" and "special", and together they'd achieve great things in this world. She became a completely different person. For a while, I thought it must be some kind of sect she'd joined. I mean, it was a good thing of course for her to get a bit more sense of order in her life, but she was going through bad depression just then, and the man's message to her was basically "pull yourself together, you can sort this out if you really want to". And when she didn't get better quickly enough . . .'

Margareta stopped. She took several deep breaths.

'When she didn't get better quickly enough, he lost patience with her and started beating her up, very violently.'

Big tears began rolling down Margareta's cheeks again. They dropped from her chin onto Tintin's fur.

'I pleaded with her to leave him,' Margareta sobbed. 'And in the end she did. It was after the time he burnt her so badly. She left him when she was discharged from hospital.'

'Burnt her?' whispered Fredrika.

'He burnt her with matches,' replied Margareta. 'He tied her to the bed and lit them, one after another.'

'But didn't you go to the police?' persisted Fredrika, sickened by what she was hearing.

'Of course we did, but it didn't help. That was why Nora moved away and got protected identity status.'

'You mean he wasn't committed of the crime, in spite of Nora's terrible injuries?'

'I mean we didn't know who he was,' screeched Margareta, her voice almost cracking. 'Don't you see? Nora didn't even know his name. He'd told her just to think of him as "The Man". And they only ever met at Nora's flat.'

Fredrika tried to comprehend what she had just heard.

'She didn't know what he was called, where he lived, or where he worked?'

Margareta mutely shook her head.

'But what was this thing they were going to achieve together, what did he say they were going to do?'

'They were going to punish all the women who weren't capable of loving their children and who rejected them,' whispered Margareta. 'And that was exactly what Nora's own mother had done, after all – reject her and then refuse to love her.'

They say Stockholm is one of the loveliest capital cities in the world. But that was lost on Alex as he stared out of his office window. He had no idea how many minutes he had spent sitting there, gazing out. It was what he liked to do when he was thinking. And since Fredrika had rung in her report, he undeniably had plenty to think about.

'He's punishing them, like Nora said when she rang us,' Fredrika shouted down the phone to make herself heard despite the poor signal. 'He's punishing them for harming their children. For rejecting them, in some situation. And the girls go along with him, because they've been badly treated themselves. It's revenge, Alex.'

'But,' said Alex, nonplussed, 'we've no data suggesting that any of these parents harmed their children. Neither Lilian nor the baby suffered any kind of mistreatment at home.'

He shuddered.

'Assuming Gabriel didn't abuse his own daughter,' he added quickly.

Fredrika protested.

'It still wouldn't fit. It's the mothers he's punishing, not the fathers. It's the mothers who've done something wrong.'

'But if a mother chose not to save her daughter from a father who was violating her, surely that would count as a crime?'

Fredrika thought about this.

'Perhaps. But the question is still: where does he find them?'

'Find them?'

'How could he know that Lilian, specifically, had been harmed? There are no official reports. And the baby? How could he know it had suffered any harm, assuming it did?'

Alex felt his heart start to thump.

'We must have missed somebody close to the families,' he said.

'Or maybe not,' said Fredrika. 'Maybe he's so far out on the fringes of their lives that he's invisible to us.'

'Could he work at a school?'

'But the baby who died had never been to school,' Fredrika objected.

Alex drummed his fingers impatiently on the desk.

'Is Peder back from the psychologist yet,' asked Fredrika.

'No,' replied Alex with a shake of his head. 'But I think he's due to see him any minute now.'

'It seems we might need to talk to Sara again. And to the baby's mother,' said Fredrika.

Alex stared angrily out of the window. He'd had more than enough of all the weird elements in this case.

'We need to get a grip here,' he said, addressing Fredrika. 'A proper grip. And it's high bloody time we found ourselves that common denominator.'

But it wasn't that easy, Alex saw as he ended the call from Fredrika. What did they really know? What didn't they know? He collated all the information Fredrika had just given him. It all needed passing on to Peder before he invested time in talking to the American profiler. There was nothing wrong in coming up with new ideas, but Alex was sceptical about bringing new parties into the investigation.

He surveyed the material in front of him. On a blank sheet of paper he had tried to construct a sort of diagram, setting out various hypotheses. It hadn't turned out as well as he hoped, but as long as he didn't have to show it to anyone else, it would serve its purpose of backing up what was in his mind.

Revenge, Fredrika had said.

Revenge? Was that the thread they were looking for?

'Right,' Alex murmured to himself. 'Right, let's take it nice and easy. What do we know? And what do we need to know?'

They knew that two children of different ages had been murdered. They also knew there was no obvious link between the children. One little girl, Natalie, was adopted, and the other wasn't. The adopted girl's parents seemed to be in a trouble-free relationship, whereas Lilian's parents had separated while waiting for their divorce. And then Natalie's family was middle class, whereas Lilian was the daughter of a man from a well-to-do family and a woman who could at best be described as middle class.

The investigative team was currently putting all its energy into identifying any junctions where the paths of the two families might have crossed in the past, but their efforts had so far yielded nothing.

Alex wrote on a sheet of paper: *He is punishing the mothers. Probably because they let their children down in some way. Probably because they rejected them.*

It was the mothers they needed to focus on, not the children. It was the sins of the mothers that had led to the children's murders. Alex brooded on the phrase 'because they rejected them' until his brain ached. In what way could Sara Sebastiansson be said to have 'rejected' Lilian? And if she had, why punish the child with death, rather than the mother?

Another perplexing thing was the location where the bodies had been found. One outside an A&E department up in Umeå, and the other in a bathroom in Bromma, outside Stockholm. The choices of location seemed bizarre in the extreme. Firstly, they were both very difficult places in which to dispose of a dead body unobtrusively. And secondly, the choices seemed illogical. Neither of the children had any apparent connection with the places where they had been left.

The only thing, thought Alex, the only thing the two have in common is the mode of operation, both the abduction and the murder itself. First the child is kidnapped, then the clothes and hair are sent back to the mother, and shortly after that, the child is dumped in some strange place where it will readily be found.

'I don't get it,' Alex said aloud to himself. 'I just don't get it at all.'

Then there was a knock on the door and one of the young DIs who had been transferred to the case stuck his head round the door.

'We dropped in on Magdalena Gregersdotter and her husband, like you suggested,' he said.

Alex had to give his head a shake to clear it before he could understand what his colleague was on about. The DI had come with Alex and Peder to break the news of Natalie's death to her parents that morning. The parents had been in a state of utter shock and despair, so Alex had decided one of them ought to go back and see the couple later in the day. The DI and another member of the team had apparently now done so.

'We showed them a picture of the house and told them where it was,' he said, gabbling so fast that Alex had to concentrate hard to keep up. 'And Magdalena, the mother, knew exactly where we meant.'

'How?' asked Alex.

'She grew up in that house. She lived there until she left school and went away to college. Do you see, this ice-cool bastard dumped her dead kid in her parents' old house, which they sold over fifteen years ago.'

Peder Rydh was sitting in his car, seething with rage. It was Saturday lunchtime and he was stuck in a traffic jam on his way back to Kungsholmen. It made no difference if it was a Saturday or a weekday: a major road accident quickly generated long tailbacks.

Looking back over the past week made him feel almost giddy. He had never for the life of him thought that the Lilian Sebastiansson case would grow into the monster it was now. Two dead children in under a week. Had he ever been on a case like it before?

Exhaust-belching vehicles passing far too close to the paint-work of Peder's car stressed him out. So did the fact of having achieved so little over the past hour. The only good idea he had come up with all day was to declare Monika Sander wanted under the name she had before she was adopted. She had apparently been called Jelena Scortz.

After that, Peder had briefly interviewed baby Natalie's parents and both sets of grandparents. None of them could think of anyone who might wish them ill.

'Think hard,' Peder told them. 'Go right back in time. Try

to think of even the slightest grudge that was never sorted out.'

But no, none of them could remember even the smallest thing.

And then his round of interviews had been interrupted by the discovery of Natalie lying dead in a bathroom in Bromma. Peder had to go back to Natalie's parents first, and was then sent to supervise the first phase of the crime scene investigation in Bromma. This time, just like last time, they were without a murder scene.

But they did at least already know how their murderer killed his child victims, so they knew roughly what they were looking for. The duty pathologist at the scene ascertained almost at once that Natalie had a small mark on her head, probably from the lethal injection. The autopsy would confirm it later, but the group was working on the initial assumption that this child, too, had been murdered by an overdose of insulin, this time injected into the child's head through the fontanelle. Was that what the murderer had tried to do to Lilian as well, but found he couldn't get through her skull?

There were also other parallels with the way Lilian had been arranged when they found her. Natalie was also naked and had been washed with some kind of spirit. She had the same lettering on her forehead as Lilian, 'Unwanted'. But she had been lying in a foetal position, not flat on her back like Lilian. Peder wondered if that was significant.

He also wondered about the word 'Unwanted'. He and Alex had just been talking about it. Words like 'Unwanted' and 'Rejected' kept cropping up in this investigation, though neither of the children seemed to have been either.

The queue of cars inched its way forward, slowly dispersing. Peder felt lousy. The idea of trying to make contact with the American profiler had seemed so obvious. And his friend had offered the ideal way in. Or so it had seemed. In retrospect, Peder doubted it had been worth it. The time it had taken him to drive out to the university and back felt wasted. Peder's friend had thought the psychologist would be prepared to have a word with him after the guest lecture, but he had in fact turned out to be extremely chilly and dismissive. Despite the potency and calibre of the current case, the psychologist intimated briskly that Peder had overstepped the mark by simply turning up and trying to pick his brains. He really had no wish to get involved with some strange Swedish case, when he was expected at Villa Källhagen for a lunch.

The psychologist unfortunately confirmed all Peder's preconceptions about psychologists, and Americans. Dim and slow, with no social graces. Not the pleasantest of people. Peder virtually threw his card at the man and made his exit. *Idiot.*

The traffic jam finally cleared. Peder put his foot down and headed for HQ.

Then his mobile rang.

He was not a little surprised to find it was a call from the psychologist.

'I'm so sorry I had to turn you down so publicly,' he said apologetically. 'You see, if I'd offered my services to you and your colleagues, every single psychology student there would have thought they were free to ask me to do the same. And to be honest, that's not what I give my guest lectures for.'

Peder, unable to work out whether the psychologist was ringing to offer assistance or merely to apologize, said nothing and wondered frantically how best to respond.

The psychologist went on:

'What I'm trying to say is that I'll be glad to help you. Maybe I could come to see you and your colleagues sometime after this damn lunch I'm obliged to attend?'

Peder smiled.

Alex did not really know what to say at first, when Peder rang and told him that the psychological profiler had agreed to come and see them later that day. Then he decided it was quite a good idea, after all. They needed all the help they could get. And what was more, Fredrika would be back from Umeå in a couple of hours' time.

Alex turned his little diagrams round, looking at them from all angles. At least they had a pattern, now. The murderer kidnapped and murdered children, and dumped them in places their mothers had some sort of link to. With savage speed.

Why had there been only a few days' gap between the two abductions and murders, Alex wondered. The murderer was taking an enormous risk by committing two such serious crimes in swift succession. *Three*, if you counted the woman in Jönköping. There were some real psychos, of course, who never expected anything other than that they would be caught. Though 'expected' wasn't the word: they *wanted* nothing better than to be caught. But was the murderer they were pursuing disturbed in that sort of way?

Alex went back to considering the locations in which the children had been found. It didn't matter that they hadn't found out exactly what Sara Sebastiansson had done or who she had met in Umeå. The main thing was that they were sure the place had some kind of significance for her, which explained why her child had been taken to that particular location and not left anywhere in Stockholm.

The truth was often much simpler than you first thought. Alex had learned that over the years. That was why it had seemed so obvious to focus on Gabriel Sebastiansson from the start. But this time, everything was different. This time, the truth seemed a vast distance away. It wasn't a close relative who was to be held to account for what had happened, but something as uncommon as a serial killer.

How many serial killers have you actually met in all your years with the police, Alex? whispered the ghostly voice in his head.

Ellen interrupted his reverie with a hard knock on his open door.

'Alex!' she called, so loudly that it made him jump.

'What is it now?' he muttered.

'We've had a call from Karolinska Hospital,' said Ellen excitedly.

Alex looked quizzical.

'They've got a woman there they think might be Jelena Scortz.'

Alex Recht briefly contemplated going straight out to Karolinska University Hospital on his own to talk to the woman the staff thought might be Jelena Scortz, but he decided it wouldn't be fair to Peder. It was thanks to Peder they had identified the woman, after all. So Alex decided they would go together. He was in buoyant mood. He had just heard that Sara Sebastiansson thought she recognized Jelena as the woman who had delayed her in Flemingsberg. She couldn't be entirely sure, since the picture they had shown her was so old, but she thought it might well be the same girl.

Peder felt a surge of euphoria when he arrived back at HQ and was told to get straight out to Karolinska to conduct – if at all possible – an initial interview with Jelena Scortz, or Monika Sander as she appeared in the files of the National Registration Service. He raced to the car with Alex on his heels, and drove to Solna breaking several speed limits on the way.

Peder had never made any secret of what he liked best about his profession. He lived for those unique adrenalin rushes that can only result from a breakthrough in an investigation. He could see Alex felt the same, even though he had been in the job so much longer.

Peder couldn't help being slightly irritated by the fact that Fredrika seemed immune to such pleasures. While everyone else was caught up in the excitement, she turned in on herself and became one big 'Is this really the solution?' and 'Couldn't it equally well be that?' On this occasion it was in fact partly thanks to her that they had reached the breakthrough, so she could at least have allowed herself a hint of a smile when she heard the news. He liked smiley people around him at work.

Alex and Peder did not really know what to expect when they got to the hospital. They had been told, of course, that the woman presumed to be Monika Sander had been very badly knocked about and was still in some form of shock. But nothing they had been told in advance prepared them for what they saw when they went into the patient's room.

Her whole face was a mess of lacerations and bruises. Long bruises disfigured her neck. Her left arm was in plaster to above elbow level, and her lower right arm was bandaged. Her forehead was covered in dressings, right up to her hairline.

'Poor thing,' were the words that flew through Peder's head. 'Poor, poor girl.'

A young nursing assistant was sitting by her bed. The nurse's face was grave. Peder guessed he wasn't the only person to be appalled by the extent of the woman's injuries.

The discreet clearing of a throat made them turn round smartly.

A man in a white coat, with thick grey hair and a dark moustache, was silhouetted in the doorway. He introduced himself as Morgan Thulin, the doctor responsible for Monika's care.

'Peder Rydh,' said Peder, squeezing the other man's hand.

The handshake felt solid. Stable. He guessed Alex was making the same judgment.

'I don't know how much you've been told about her injuries,' said the doctor.

'Not a great deal,' admitted Alex, stealing a glance at what was left of the woman in the bed.

'Well in that case,' Morgan Thulin said firmly but kindly, 'I consider it my duty to inform you. She is still, as you see, in a very serious condition. She's drifting uneasily in and out of consciousness, and finds it hard to speak when she tries to. The whole jaw area has been damaged, and until this morning her tongue was so swollen that it almost entirely filled the oral cavity.'

Peder swallowed, and the doctor went on.

'Your police colleagues who are looking into the assault were here earlier to ask who did this to her, but she wasn't able to tell them anything coherent or comprehensible. My guess is that she's still in a state of shock, and then there's the effect of the pain relief we're giving her. Apart from the injuries you can see, she's got several broken ribs. She doesn't seem to have been subjected to any kind of sexual assault, but she has a number of severe burns.'

'Burns?' echoed Peder.

Morgan Thulin nodded.

'Match burns, about twenty of them all over her body, including the inside of her thigh and the front of her neck.'

The room shrank, there was no air, and Peder wanted to go home. All his enthusiasm evaporated. He stared listlessly at the leaves of a plant on one of the window ledges.

'The burns will leave her with permanent cosmetic scarring, but no functional impairment, clinically speaking. As for the mental scars, it's too early to say, but I'm sure she's going to have a long road to recovery. Very long indeed.'

Strange, the plant seemed to be moving. Was it the draught

from the open window making it sway like that? Peder's eyes followed the plant from side to side several times before he was brought back to reality by the fact that everything had gone quiet. Why wasn't the doctor talking any more? Alex gave a little cough.

'Sorry,' said Peder in a low voice. 'Sorry, it's been a mad couple of days, that's all . . .'

He could scarcely believe he was hearing his own voice. What was he saying?

Morgan Thulin patted him on the shoulder. Alex raised one eyebrow, but said nothing.

'There's more I should tell you, if you're sure you can take it?'

This made Peder so embarrassed that he wished he could hide behind the goddamned pot plant.

'Naturally I shall listen to everything you can tell us,' he said, in an attempt to sound in command of the situation.

Morgan Thulin eyed him dubiously, but was charitable enough not to say anything. Alex followed his example.

'There are signs of previous injuries, too,' the doctor said. 'So it seems this was not the first time she was beaten up.'

'Not the first time?'

'No, definitely not. The X-rays of her fingers show scarring on most of them indicative of fractures left to heal by themselves. Both arms have been broken, and there are signs of previous injuries to the ribs. She also has marks left by previous burns. We've counted about ten, so the assault this time seems to have been on a whole new scale.'

When Morgan Thulin had finished his account, they stood there nodding. Morgan Thulin nodded to show his story was at an end, and Peder to indicate he understood what he had just been told. Alex nodded mainly because the others were nodding too.

Then the woman in the bed made a sudden movement.

She whimpered quietly and tried to sit up. Immediately the nurse was there, gently restraining her. If she could just lie still, they would raise the head end of the bed so she was sitting up a bit.

Peder rushed over to help with the bed. Partly he wanted nothing more than to help, partly it gave him a chance to get nearer the woman. He saw she was barely able to open her eyes, but was still intently tracking his movements, first across the room and then as he helped to adjust the bed.

Morgan Thulin left them, saying, 'I shall be in my office if there's anything else you need to know.'

Peder wondered where to sit. It felt too intimate and intrusive to perch on the edge of the bed. But the easy chair on the other side of the room felt much too far away. He promptly pushed the chair closer to the bed, so he was about the right distance from the woman. Alex stayed over by the door.

Peder introduced himself and Alex by their forenames and surnames, and said they were from the police. He saw the woman's gaze change and darken. She held up her hands as if to keep them at bay.

'We only want to talk to you,' he said cautiously. 'If you aren't up to answering, or don't want to, that's fine. We'll just go away.'

He restrained himself from adding, 'And come back another day.'

'Can you nod if you understand what I'm saying?'

The woman regarded him in silence, and then nodded.

'Can you tell us your name first?'

Peder waited, but the woman didn't speak. The nurse helped her take a sip of water. Peder carried on waiting.

'Jelena,' came a whisper.

'Jelena?' repeated Peder.

The woman nodded.

'And what's your surname?'

A further pause. Another sip of water.

'Scortz.'

A light breeze from the slightly open window brushed across Peder's cheek. He tried not to smile, not to show how pleased he was. It was really her. They'd finally found Monika Sander.

He felt suddenly unsure how to proceed. They didn't even know for sure that this woman – Monika Sander – was the one who delayed Sara Sebastiansson at Flemingsberg. But they needed to know. Peder thought frantically. Mainly about why he hadn't got this all worked out before they got to the hospital.

He decided to start from the other end.

'Who did this to you?' he asked quietly.

The woman in the bed rubbed her plaster cast on the sheet. Perhaps it had already started itching.

'The Man,' she whispered.

Peder leaned forward.

'Sorry, I didn't quite . . .'

The nurse at the bedside was clearly irritated, but made no comment.

'The Man,' said the woman again, and it was obvious she

was making an effort to speak clearly. 'That's . . . what I . . . call him.'

Peder stared at her.

'The Man?' he repeated.

She nodded slowly.

'Okay,' said Peder carefully. 'But do you know where he lives?'

'Only . . . see him . . . my . . .' slurred the woman.

'You only see him at your place?' Peder supplied.

She nodded.

'So you don't know where he lives?'

She shook her head.

'Do you know where he works?'

She shook her head.

'Psy-chol–o . . .'

'Psychologist? He told you he was a psychologist?'

The woman seemed relieved that he understood what she was saying.

'But you don't know where he works?'

She shook her head, looking very miserable.

Peder racked his brains.

'Do you know what sort of car he drives?'

The woman thought. She seemed to be trying to frown, but her face muscles refused to obey her. She must be in dreadful pain, thought Peder.

'Diff . . . rent,' she whispered at last.

Peder waited.

'Hardly . . . ever . . . the same . . .'

Peder was taken aback. Did the guy go round in stolen cars, or just hire one when he needed to?

'Work . . . car . . . ?'

'You think he uses different cars from work?'

'He said . . . so . . .'

He'd clearly lied about everything else, so why not lie about his car, too, thought Peder in frustration.

'Where did you meet him?' he asked curiously. 'The very first time, I mean.'

His question prompted an immediate reaction from the woman in the bed. She turned her head away, with a look of what seemed to be anger. Peder waited a few moments and decided not to force it.

'Maybe you don't want to talk about that part?' he said tentatively.

The woman shook her head.

Alex shifted slightly on the other side of the room, but said nothing.

Peder decided to focus on the woman from Jönköping and what she said when she rang the police anonymously. It should have occurred to him at the start that she was the obvious starting point for the interview.

He began a little hesitantly.

'We think the man who beat you up might have done the same to other women, too.'

Jelena Scortz, exhausted, rested her head back against the pillow, but her eyes were following him with interest.

'We think he approaches women and asks them to join him in some kind of battle or campaign.'

The woman dropped her eyes but even Peder, with no medical expertise, could see the colour draining from her face. The nurse made an impatient movement and tried to catch Peder's eye. He avoided her gaze.

'It's terribly, terribly important that we find him,' Peder said, trying not to sound too stern.

After a pause, he went on:

'It's absolutely vital that we find him before any more children get abducted and murdered.'

The woman gave a whimper and started to toss helplessly in the bed.

'I really think . . .' began the nurse, stroking Jelena's hair over and over again.

Delicately, delicately, so as not to hurt her.

Peder, however, felt very satisfied with the reaction he had elicited from Jelena. He knew now that she was implicated. In Lilian's disappearance, at the very least.

He moved over and sat on the edge of the bed. Jelena refused to look at him.

'Jelena,' he said gently, 'we do know you must have been forced into all this.'

That wasn't true, either, but it didn't matter at the moment. The main thing was to get Jelena to calm down, which she did.

'I need all the information I can get,' Peder pleaded. 'How does he locate these children? How does he pick them?'

Jelena was breathing in a strange, jerky way. She still wasn't looking at him, or at the nurse.

'How does he pick them?'

'Their . . . mothers.'

The answer came so softly that he could hardly hear what she was saying. Yet he had no trouble at all in understanding what she said.

'Right,' he said, hoping she would have something to add.

But she said nothing, so he asked:

'Are they women he knew before? How does he find them?'

She turned her head slowly until she was looking straight at him again. He felt a chill run through him as he saw how dark her eyes were.

'You don't . . . choose,' she hissed. 'You love . . . all the ones . . . you get. Or none . . . of them.'

Peder swallowed, several times.

'Don't choose what?' he asked. 'I don't understand, what is it you don't choose?'

'The . . . children,' Jelena whispered feebly, and her head lay still on the pillow again. 'You . . . have to . . . love . . . them all.'

With that, Jelena lapsed into silence, and Peder realized the interview was at an end.

Fredrika was surprised to see that the investigation team corridor was such a hive of activity when she got back to HQ. She located Alex and Peder in the Den. Mats, the analyst from the National Crime Squad, was there – *hadn't he had enough yet?* – along with another man whom Fredrika didn't recognize. She said hello and introduced herself.

'Fredrika Bergman.'

'*Excuse me?*'

Rather taken aback, Fredrika said her name again in what she hoped was a less Swedish-sounding way. The man got it that time, and introduced himself as Stuart Rowland. He took a seat again on the chair that was unobtrusively positioned in one corner of the room.

Peder sprang to his feet when he saw Fredrika introduce herself to the mysterious Stuart Rowland. He explained in English why their visitor was there.

'Dr Rowland is a psychologist, a so-called profiler,' he explained in a voice almost quivering with reverence. 'He has promised to give us the benefit of his knowledge at our meeting.'

As if the Pope himself were paying them a visit, thought Fredrika.

Peder turned to Fredrika and asked her discreetly, in Swedish:

'I hope you won't feel uncomfortable if we hold the first part of the meeting in English?'

When she realized he meant the question seriously, she felt her cheeks start to turn crimson.

'As long as the meeting's in English, German, French or Spanish, I'll be absolutely fine,' she said with a stiff smile.

Peder blinked, completely failing to grasp the implication of her words.

'Great,' he said, and sat down again.

Alex, observing Peder and Fredrika from a distance, allowed himself a smile.

'Fredrika, I'm glad you're back in time for the meeting. Take a seat, and we can start.'

Fredrika, who had not realized until that moment she was the only one they were waiting for, sat down. Ellen gave her a little grin and pushed the door of the Den shut with her foot.

Every investigation has its critical moment. Alex had a distinct feeling the violent investigation in which he was currently embroiled had reached precisely that point. There were not that many more facts to be gathered, Alex convinced himself. They already had most of them in front of them.

He took a surreptitious look at the psychology professor Peder had virtually hijacked from the university. In his brown jacket with suede elbow patches and suede breast pocket, and an enormous moustache bristling under his nose like a squirrel's tail, he looked as if he had wandered into the Den straight off the set of some British film.

But Alex knew he couldn't afford to be choosy. Any form of help had to be seen as worth having at this stage.

'Okay,' he said, surveying all those present.

You could have cut the atmosphere with a knife. Alex swallowed, hard. People this tense could hardly come up with any masterly theories. He glanced at Fredrika. She would be the exception, of course. Fredrika seemed to be able to focus her thoughts on absolutely anything at any time, as long as she was told it was important. And it didn't get any more important than this.

He went on in English.

'We say a special welcome to Professor Rowland,' he said, hoping he sounded formal enough. 'We are very pleased to have you at our meeting.'

The Professor gave a gracious nod and smiled under his moustache.

Alex had had to get approval for Professor Rowland to attend the meeting from the next level of the police hierarchy. Desperate though the situation was, there were still rules to follow and confidentiality to be observed.

As Alex switched on the overhead projector, he hoped this was clear to everybody round the table. With the help of the analyst, whose name he now knew to be Mats, he had put together an easy-to-use overview of all the material they had amassed in the course of the investigation, including the recent information supplied by Fredrika over the phone.

Alex summed up the case and their findings with exemplary brevity. He avoided looking at their foreign guest. He took it for granted that the FBI must be a lot more fun than working for the Stockholm police.

As if he could read Alex's thoughts, the Professor suddenly spoke up.

'I have to say, this is an extremely interesting case,' he said.

'Really,' queried Alex, feeling perversely flattered.

'Yes,' said Rowland. 'But I'm afraid I can't quite see from your diagram exactly what help you need from me right now. What is it that's not clear?'

Alex stared at his own sketch. Surely there was plenty that wasn't clear?

'It's quite clear – beyond all reasonable doubt – that the same man kidnapped and murdered both girls,' the Professor began. 'But if the woman you've identified at the hospital really is the man's accomplice, and I think we can assume that on the basis of your interview, then he must have carried the second crime through on his own, without her. The question is: did something go wrong in the first murder? Serial killers very rarely start their careers with two such major crimes in the course of just a few days, crimes that would attract such attention.'

The Professor paused, as though to check everyone understood what he said, and that he was not speaking out of turn.

Alex put his head on one side.

'So what you mean, Professor Rowland, is that you think the fact that the woman was able to get out of the flat on her own after the attack, and went to hospital, made him act more quickly?'

'I'm convinced of it,' the Professor said firmly. 'The woman was probably punished for not completing some part of her task to the letter during the first murder. The nature of her injuries seems to indicate that he was in a rage when he attacked her, wild and out of control. That in turn shows that she must have been careless about something she didn't understand to be of crucial importance to the killer *at a symbolic level*.'

Alex sat down, leaving the stage to the Professor for a while.

'We must have our picture of this couple clear in our minds,' Rowland said emphatically. 'Both the women the man tried to collaborate with were weak individuals in the sense that they had been in very vulnerable positions and had a hard time, even though they were young. They were probably attracted to the man because no one like him had ever shown any interest in them before.'

Fredrika's mind went back to what Nora's grandmother Margareta had said: that it had seemed like a real life Cinderella story when Nora met the man who was later to destroy her life.

'You are almost certainly looking for a very charismatic, determined person,' the Professor continued. 'He may have a military background, but whatever his exact background, he's well-educated. He's good-looking. That's how he attracts these abandoned girls and gets them to worship him to the point where they'll do anything for him. If he is a psychologist, as both girls claim he told them, that scarcely makes him less of a threat to us.'

'But the first woman walked out on him,' Fredrika objected, thinking again of Nora in Jönköping.

Who had had the strength to break free and make a new start.

'True,' said the Professor, 'but then she wasn't entirely alone. She had a strong grandmother behind her. Our killer would certainly have learnt from that mistake the first time – if it was the first time. The woman he seeks has to be weak, and entirely on her own. There mustn't be anyone in her life

with any influence over her. He alone must be able to domi-
nate her and dictate the terms of how she lives.'

Professor Rowland shifted his position on the hard chair. It
was apparent that he liked talking, and would carry on as
long as no one interrupted him.

'He thought he had complete control over this last woman,
Jelena, yet even she sprang a surprise and left him. His woman
is important to him, practically but also mentally. She affirms
him; she intensifies his perception of himself as a genius.
And . . .'

Professor Rowland looked serious, and held up a warning
finger.

'And, my friends, he *is* a genius. Neither of the women
knows what his name is, where he works, or even what type
of car he has. They never call him anything but "The Man".
He could be absolutely anywhere. The best you can hope for
is that you pick up his fingerprints in the woman's flat, but I
rather doubt you will. Bearing in mind how strategically this
man seems to operate, I wouldn't be surprised if he's disfigured his own fingers.'

There was a spontaneous murmur from his audience, and
Alex impatiently hushed them.

'What do you mean, disfigured?'

'Oh, it's not difficult,' Professor Rowland smiled. 'Nor
even particularly uncommon. A lot of asylum seekers do it, to
make it hard to register their fingerprints. Then they can seek
asylum in a series of other countries if their application is
turned down in the first one they go to.'

There was not a sound in the Den. Alex had been pinning
his hopes on fingerprints or DNA from the flat providing the

solution to the case, always assuming the man had a previous conviction. He straightened his back.

'Wait a minute, you mean you think the man has been convicted before?'

'If he hasn't, then there's more likelihood of your finding his fingerprints in the flat,' said Professor Rowland. 'If he has, and I believe that to be the case, then I would be very surprised if he'd been careless enough to leave any concrete traces behind him.'

Fredrika considered what the Professor had said about the perpetrator seeming to speed up the pace once the woman escaped from the flat.

'Can we infer that more children will go missing?' she asked, frowning.

'We certainly can,' replied Professor Rowland. 'I think we can more or less assume he has a list of kids he's planning to abduct. It's not something he decides as he goes along – he already has this all worked out.'

'But how does he find them?' blurted Peder in frustration. 'How does he choose the children?'

'It's not the children he finds,' said the Professor. 'It's their mothers. It's the mothers being punished; the children are just a means to an end. He's taking revenge on someone else's behalf. He's putting things to rights.'

'But that still doesn't answer my question,' Peder said in desperation. 'And what's driving him?'

'No,' the Professor agreed, 'not exactly. But almost. Both women have been punished in the same way: he stole and killed their children and dumped them in a place to which they had some link. So one possible conclusion is that both women had committed the same crime. And that the answer to what's driving him is vengeance.'

Professor Rowland adjusted his glasses and scrutinized Alex's diagram.

'He is punishing the women for not loving all children equally. He is punishing them because if you don't love all children, you are not to have any at all.'

He furrowed his brow.

'It's hard to know exactly what he means,' he sighed. 'It seems as if these women, wholly or partially unconsciously, have wronged their own children, or some other child. Again, I don't think the women themselves necessarily remember the precise occasion. They almost certainly haven't broken any law. But *he* thinks they have.'

'And so does the woman in the hospital,' Fredrika put in.

The others looked at her and nodded their agreement.

The Professor made an expansive gesture.

'The word he uses to mark the children, "Unwanted", identifies the subject for us with absolute clarity, especially now we know the backgrounds of his two female companions, but we still don't know exactly what the trigger is, so we do not know either exactly how he once encountered these women who have lost their children. But we know, we *know*, that he must be aware of their pasts, since both bodies were dumped in a town or a place the women have had no contact with for many years.'

Professor Rowland drank some of his now cold coffee.

Fredrika asked tentatively:

'The places where the children were found, might they be linked to the so-called crime?'

'Perhaps,' replied the Professor. 'On the other hand, it could be that the first body was not presented precisely as the man had envisaged. You're working on the hypothesis, aren't you, that the woman now in the hospital drove the car, while the man went to Jönköping to silence Nora? That hypothesis is probably quite correct, so we can't assume Lilian was found exactly the way the man planned. He delegated the important final stage of the plan to the woman, so he relinquished control of the situation for a brief period.'

Alex and Peder exchanged looks. To hell with confidentiality, thought Alex.

'The little girl was lying on her back,' he said. 'The baby was found curled up in a foetal position.'

'Really? That's extremely interesting. That could have been the detail the woman missed, and that's why he beat her up.'

'But how can a little detail like that be so significant in the overall context?' asked Fredrika.

'We mustn't forget that although our adversary is very sharp, very intelligent, he's far from rational. For you and me, it wouldn't matter a damn whether the child was on its back or curled up, we'd be focused on getting rid of the body as unobtrusively as possible. But this man's focused on something else. He's *arranging* the dead children; he wants to tell us something.'

It all went quiet again. The only sound was a fan whirring in one corner. Nobody said a thing.

'There are two gaps in your theory,' Rowland summed up. 'You don't know what form of contact the man had with the women, but you can say almost for sure that it must have been a long time ago. The concrete role played by the locations he selected remains unclear, but look more closely into whether the women have any *special* link to those particular places that hasn't emerged up to now. The other thing you don't know is exactly what the women were punished for, but it's to do with their inability to love all children equally. Look into their pasts. Maybe they worked with children, and were involved in an accident of some kind.'

Alex looked out of the window. More cloud was rolling in over the capital.

'You all look dejected,' said Professor Rowland with a smile. 'But I don't think it'll take you long to solve this one. We mustn't forget, either, that we can reasonably expect to find there's a reason for his becoming such a sick person. When you do find the perpetrator, there's every likelihood you'll discover he had a very disturbed childhood himself, probably without one or both of his parents.'

Alex gave a wan smile.

'Just one more thing,' Peder put in swiftly before the meeting broke up. 'That woman Nora met him, er, seven years ago. Does that mean there were earlier murders? And why did it take him almost ten years to find a new partner?'

Professor Rowland looked at Peder.

'That's an excellent question,' he said slowly. 'And I recommend that's where you start. Where was our man in the years that elapsed between his first and second accomplice?'

The meeting did not go on for long after Professor Rowland had left the Den to be escorted to the exit by Ellen. Everyone in the team, whether old, new or borrowed, was on tenterhooks round the table.

Fredrika had rather the same feeling she used to get when she watched a thriller and could sense in every fibre of her body how near the plot was to its denouement, but still had no idea how it would end. Inviting Professor Rowland had been a stroke of genius. Fredrika made a mental note to tell Peder later what a great initiative it had been.

She was pleased to see everyone in the room looking equally elated. It certainly said something about the case, the fact that so much energy could be generated even on a Saturday.

Alex set out the two main lines of enquiry they were to follow from there. Their top priority was to be individuals who had served sentences and been released that year, or at the end of the previous year. Alex admitted they didn't know exactly what they were looking for, but there were a number of indications as to the age of the murderer, and he was probably an educated man. He might even be a psychologist, as he had told Nora and Jelena. To get a better fix on the time, they would need to interview Jelena Scortz again about when she first met the man. They could also check with her whether he had disfigured hands or fingers.

The other priority was investigating the pasts of Sara Sebastiansson and Magdalena Gregersdotter. At what stage of their lives had they been associated with the places where their children were later found murdered?

The division of labour was covered in just two sentences: Peder would be in charge of the task of identifying released prisoners who fitted the criteria. Fredrika would be in charge of the task of mapping the two women's earlier lives. Alex laid a heavy hand on Fredrika's shoulder.

'It would make things a whole lot easier if you, being so keen on cause and effect, could find a link between a bathroom in Bromma and a child losing its life.'

He gave a tired wink as he said it.

Fredrika found nothing to complain about in terms of the task she had been allocated. Quite the opposite: she was very happy with it. She gave a melancholy smile as she thought of Alex's words: 'You being so keen on cause and effect . . .' There was nothing much she could say at times like that, she'd discovered. It was best just to go along with it.

Fredrika closed her eyes and put her head in her hands.

An A&E department in a town Sara Sebastiansson went to over fifteen years ago.

A bathroom in a house where Magdalena Gregersdotter lived over twenty years ago.

She repeated the words to herself several times. An A&E department in a town . . .

She tried leaning back in her chair. She was filled with a feverish kind of tension. They were missing something. Something fundamental.

Alex's words echoed in her head again. *It would make things a whole lot easier if you, being so keen on cause and effect, could find a link between a bathroom in Bromma and a child losing its life.*

Then she heard Professor Rowland's voice. *The women are probably both being punished for the same crime.*

A thought slowly began to take shape in her mind. Afraid of losing focus, she groped for pen and paper without changing her position in her seat.

Her pulse started racing when she finally gave the thought its freedom.

Of course.

You just had to play around with the words a bit, and they fell into place.

The common denominator of a bathroom in Bromma and a town in Norrland. That was what Fredrika had said with a bitter laugh when Alex rang and she went out onto Margareta Andersson's balcony in Umeå to take the call. But Alex had said something else. *Something about finding a link between a bathroom in Bromma and an A&E department in Umeå.*

Of course. It was only when the thought occurred to her that she realized what they had overlooked, and not followed up in the investigation. It wasn't Umeå that was relevant here, but the A&E department itself.

The wrong questions inevitably yielded the wrong answers. Bearing in mind that the other child was found in a bathroom, it seemed very odd if the intention had been for the first one to be lying outside the hospital. By that token, the baby could just as well have been left on the pavement outside the house where it was found. So the person who dumped Lilian in Umeå had made more than just one mistake. And paid dearly for it.

With the last piece of the puzzle finally in place, Fredrika felt nothing but relief. It wasn't the children who had links to the geographical locations where they were found, but their mothers. So Alex had said the wrong thing, and thought the wrong thing, when he asked her to see a connection between a bathroom in Bromma and a murdered child. But he had been right the first time. The connection was between a bathroom in Bromma and a woman who had once lived in the house. So the equivalent connection must be between Umeå University Hospital and . . .

Fredrika was already reaching for the phone as she thought her idea through to its logical conclusion. There was just one more person she needed to speak to before she had a full picture of what had really kept Sara Sebastiansson up in Umeå that summer so long ago.

It was Saturday evening, yet Peder was still at work. It was summer and it was cloudy. It was cool and it was clammy. Nothing was how it should be.

Peder again felt himself being tossed between conflicting extremes of emotion. He hadn't spoken to Ylva all day, and now he was anguished at feeling regret about the fact. He had begun the day feeling worthless and unproductive at work, and now he suddenly felt his career was practically at its peak. Inviting the American professor in had been a lucky throw of the dice. Above all for the investigation, but also for Peder himself. He felt so much more than adequate. He felt energized and ready.

The car almost found its own way back to Karolinska. This time he hadn't rung to warn them he was coming. If it wasn't convenient, he'd just have to come back the next day.

He tried to feel sorry for Jelena Scortz, who had suffered so much misfortune in her relatively short life. But at the same time, he was possessed of an unshakable faith in what was known as Free Will. No matter that Jelena Scortz's life had been shit, there was a time limit on how long a lousy childhood was allowed to affect the rest of your life. And if you allowed yourself to go in for crazy things like murdering children, you were worth less than nothing in Peder's eyes. That went for Jelena Scortz, too. That went *especially* for Jelena Scortz, in fact; that dark, angry look Peder had seen in her mangled face when she spoke of why the women had to be punished was burnt into his memory.

She knew what she was doing when she held Sara up in Flemingsberg, thought Peder bitterly. She bloody well knew.

Even so, Peder softened when he got up to the ward and saw Jelena. He was no fan, either, of anyone who could inflict such extensive injuries on a fellow human being.

There was a nurse at Jelena's bedside, helping her drink through a straw. The nurse jumped at the sound of Peder behind her.

'You startled me,' she said, and gave a laugh when she saw his ID.

It wasn't the same nurse as before.

Peder smiled back at her. Jelena didn't move a muscle.

'I'd like to have a little talk to Jelena, if she's up to it,' he said. 'I was here this morning, as well.'

The nurse frowned.

'Well I'm not sure . . .' she began.

'I'll be quick,' Peder added hurriedly, 'and only if Jelena doesn't mind.'

The nurse turned to Jelena.

'Do you think you can talk to the policeman for a minute?' she asked uneasily.

Jelena said nothing.

Peder slowly approached the bed.

'I've got a couple of follow-up questions,' he said softly. 'Only if you feel up to it.'

Jelena still said nothing, but she kept her eyes on him and didn't shake her head in protest. Peder decided to interpret that as tacit consent.

'Can you tell me how long you've known the man?' he asked.

Jelena turned her head very slightly on the pillow. Was she starting to regret having run away from the man? Did she feel she had betrayed him by quitting the battle? If so, she was unlikely to say a word more to anyone in the investigation team.

'Since . . . New Year . . .'

She spoke so quietly that Peder could hardly hear what she said.

'Since New Year,' the nurse interpreted, enunciating more clearly than she needed to.

Peder nodded eagerly.

'How did you meet? Please tell me . . .'

He was pleading. A thing he very rarely did.

Small, solitary tears began slowly rolling down Jelena's bruised and battered cheeks. Peder swallowed. The job could

Kristina Ohlsson

never be allowed to get personal, but you could never let yourself be so aloof that you lost your human touch.

'The street,' Jelena said, quietly but so clearly that both Peder and the nurse heard what she said.

But the nurse still opened her mouth to clarify the woman's words again. Peder indicated to her to be quiet.

'The street,' he repeated slowly. 'Were you . . . Were you working as a prostitute when you met the man?'

Yes and no questions were easier. Then she could just nod or shake her head. This time she nodded.

Is he a kerb-crawler? wondered Peder. Is that how we're going to find him?

Jelena seemed suddenly very drowsy. The nurse began to look very concerned. Peder got up to go. He had the information he needed.

He said thank you and took his leave, but pulled up short in the doorway.

'Just one more question, Jelena,' he said.

She turned her head and looked at him.

'Was there anything odd about his hands? Were they damaged in some way?'

She swallowed several times. Peder could see she was in a lot of pain.

'Burned.'

Peder frowned.

'Burned,' repeated Jelena. 'He said . . . they got . . . burned.'

She was utterly exhausted. Peder stared at her until he felt his eyes were going to pop out of his head. It couldn't be true.

'He told you they got burned?'

Another nod.

'And they looked as if they had?'

More nodding.

Peder tried to think, though his thoughts were stampeding all over the place.

'Where,' he began. 'How . . . ?'

He cleared his throat.

'Were the scars on the backs or the palms of his hands?'

'Palms.'

'Did they look old, these scars?'

Jelena gave a weary shake of her aching head.

'New,' she whispered. 'New . . . when . . . we . . . met.'

Bloody hell. Was there anything this man hadn't thought of?

Peder swallowed again.

'Jelena, if there's anything, anything at all, you want to tell us, you can do it whenever – *absolutely whenever* – you want. Thank you.'

Peder had turned to go, when Jelena made a sound.

He looked at her enquiringly.

'Doll,' whispered Jelena, who had stopped crying now. 'He . . . calls . . . me . . . Doll.'

Peder thought she looked as though she was attempting to smile.

Fredrika received a call from someone who introduced herself as Dr Sonja Lundin.

For a moment, Fredrika was at a loss. She didn't recognize the voice or the name.

'I'm a hospital pathologist in Umeå,' she clarified. 'I was the one who carried out the first proper examination of the little girl who was found murdered up here.'

Fredrika felt embarrassed at not recognizing the woman's name. But then it was Alex who had dealt with that part of the investigation.

'I don't think we've been in touch before,' said Sonja Lundin, in answer to her unspoken question, 'but I rang to speak to your colleague Alex Recht, and they referred me to you because he's in the middle of an important call. One of you left a message for me about a patient file.'

Fredrika's heart skipped a beat.

'I can deal with it,' she confirmed. 'I was the one who rang.'

She was profoundly grateful that Alex was unavailable, because this was not a conversation intended for his ears.

'Strictly speaking,' Sonja Lundin said dubiously, 'this sort of information is confidential.'

'Of course,' Fredrika hastened to say.

'But given the nature of the crime and the fact that your

enquiry is no more specific than it is, I see no problem in answering your question,' Sonja Lundin announced briskly.

Fredrika held her breath.

'There is a file in the name of the person you enquired about,' Sonja Lundin informed her.

Fredrika blinked. There, she'd thought so.

'Can you give me a date?' she said quietly, afraid of over-stepping the mark and demanding too much information.

Sonja Lundin was silent for a moment.

'29 July 1989,' she then said. 'The patient was discharged the same day. But I'm afraid I can't tell you what she was here for unless . . .'

Fredrika interrupted her.

'That's all I need to know for the moment. Thanks very much indeed for your help.'

Evening was drawing in. The sky had an almost autumnal look as the evening sun went behind a cloud. What had happened to summer this year? Alex let his eyes rest on the view from his window. It felt like a different sort of evening. An exciting one.

Alex's reflective mood was punctured by Peder, who came galloping into the room. Alex smiled. Whereas Fredrika was forever slipping out on secret little missions and dramatically revealing her findings at group meetings, Peder liked to report back frequently on his achievements and conclusions.

'They've known each other since New Year,' he announced, sinking uninvited into the armchair Alex kept for visitors.

'Who?'

'Jelena and the so-called Man.'

'And how do you know that?'

Peder drew himself up.

'I told you I was going out to Karolinska,' he replied, with a slightly defiant air.

When Alex said nothing, Peder went on.

'He picked her up off the street; she was a prostitute.'

Alex sighed, and propped his chin in one hand.

'Wasn't the other girl, as well? The Jönköping murder?' asked Peder.

Alex's brow furrowed.

'I don't think so,' he said uncertainly. 'You'll have to check with Fredrika, but I don't think so. She was in with that sort of crowd, though, so she might very well have met him on the street, come to think of it.'

Peder made an impatient gesture.

'Oh come on,' he said. 'What would she be doing on the street if she wasn't a prostitute?'

'How the fuck do I know?' Alex said tetchily. 'It's what her grandmother said. And if Grandma wants to varnish the truth a bit, that's up to Grandma. But she might also be right. Nora isn't on our files in connection with any prostitution rackets.'

'But how does she fit into all this?' asked Peder. 'I just don't get why he bothers at that critical stage to shoot over to Jönköping and bump off an ex-girlfriend.'

'An ex-girlfriend he long since let in on all his plans,' Alex reminded him.

'Sure,' said Peder. 'Sure. But still . . . What the hell was the point?'

'I'm with you on that, but I say we leave it aside for now,'

Alex said doggedly. 'I've spoken to the Jönköping police. They didn't manage to secure a single clue to the identity of the killer except that Ecco shoeprint. The Jönköping line of enquiry isn't going to get us anywhere.'

'But we suspected for a while that he had some way of knowing what stage we'd reached in the investigation,' began Peder.

'That must have been a coincidence,' Alex broke in. 'At that point we scarcely knew ourselves that she'd rung in and tipped us off about him.'

Peder shut his mouth. Then he said:

'The reason they can't find anything is that he's sabotaged his own fingers.'

Alex stared at him.

'Are you joking?'

Peder shook his head.

'Christ almighty,' groaned Alex. 'What kind of pervert are we dealing with here?'

Peder was quick to supply the information.

'Could he be a kerb-crawler?'

Alex was brought up short.

'Kerb-crawler?'

'That's how he finds his girls.'

Alex put his head on one side.

'That's not a bad idea,' he said slowly. 'Not a bad idea at all. And there are kerb-crawlers from all social classes, as we know.'

'Right, I'll start looking there, then,' Peder declared.

'You do that,' Alex said with equal determination, adding: 'And check out particularly anybody who's been had up for gross violation of a woman's integrity, or any other crimes of violence directed at women. This might not be the first time he's assaulted a woman.'

Peder gave a keen nod.

Then they both just sat there, trying to summon the energy to stand up and get to grips with everything that needed to be done.

'She said he calls her "Doll",' said Peder, breaking the silence.

'Doll?' echoed Alex.

Any bereavement is hard to bear.

But the grief of losing a child is not just heavy: it is as dark as night.

Fredrika tried to hold that thought in her mind as she got out of the car outside Sara Sebastiansson's flat. Once she had had the phone call from Umeå, there was no reason to delay, so she had come straight round. She wondered if she was overstepping the mark by coming to see her on a Saturday evening, and found the answer to be an emphatic no. No, given the circumstances it wasn't wrong. Not in the slightest.

Fredrika tried to keep her anger in check. She tried to understand, and above all she tried to convince herself there was a reason why Sara had behaved as she had done.

But she could feel the frustration pounding away inside her. A piece of the puzzle had been missing all this time, and Sara had been coolly sitting there with it in her hand. She had not just obstructed the investigation of her own daughter's death; she had also obstructed progress in the baby Natalie case.

Fredrika wished instinctively and with all her heart that Sara would be alone in the flat when she rang the doorbell. Otherwise she would have to ask the parents to leave.

Sara opened the door at Fredrika's second ring. She looked pale and haggard, with such dark rings under her bloodshot eyes that all Fredrika's anger and frustration melted away. Reality landed right in front of her: this was a woman who had just experienced her worst nightmare in real life. Criticism had very little place here.

'I'm sorry to turn up unannounced,' Fredrika said in a low but steady voice, 'but I need to talk to you.'

Sara stepped back from the door to let Fredrika in, and showed her through to the living room. It seemed to be serving as an extra bedroom; there were mattresses on the floor. Presumably her parents hadn't gone home yet, though to Fredrika's relief they weren't anywhere to be seen.

'Are you on your own?' asked Fredrika.

Sara nodded.

'Mum and Dad are out doing some food shopping,' she said in a thin voice. 'They'll be back soon.'

Fredrika unobtrusively took out her notepad.

'Have you found him?' The words burst out of Sara.

'You mean . . .' Fredrika began, rather confused.

'I mean Gabriel,' replied Sara, and when Fredrika met her gaze she felt cold all over.

Sara's eyes were blazing with pure, unadulterated hatred.

'No,' said Fredrika, 'we haven't found him. But we've issued a nationwide alert and arrested him in his absence.'

She swallowed and paused.

'But we no longer suspect him of Lilian's abduction and

murder. In purely practical terms, he can't possibly have done it.'

Sara gave Fredrika a long look.

'I don't think he murdered our daughter either,' she said. 'But now I know he had his computer full of disgusting child porn, I can't wait for you to find him and lock him up for all the time he's damn well got left to him.'

Fredrika did not even consider getting into a discussion of the sort of sentence that might be waiting for Gabriel Sebastiansson when they found him, if they ever did. She kept it all inside her, and tried to say something comforting instead:

'There's nothing to indicate he abused Lilian.'

Sara stared straight ahead through empty eyes, and said on a rising note:

'So I was told. But that's no guarantee he didn't touch her, the total arsehole.'

She shrieked the last words so loud that Fredrika began to wonder if it had been such a good idea to come alone and unannounced, but she held her apprehension in check. Her business with Sara was vital to the investigation.

'Sara,' she said resolutely, 'we need to talk about Umeå.'

Sara wiped away a few tears that had found their way down her cheeks.

'I've already told you about Umeå,' she said.

'But I wonder if you've any idea why Lilian ended up outside the hospital,' Fredrika said.

'I haven't got a clue,' Sara said, but she avoided looking at Fredrika.

'We, the police, think she was left there for a special reason,' Fredrika went on implacably. 'We think you might have some connection to the place, which the murderer knew about, and that was why he chose that precise location.'

Sara stared uncomprehendingly at Fredrika.

'Is there something you haven't told us?' asked Fredrika. 'Something you thought wasn't important, that couldn't possibly have any bearing on the case, so you didn't need to tell us about it? Something private that you'd rather not talk about?'

Sara dropped her eyes and shook her head. Fredrika suppressed a sigh.

'Sara, we know you have a patient file at Umeå University Hospital,' she said firmly, 'and we're convinced there's a link between your visit and the fact that Lilian was left there.'

'I had an abortion,' whispered Sara, after a long hesitation.

Fredrika did not take her eyes off Sara's face. That was what she had suspected, but she had needed confirmation.

'I got pregnant about the time I broke up with my boyfriend that spring, and of course I couldn't tell them about it at home. So I decided to have it done when I was up in Umeå on the course. It wasn't very difficult to arrange. I told the course tutor I had to have a day off to meet someone I knew, and then I went to the hospital instead.'

What was the loneliest thing imaginable? Going through a covert abortion had to be high on the list. And more importantly, was that why Sara was now being punished so cruelly?

'I'm really sorry we have to drag up this old business,' said Fredrika, 'but we have to know for the sake of the investigation.'

Sara nodded and shed silent tears.

'Did anyone – anyone at all – know what you had done in Umeå?'

Sara shook her head hard.

'Nobody knew,' she sobbed. 'Not even Maria who came on the course with me. I didn't tell a single person. I've never spoken about it until now.'

Fredrika's body registered pain. Sara's living room felt as if it was closing in around her.

'And that was why you made sure you stayed on in Umeå longer than Maria?' she asked.

'Yes, I couldn't very well have it done while Maria was still there,' said Sara, suddenly very tired.

Then she pulled herself together.

'It would be extremely unfortunate if my parents found out about this,' she said, her voice shaking.

'I can assure you that we won't be letting the information go any further,' Fredrika swiftly assured her, and very much hoped she wasn't lying.

Then she asked again:

'You're sure you didn't tell anyone? Not even your boyfriend? Wasn't there anyone who knew or could have suspected something?'

Sara shook her head.

'I didn't tell a soul,' she said doggedly. 'Not a soul.'

But somebody knew, thought Fredrika. *Some evil person knew*.

And then, without thinking what she was doing, she leant forward and laid a warm hand on Sara's shoulder. Almost like the pastoral carer she had said she didn't want to be.

Ellen Lind didn't feel guilty about going home earlier than the others in the team. Her role wasn't the most vital, after all.

All the time she was growing up, Ellen had been the classic overshadowed child. She lived permanently in the shadow of her older and more successful siblings. She also lived in the shadow of her attractive, successful parents. She was very aware of being the unplanned afterthought, while the other children had been very much wanted. Ellen wasn't even a family name, unlike those her two elder brothers and sister had been given.

Her sense of exclusion intensified and became permanently ingrained. Ellen was different. She even looked different. She was differently proportioned, with blunter facial features. Her sister and brothers were tall, good-looking, and self-assured from an early age. But not Ellen.

Ellen, however, had put all that behind her long ago. Now that she was a grown-up woman with a family of her own, she viewed her parents and siblings as little more than distant relations.

Past experience meant Ellen felt fairly resigned to the sense of exclusion she experienced at work. She was used to being the outsider, used to not fitting in. She and Fredrika had had a few discreet chats about it – everything about Fredrika was discreet – when Fredrika first joined the team, but they hadn't exactly become close friends. Ellen thought that was rather a shame, because she was sure she and Fredrika would have made ideal friends.

But neither Fredrika nor work was uppermost in her mind as she went home that Saturday night. She was thinking about Carl, and about her children. Most of all, she was thinking about Carl.

She was concerned that he hadn't replied to her text, not yesterday and not today either. Nor had he answered when she rang him. She didn't even get through to his voicemail, just to a robotic monotone telling her syllable by syllable that 'this subscriber is currently unavailable. Please try again later.'

It was as if he had gone to ground.

Ellen tried not to worry. It had all gone swimmingly last time they met. She knew she'd been over-sensitive about relationships since her marriage fell apart. She easily got a touch paranoid, and there was undoubtedly no less desirable quality you could possess in the marriage market. She felt her chest tightening and a sort of pressure building there. A few deep breaths made her feel better. But a bit later she found her stomach aching instead.

She knew it was idiotic, of course. There would be a perfectly natural explanation for Carl's silence. She couldn't expect him to be permanently available for her.

Ellen tried to laugh at herself.

She had really got it badly. She was seriously in love, for the first time ever.

The pathologist who carried out the autopsy on baby Natalie finally managed to get hold of Alex. She told him in brief that the procedure appeared identical to the way Lilian Sebastiansson had been killed. Insulin had been injected into her fontanelle. No fingerprints and no traces of another person's DNA had been found on the body.

There had been no trace either, however, of the talc product found on Lilian.

'Which is rather strange,' the pathologist remarked. 'It means the murderer decided he didn't need to wear gloves for this murder.'

'There's nothing strange about it,' Alex said bluntly. 'Our man doesn't have to worry about leaving fingerprints; only the woman, and his previous female accomplice, needed gloves. And the woman didn't handle the second child.'

'Why doesn't he need gloves?' asked the pathologist in surprise.

'He burned his own hands to make sure he wouldn't leave fingerprints.'

'Incredible,' the pathologist whispered, mainly to herself.

Alex asked whether she could tell him anything else.

There was silence while she thought.

'No,' she said eventually. 'No, nothing at all. Well yes, actually.'

Alex waited.

'We found no traces of sedative in the baby like those we found in Lilian.'

Alex pondered this.

'The baby was asleep when she was snatched from her pram,' he mused aloud. 'The murderer probably didn't feel the need to sedate her.'

'Of course,' said the pathologist. 'Of course.'

Then she added:

'There's nothing more I can tell you about the baby. No violence was done to her other than the lethal injection, and I found no bruising on her body, new or old.'

'Old?' queried Alex, frowning.

He could sense the pathologist blushing at the other end of the line as she answered:

'There are so many sick parents. It was just as well to check . . .'

Alex gave a sad smile.

'Yes, you're quite right.'

It had initially surprised Alex to find how often the executioner was to be found in the victim's immediate vicinity. It had taken him years to understand how it was even possible. He could comprehend how someone might lose their head in the heat of the moment and hit out at another person. But the step from there to the cold-blooded killing of another human being, often fully conscious of what you were doing, was too big for him to take. What was more, people seemed capable of killing each other for the most bizarre reasons.

'It's a mad world,' Alex whispered to his wife one evening when they were newly married and about to go to sleep.

She had chosen that moment to tell him they were expecting their first baby. Her timing in breaking the news had done nothing to dispel his conception of the world: it *was* mad.

But however hard Alex struggled to make the Lilian case fit the mould of all the other missing children cases he had dealt with in his career, however hard he wished it would end in some way he would later find hard to call to mind, he knew that the case of the abduction and death of Lilian Sebastiansson was quite unique, and that he would never forget it.

He peered at the clock. How long were they going to carry on? Was it really worth their while to work all night? How would everyone feel tomorrow if they did? The team had got to be able to stay the course.

The pathologist gave a little cough. The sound interrupted Alex's thoughts and made him feel foolish.

'Excuse me,' he hastened to say, 'but I didn't quite hear that last bit.'

The pathologist seemed to be hesitating.

'The fact that he injects the toxic substance into the child's head,' she started slowly.

'Yes?'

Further hesitation.

'I don't know, maybe I'm completely wrong and it's got nothing to do with the case, but . . . in some countries that's an entirely legal method of carrying out a late abortion.'

'Sorry?' said Alex, raising his eyebrows.

'Yes, it's true,' said the pathologist, rather more sure of herself now.

When Alex said nothing, she continued.

'It was practised in a number of countries where very late

abortions were allowed. It was really more of a delivery than an abortion. When the baby's head appeared, the lethal substance was injected straight into the skull, so the child was by definition stillborn when it came out.'

'Good God,' said Alex.

'Well that's how it was,' the pathologist said in conclusion. 'But as I say, it may not be relevant to this case at all.'

The thoughts went chasing round inside Alex's head.

'I wouldn't say that,' he told the pathologist. 'I wouldn't say that.'

Alex returned with renewed energy to the material spread out in front of him.

The atmosphere in the Den had been magical when the American psychologist was talking. It was actually a long time since Alex had encountered someone who spoke that much sense. He had practically laid out the whole structure for the investigation from that point on.

Alex grabbed the report he had just had from the squad that had searched Jelena Scortz's flat. It had been hard work, very hard work, extracting a search warrant from the examining magistrate. Jelena was considered to have admitted far too little to confirm that she was implicated in Lilian's murder. It was only when Alex made the point that regardless of the degree to which they could prove she was an accessory to murder, she had at the very least admitted that the main suspect had stayed in the flat. That was enough to justify a search warrant.

But just as the psychologist had predicted, the search of the flat yielded nothing to help them identify the killer. They naturally found huge numbers of fingerprints in the flat. And when they were checked against the National Police Board's fingerprint register, they nearly all turned out to belong to Jelena herself. Her fingerprints were stored in the system because she had been arrested and charged with theft and receiving stolen goods some years before.

None of the other fingerprints had matched anything in the register. And the perpetrator himself left no fingerprints at all, of course.

Alex felt ill looking at the photos taken in the bedroom where Jelena had been left after the assault. Blood on the sheets, blood on the walls, blood on the floor.

The search team had not found a single object that looked as if it could belong to a man. There was only one toothbrush in the bathroom, and that had been taken for analysis. Alex was absolutely certain they would find no one's DNA on it but Jelena's. They found no men's clothes, either.

There were in fact only two items of potential interest that the police had brought from the flat. One was some individual strands of hair, found on the bathroom floor. With luck they might prove to be Lilian Sebastiansson's, and then there would be no need to worry any more about linking Jelena to Lilian's murder. The other was a pair of dark Ecco shoes, size 46. They had been standing neatly in the hall.

Alex was entirely nonplussed. How could anyone as strategic and intelligent as the murderer clearly was make such a blunder?

Then he realized there could only be one answer, and his pulse rate accelerated to an almost dangerous level.

It was obvious – *obvious* – that the murderer must have

returned to the flat after the assault on Jelena. Returned and discovered her gone. It must have been quite easy for him to work out that the police would link Jelena to the crime sooner or later, especially if he had seen the appeal for information about her in the national press.

'Shit, shit, shit!' shouted Alex, thumping his fist on the desk.

He stared at the picture of the Ecco shoes, which seemed to be jeering at him. The sheer cheek of it made him feel weak at the knees.

He knew we'd be able to identify Jelena sooner or later, and that would eventually lead us to the flat as well, Alex thought. So he left the goddamn shoes as a greeting.

It was almost half past seven and Fredrika Bergman was wondering whether to drop in on Magdalena Gregersdotter before nightfall or to leave it for the next day. She decided to go back to the office and talk it over with Alex before making up her mind.

Fredrika was so worked up that she could hardly sit still in the car. Music blared from the loudspeakers at top volume. *Swan Lake*. For the briefest of brief moments, Fredrika was back in the life she had lived before The Accident. Music that made her feel alive, an occupation to which she devoted herself passionately.

And then her mother's voice:

Play so somebody could dance to the music; always remember the Invisible Dancer.

Fredrika could almost see the Invisible Dancer dancing *Swan Lake* on the bonnet of her car. For the first time in ages, she felt alive. She hadn't the words to describe how glorious it felt.

From pure euphoria, she texted Spencer as soon as she had parked outside HQ and thanked him again for a wonderful night. Her fingers wanted to write something more amorous. Reason won as usual, and she slipped the phone into her bag without firing off any declarations of love. But she had that feeling again. That feeling of something being different, something having changed.

We've been pushing the boundaries recently, she thought. We see each other more often and we've started putting how much we mean to each other into words.

There were still people working at their desks as Fredrika offloaded her handbag and jacket in her little room. In the police world, success was measured in terms of the number of square metres of office space you were given. Rumour had it that the security services were planning to move out of HQ and house their staff in a new building with open plan offices. Fredrika sniggered at the thought of the outcry there would be if a plan like that were ever put forward in her department. She could hear her colleague Håkan raising his voice in protest:

'You expect *me* to work in an open plan office? When I've waited twenty-two years to move into the office next to mine!'

Fredrika was in a good mood, to put it mildly. But as she stood in the doorway of Alex's room a moment or two later, she felt all the energy and appetite drain from her.

'Has something happened?' she asked automatically when she saw the grim look on Alex's face.

She immediately regretted her choice of words. Two little

girls had been murdered in under a week – that alone made the phrasing of her question ludicrous.

But Alex wasn't one to notice the choice of words. Fredrika more than made up for him in that respect.

'So did your sudden flying visit produce anything?' was all he said.

Fredrika had surprised him several times in recent days. He had high expectations of her now.

'I think I know what crime the women had committed, and the reason why he's punishing them,' she said.

Alex raised his eyebrows.

'I've got a theory, too,' he smiled. 'Shall we see if they match?'

Peder started by looking at all the men serving sentences for violation of a woman's integrity who had been released since the previous November. There were far too many of them. He refined his search to a particular age group, men between forty and fifty.

He saw that most of the men had only served very short sentences. It was seven years since Nora had known the man; what had he been doing since? Were there other women who had been through the same thing, but who they just hadn't found yet? Worse still, were there more children who had died in similar circumstances? Peder felt close to panic. Why hadn't he thought of that before? Why had they assumed these were the murderer's first victims?

Then he calmed down a bit. If there were any police officers in the country who had worked on similar cases over the past twenty years, they would undoubtedly have been in touch with their Stockholm colleagues by now. Unless the murderer had tried, and failed? Maybe he had abducted a child, but not gone through with the actual murder?

Peder shook his head in frustration. They had to take the risk of concentrating their efforts, had to dare to choose which line to pursue first. Peder jotted down the options he had ruled out. 'Glad to see you prioritizing!' Fredrika would have said if she'd seen him.

Peder decided to ask Alex to delegate to some other member of the team those lines of enquiry he still considered important, but less pressing.

He looked at the lists he had collated. There were altogether too many people on them with sentences way too short. If he bore in mind what the team had agreed on:

1. that their murderer had for some reason been inactive since he lost control of Nora, and had 'recruited' Jelena in her place;
2. that he was probably on their files and might have been convicted of some grievous crime of violence that had kept him locked up for most of the period since Nora left him;
3. that he was in all probability mentally ill;
4. that he possibly visited prostitutes

then there shouldn't be that many names left on the list. But how did you sift out that kind of information?

Peder worked frantically at his keyboard.

Police files weren't damn well designed for this kind of investigation, he thought angrily.

He'd had help in retrieving the first set of data he had worked on. But the help, that is to say Ellen, had finished for the day, and wouldn't be back until tomorrow. Perhaps it was time for Peder to call it a day, too, go home and get some sleep.

The very thought filled Peder with anxiety. He didn't feel the least bit inclined to go home and be confronted with his crumbling marriage. He missed the children. But he was intensely tired of their mother.

'What the hell shall I do?' muttered Peder. 'What in fuck's name shall I do?'

He'd heard nothing from Pia Nordh since he left her flat. He was thankful for that. He felt thoroughly ashamed of the way he had behaved that morning. And it scared him that it felt like several years ago, when it fact it was only a few days.

Peder looked down at his conscientiously scribbled notes. He read through them. He read through them again.

He opened his filing cabinet and got out the diagram he and Fredrika had drawn up with timelines for Gabriel Sebastiansson's movements the day his daughter was kidnapped. He took a blank sheet of paper out of his desk drawer and started drawing a new timeline.

It's all too rushed, he thought as he drew. There are too few of us with too much to get into our heads too quickly; that's why we keep missing little things.

Magdalena Gregersdotter's parents had sold their house in Bromma over fifteen years ago. If Natalie's murder had anything to do with Magdalena's family home, then the murderer must have had contact with Magdalena – in some unfathomable way – before her parents sold the house.

So let's see. First the murderer was in Stockholm for a time.

Somehow he became aware of Magdalena, probably when she committed the 'crime' that she was now being punished for. Then he moved – temporarily or permanently – to Umeå. He stayed there long enough to come across both Sara Sebastiansson and Nora from Jönköping, now deceased.

Peder paused for thought, then decided to try refining his search through the bulk of material still further. The man they were looking for had probably committed the crime for which he served his prison sentence in Umeå, or somewhere nearby.

Peder went through his list. Then he added a final bullet point:

The man had not necessarily been in prison for seven years. He could have been sentenced to psychiatric care.

There was a knock at Peder's door.

'Can you come along for a very quick meeting in the Den before we call it a day?'

'Sure,' answered Alex, as he fired off his email request to Ellen.

She would have to deal with it in the morning.

'Abortion?' Peder said in amazement.

'Yes,' replied Fredrika.

Peder's drooping eyes were suddenly wide open.

'Did Magdalena Gregersdotter have an abortion, too? Remember the psychologist said the women had probably both committed the same "crime" . . .'

Fredrika gave an eager nod.

'I remember,' she said. 'But I haven't had a chance to talk to Magdalena yet. I'll get round there tomorrow morning.'

'Could he have been the doctor who performed their abortions?' Peder wondered aloud.

'We mustn't get ahead of ourselves,' warned Alex, holding up a hand. 'First we need to establish that Magdalena did have an abortion. And if so, we must try to clarify why he crept in and put her dead child on the bathroom floor of her parents' old house, and not at the hospital where the abortion was carried out.'

'In the old days, women did their own abortions,' began Peder, but was silenced by both Fredrika and Alex.

Peder decided to keep his mouth shut.

'And we must certainly find out,' said Alex in a businesslike tone, 'why we weren't told this earlier.'

'Because you think in the way you just sounded,' Fredrika said frankly.

Peder and Alex looked blank.

'What you just said was: "why weren't we told this earlier?"' she explained. '"Weren't told", rather than didn't find out. If we thought of facts as things we have to uncover – by asking the right questions, for example – then we wouldn't be so vulnerable and reliant on the information other people feel like giving us.'

Alex and Peder exchanged glances. They both wore a faint smile.

'Don't you think?' asked Fredrika, suddenly unsure.

Alex laughed out loud for the first time in days.

'You could well have a point,' he grinned.

Fredrika flushed.

'Sara didn't want to say anything about the abortion, but we all kind of assumed that if she had some specific connection to the hospital and not just Umeå in general, she'd tell us about it of her own accord,' Alex said thoughtfully, looking serious again. 'That was a mistake. We should have stuck to our guns, pressed her harder even though it didn't feel quite right.'

He gathered up his papers.

'We'll carry on in the morning,' he said. 'It's late and we've come a long way today. I'd even say a very long way.'

'That's why it doesn't feel right to go home just now,' Peder said grumpily.

'I know it seems tough, but we all need a bit of rest,' Alex insisted. 'We'll reconvene in the morning. I've already rung round to warn everyone it'll be a full day's work tomorrow. We'll have to take our days off some other time.'

Fredrika glanced out of the window at the dull grey, cloudy summer sky.

'We can take them when summer comes,' she said drily.

THE LAST DAY

Ellen Lind was the first one in on Sunday morning. She was the first to arrive and the first to leave. She liked working that way.

She sent a text to her daughter as she turned on her computer. She had asked the children about a hundred times if they really thought they'd be all right at home on their own without a babysitter. They had assured her at least as many times that they'd be absolutely fine.

Peder's request was at the top of Ellen's inbox. She opened the email. Good grief, what sort of searches did that man think you could do in the police files? He still hadn't registered that he wasn't on the set of some American TV crime series, but in the real police world.

Ellen decided to give it a go anyway. She rang her contact at the National Police Board for help. The woman sounded cross and moaned about having to go in.

'Bloody hell, on a Sunday,' she muttered.

Ellen made no comment. For her, these were exceptional circumstances. And though they were downright grotesque ones, she had to admit she thought it was all rather exciting.

Less exciting, and more frustrating, was the fact that she hadn't heard a word from Carl. She had kept her mobile switched on overnight in the hope that he'd be in touch, but he hadn't sent so much as a line. Ellen didn't really think there was any reason to doubt Carl's love, and felt it was more likely that something had happened to him. If she had heard nothing by that evening, she would start ringing round the hospitals.

And yet.

And yet there was something not quite right. A scarcely perceptible feeling of anxiety began to grow and creep over Ellen. However hard she tried, she couldn't shake it off.

Feeling restless, she went to empty the fax machine, which had been receiving messages during the night. Fredrika had a number of faxes from Umeå University Hospital. Ellen frowned as she leafed through the pile. It was clearly the medical record of somebody called Sara Lagerås. There was a short message for Fredrika, too.

'Patient file herewith. Permission received from Sara Sebastiansson by phone. Regards, Sonja Lundin.'

Ellen was immediately curious.

Whatever had she missed by going home first last night?

Fredrika Bergman's head was as heavy as lead when she woke up on Sunday morning. She reached wearily for the alarm clock. It wasn't due to ring for another ten minutes. She burrowed her head as far into the pillow as it would go. Must rest, must rest.

Leaving the flat an hour later, she remembered she hadn't devoted much attention to the phone message from the Adoption Centre. Not *enough* attention, at any rate. Fredrika excused this by concluding it was far too big a decision to make while she was caught up in such a weighty and far-reaching police investigation.

Fredrika focused on the job in hand. She drove straight round to Magdalena Gregersdotter's and rang on the way to say she was coming. She stressed that she would need to speak to Magdalena alone.

A tall, dark-haired woman opened the door when she rang the bell.

'Magdalena?' asked Fredrika, realizing she hadn't the faintest idea what Natalie's mother looked like.

'No,' replied the woman, holding out a cool hand. 'I'm Esther, her sister.'

Esther showed Fredrika into the family living room.

Neat and tidy, she thought. This family has no truck with any kind of messiness or disorder. A very appealing characteristic, in Fredrika's world.

She stood alone in the middle of the living room. So many homes were opened to you when you rang at the door in your professional police capacity. What an enormous stock of trust her employer enjoyed in ordinary domestic settings. The thought almost made her head swim.

Then Magdalena Gregersdotter came into the room, and Fredrika was dragged back to reality.

It struck her that Magdalena was not at all the same kind of woman as Sara Sebastiansson. A woman who would never paint her toenails blue; you could tell by the way she carried herself, by the impression of integrity she gave, that her experiences were far removed from those of the more exuberant Sara. If she admitted to seeing through an abortion in her parents' bathroom, Fredrika was going to have a bit of difficulty believing it.

'Shall we sit down?' she prompted gently.

At least she hoped it sounded gentle. She knew all too well how abrupt she could appear in certain situations.

They sat down. Magdalena perched on the edge of the sofa, Fredrika in a huge armchair. It was upholstered in a multi-coloured fabric that contrasted starkly with the white walls. Fredrika couldn't make up her mind if she thought it was attractive or disgusting.

'Have you . . . got anywhere?'

The look in Magdalena's eyes was plaintive.

'I mean . . . in the investigation, that is. Have you found someone?'

Someone. The magic word that hounded every police officer. Find someone. Pin someone down. Hold someone responsible.

'We haven't identified an individual, but we're working on a theory that could prove very fruitful for the investigation,' Fredrika said.

Magdalena nodded and nodded. Good, good, good.

'And it's our theory that brings me here today,' Fredrika went on, now she had been given a starting point. 'I really only have one question for you,' she said, catching the other woman's dulled eye.

Fredrika deliberately paused to make sure she had Magdalena's undivided attention.

'It's a terribly private question, and it feels grotesque to have to ask it, but . . .'

'I'll answer anything you ask,' Magdalena broke in. 'Anything at all.'

'All right,' said Fredrika, feeling oddly reassured. 'All right.' She took a deep breath.

'I wonder whether you've ever had an abortion.'

Magdalena stared at her.

'An abortion?' she repeated.

Fredrika nodded in confirmation.

Magdalena did not drop her eyes.

'Yes,' she said huskily. 'But it was a long time ago. Almost twenty years.'

Fredrika waited with bated breath.

'It was just after I left home. I was with a man almost fifteen years older than me. He was married, but he promised to leave his wife for me.'

Magdalena gave a hollow laugh.

'But he never did, of course. He went into a total panic when I told him I was pregnant. He shouted at me, told me to get rid of it straight away.'

Magdalena shook her head.

'It wasn't a lot to ask,' she said curtly. 'I got rid of it, of course. And I never saw him again.'

'Where was the actual abortion done?' asked Fredrika.

'Here in Stockholm, at Söder hospital,' Magdalena said quickly. 'But it was so early in the pregnancy that I had to wait several weeks before I could have it done.'

Fredrika could see the other woman's eyes clouding again.

'It was all very weird. You see, the abortion didn't work, but they didn't realize. So I went home thinking the baby was gone, when in fact it was still inside me. A few days later I felt very ill, and miscarried. My body completed the abortion by rejecting the baby, as it were. I think that's why I never managed to get pregnant again. The infection I got afterwards made me sterile.'

She fell silent. Fredrika swallowed and looked for the right words to formulate the vital question:

'Where was the abortion completed?' she asked in a low voice.

Magdalena looked troubled, as if she did not understand.

'Where did you lose the baby?' whispered Fredrika.

Magdalena's face dissolved and she put her hand to her mouth, as if to smother a scream.

'In the bathroom at Mum and Dad's house,' she wept. 'I lost the baby where he left Natalie.'

Peder Rydh was in a bad mood when he got to work on Sunday. The only bright spot was that he'd managed to make Jimmy's day when he rang him on the way in.

'Posh cake soon, Pedda?' cheered Jimmy on the phone.

'Posh cake very soon,' Peder agreed. 'Maybe even tomorrow.'

Assuming there's anything to celebrate by then, he added silently to himself.

Peder's early morning grumpiness was not improved by the fact that Ellen still hadn't been able to get the results from the files that he'd asked for.

'That sort of thing takes time Peder; just be patient, please,' she begged.

He couldn't stand that phrase, but he had no grudge against Ellen and didn't want to fall out with her. So he went back into his room before he said something he'd regret.

That night had not afforded him the same peace of mind as the one before. He had slept on the settee, and that had never happened before. He had briefly considered driving to Jimmy's assisted living unit and bedding down there instead, until he realized how confused and anxious it would make his brother.

Lack of sleep made Peder less than rational, and he knew it. That was why he hadn't exchanged a single word with Ylva before he left home that morning, and had started his working day with two big cups of coffee.

He sat down at his computer and looked up a few things at random in various registers, but found the task beyond him. He didn't have full access to the files, and there were some to which he had no access at all.

He opened his filing cabinet and got out all the material he had amassed. He repeated the phrases they had all been trotting out in recent days. *What do we know? What don't we know? And what do we definitely need to know to solve this case?*

They thought they knew why: the women were being punished because they had once had abortions. That fitted with the words 'women who don't love all children equally are not to have any at all'. To begin with, Peder had interpreted the phrase to mean that the man somehow wanted to punish all women who didn't literally love all children equally, but now he knew that to be wrong.

What the team did *not* know, however, was how the man selected these women from among all those in Sweden who had had abortions and then gone on to have children. Could the murderer actually be the father of the 'rejected' children? Peder didn't think it very likely. The murderer was, or had been, on the margins of the women's lives when they had their abortions. So he could be a doctor, for example. Unless he came across their names later, in old case notes or

432   Kristina Ohlsson

something like that. In that case, he might not even have known them at the time of the abortions.

Peder sighed. There was an almost infinite number of alternatives to choose from.

He returned doggedly to his notes.

There were several indications that the man they were looking for could be linked in some way to a medical setting, like a hospital. There were the traces of talc from hospital gloves; there were the drugs to which he seemed to have access. Sedatives, but also more lethal substances.

Peder reflected. The drugs weren't that uncommon in themselves. They were no doubt to be found in every hospital in Sweden. But not all hospitals had staff members who had served sentences for serious crimes of violence. Was that sort of thing checked up on? And if it was, could the man they were looking for have been working in a hospital under a false identity?

Peder doubted it. Surely hospitals kept tabs on that kind of thing? Unless of course the change of name had been done entirely legally.

Peder shuffled his facts this way and that. All the while, the phrase 'There must be a way of checking this' was echoing in his head. It became a mantra, a life-buoy to cling on to. Somewhere out there was the man they were looking for. All they had to do was find him . . .

Peder had no idea how long he had been sitting there, deep in thought, when Fredrika rang to confirm what they had suspected, namely that Magdalena Gregersdotter had also had an abortion years ago. For Peder, the link to the bathroom in Bromma was both tragic and fascinating.

Half an hour later, Fredrika walked into his room. She looked different, in jeans and a cord jacket, with a sleeveless top underneath. Her hair was pulled back from her face in a tight ponytail and she had scarcely any make-up on. Peder was surprised to find how pretty he thought she looked.

'Have you got time?' asked Fredrika.

'Sure,' he replied.

Fredrika sat down on the other side of the desk. She had a sheaf of papers in her hand.

'I've had the women's hospital records faxed over,' she said, brandishing the papers. 'From the time of their abortions.'

Peder felt reinvigorated.

'You think the murderer works at a hospital, too?'

'I think the murderer works, or worked, in some part of the healthcare system,' Fredrika said guardedly. 'And I think that's where the women might have met him. They didn't *necessarily* meet him in person, but I still tend to think they did. And I think the reason they don't remember him today is that his role in their treatment was a very minor one.'

'A man on the margins,' Peder mumbled.

'Just so,' said Fredrika.

She tossed half the pile of paper onto Peder's desk.

'Shall we do this together, while you're waiting for Ellen to get you your results? Who knows, maybe it could be the shortcut we've been looking for.'

It was getting hotter and hotter in Ellen's office. She could feel her deodorant evaporating and the sweat prickling her skin. She knew this was yet another sign that she was nervous. She always sweated at times like that.

Why had she still heard nothing from Carl? And why had she decided to wait until the evening before she started ringing the hospitals? It felt an indescribably long time away.

Ellen was so anxious she was close to tears. What had really happened? She touched the bouquet of flowers Carl had sent her a few days before. She had so much love to give; why did he have to make it so hard?

My emotions are all over the place, thought Ellen, smiling at what she was finding harder and harder to see as a coincidence.

Then she felt her anxiety and dejection turning to sheer frustration. Not hearing from Carl was one thing, but why weren't the children answering her texts? Didn't they realize she'd be worried?

It was late morning, so she was sure they wouldn't still be asleep. She lifted the receiver of her desk phone and tried ringing the landline instead. She must have let it ring twenty times, but there was no answer.

Anxiety gnawed inside her. The children certainly wouldn't be asleep at eleven in the morning, but they could hardly have gone out, either. Or was she so stressed she'd forgotten one of their activities? Some gym display or football training session?

Ellen tried to work for a while. She was still waiting for Peder's results. After a while she rang home again. Still no answer. She rang both children's mobiles. Neither answered.

Ellen sat silently at her desk. She was worried about the children. She was worried that Carl hadn't been in touch. She looked at the flowers on her desk. She thought of all the confidences she and Carl had exchanged. She remembered him saying that she was so important to him. That she gave him 'everything he needed'.

Then Ellen realized how everything fitted together. Suddenly she wasn't worried or irritated any more. She was terror-stricken.

A lex Recht barely had time to hang up before Peder and
Fredrika came into his room and lined up in front of his
desk. Like two schoolchildren. Alex smiled to himself.

'I assume you two have heard the good news?'

Peder and Fredrika looked at each other.

'That we've got him?' Alex clarified.

Fredrika and Peder both stared at him.

'But how's that possible?' exclaimed Fredrika.

'Simple,' Alex said delightedly. 'He tried to take a flight
from Copenhagen to Thailand and was stopped at passport
control. We were just in time getting Interpol on side, to block
his passport.'

'Sorry, but who are you talking about?' asked a confused
Peder.

Alex frowned.

'Gabriel Sebastiansson, who else?'

A heavy sigh escaped Fredrika and she was obliged to sink
into Alex's visitor's chair.

'We thought you meant the murderer,' she said under her
breath.

'No, no,' Alex said irascibly. 'We've scarcely even identified him yet.'

Peder and Fredrika exchanged looks again.

'Well, we might have,' said Peder.

Alex gestured to him to take the other chair.

Fredrika was about to say something when Ellen came rushing in.

'I'm sorry,' she said in a choked voice, 'but I've got to go home for a little while. I'll be back soon.'

'What's happened?' asked Alex, concerned. 'We really do need you here just now . . .'

'I know,' sighed Ellen, 'but the children aren't answering any of the phones and they're not used to being left on their own at home. I rang their dad as well, and friends they sometimes go to. Nobody's seen them. I just want to pop home and check everything's all right. And give them a good telling off for not answering when their poor, worried mum rings.'

'Okay, but hurry back,' said Alex.

Alex had raised children of his own. He would have done exactly the same thing in Ellen's place. And he would most certainly have told them off. In no uncertain terms.

'Tell them you'll send me round next time,' he called after her.

Then he turned his attention back to Fredrika and Peder.

'We think he's a psychologist, just like he told Nora and Jelena,' Fredrika began eagerly, her eyes gleaming.

'And we think it was his work as a psychologist that brought him into contact with the women whose children have been murdered,' Peder went on.

Alex hoped they weren't going to carry on with this double act. It would only end up confusing him.

'It's standard procedure, you see, for women to be offered counselling when they have an abortion,' Fredrika explained.

'And we've found entries in both women's hospital notes saying they accepted the offer.'

Peder flicked through the sheets of paper he was holding.

'According to her file, Magdalena Gregersdotter had a session with a psychology student who was on a placement at Söder Hospital at the time. Because of the trauma that resulted from the complications she had after the abortion, she also saw a fully qualified psychologist later on. But initially, when they thought the abortion had gone to plan, she spoke to a youngish guy who was still in training. According to her notes, his name was David Stenman.

Alex frowned. *David?*

'Sara Sebastiansson's abortion was done some years later, in Umeå. She had a counselling session, too,' reported Fredrika. 'According to her file, she saw a psychologist, but unfortunately there's no name, just some initials: DS. I rang Umeå Hospital and they confirmed it was the same person.'

Alex looked from one to the other.

'Did Ellen have time to give you the list of potentially interesting people from our own files?' he asked Peder.

'No,' said Peder. 'And we've looked up David Stenman in the National Registration Service records, and there's nobody of that name.'

'But we did find he had a criminal record,' Fredrika put in. 'He was sentenced to psychiatric care in early 2000 for arson, and released last autumn. There were extenuating circumstances: the person who died in the fire was his grandmother, who apparently abused him dreadfully when he was growing up in her care. For example: she used to burn him with matches to punish him if he'd done something stupid.'

'And now he's punishing others the same way,' Alex said quietly.

'Yes,' responded Peder. 'There are various other interesting details. Such as the fact that he was never meant to be born. His mother was an addict and tried to abort him herself with a knitting needle.'

'Hence his hatred of women who allow themselves the luxury of choosing and thus – in our murderer's eyes – commit a sin,' Alex said matter-of-factly, and leant across the desk. 'But if you found he had a criminal record, you must presumably have found his personal ID number and been able to check it against the registration records? Perhaps he's changed his name?'

'That was exactly what he did on his release,' said Fredrika, putting a computer print-out in front of Alex.

'He changed his name to Aron Steen. According to the National Registration Service records, he's registered at an address in Midsommarkransen. And here's an old passport photo, too.'

Fredrika put another sheet of paper on the desk.

Alex felt his heart pounding as he scrutinized the photograph of a rather distinguished-looking man.

'What do you say then, Alex?' asked Peder uneasily.

'I say we've bloody well found our murderer,' Alex replied grimly.

He clapped his hands.

'Right,' he said firmly. 'Here's how I suggest we proceed. Peder, you contact our friends in the emergency response unit. I want them to go to that address straight away and bring him in. With any luck, he may not have realized how warm we're getting and not had time to go underground.'

Alex cleared his throat and went on.

'Gather all the information about this bloke you possibly can on a Sunday. Talk to Magdalena and Sara again if you need to. Ask them if they remember him. It's vital to be thorough. We mustn't leave any stone unturned here. We need to chart every step he's taken since they let him out. And don't forget to report to the examining magistrate asap. Get hold of the poor bugger who's on call today. He's going to have plenty to do today. And go through the list as soon as you get it from Ellen. I don't want to exclude the possibility that it's someone else we've got on our files.'

Fredrika and Peder nodded eagerly, hardly able to contain themselves. Even Fredrika had been swept up in the excitement this time.

'We've managed to locate his probation officer,' she said. 'Our friend Aron Steen's been behaving impeccably since his release, and he's even managed to find a job. With a cleaning company. It wouldn't surprise me if that company happened to have had a contract with a hospital these past six months. Then we'd know where he got hold of the drugs and the surgical gloves.'

Fredrika was smiling as she spoke. Her voice was insistent, her body language full of pent-up energy.

She's got it in her, thought Alex. I was wrong. And so was she. She's deluding herself when she says she hasn't got the hunger for it.

They heard quick footsteps in the corridor outside. Ellen stuck a flushed face round his door.

'I'll forget my own head next,' she said, clearly under pressure. 'Left the car keys in my room.'

She stopped when she saw their exhilarated expressions.

'What's happened?'

The question made them all start to laugh. It was the laughter of relief, Alex noted.

'We think we've got him, Ellen,' he said with a grin.

'Are you sure,' asked Ellen, blanching.

'Well,' said Alex. 'You can never be a hundred per cent sure, but we're as sure as we can be at this stage.'

He pushed the sheet of paper with the print-out of the passport photo across the desk to her.

'Let me introduce . . .' he began, but then stalled. 'What was this joker's name again?' he asked irritably.

Fredrika and Peder smiled.

'Well, if you're not going to listen to what we tell you, we'd better start reporting to some other boss,' sighed Peder with a flamboyant sweep of his hands.

None of them noticed how Ellen reacted as she took two steps towards the desk and stared at the man in the photo. None of them noticed her cheeks turning pink and her attempts to blink away the tears that were blurring her vision. But they all heard her murmur:

'Thank you God.'

They all fell silent.

She pointed a trembling finger at the picture.

'I thought for a while it was . . . I thought it might be the man I was . . .'

She gave a laugh.

'What daft ideas we get into our heads sometimes,' she said with a sob, smiling through her tears.

Then her mobile rang. Her son was gabbling at the other end, his voice strained.

'Mum, you've got to come home right now.'

'What's happened, love?' asked Ellen, still with the smile on her lips.

'Mum, please come now,' her son repeated nervously. 'He says you've got to come now. Come home as quickly as you can. He doesn't seem very well at all.'

It came like a bolt from the blue when the last child disappeared. They got the news just as they were making final preparations for the swoop on Aron Steen.

Alex charged out into the corridor and found Fredrika and Peder in the Den, the latter in the middle of strapping on a bulletproof vest. Fredrika was poring over some papers, frowning.

'He's taken another child,' Alex said. 'A four-year-old boy's gone missing from a children's playground in Midsommarkransen, near where Steen lives, half an hour ago. The parents rang in and said they'd found his clothes and what looked like tufts of his hair left behind a tree on the edge of the playground.'

'But we've got his place under surveillance,' exclaimed Peder. 'They reported seeing him through the window of the flat, and they haven't seen him come out.'

'Well he must have done,' said Alex tersely, 'because another kid's been snatched.'

'Well he can't have got very far,' said Fredrika, fiddling with a piece of paper in front of her.

'No, we don't think he can,' Alex said urgently. 'And this time he must have been in a real fucking hurry. The clothes were just chucked down in a heap and he hadn't scalped the boy but just chopped off a few chunks of hair at random.'

'He knows we're on his tail,' said Peder resolutely, fixing his service pistol to his belt.

Fredrika looked askance at the gun but said nothing.

'What do we do now?' she asked.

'We carry out the operation as planned,' Alex said firmly. 'We need to get into the flat and see if we can pick up any leads to where he might have taken the boy. But he won't get far, as I say. We've got roadblocks on all routes out of town and a nationwide alert's gone out for him.'

Fredrika looked troubled.

'I assume we're interviewing the boy's parents?' she said. 'About the background to the abduction, I mean.'

'Of course,' said Alex. 'We've got a couple of detectives round there now. This time we know what we're looking for. The mother will need to be asked where the final stage of her abortion took place, and then we'll have to be there when he shows up with the child.'

Fredrika nodded, but her brow remained furrowed.

'If it's not already too late. If he's in as much of a hurry as he seemed to be in the playground, the boy could already be dead. We can't rule it out.'

Alex swallowed hard.

No,' he said. 'No, of course we can't. But we can work as hard as hell to prevent it being that way.'

Peder was thinking.

'But if we assume he knows we're looking for him?' he began tentatively.

'Yes?'

'Either he's as off his head as we thought, in which case he'll cut it short with the kid, even though the whole thing's a lot less tidy than he planned it to be. Or parts of him are still rational in spite of everything, in which case he won't dispose of the boy at the very start.'

'But use him to bargain for his freedom,' Alex added.

'Exactly,' said Peder.

The Den went very quiet.

'Has anybody heard how Ellen got on, by the way?' asked Fredrika.

Alex shook his head.

'She was adamant she wanted to go home on her own, said she'd be fine, but I sent a patrol car round anyway. There was something about that story that didn't feel right.'

Enthusiastic rays of sunlight were finding their way into the Den, spreading heat. Little balls of fluff went rolling across the floor. The air conditioning had spluttered into life.

Rapid steps were approaching. A young DC came rushing in.

'The surveillance team at Steen's place just rang,' he blurted. 'He's back home again.'

'Who's back home again?' asked Alex in irritation.

'Aron Steen. He's just got back to his flat.'

'What about the kid?' asked Peder.

'He was carrying him naked in his arms. As if he knew we were watching but didn't care.'

For a few short hours, Ellen had fully believed the reason she hadn't heard from Carl was quite simply that he was the child murderer they were hunting. And that the reason her children weren't answering the phone was that Carl had kidnapped them.

But it wasn't true.

Ellen couldn't fathom how she'd let her private and professional lives get entangled to that extent. When had she lost
control of her own imagination? When had work become
such a major part of her existence that she couldn't distin-
guish it from other important parts any more?

I've really got to think this through, Ellen decided. I need to
work out what's truly important to me.

The children hadn't answered the phone because they'd
been round at a neighbour's enjoying a nice brunch. And
forgotten the home phone lines. It was no stranger than that.

But as for Carl.

Ellen peered sideways at him as she sat there on her living
room floor. The children had immediately retreated to their
rooms when she got home.

'He was sitting on the front steps when we got back from
brunch,' her daughter had told her, nodding towards Carl
who was sitting on the bottom step with his legs stretched
straight out in front of him. 'You'd better talk to him. He
seems totally out of it.'

Ellen was initially dubious.

Should she let him into her home?

A patrol car went slowly past her house and pulled up.

Ellen invited Carl in, but left the front door open. The
patrol car waited.

The first thing Carl did was to collapse onto Ellen's old
chesterfield sofa and burst into tears. Ellen decided to sit on
the floor at a slight distance. And that's the way they had been
ever since.

Life was so peculiarly unpredictable. Who could possibly
have foreseen that this somewhat rigid and self-controlled

man, who always chose his words carefully and always seemed so strong, could break down in such an unconstrained way? Since Ellen had no words for occasions like this, she remained mute. She could hear her son talking on the phone through his closed bedroom door, and her daughter getting out her guitar.

'I'm married.'

Ellen jumped as Carl broke the silence.

'I'm married,' he said again.

'But . . . ,' began Ellen.

'I told you I was single, but I lied. I've been married to the same woman for over fifteen years, and we've got two children. We've a house in Borås.'

Ellen slowly shook her head.

A knock on the open front door interrupted them.

A uniformed police officer came into the living room.

'Is everything all right?' he asked.

Ellen nodded.

'Because if it is, we'll be moving on,' the policeman said hesitantly.

'Everything's fine,' she said in a monotone. 'Everything's absolutely fine.'

The policeman left, the front door closed behind him. Her daughter played the opening chords of 'Layla'; her son gave a loud, shrill laugh into his phone.

How remarkable that everything just carried on as if nothing had happened.

'That was why I didn't want to meet your family, Ellen,' Carl said in a softer voice.

He blew his nose on a handkerchief with his initials

embroidered on it. Was it his wife who was so handy with the needle?

'I was desperately unsure about this,' he sighed. 'About us. What it was. What we had. What it could turn into. And whether I was brave enough.'

Ellen's chest rose and fell as she tried to breathe without the air getting stuck anywhere on the way.

'Brave enough to do what?' she asked in a low voice. 'Brave enough to do *what*?'

'To do what I've just done. Leave my family.'

Ellen remembered afterwards that she had never lost eye contact with him in the course of the conversation.

Carl began to speak faster.

'I know I've done everything wrong; I know I've behaved badly. And I realize you must have wondered where I'd got to when I didn't answer your calls. But I've still got to ask . . .'

Silence again. Silence beyond Eric Clapton on guitar and hoots of laughter into a telephone.

'I've still got to ask, whether you think . . . Whether you think it could be the two of us.'

Ellen met his dark eyes. For a brief moment she saw him the way she had seen him when they first met. Life-affirming and whole.

But that had been then. What could become of what she saw ahead of her now?

'I don't know, Carl,' she whispered. 'I just don't know.'

The emergency response squad found the door of the flat ajar when they got to Aron Steen's flat. Alex and Peder held back, firearms at the ready. They had made Fredrika stay at HQ. Alex had no intention of being responsible for unarmed, civilian personnel in a critical situation like this.

'Aron Steen,' Alex shouted in a commanding voice.

No answer.

The officers kicked the door back on its hinges.

No one to the right, no one to the left.

The squad advanced into the flat.

A dark hall. Dark, undecorated walls.

Alex was aware of a pungent smell assaulting his nostrils. Petrol. *The flat stank of petrol.*

They found him in the kitchen. He was sitting on a kitchen chair with the drugged and unconscious child in his arms, soaked in petrol, with a lighter in his hand.

Subdued voices among the officers. 'Take it easy' and 'Hold it right there' and 'Keep back; there's petrol all over the floor.'

They did not enter the kitchen.

Nor did Alex.

But he put away his gun and stood there, balancing on the threshold that marked the end of the hall and the start of the kitchen. Where Alex's field of play ended and Aron Steen's began.

They regarded each other. Aron Steen smiled a placid smile.

'So we meet at last, Alexander,' he said, breaking the tense silence.

'Yes, we do,' Alex said quietly.

Aron shifted the child slightly on his knee. The squad monitored his every movement. Aron smiled again.

'I really think we ought to be able to sort this out without a lot of unnecessary violence,' he said, his head on one side. 'Can you ask your companions to wait in the hall, Alex? So we can talk in peace.'

It was the voice of a teacher. He was talking to Alex as if he were a child, a pupil. Alex felt a surge of anger. Aron Steen had nothing to teach him. That would have to be made very clear to him.

Peder was suddenly at Alex's shoulder. He had his gun in his hand. Alex waved him away and signalled to the men behind him to fall back into the corridor and hall. They would still have a line of sight from there, but be less obtrusive.

Aron watched them. His mouth was smiling, but his eyes were ablaze.

'There's something special about fire, isn't there?' he whispered, fingering the lighter. 'I learnt that at a very young age.'

Alex held off. Later, he would wonder why.

Aron looked at Alex and the men behind him.

'I'll exchange the boy for free passage out of the country.'

Alex gave a slow nod.

'Okay.'

'This is how it's going to work,' Aron Steen went on in a smooth voice. 'The boy and I are going to leave the flat and get into a car and drive away. You are *not* going to follow us.

Once I've gone far enough, I'll ring and tell you where to find the boy.'

Sunbeams were dancing on the window ledge behind Aron and the boy. Alex let his eyes follow them and then looked back at Aron.

'No,' he said.

Aron looked startled.

'No?' he repeated.

'No,' said Alex. 'The boy's not leaving the flat.'

'Then he's going to die,' Aron said calmly.

'He'll do that if he goes with you, too,' countered Alex in the same calm tone as Alex. 'That's why we can't let you take him with you.'

Aron seemed exasperated.

'But why should I kill him? I told you, I want to exchange him for free passage.'

'And I said okay,' replied Alex. 'But the exchange happens here. You give me the boy and then we leave the flat.'

Aron laughed out loud and then got up so abruptly from the kitchen chair that Alex took an involuntary step backwards. The squad members moved forward from the hall, then stopped and waited. An utterly absurd sense of security beamed through Alex's body as he felt the kinetic energy behind him. As if their presence made any difference to the situation.

'I've shown you how I work, haven't I?' asked Aron, raising his voice. 'I've shown you the precision I apply to my mission?'

Alex heard the raised voice and felt very concerned. It was crucial for everyone's safety that things did not escalate.

'We've noted your way of working,' he said softly. 'And we're very impressed, of course.'

'Don't try to flatter me,' Aron hissed.

But it worked.

Aron sat down again. The child was limp and heavy, and the petrol had made him quite slippery. Alex could see a little trickle under the boy's nose. Aron shifted to get a better grip.

Alex could feel the smell of the petrol making his own head heavy.

He opened his mouth to say something, but Aron got there first.

'The child and I leave the flat together, otherwise there's no deal,' he said in a low voice.

'We can negotiate,' said Alex, squatting down on his heels. 'We're both completely clear what we want to achieve; I want the boy and you want your freedom.'

Alex threw his arms wide in a gesture of appeal.

'We should be able to come to some agreement, shouldn't we?'

'We certainly should,' Aron said placidly.

There was a moment's silence. A cloud moved across the sun. The flat was cast into shadow.

'But the boy can't leave the flat?' Aron said eventually.

Alex shook his head.

'No, he can't.'

He scanned the room. The only way out of it was through the door where Alex was standing. An urgent sense of anxiety found its way through the petrol fumes and gripped him. Why wasn't Aron sitting in the living room with the boy? There was an unguarded balcony door in there to escape through. *Why had he backed himself into a corner?*

Aron provided the answer to Alex's unspoken question.

'Just as I thought,' Aron said with a smile. 'You never had any intention of letting me leave the flat.'

Before Alex could reply, the lighter flared, and in a second the whole kitchen was on fire.

PART III

Signs of Revival

THE END OF SEPTEMBER

Before summer had ever really arrived, autumn came creeping in. Only then did the rain stop. The sky was high and cloudless above the land, but the evenings grew ever cooler, and the nights were drawing in.

Alex Recht came back to work in the third week of September. He stopped in the doorway of his office and smiled. It was good to be back.

In the staff room, they all celebrated his return with coffee and cake. His boss made a short speech. Alex bowed and thanked him, accepted a bouquet and said thank you again.

Alone in his office a while later, he shed the odd tear. It really did feel great to be back.

His hands had healed better than anyone had expected, the doctors said, and they promised he would get full movement back in both of them.

For probably the thousandth time, Alex inspected the scar tissue decorating the backs and palms of his hands. Thin skin in a haphazard pattern of various shades of pink covered his hands and spread up over his wrists.

Alex was staggered not to be able to recall any pain when his hands were on fire. He remembered the whole course of events: Aron Steen's kitchen turning into a blazing inferno; Aron just sitting there on the kitchen chair, engulfed in flames, the burning child in his arms. Alex saw himself in his mind's eye, lunging forward into the fire and tearing the child from Aron's grip. He could hear his own cries echoing in his head:

'Out of the fucking way. The boy's on fire!'

And the boy was indeed on fire. He was so much on fire that Alex didn't have time to register that he was, too. He dragged the boy down onto the hall floor and rolled on him, over and over again, to put out the flames. Then Peder threw a large bath towel over Alex and tried to trap his thrashing arms. The fire crackled and spat, burned and cursed.

The emergency response squad advanced into the kitchen, armed with a hall rug, a bathmat and more towels to protect themselves against the fire. It proved impossible to reach the kitchen table, at which Aron Steen sat like a flaming brand. Not a sound escaped him as the fire took his life. And that, it later emerged, was what most of those involved in the operation saw in their nightmares. The burning man sitting stock still at the kitchen table.

A neighbour who had heard all the disturbance came running up with a fire extinguisher. With that they were able to contain the fire until the fire engine and ambulance got there, but by then one person was dead and a little child was badly burned. The ambulance crew found Alex in the bathroom, trying to soothe his poor hands under cold running water.

Alex found it harder to remember what had happened after that. He knew they had kept him under sedation for several days. He knew it had hurt like hell when he came round. But once he had embarked on the rehabilitation programme, everything had gone better than he could have hoped.

In the time Alex was on sick leave, the papers did nothing but write about the events of the case. Countless newspaper reports detailed the murders of the children and of Nora in Jönköping. There were timelines, and maps with arrows, and red dots, telling the story over and over again.

Alex read them all. Mainly because he had nothing better to do with his time, or so he claimed.

The fates of Nora and Jelena were recounted in many different versions. The press found so-called relatives of the girls, relatives who had never actually had any contact with either of them, but were keen to see themselves in the papers. Former classmates told strange tales of their schooldays, and the articles had quotes from former teachers and even employers who had been located and interviewed.

The police investigation came under scrutiny. Could the police have acted earlier? Could the perpetrator have been identified sooner? A variety of experts were asked to give their opinion. Several of them thought the police had managed to make a mess of what was basically a 'very simple investigation', while others made the reasonable point that it had been right for the police to make Lilian Sebastiansson's father their main suspect in the initial phase. It had been right, even though it had cost the investigation valuable time.

But the body of experts was unanimous in its criticism of the raid on Aron Steen's flat in Midsommarkransen. Some thought the police should have pulled out as soon as they smelled the petrol and come back with fire blankets and extinguishers. Others thought they should not have engaged in any kind of dialogue with Aron Steen, but tried to put him out of action with a shot through the window, since he was sitting in full view.

None of the pundits whose views were in print had been

present at the raid. But Alex had been. He would maintain until the day he died that the raid could not have been done in any other way. If they had made their presence known at the door and then retreated for firefighting equipment, the boy's life would have been in dire jeopardy. The moment they went into the block of flats, there was only one way for them to go. Forward.

The articles Alex found less infuriating and more interesting were the big features about the murderer. Here, the newspapers had been more thorough in their research and got access to better background material, which made for more satisfactory reading. For Alex, the features showed that the journalists didn't really know which leg to stand on. It was impossible to relate Aron Steen's tragic story without an element of understanding and sympathy creeping in. Not forgiveness, they stressed, but understanding.

Aron was really one of those people who never had a chance, Alex thought grimly. Even as a babe in arms he had been horribly mistreated by his mentally unstable grandmother, who went on to spend years belittling him as a person, distorting his perception of right and wrong, and preventing him from developing even the most basic capacity for empathy. He turned up at school in soiled clothes, looking wild and angry, day after day. He stank of his grandmother's cigarette smoke. The other children teased him, called him grandma's little girl. He was so skinny and had such long hair that it was hard to tell if he was a boy or a girl, they said. His worst tormentors were inspired by the smell of smoke and his dirty appearance. They called him Cinderella.

The boy was fifteen before social services finally intervened and he was placed in a foster home. His grandmother made no bones about blaming him for his mother's, her daughter's, death, and told social services that she couldn't for the life of her see that he would ever develop into a normally functioning person.

It seemed at first as though Aron Steen's grandmother was wrong. He completed his school career, went to university and qualified as a psychologist, and left home. But there were warning signs. His nursery school teacher had reported that even at a very young age he took great pleasure in inflicting pain on animals. He found it hard to make friends and maintain relationships. Yet he was outgoing and good at expressing himself verbally. In adult life he was considered good-looking, which helped him socially.

He found it hard to adapt to new workplaces, and was constantly changing job. He was always on the move, and seen by those around him as a restless soul.

At the time he met Nora, he was back in Umeå where he grew up, working at the hospital. According to the papers, the break-up with Nora must have triggered some kind of psychosis, because that was when he went to his grandmother's home in the middle of the night and set fire to it, burning her alive in her bed.

The rest was, as they say, history. Alex had recently spoken to the parents of the little boy Aron Steen had taken hostage. The boy was slowly recovering. His injuries were much more extensive than Alex's, but at least he was alive. His parents were very grateful for that. Only time would tell whether the boy felt the same gratitude.

Though resolute police work had uncovered the identity of the perpetrator, many other questions remained unanswered.

It was impossible to establish exactly where Aron had murdered the children. In all probability, Lilian had been killed in Jelena's flat, and Natalie in Aron's, but nothing could be proved. Nor had the investigation reached any conclusion about why Nora had been murdered at precisely that point in time. When they interviewed Jelena Scortz, she claimed she knew nothing about it.

As for Jelena, she had been discharged from hospital and was being held on remand in Kronoberg Prison, awaiting trial. She denied all the charges, but there was technical evidence confirming Lilian had been in her flat. Lilian's panties had been found in a bag in the rubbish collection area in the basement of her block. Jelena refused to say anything about how they came to be there. Alex couldn't decide if he felt sorry for her or not.

Alex switched on his computer and flicked through his desk diary. He only had a couple of weeks at work before he and Lena were off on their trip to South America to see their son. It was going to be a wonderful and exciting trip, Alex was in no doubt about it.

There was an unobtrusive little knock at Alex's door.

Fredrika was loitering hesitantly in the doorway.

'Come in,' said Alex with real warmth in his voice.

Fredrika smiled as she came in and sat down in the visitor's chair.

'I just wanted to see how you were,' she said. 'Is everything okay?'

Alex nodded and smiled.

'Almost everything's very okay indeed,' he said. 'How about you, are you okay?'

It was Fredrika's turn to nod. Yes, she was fine.

'Did you have a good holiday?' asked Alex, sounding genuinely interested.

Fredrika was caught out by the question. The summer and her holiday both felt so very far away.

But his query brought back happy memories of the week she and Spencer had spent at a little guest house in Skagen.

She smiled, but her eyes clouded over.

'I had a lovely holiday,' she replied emphatically.

Saying it conjured up the image of Spencer, sitting on the sand, looking out over the sea. The wind in his face and his eyes like narrow slits, protecting themselves from the sun.

'It won't get any better than this, Fredrika,' he said.

'I know,' she answered.

'Just so you don't feel I'm misleading you.'

'You don't need to worry about that. I've never felt anything but safe with you.'

Then they sat there on the sand, looking out over the water where the tall waves chased each other back and forth, until Fredrika, agonizing, hesitantly broke the silence.

'Talking of misleading each other, there's something else I think we should talk about . . .'

Alex cleared his throat as Fredrika's attention drifted away.

'Thanks for the CD you sent,' he said. 'Lena and I both love it. We play it almost every day.'

'Oh, I'm glad,' she said. 'I'm very fond of that one myself.'

Then there was silence.

Alex shifted uneasily in his seat and decided to ask a more urgently topical question, but Fredrika got in first.

'When's Peder expected back?'

Alex had to think.

'The first of November,' he said. 'Unless he opts to be a stay-at-home dad.'

Fredrika had to smile.

Peder and Fredrika had joined forces to conclude the investigation that started when Lilian Sebastiansson went missing from a train at Stockholm Central Station. It had been a fruitful collaboration that had given them new respect for each other, and they had parted as good colleagues when Peder went on paternity leave at the start of August.

That was the last they had heard of each other. Fredrika wondered a few times whether to give him a ring, but never got round to it. Perhaps it was because she saw him as just that, a colleague, rather than a friend. And now too much time had passed for it to feel a natural thing to do. There was also quiet but persistent gossip on the corridor about Peder and his wife having a 'trial separation', as it was put, though he was also said to have asked a lawyer friend to act for him in the question of divorce proceedings and dividing the joint property.

Tragic, thought Fredrika.

Alex thought the same.

But neither of them put it into words, simply letting it hang there in the air.

In the resulting silence, Alex again tried to ask the question he needed answering.

'And what about you, Fredrika? Are you going to stay on here with us?'

Fredrika drew herself up and looked Alex straight in the eye.

'Yes,' she said with composure. 'I am.'

Alex smiled at her.

'I'm glad,' he said honestly.

More mutual agreement that didn't need words. Fredrika briefly considered whether this was the time to say that although she wanted to stay with Alex, certain things would have to change. Certain things to do with his assessment of her competence, and how her background was valued. The media had drawn attention to her involvement in the case, which had turned a spotlight on tensions between police and civilian personnel in the force. Fredrika had refused no fewer than two invitations to take part in discussion programmes. But she felt no urge whatsoever to give vent to her personal opinions on television.

Fredrika decided the issue could wait. It was Alex's first day back at work since the fire; it didn't feel right to force him into such a major discussion.

And anyway, there was another question she wanted to take up with him.

'I've got to tell you that I shall be on parental leave from the end of April next year.'

Alex gave a start. Fredrika had to bite her bottom lip to stop herself bursting out laughing.

'Parental leave?' Alex repeated in amazement.

'I'm going to be a mother,' said Fredrika, feeling her cheeks glow with pride.

'Congratulations!' Alex said automatically.

He studied her.

'It doesn't show yet,' he blurted out before he could stop himself.

Fredrika simply smiled, leaving Alex free to put his foot in it a second time.

'Is there going to be a shotgun wedding?'

It was Fredrika's turn to flinch, and Alex made a defensive gesture with his damaged hands to show he took the comment back. Fredrika found herself giggling, entirely involuntarily. Shotgun wedding. What a phrase.

I owe him this one, thought Fredrika, and answered the question.

'No, I'm afraid not. The father's already married, you see.'

Alex stared at Fredrika with a foolish grin, waiting for her to take back what she had just said. But she didn't.

Alex turned to look out of the window instead.

It'll do me good to get away to South America, he thought.

AUTHOR'S ACKNOWLEDGMENTS

This is my first book and therefore the longest list of thanks I shall probably ever write.

This book would have been impossible to write if I had not already spent twenty years amusing myself writing endless tales and stories. You have to start somewhere, after all. And for me that was when I wrote my first so-called storybooks at school, at the age of seven. I owe a great debt of gratitude to the amazing teachers in primary and lower secondary school who taught me at an early stage to love reading and writing, and then didn't stop encouraging me to write more when they saw how much I was enjoying it: *Kristina Göransson, Kristina Permer* and *Olle Holmberg*.

I have no idea where the idea for this book first came from. It was like all my other ideas: one day it was just there, begging to be turned into a story. It was August 2007 and I had eight days of holiday left. By January 2008 the first draft was finished. It was an emotional moment. I had never seen a book project through before. There are several reasons why it was different this time, and I want to thank my writer colleague *Staffan Malmberg* for one of them. His words '*You just have to get past page 90 when you're writing! Then you'll be able to go on as long as you want!'* helped convince me that not all my stories had to end up in the desk drawer as fragments of novels.

The book is a detective novel, and entirely the product of my own imagination. At least as far as the plot is concerned. I have been employed in a police organization since the autumn of 2005. That doesn't make me into a fully trained police officer, though I have learnt a lot in those years. So I must thank *Sven-Åke* and *Patrik* who made useful and amusing comments on my manuscript, drawing on their own extensive police experience, and also taught me what I needed to know about the sharp end of detection. Both of you, in your different ways, make a great contribution to the Swedish police force. Any mistakes (or conscious departures from standard police procedure) that remain are entirely my own.

The act of writing, contrary to what one might think, is actually a relatively small part of the job of producing a finished book. I write very quickly. But everything else happens at a much slower speed. Every author realizes sooner or later that Stephen King, genius that he is, was right when he wrote: 'To write is human. To edit is divine.' Editing is something with which one almost always needs help. Help is what I have had, and of the most superb calibre.

First of all: A huge thank you to my publisher Piratförlaget and its amazing staff, who had faith in me and decided to publish my book. The very first time I came through the door into your offices, I knew I was going to be happy there. Particular thanks go to *Sofia Brattselius Thunfors* and *Anna Hirvi Sigurdsson*. Sofia introduced me to the world of publishing with great enthusiasm and patience and guided me through the process that leads up to the actual publication of a book, as well as making sound, constructive comments on my manuscript. Anna, with incredible feeling for the written word and a firm grip on her magic pen, was a real rock in the editing of the text.

Thanks also to my peerless sister-in-law *Caroline Ohlsson*, who not only asked me to be godmother to her firstborn daughter Thelma but also, in spite of being in the advanced stages of pregnancy, took the time to read and comment on my very first draft, which at that stage was in a fairly wretched state.

Many thanks to *Helena Carrick*, who read the book at a later stage and contributed vital views and comments. A terrific reader, a sharp-eyed critic and most of all a wonderful friend. It is a real gift to have such an inspiring, energizing person on hand.

And finally *Sofia Ekholm*, who has not only shown uncompromising and unbounded loyalty, but who also rose to every occasion and made me believe by her words and actions that this really is something I can do, and do *well*. You are part of this book in many respects, and there is so much that would be a lot less fun without you.

Thank you.

At my desk, Stockholm, spring 2009

Coming soon from Simon & Schuster

SILENCED
by Kristina Ohlsson

Trade Paperback ISBN 978-1-84737-961-0
Ebook ISBN 978-1-84737-962-7

Available from September 2012

Turn the page to find out more about Fredrika
Bergman's next gripping case . . .

Fifteen years ago . . .

In a meadow near her parents' summer home, a teenage girl is picking flowers for a traditional Midsummer's Eve ritual. The ritual calls for seven different flowers, and she's only missing one: a daisy. But just as she picks the final flower, she realises she is being watched. A man has followed her from the house. Still clasping the daisy in her hand, she is brutally raped and beaten. This terrible episode will sow discord among her family as each tries to come to terms with what has happened in their own way.

Present day . . .

On a damp February morning in Stockholm, Alex Recht's special investigation unit is frustrated by the run of the mill cases they have been working on recently. Two new cases have just come their way and these too seem insignificant and unexciting . . . but appearances can be deceiving.

Case One: A priest and his wife are found shot dead in their apartment. Discovered by local police officer Viggo Tuvesson, a close friend of the family, all evidence indicates that the priest shot his wife and then committed suicide. But is that all there is to it?

Case Two: A hit-and-run victim who cannot be identified. He hasn't been reported missing and he is not wanted by the police, so a heavily pregnant Fredrika Bergman is assigned the task of finding out who he is.

Two different cases, seemingly unrelated. But it is not long before the two investigations converge and the special unit begins to uncover an astonishing crime organization – a clandestine people-smuggling network operating out of Bangkok.

As the police slowly reveal the shocking hypocrisy behind the network, they will find a trail that runs all the way back to the 1980s, to a crime that went unreported, but whose consequences will reach further and deeper than anyone ever expected.

Silenced is intense, fast-paced and urgent. Kristina Ohlsson uses her expert knowledge on international politics as well as her inside experience of the Swedish Police to create a totally gripping and utterly convincing new novel.